Mirrors of Life

debut novel by

Neal Owens

Edited by: Rick Taubold

Cover Design by: Rick Taubold

Published by: Owens LLC

www.owenspublishing.com

ISBN: 978-1-7331503-0-9

Dedicated to my Mother (Helen) and Grandmother (Ruth)

Special Thanks to my Aunt Loretta.

I extend thanks to Rick Taubold, Writers Café, Silver Pen Writers, FanStory, and all who read this novel.

INTRODUCTION

The earth turns in unperceived movement that opens and closes windows into people's lives—locks and unlocks doors in their paths—and unseen mirrors reflect the days of the expected and unexpected.

Take the plight of Yvonne Baker, a beautiful, dark-skinned, gullible fourteen-year-old.

Pregnant, with a distorted fantasy of motherhood, her euphoria turned to sorrow when her seventeen-year-old boyfriend abandoned her as if she didn't exist.

Heartbroken and embarrassed, she prayed with the faith of her grandmother's persuasion, and the tears of a naive teenager awakened the conscience of a woman determined to guide her child out of poverty.

Like a drooping plant when watered, Yvonne saw education as the key, and spoke to her womb every day as if she was teaching the alphabet and how to count.

In the hope of ending the family cycle of generational welfare, Yvonne gave birth to a son named Mister.

CHAPTER 1

The voices of children at play resonated across the stellate courtyard. Seniors ushered intergenerational games of chess at the edge of the complex. Young mothers pushed strollers on the paved path that led to the mart. Teenagers with concealed guns lingered on the wooded trail as drugs for money inconspicuously exchanged hands.

Three apartment buildings towered over these scenes in the autumn twilight. Inside one of the structures, Yvonne lay on a black, faux-leather sofa, her ten-year-old tabby cat sprawled on the coarse carpet. Knuckles beating on the door interrupted her deep sleep.

"Who is it?" She yawned with one eye half-open.

"It's me, baby."

A voice that she hadn't heard for nine years widened her eyes. She leaned up onto her elbows. Jumbled images sped through her mind with raised brows.

"Yvonne, open up. It's me, Justin."

What does he want? She scurried into the small, narrow kitchen and grabbed the biggest knife out of the wooden block.

"Open up, baby," he bellowed.

Damn, he knows I'm here. I gotta open the door.

She held the knife behind her thigh, and with the security chain attached, she cracked it open.

Justin, his skin yellowish and eyes drooping, was standing in an oversized black jacket, baggy blue jeans, and untied buff boots. He leaned against the door and tried to see more than her partial face.

"What do you want?" she snarled.

"You gonna greet me like that? Why you hiding? Open up. I came to see you and my son."

"Why?"

"Why? Why you frontin? Let me in."

"No. Ain't nothing here for you."

"What you mean ain't nothing here for me? My son is here! Let me in so I can see my son! You got a nigga in there or something?"

She rolled her eyes. "It's none of your business who's here. Go before I call the police."

He took a step back and lowered his head. "Call the police? What's up like that? I just came to talk to you and see my son. Don't let me stand out here in the hallway. Let me in so I can see my son, then I'll go."

"He's not here."

"Where he at?"

"Why do you wanna see him? You dogged me when I told you I was pregnant. You remember what you said?"

"Nah, that was ten years ago."

"I haven't forgotten. You said, 'That baby's not mine.' You slapped me and said I better not tell anybody you're the father. You called me, 'young and dumb and full of cum.' You laughed at me in front of your boys like I was a fool for believing you cared about me. You remember that?"

He took a step forward and leaned his shoulder against the crack and spoke softly. "I'm sorry, baby. My bad. I was young and stupid. I haven't been around to see you because I been locked up for seven years. Just got out yesterday. I've changed, baby. I matured in the joint. I'm trying to make things right. I stopped smoking trees and all that. I'm out of the game and looking for an honest job. I love you, Yvonne. I've always loved you, baby. I want us to start over. I know you remember the good times we had."

"I'm sorry, Justin, but I've moved on. You're not my type."

His shoulders jerked as his expression turned hostile. "Your type? What the fuck you mean I'm not your type?"

"You're not my type. That fourteen-year-old virgin you knew is a woman now, and you're not the man I want in my life."

"Bitch, you the same freak that like to roll with big dicks. Stop frontin! Let me in!"

"Justin, you're still a kid in a man's body. P-please go away. I don't want my son influenced by you."

"What the fuck you saying? You don't want me to influence my son? What kind of shit is that? I told you, I'm out of the game. Call my son before I kick down this fucking door!"

Yvonne pointed the edge of the knife. "If you force your way into my apartment, I'm gonna kill you."

"So you gonna stab me now? You think I'm scared? Bitch, I've fought niggas with shanks. You don't scare me. Open the fucking the door before I kick this motherfucker in, and your ass too!"

She slammed the door and quickly turned the deadbolt.

He rammed the sole of his boot against the door. "Bitch, tell that punk-ass nigga you got in there to come out here! Open the fucking door so I can see my son! Mister, come out here and talk to your father!"

Yvonne thought of running to the phone, but she believed her back pressed against the door would keep the velocity of kicks from busting through, so she didn't move. The door was old and worn, but the wood was solid enough. With both hands gripping the knife, her eyes searched for an escape route. She shuddered. "G-God, help me."

"Bitch, I'm gonna kick your ass when I catch you on the street! I'm gonna see my son! You fuckin' ho!"

In the following silence, she felt him waiting. She smelled his scent; she heard his breath. Then she heard him strut down the worn steps and pound his fist against the wall.

She sighed with relief, scampered to the phone that sat on a coffee table handed down through her family, and dialed her grandmother. "Where's Mister?"

"He's watching television. What's wrong?"

"Keep him inside. Justin came here looking for him."

"Justin's out? Why he looking for Mister? He told everybody Mister isn't his son."

"I think he heard about the college scouts."

"Oh, he sniffing for money. So what you gonna do?"

"I have to tell him. I don't want Justin to tell him."

"You want me to call Mister to the phone?"

"No. I'll wait until the morning. I don't know how he's going to react. I need to think about what I'm going to say. He hasn't asked about his father, but I'm sure he wants to meet him. I wanted to meet mine."

"But you asked about your father. He hasn't asked about his. Maybe he already know or don't care."

"Maybe. But I have to tell him before he hears it from Justin."

"Okay, if he come here, I'll call the police."

"He won't come there. He thinks Mister and a boyfriend are with me."

"Do you have a man there?"

"No."

"Are you all right?"

"Yeah. He tried to kick down my door, but I'm all right."

"What? Call the police!"

"I will if he comes back."

"You should spend the night here."

"I'm good. He's probably out in the courtyard."

"Okay, but if he come back, call the police."

"I will."

* * *

The rays of the morning sun peeked through Yvonne's bedroom blinds and shined on her face. After spending a sleepless night, she was propped against the headboard—another piece passed down through her family—watching the morning news as usual. Her feline was curled beside her.

Breaking News flashed across the screen and the reporter said, "In this alley behind me, police found the dead body of an African-American male shot multiple times. The victim, identified as twenty-eight-year-old Justin Kendricks, was released two days ago from federal prison after serving seven years for manslaughter. Mr. Kendricks was a known gang member, but we are unable to confirm if his murder was gang related. The police are not releasing any additional details at this time."

"Ohhh my God!"

Yvonne didn't see a problem removed, but a person lost in translation like the many led astray by the illusion of grandeur.

9

Tears wet her naturally long eyelashes as she phoned her grandmother. "Justin is dead!"

"What happened? You killed him?"

"Nooo. He was found shot in the alley."

"The Lord works in mysterious ways."

"Why do you say that? He had a good side to him."

"A serial killer has a good side, but that don't make him less evil. I feel sorry about his death, but I'm not gonna cry over it. God don't like a man that hit women. You still gonna tell Mister?"

Yvonne was silent. Her grandmother didn't break the silence. After a few seconds, Yvonne said, "No."

"Good. Are you going to the funeral?"

"No."

"Are we still going to church?"

"Yeah. I'm going to get ready now."

"Don't forget to bring Mister's suit."

"I won't."

* * *

In a community where gossip was prevalent, several told Mister the name of his father. But he didn't show any emotion, and he didn't ask his mother if the rumors were true.

On the morning of Justin's funeral, guilt filled Yvonne's consciousness and she felt compelled to tell her nine-year-old son. She sat on the edge of her queen-sized bed and called him into the neatly kept room where three framed Scriptures hung on the spotless walls.

When he entered, he said, "Ma, you are my mother and my father."

On the verge of tears, she opened her arms. "I love you."

He hurried into her embrace. "I will always love you, Ma."

Tears leaking now, she squeezed him harder.

"Do you want to go to the funeral?" she asked.

"No."

CHAPTER 2

As the days moved forward with the hope of dreams, Yvonne and her best friend Cynthia, whose birthday was today, were walking towards a popular nightclub in the heart of downtown. The sight of two attractive and fashionably dressed women snatched the attention of men on the street and in passing vehicles. A tall and burly man, who wore a long, black leather coat, was guarding a red velvet rope that kept more than sixty people dressed to impress waiting to enter.

"I didn't think it would be this crowded on oldies but goodies night," Yvonne said, surprised.

"We aren't getting in that line," Cynthia whispered. "Follow me."

Heads turned as they walked past and stopped at the VIP entrance as if they belonged.

"Who are they?" a few at the front of the line murmured.

The fourteenth person yelled, "That's Apollonia."

Necks stretched.

The people at the front muttered, "That's not her."

The gatekeeper whispered in Cynthia's ear, "You're close enough," and unhooked the second red velvet rope. "Enjoy," he said as he opened the gold-handled black door.

They stepped onto a white-pebbled, mosaic marble floor lighted by the high-ceilinged crystal chandelier. A Victorian-style couch and caprice chairs furnished the entrance hall of the open space. Brawny bouncers in black suits and neckties stood along the walls like statues. The hostesses wore black, fitted dresses and were swiftly moving up and down the marble stairs.

Behind the green jade, granite coat-check counter stood a red-haired woman. Her plum lipstick and hooded brown eyes were distinctive. "Would you like to check your coats?"

They handed her their coats and scarfs.

The thin, jovial woman issued each a ticket and stamped the back of their hands.

"What's the stamp for?" Yvonne asked with her head leaning down.

The woman broadened her smile. "It's to return to the VIP lounge if you enter the main floor." She pointed. "That door leads to the main floor."

Yvonne swung her head to Cynthia. "Where do you want to go first?"

"Let's go upstairs."

They rode the swanky elevator to the second floor and entered the fluorescent lounge.

Yvonne whirled. "Wow, they got a dance floor and private rooms up here."

Cynthia grabbed Yvonne's arm and led her to the four-sided gold-plated rail balcony. They looked below.

Yvonne frowned. "It's not packed. Why are they not letting the people inside?"

"It's all about image. Not sure if you should blame the club or the people willing to stand in line."

"Both."

"I agree. C'mon, let's look around."

They strolled and peeked into the rooms that had open doors.

"Ain't nothing but women up here," Yvonne said.

"They're waiting for the NBA players who are coming after the game. You wanna stay up here, or mingle with the general public?"

"It's your birthday."

"Let's go downstairs. We'll have more fun. Those fly-girls at the bar are hating on us. I ain't time for all that."

Yvonne chuckled softly. "Well, the men do pause when we walk in the door."

Cynthia laughed and said, "Yeah, they do, since we were twelve."

"I love you. Happy Birthday."

"Thank you. I love you too."

They embraced like biological sisters, sauntered down the stairs, entered the main floor, and sat at an unoccupied four-person table.

While they waited for the waitress to return with their drink orders, their bodies were swaying to the beat of Whodini and their eyes discreetly searched for single men.

"A lot of nice-looking guys are here," Yvonne said, and puckered her full lips.

"I heard it's always like this." Cynthia pointed with her straight nose. "Check out the guys over at the bar in the smooth operator suits."

Yvonne gave each the once-over. "I hope they got a brain."

Cynthia chuckled. "I don't think so. If they did, one of them would've been over here by now."

They were laughing when the energetic waitress returned with their drinks. "Are you starting a tab?" she amiably asked.

"We are," Yvonne replied, and lifted her drink to Cynthia. "Happy Birthday!"

She smiled with glistening catlike eyes. "Thank you."

They clinked their wine glasses, sipped, and chatted over the clear acoustics of powerful surround speakers.

Yvonne angled her head towards a group of men. "Those guys keep looking at us. Why don't they just come over and ask us to dance?"

"Because they lack confidence and nerve. They're waiting for a woman to ask them because they're afraid of rejection."

"Well, I'm not going to ask them. Let's dance."

They capered to the middle of the dance floor and were cavorting under the colorful lights to the beat of Marvin Gaye when a stranger emerged from the shadows of men standing around.

Dressed in a tailored military uniform, the tall, dark man squeezed his handsome physique in-between and turned his rhythm towards Yvonne. His dark-brown satin eyes were clearly fixed on her hourglass figure in a lavender fit-and-flare dress.

Cynthia, a shapely amber skin with well-proportioned breasts and rear, continued to dance while Yvonne and the stranger flirted without a word.

When the song ended with the beat into the next, he stopped dancing and asked over the loud music, "What is your name?"

She raised her voice, "Yvonne. Yours?"

"Cedric. Can we sit and talk?"

"Sure. Your table or mine?"

13

"I don't have a table."

She grinned and led him past a row of men with envious eyes.

Cynthia stayed on the dance floor; two Marines vied for her attention.

Cedric sat facing Yvonne and signaled the waitress.

With a black tray under her arm, the waitress maneuvered to the table. "What can I get for you?" she asked with a bubbly smile.

After they ordered, he slid his eyes back to Yvonne. "Why are you looking at me like I'm a ghost?"

She chuckled. "You showed up like a ghost."

He laughed.

She beamed. "You look like the identical twin of Big Daddy Kane. I'm serious. The resemblance is amazing."

"I know. I hear that often. But white people say I look like a tall Wesley Snipes. Probably because they don't know who Big Daddy Kane is."

She gave him a sideways smile. "I think you're right. So, where were you hiding?"

He slowly rubbed his index finger across a manicured mustache and gazed at a complexion that matched his. "I wasn't hiding. I just got here."

"I didn't see you in that long line."

"Formal military attire can just walk up and enter. We don't even have to pay. I heard the owner was in the Air Force."

"Ah, you didn't waste time making your move when you got in here."

"Why should I when I see what I want? Are you attached?"

"I'm attached to my nine-year-old son."

"What's his name?"

"Mister."

"Mister? That's a unique name."

"Thanks. Do you have children?"

"I have a six-year-old daughter back home in Mississippi. Her name is Erin."

"Erin is a pretty name."

"Thank you," he said. The beat of Grover Washington Jr. emptied the tables around them.

Their eyes locked, oblivious to the music and people around them.

The waitress interrupted the moment of silence and set their drinks on the tablecloth.

Yvonne circled her finger around the top of the glass of white wine. "Are you and the mother of your daughter still together?"

His eyes sparkled behind a grin that became a full smile. "We're not a couple, but I will always be a part of my daughter's life. I believe a father's role is to support his child emotionally and financially, regardless of his relationship with the mother."

Engrossed, she leaned forward. "Tell me about yourself."

"What do you want to know?"

"I want to know who you are, where you come from, and where you're going."

"You are very direct."

"I want to know if you're more than just a handsome face."

He sipped his gin and cranberry juice, set it down, and leaned back on the leather barrel chair. "I was born in the slums of Mississippi—a state where slavery still exists in the backwoods. I grew up without a father, but I didn't miss him because of my mother. I don't have any brothers or sisters. I was very reclusive as a child but had an active imagination, so I created a way to play football and basketball games alone. I'm a thinker. I've grown to learn that the things most call imagination, coincidence, and dreams are God's presence in their lives."

She widened her eyes in surprise.

"I'm trying to live as God intended man to be. I describe myself as spiritual and not religious because I believe God dwells in every faith."

She lightly double-tapped the table with her long nude-polished nails and leaned back. His mysteriousness excited her. "Tell me about your mother?"

"My mother is a God-fearing woman. She is my best friend."

Yvonne expressed a smile that she had never felt before. Her eyes drifted; her thoughts floated on moments with her son.

Cedric was nodding to the music. "I love this song by Gil Scott-Heron. He's one of my favorite recording artists."

"Unh, I like him too!"

"So we have something else in common." He leaned forward, fingers clamped and edge on the table. "Do you like movies?"

She grinned. "Yes."

"My favorite movie is *The Spook Who Sat By The Door*."

"I never heard of that movie. I don't like horror movies."

"It's not a horror movie. It's about a black revolution. I won't go into details because I want you to see it. I read the book too. But my favorite book besides the Bible is the *True Story of Black Wall Street*."

"I've heard of Wall Street, but what is Black Wall Street?"

"Economic empowerment in a black community. The path to self-sustainability."

"So what happened to Black Wall Street?"

"You have to read the book."

"Aww, c'mon, tell me, please?"

"I'm not going to tell you."

"Oh, so you're one of those selfish guys. You don't want to tell me about the movie; you don't want to tell me about the book. You want a sista to find her own way, huh?"

"No, I'm not like that. I'm trying to teach you to check things out for yourself."

"Yeah, right," she said and turned her face away.

"Ah, don't be like that. Are we having our first argument already?"

She pouted. "Nooo."

"I can see you were a spoiled child."

"I wasn't spoiled. I just like to have my way."

"Well, I'm not going to let you have your way just because you want it."

"Okay, Mr. Selfish, is that why you joined the military?"

He chuckled. His smile enhanced his comeliness. "I'm far from selfish. To answer your question, I joined to escape poverty because the only job for a black man without a college degree in Mississippi is washing dishes or cleaning toilets. The military took me out of poverty, but not my family. So, because

16

they're still in poverty, I'm still in poverty. If a black man isn't a professional athlete or artist, the only way for him to escape poverty is with a quality education or entrepreneurship. I dream of starting my own business one day."

"Hmm, what type of business?"

"Gold commodities. I believe I can convince the Nigerians to sell their gold below market price. Then I'll sell it to the Europeans at market price."

"Sounds like a good idea, but why would the Nigerians sell gold to you below market price?"

"Because they respect a black man who isn't afraid of the White Establishment, a man that will use the financial loopholes of this country to benefit Africa. Since ancient times, Europeans have raped Africa for its natural and human resources. My plan is to act as a liaison to help Africans regain some of their lost wealth. Everything that anyone has created or accomplished started with a dream. Dreams come true with the will to succeed and a dedicated focus towards achieving one's potential. If your dream is to become a professional basketball player, but you don't have the talent to play at that level, you need to be brutally honest with yourself and pursue a more suitable dream. If your dream is to become a lawyer, but you don't like to read, write, or conduct research, then you're just daydreaming."

"Mm-hmm. My son's future is my dream. From infancy, I taught him the values and personal leadership to resist peer pressure and avoid the unscrupulous role models."

She sipped her wine. "He's an excellent basketball player. College scouts are already attending his games. But I made education his priority. I told him, God forbid, that he could have an injury that would end his dream to play basketball professionally. But a good education will last until he dies. He's a straight-A student. I'm determined to help my son escape poverty, and never return."

"That's good. You should live for what will be, remembering what has been, and knowing what is."

"Wow! That's deep. Please explain?"

"Reality surpasses actuality, because reality is not only the past and present, but the future too. Let me break it down this way. Today, you live in poverty—that is your actuality. But you're doing the necessary things today that lead toward escaping poverty tomorrow—that is your reality—so continue to live for tomorrow."

He wet his lips with his drink. "Tell me about yourself."

"Okay. I'm the oldest of four sisters and two brothers. I grew up without a father. I think I was looking for a father's love when I got pregnant at fourteen. If it wasn't for my grandmother, Ruth, I don't know what my life would be like today. She told me that education is the key to escaping poverty.

"She jump-started my motivation to finish school. She said, 'Don't have another child until you get married.' She told me about the mistakes she made when she followed her mother's advice to have one child after another to receive a monthly welfare check. She didn't graduate from high school and made me promise to graduate. She babysat my son while I went to school and worked at the Eatery on the weekends.

"Life was hard, but I graduated with honors and received a scholarship to attend community college. I had planned to get an associate's degree, transfer to the state university, and get my bachelor's in nursing. But after I received my associate's, I was promoted to a manager position at the Eatery and decided to postpone my education so I could spend more time raising my son. So here I am today, trying to break the family cycle of generational welfare."

"Inspiring story. Where is your mother?"

She paused before she said, "I love my mother, and I know she loves me. She just doesn't realize the importance for a parent to continue hugging their child throughout adolescence. I was five years old the last time she hugged me. At the time, I thought she was just too busy taking care of my siblings. But even now, she doesn't hug her children unless we hug her."

"Where do you live?"

"I have a two-bedroom apartment at the Hilltop. My mother and grandmother live in the same project. They told me that men who leave the projects don't come back for a project woman."

"Sounds like foolish men to me. There are lots of virtuous women in the projects. I can see that you are one of the many."

She blushed and turned her eyes in search of Cynthia.

His eyes followed.

At a table on another side of the dance floor, she saw Cynthia having a seemingly pleasant conversation with the two Marines.

"Are those your friends with my friend?"

"No, I came alone. But we have Marines on the base."

"Mr. Williams, is this your first time here?"

He seemed startled for a moment. "Oh, my name tag. First time. What about you?"

"My first time. I'm here to celebrate my best friend's birthday."

"She looks like she's having a good time. Are you having a good time?"

Yvonne answered with her eyes and sipped her wine.

He smiled and sipped the last of his drink before he said, "Well, Ms...."

She looked at him sideways. "Baker."

"Would you like to dance?"

"Sure."

After their trip to the dance floor, they sat and conversed about God, politics, society, and the things they liked to do at their leisure. They exchanged contact information.

When the DJ announced the last call for alcohol, Cedric asked, "When can I see you again?"

"When do you want to see me again?" Yvonne slowly rubbed the rim of the empty glass.

"Tomorrow."

She batted her lashes. "Maybe."

Their moment of silent flirtation was interrupted when Cynthia sat and said, "Your name?"

"Cedric," he answered with his patented smile.

"If you weren't wearing that uniform, I would've believed that you were Big Daddy Kane."

His smile broadened. "Your name?"

"Yvonne hasn't told you?"

"I didn't ask."

19

"My name is Cynthia."

"Nice to meet you, Cynthia. Happy Birthday, and I like your hairstyle."

Her skeptic expression became a smile. "Thank you. It's called a razor cut." She turned to Yvonne. "Are you ready to go?"

"I'm ready."

Cedric stood. "Can I walk you to the car?"

Cynthia interjected, "How do you know we have a car?"

With a stolid expression, he asked, "What did the Marines do to piss you off?"

She didn't answer and headed towards the VIP lounge.

Cedric turned to Yvonne. "I need to get my coat."

"Okay, I'll meet you out front."

At the coat check, Yvonne asked, "What's wrong?"

Cynthia hesitated before she said, "Nothing. Where's your friend?"

"He will meet us outside."

When they exited, Cedric was standing on the sidewalk, wearing a long green military coat and beret.

Cynthia walked by as if she didn't see him. Yvonne smiled and nudged him to follow.

He tried to include Cynthia in the conversation during the three-block walk, but she remained standoffish. He lowered his head and whispered to Yvonne, "She doesn't like me."

"She probably thinks you're just out for one thing."

He halted. "You think I'm just out for one thing?"

Two steps away, she turned and faced him and tried to see his soul. He opened up to let her. After a few seconds, she turned and entered the parking garage. He followed with the silence she dictated.

Cynthia picked up the pace. She opened the driver's door and stared at Cedric before she entered.

Why is she gritting? Yvonne wondered.

Cedric opened the passenger's door. Yvonne entered and rolled down the window.

He bent down and cuffed the door. "Is it too late to call you when I get back to the base?"

"I'm not sleepy," she said. *Is he going to try and kiss me now?*

He flashed his pure whites as if reading her thoughts, stood, and backed away from the vehicle.

He didn't kiss me. I wanted him to kiss me. She smiled, rolled up the window, and waved as Cynthia drove away.

CHAPTER 3

Yvonne and Cedric had entered the second month of dating and were chatting over the phone when gunfire-like sounds erupted through her bedroom window.

"Happy New Year!" she said.

He replied, "Happy New Year."

"So, what's your resolution for 1989?"

"To continue living a righteous life."

"A righteous life? What's a righteous life?"

"A life that tries to do the right thing. A life that believes you reap what you sow. What's your resolution?"

"Mine is to find time to attend my son's basketball games. He tells me that he understands I have to work, but I know he wants me there, and I want to be there. Thanks again for going to his games."

"I told you before not to thank me. I don't go as a favor. I enjoy watching him play. He's awesome. Your son is destined to play in the NBA."

She cracked a smile and said, "The first time you told me that, I thought you were saying it to be nice, but now I know you mean it."

"I don't say things I don't mean."

This man is too good to be true. "My son told me that you taught him a lot. What do you talk about?"

"I can't divulge the secrets of our man talk, but I can tell you that we talked about the birds and the bees, and the knowledge of life."

"The knowledge of life? What is the knowledge of life?"

"The knowledge of life is a series of relationships that categorically begins with self. Knowing one's self leads to knowing one's purpose, which leads to fulfilling one's life."

"You are very wise for a man who didn't attend college."

"The most important knowledge is common sense. And the Bible says, 'The fear of the Lord is the beginning of wisdom, and the knowledge of the holy is understanding.'" (Proverbs 9:10)

She curled and snuggled the teddy bear that matched her white sheets and comforter. Her head rested on an excess of fluffy pillows. "Hmm," she whispered as if she felt his touch. "I wish you were here."

He soothed, "I am there. My spirit is in the room. Tell my flesh what you're wearing."

She rolled onto her back, her eyes closed, and bashfully said, "Bra and panties."

"What color?"

She whispered, "A shade of blue."

"Mmm. Can you feel me looking at you?"

"Uh-huh."

"Can you feel me touching you?"

"Yesss, I feel it."

"Can you feel my tongue caressing yours?"

"Mmm. I feel it."

"Tell me what you feel."

"You. I feel you kissing me, and touching me."

"Feel me, Yvonne. Feel me like I'm feeling you. Feel the imagination made real by my voice."

"Mmm, I feel you."

She entered the realm of imagination and allowed his voice to guide her fingers to a climax.

Silence held her last moan before she screeched, "I can't believe it," and grinned.

"Did it feel real?"

"Yes."

"Then believe it. Everything we feel is real. It's called the spiritual world."

"I really felt you."

"I felt you too. The real world is the spiritual world."

With half of her face sunken into one of the pillows, she said, "I love you."

"I love you too."

* * *

Yvonne planted her footsteps on the snow-covered courtyard as she darted to her grandmother's building.

The bitter cold and howling wind didn't remove her beatific expression.

She entered the unlocked girded green door, stomped on the tattered terra-cotta tile, removed her white, faux-fur pom-pom beanie hat and goose down ski jacket, and rode the elevator to the sixteenth floor.

The door opened to the strong smell of chitterlings that faded as she walked down the impoverished hallway.

She used the spare key to enter the apartment.

Ruth was in the bathroom. "Vonnie, that's you?"

"Yeah, it's me, Grandma!"

"I'll be out in a minute."

"Okay."

Yvonne hung her jacket and hat in the closet across from the front door, and placed her black, knitted gloves inside the pocket.

She sat on the plastic-fitted sofa—a picture of Jesus centered on the egg-white wall behind. An array of family photos was on the brass table at the side. A crafted white mermaid with silver scales that Yvonne had made during her youth at the Police Boys & Girls Club decorated the tawny coffee table.

Her grandmother limped into the room with a rubber-handled aluminum cane.

"Grandma, when I get money, I'm going to pay for the operation on your knee."

Ruth's smile broadened. "You and Mister don't have to keep saying that. I know you will. Until then, Jesus will continue to take care of me. I made a cake last night."

"Mmm," Yvonne said, and started to rise from the couch.

"Don't get up; I'll bring you a slice."

"Thanks, Grandma."

She grabbed the saucer from the brown wooden cabinet over the stove, sliced the cake, and handed Yvonne the dish and a fork.

"You know I don't need a fork for this." Yvonne used her fingers to carry a piece of the tender cake to her mouth and swallowed. "Mmm, Grandma, your cake is sooo good. When I get the money, I'm going to open a bakery for you. Everybody will buy your cakes and pies."

Ruth giggled and sat beside her.

Sporting a childhood grin, Yvonne said, "Grandma, I think I'm in love."

"You think?"

"Okay, I know."

"How do you know?"

"The way I feel. I never felt like this before. It's the way Cedric looks at me, and touches me. I've never made love until I met him. There's a difference between having sex and making love. You know what I mean?"

Ruth went back in time. Her face was unable to hide the recollection of a lingering passion. "I-I know what you mean."

"Most importantly, Mister likes him. They are always talking. When I asked Cedric what they talk about, he said he couldn't share the secrets of their man talk. When I asked Mister, he smiled and said, 'It's a secret.' He is always asking 'Where is Cedric'—like Cedric is his father. My son hadn't felt that way about the other men I dated. Can you believe he picked up Mister in this weather and took him bowling on the base? I love him, Grandma."

"Are you sure it's love and not infatuation? You've only dated a couple of months."

"It's both. I know it's still early in our relationship, but Cedric has a way of making a minute feel like a day."

"Has he told you that he loves you?"

"Uh-huh."

"Do you believe him?"

She leaned back on the sofa and shifted her body to face Ruth, and said, "Yes."

"I believe him too. I could see it in his eyes when I met him. Have you told him that you love him?"

"Yes. Last night, after phone sex."

"Phone sex?"

"Yeah, Grandma. It was like I could feel his body on top of me."

"Child, don't say any more. I'm starting to get goose bumps. Have you told your mother how you feel about him?"

"You know I can't tell her. She's only gonna say something negative."

"She's your mother, and being in love for the first time as a woman is an important moment in your life. You have to tell her."

Yvonne turned to the window and stared at the swirling snow. Her spirit dampened by the thought of visiting her mother.

After she had eaten another slice of the three-layer yellow cake with chocolate frosting, she wrapped slices for Mister, Cedric, herself, and her mom before she trudged to the building at the far side of the courtyard.

An "out of order" sign greeted her as she approached the elevator. *This is unacceptable. It's been more than a week.*

She climbed six flights and knocked several times before her mother, Beverly, a dreary-looking, forty-year-old opened.

"Hi, Ma."

Beverly didn't look her in the eye, and didn't say a word. Zombie-like, she turned and drooped towards the royal-blue sofa.

Yvonne entered the apartment that reeked of burnt pork chops and neglected filth. "You fell asleep again while you were cooking?"

Beverly plopped. "No," she said with a befuddled look.

Yvonne closed the door, removed her hat and coat. "Why haven't the girls cleaned the house?"

"Your sisters are frolicking in the streets like you did."

Yvonne rolled her eyes, placed her hat and gloves inside the pocket of her coat, and hung it in the closet that faced the front door.

She sat next to her mother on the stained and torn sofa. "Have you talked to Ruben and Steve?"

"They call, but I don't answer."

"Why? They need to hear your voice since you don't visit them."

"They don't need me."

"Ma, why are you talking like that? You're their mother. Are you mad at them because they are locked up, or because they can't give you money anymore?"

26

She turned away.

"Ma, I brought you a slice of Grandma's cake."

Beverly snatched it, unwrapped the foil, and ate, head down as if ashamed.

Yvonne turned away. Her welled-up eyes were fixed on the sullied carpet where she'd slept at the age of thirteen to eighteen. The painful memories pushed her eyes back to her mother.

"Ma, look at me."

Beverly shifted her eyes to her daughter.

"Ma, I'm in love with Cedric."

"Why?"

"Because he makes me happy."

"He's only having fun with you, Yvonne. Men like him won't marry a project girl."

"Why are you always so negative? All men are not the same."

"Yes, they are."

"No, they're not!"

"You'll see. Your father was like him. A smooth talker. Telling me how much he loved me, but sleeping all over town, even with some of my friends. Where is he now? God only knows."

"I knew I shouldn't've told you."

"Praise God, you did. You need to hear the truth. All men are the same, roaming dogs looking for a bitch in heat. The only reason he's still around is because he hasn't gotten you pregnant. He probably got more than one kid in Mississippi, and God knows how many others since he's been in the military."

"Ma, I gotta go."

"Go ahead, run from the truth like you always do. If he marries you, it's only because he knows Mister is going to be a millionaire."

Yvonne bit down on a corner of her lip. "I gotta go, Ma. I love you."

She sprang off the sofa and opened the closet. She grabbed her jacket, kissed her mother on the cheek, and hurried out of the apartment on the verge of tears.

After a few steps, she leaned against the graffiti-covered wall, unable to hold back tears that removed mascara.

"God, please help my mother," she mumbled down the stairwell.

A group of youths were standing at the exit landing. The oldest was nineteen and the youngest eleven.

"Hi, Ms. Baker," each one respectfully said.

She tried to hide her tears and said, "Hi," as she walked through the circle they opened.

Memories of her youth came back. She turned and said to the group of nine, "Don't give up on your dreams. You can make it out of this place without jail or a casket."

They smiled with hope in their eyes.

She mirrored the smile, put on her gloves and hat, zipped up the jacket, and plodded through the snowdrifts that hindered visibility. Disheartened, she hurried up the steps to the door of her second-floor apartment. But happiness replaced the sadness when she saw Cedric cooking with her son beside him.

"Ma, I got a strike!" He embraced her.

Cedric lowered the chicken wings and joined the picture that reflected in the oval mirror mounted on the wall of the dual living and dining room.

She looked at the reflection and tightened her embrace. *Thank you, God.*

* * *

Eight days later, on a Saturday morning, there was a knock on Yvonne's apartment door.

"That must be Cynthia," Yvonne said, on her knees, wiping the dust off furniture.

Mister was washing dishes, and said, "Cynthia is coming to help us clean?"

"No, she's moving to Atlanta tomorrow."

"Oh, you want me to get the door?"

"No, I'll get it."

"It might be Cedric, Ma."

On her way to the door, she said, "Don't get excited. It's not him. Your buddy is home visiting his family."

She opened the door.

A delivery man stood with a large square package. "Special delivery for Yvonne Baker."

"I'm Yvonne Baker."

"Please sign here."

She carried the light, but large, plain package to the sofa. *This must be from Cedric.*

Mister shook the suds off his hands and scooted beside her.

"Ma, hurry up and open it."

She ignored her son's anxiousness and despite her inward excitement, slowly unwrapped. Her eyes brightened at the sight of a decorated box that had a yellow ribbon tied in a bow. She smiled, untied the bow, ripped the wrapping, opened the box, and saw a smaller decorated box with a blue bow.

Mister became impatient and tried to open the package.

Yvonne slapped his hand. "Stop. It's my present."

She untied the bow, ripped the wrapping, and lifted out a tiny decorated box with a red bow. Her eyes widened. A ring was her thought, and she vigorously tore the wrapping.

Engraved with gold lettering on top of the black suede case was, "Earrings 4U." She smiled behind her minor disappointment, and opened the case.

"OOHH MY GOD! A RING!" Tears of joy streamed down her cheeks.

She leaped and jumped like her double-dutch days.

Mister watched, then he jumped as if his mother had made the game-winning basket.

Seconds later, a knock on the door.

"It's Cedric!" she screamed, and put on the ring. Finger extended, she opened the door.

The delivery man said, "I'm sorry, Miss. I asked you to sign for the wrong package."

Her smile retreated; her eyes closed; her face darkened; her head dropped. She was baffled, disappointed, and embarrassed all at once.

But in a moment of the unexpected and needed, Cedric jumped out from hiding and fell to one knee. "Will you marry me?"

"YESSSS! I LOVE YOU! I LOVE YOU! I LOVE YOU!"

She yanked him off his knee and their tongues locked.

Mister joined their embrace. When the passionate kiss ended, he looked up with his light brown eyes and said, "Ma, you gonna marry my father?"

She was startled but happy to hear him say those words, and affectionately rubbed his slender back. "Yes, I am." She kissed the top of his head.

Cedric turned to Mister with a broad smile and patted his shoulder. "We're going to be a family."

Mister placed the side of his face on Cedric's chest and closed his eyes. Then he lifted his head and faced his mother. "I'm going to go tell Great-Grandma." He grabbed his gray hoodie from out of the closet and scooted.

"Are you sure you want to marry me?" Yvonne asked.

He held her hands. "I told you before, I don't say what I don't mean."

"I love you."

"And I love you."

After a couple of short kisses, they sat at the square four-seat wooden dining table and made plans to wed when he returned from his ninety-day deployment to Lebanon.

"I can talk about our wedding all night, but I have to get back to the base. I leave tomorrow."

"Tomorrow? What happened to Thursday?"

"My orders were changed."

"You can't leave here yet. I'm not going to see you for twelve weeks." She gave him the look, and held it as she walked towards the bedroom.

He followed her, with fervent desire written on his face.

* * *

Six weeks later, Yvonne learned that she was pregnant and phoned Cedric to share the news but was unable to reach him. She left an urgent message.

30

The next day without a response, she called again without success.

Eager to share the news, she sent a message through the military email on the computer Cedric had given as a Christmas gift, but days passed without a reply.

After various and multiple attempts, all types of negative thoughts settled, and worry turned to fear.

Several days later, Yvonne received a long-distance phone call.

A hesitant voice said, "Hi Yvonne, it's Kenneth."

She screeched, "Where is Cedric?"

He stuttered, "...C-Cedric was captured and killed by extremists."

Her eyes widened and her mouth hung open. Her fingers collapsed as if melted, and the coil cord handset dropped onto the bedroom carpet.

She flopped on the edge of the bed with her eyes wide open. She tried to gather thoughts, but none stayed. She turned to the framed Scriptures and inwardly read each one.

The rapid beeps from the phone off the hook broke the silence.

She stared at the handset, angry that she wasn't able to turn back the hand of time.

Numb, she listened for a few seconds to the annoying sound before she picked up the phone and returned it to the base that sat on the small pink dresser beside the bed.

She cried, "Why?" She clutched the framed picture of her and Cedric that stood next to the phone and lay in a fetal position, brooding. The fond memory of that day brought relentless tears.

Mister ran into the room. He embraced his mother as she lay there, and cried because she was crying. The harder she sobbed, the tighter he held her in his ten-year-old arms.

"What happened, Ma?"

Only tears and convulsive gasps came from her mouth.

"Ma, there is a positive side to every negative thing."

The familiar words lessened her pain as she recalled an occasion when Cedric had turned her sadness into a smile with that phrase.

Her eyes opened and locked on his. "Cedric died."

His tears suddenly had a meaning. Sobbing, he asked, "Why did my father die?"

"He died a hero, baby."

His body relaxed. "A hero?"

"Yes. Cedric died protecting the country."

Mister's teary eyes fell on his mother's breast. She rubbed his head, and tearfully said, "There is a positive to every negative. I'm pregnant."

"Pregnant!" he shouted, alleviated from sorrow, and planted the side of his head on her stomach.

Silent tears rolled down Yvonne's face as she watched her son fall asleep in that position. After several minutes of reflection, she woke Mister and sent him to his bedroom.

Unable to sleep, she phoned Cynthia.

"I'm sorry," Cynthia said tearfully. "You know I thought he was a player. But he really loved you. He died loving you. And he left you with the most important thing, his seed."

Yvonne wept.

"You need to cry. Get it all out, and tomorrow start planning on how you will raise another child. You have to do it for Cedric."

"It's going to be hard."

"What hasn't been hard in your life? But you got it done every time. You know God will help you."

Yvonne paused. Her eyes closed in a flood of tears. Her head lowered. "I loved him so much!"

"And he loved you, and still loves you. He left you with his seed. God blessed him, and you."

Yvonne used her index finger to wipe the lingering tears. She lifted her head, exhaled, and said, "You're right. In my womb is the continuation of his life."

CHAPTER 4

After a week of self-imposed seclusion, Yvonne listlessly gazed out her grandmother's window at the golden glow of the sunset behind thin clouds.

Ruth was sitting next to the sofa in her favorite chair, a rust-colored recliner. "When are you going to visit your mother?" she asked.

Yvonne didn't turn from the view of solace. "Grandma, I'm not in the mood for her right now."

"You know she's gonna be upset that you came to see me and not her."

"I don't want to hear her negativity. Don't mention I was here."

"I won't. But I'm sure she'll find out. You know how much people around here love to gossip."

"Doesn't the Bible say something about busybodies?"

"I'm sure it does. The Bible speaks about everything."

"I'll stop by and see her in a few days. I'm not feeling her right now."

* * *

The next morning, knuckles on Yvonne's door interrupted a reminiscent moment.

Damn, I know that's my mother. Yvonne reluctantly opened the door. "Hi, Mom."

Beverly forced a smile to disguise her balled-up face. "Are you all right?"

Yvonne turned without a word and dragged herself into the kitchen.

Beverly stepped inside and closed the door. "Why haven't you returned my calls? I've been worried to death."

"Ma, I'm not in the mood to talk."

"That's what Mister told me, so I didn't bother you, but you went to visit my mother. Why didn't you come to see me?"

Yvonne didn't answer. She poured a cup of coffee and sipped. She shifted her eyes to the wooden clock that hung on the yellow wall and shuffled to the sofa.

Beverly plopped next to her. "I'm sorry to hear what happened to Cedric."

"I don't want to talk about him right now."

"I do. I want to apologize for what I said. I was wrong. He was a good man. I'm sorry."

The words melted Yvonne's resistance, and with a flood of tears, her head toppled onto her mother's shoulder.

They cried together.

The picture of a missing mother found and an ailing daughter healed was the moment at hand.

After the tears subsided, they chatted, smiling and laughing, for nearly three hours.

"I gotta go and cook dinner," Beverly said.

"Okay, Ma. Thanks for stopping by."

Yvonne was walking her to the door when Beverly noticed a stack of letterhead envelopes on the small table. "Look at all that mail. Are the private schools still recruiting Mister?"

"Yeah."

"You should send him to private school. They got the best teachers and coaches. Why you keeping him in that public school? You always talking about the importance of education. Private schools got the best education, and it's free for him."

"Ma, he likes his public school. He's a straight-A student. Some of his teachers were my teachers. Mr. Ramey and Mr. Watson are excellent instructors. Mister likes his coach too."

"You should still send him to private school."

"Public schools are as good as private schools. The only difference is the class size. It's harder for a teacher with a class of thirty-five students compared to only fifteen at a private school."

"That's why you should send him to private school."

"Ma, I'm not going to send him where he doesn't want to go."

"He's too young to know what's best for him. You need to be the boss and make him go to private school. He need to get away from this neighborhood."

"Ma, I'm not going to send Mister to a school he doesn't want to attend. He's happy at his school, and that is where he is going to stay."

"Okay, you're his mother."

"Thank you."

"But you still should send him to private school."

* * *

Six months pregnant, Yvonne attended a prayer breakfast for past loved ones and saw a familiar face weeping. She watched the man who sat alone and felt compassion.

After the service, she approached, rubbed his back, and sympathetically said, "True love never dies."

Little did she know how much her kindhearted gesture meant to the man who had been wrestling with suicidal thoughts.

"What's your name?" he asked as he looked up at her from his seat on the burgundy cushioned pew.

"Yvonne. I'm here because my fiancé recently died."

"My condolences, Yvonne. My name is Charles. My wife and daughter were killed ten years ago by stray bullets from an eleven-year-old. I will never forget that day."

"I won't either. I was across the street when it happened."

"You witnessed it?"

"I wish I hadn't."

"I wish it hadn't happened. I still pray for that boy and his parents. I don't blame him. I blame the system that confines at-risk youth to juvenile delinquency."

She nodded.

Charles, a ruddy freckled-face forty-nine-year-old gave Yvonne a look she recognized as skepticism. He must have noticed she was pregnant and maybe wondered why she was being so nice, maybe another gold digger looking for a sugar daddy, like the others.

Yvonne sensed his distrust but didn't walk away.

"Are you staying for lunch?" she asked.

He stared blankly.

She said, "You shouldn't be alone right now. We can eat together if you're not in a hurry."

His eyes twinkled. "Okay. I'll stay for lunch."

The two entered the church basement and sat together amid whispers from some who likely speculated that Yvonne was trying to fleece him. She noticed the stares and subtle glances but wasn't bothered. *A bunch of busybodies.*

Charles must have read her expression. "They think you're like the other young women who conned me out of money."

Her brows lifted. "Who conned you out of money?"

He lowered his eyes and head.

"No need to be ashamed now. You already told me that women stole from you. I'm not interested in your money. I invited you to eat with me because you need a friend."

He lifted his head in silence.

"I'm waiting for you to answer the question," she said with one hand on top of the other.

"When I got the life insurance for my wife and daughter, I became a favorite of the young women in the neighborhood who told me about their problems. So I gave them money, but they lied. One said she was in school and needed a computer to study at home, but I found out later that she wasn't in school. One said her mother needed an operation, but she lied. One told me that she was going to be evicted from her apartment if she didn't pay her landlord two thousand dollars in cash. I gave her the money, but she lied too."

He paused and centered his eyes on her. "It's sad that people take kindness for weakness. I guess I was the fool. I shouldn't be so willing to help. But I'm a Christian. How do I balance helping and not helping?"

She leaned forward and stretched her hand on his shoulder. "Kindness is not a weakness. To lie and steal is a weakness."

His eyes squinted as if a bright light was in front of him.

"Can I ask you a question?"

"Yes."

"What was the real reason for trying to help them? Please be honest?"

He again lowered his head, this time as if an arrow had pierced his heart. "What do you mean the real reason?"

"You know what I mean. Tell me the truth."

He lifted his head. "They told me that they liked me."

"So you were trying to buy their love?"

"They said they liked me. I told them my age, and they said, 'age doesn't matter.' I was lonely when my wife and daughter died. That's a natural emotion."

"True, but our emotions can easily deceive us. If you're afraid of being alone, that feeling will lead you to commit foolish acts. You were tricked three times because you allowed your loneliness to control you."

"I just wanted a friend. Someone to talk to."

"Where is your family?"

"My parents were killed when I was six. I came to North Carolina to live with my grandmother, who died thirteen years ago. I don't have any family or friends outside of work. Will you be my friend?"

"I've been your friend from the first moment I spoke to you. Will you be mine?"

"Yes."

To the chagrin of some, they exchanged contact information and left the building together.

* * *

Charles held Yvonne's hand when she gave birth to a son named Derrick Cedric Williams. The next day, he drove Mister, Ruth, and Beverly to visit her at the hospital.

Yvonne was sitting upright on the bed with her baby cradled. Mister was the first in the room and kissed him before he kissed his mother. Beverly and Ruth crowded around the baby—oohs and ahhs were their voices.

When they backed away to sit, Mister whispered in Derrick's ear, "I'm your brother and father."

His eyes opened as if he understood the words.

"Ma, he can hear me! He opened his eyes!"

Beverly and Ruth leaped and leaned over Mister's shoulders.

37

"Ahh, they're closed," Beverly said.

"He looks just like his father," Yvonne said with joy.

Ruth said, "He looks like Mister to me."

Beverly interjected, "Naw, he looks like Grandaddy Earl."

Yvonne lifted Derrick towards Charles, who was standing celebratory beside her. "Who does he look like to you?"

"He looks like Derrick Cedric Williams."

She smiled. "Great answer."

* * *

Two days later, at the tail end of the morning rush hour, Charles was driving Yvonne from the hospital when she turned her newborn towards him.

"Will you be Derrick's godfather?"

A tear from the corner of his eye rolled under the arm of his glasses. He pulled over to the shoulder and parked his twelve-year-old minivan.

Yvonne's expression turned blank.

He sighed and lowered his head, with both hands on top of the steering wheel.

"What's wrong, Charles?"

He sniffed. "I'm sorry. I'm just surprised you asked."

"Why are you surprised? We go to church together; we go to the movies together; we cook and clean for each other. I cried on your shoulder when my cat died. You're the one who took me to the hospital when I was in labor. I love you, Charles. I love you as a friend."

He lifted his head and removed his glasses.

With the sleeve of his colorful polyester shirt, he wiped tears, and turned his head towards her. "I love you too. But more than a friend."

"I know you do. I'm sorry I can't share those feelings right now... but I appreciate you for not pressuring or making me feel obligated. We have a good friendship. Let's just see what happens."

He nodded. "Thank you for being honest. Of course I will be his godfather."

She widened her smile and kissed him on the cheek. "Thank you for being my friend."

CHAPTER 5

A college gymnasium in Washington, D.C., was the setting of a prestigious thirteen-and-under national basketball tournament. Yvonne and Charles were sitting in the first row.

The ardent fans beside and behind shouted, "Let's go, NC!"

As if there was a competition as to who could scream the loudest, the fans on the other side roared, "Let's go, Indiana!"

Charles yelled, "Get the rebound, Mister!"

Feeling the stress of the game, Yvonne was silent.

The Indiana team was trailing by one point, with a player at the free-throw line. In the spirit of sportsmanship, the gym quieted when the referee handed the thirteen-year-old the ball.

He made the first shot, and the Indiana fans roared and stomped.

The North Carolina coach, a police officer, called a time-out and huddled his team as the Indiana crowd chanted.

Yvonne's hands, formed in prayer, covered her nose and mouth.

Charles gripped her arm. "That was a good time-out. He's freezing the shooter. That kid won't make the second free throw. We're going to overtime."

Two play-by-play announcers were broadcasting the game for tape delay on the community channel.

Announcer #1: *"This is a great game."*

Announcer #2: *"It's amazing how these young kids can play so well. Mister Baker is better than advertised. Man, he's exciting. Only eleven years old and already five foot nine. He's the fastest kid I've seen dribbling the basketball... and he plays every position."*

Announcer #1: *"He is indeed an outstanding talent. The same for Effi Giles of Indiana. Thirteen and six foot two. He has dominated the paint on both ends of the floor with nineteen blocked shots, twenty-four rebounds, and twenty-three points. He is very impressive. Those two players are the reason for all the scouts in the building."*

Announcer #2: *"We seem to have a delay. Both of the referees went to the scorer's table."*

Announcer #1: *"While we wait for the game to resume, I will recap if anyone is just tuning in. The score is 49-49 with 6.9 seconds remaining. The kids from North Carolina have erased a twelve-point halftime deficit with their outside shooting—led by Mister Baker who has scored twenty-nine points.*

"It looks like we are ready to resume. Effi Giles has one more free throw that can give his team the lead and possibly send them to the championship game tomorrow against Washington, D.C."

The buzzer sounded, and both teams returned to the floor. Effi Giles stood confidently at the free-throw line. The only sound was three bounces of the ball.

The North Carolina fans and players were praying for a miss but he made the free throw, and the Indiana fans celebrated as if the game was over. Unfazed, the North Carolina coach called his last time-out.

"Oh my God, this is too much," Yvonne said as she squirmed.

Charles looked at the clock. "They need a miracle now."

Yvonne said, "I believe in miracles."

Charles replied, "Mister can do it."

The buzzer sounded, and the teams returned to the court. Unnerved, Mister glanced at his mother.

She returned the confident expression and yelled, "You can do it."

Announcer #1: *"Indiana has set their defense to protect against the outside shot. They are daring North Carolina to attack the basket."*

Announcer #2: *"You're right. They're in a 1-3-1 zone with the point man at half-court—three players are guarding the three-point line—and Effi Giles is alone under the basket to deter a lay-up attempt. It's a very aggressive defense. Smart move by the Indiana coach. North Carolina has to travel the length of the floor in less than seven seconds. Not a lot time for thirteen-year-olds."*

Announcer #1: *"The North Carolina kids look confused. I think they were expecting Effi to be on the inbound passer. That's the only reason I can conclude as to why Mister is inbounding the ball.*

"Here we go. Mister inbounds the ball and gets it back with a figure eight!

"He avoids the half-court trap with a behind-the-back dribble!

"Oh, they got him trapped on the left side.

"He escapes with a dribble between his legs!

"He's going all the way to the basket!

"Effi goes for the block!

"Mister shoots a reverse lay-up.

"It's good! He made it at the buzzer! North Carolina wins on a spectacular shot from Mister Baker!"

Yvonne and Charles erupted along with the impassioned North Carolina crowd. While players and fans stormed the court, Charles and Yvonne found themselves in a moment. They were captured by an urge and stood in silence with their eyes fixated on each other. Charles' eyes reflected uncertainty. He paused like a man who hadn't kissed a woman.

Yvonne sensed the lack of nerve and kissed him first.

"Was that gratitude?" he asked.

She leaned back, eyes wide, mouth open, hands on hips. "Did it feel like gratitude?"

Charles dropped to one knee, and said, "Will you marry me?"

She widened her smile and said, "Yes."

He leaped like an eighteen-year-old and shouted, "She said yes!"

After congratulatory hugs from the coaches, players, and fans, Mister ran into the arms of his mother.

"I'm so proud of you. I knew you could do it."

Charles squeezed his arm around Mister's shoulder. "How did you make that shot?"

Mister leaned into him as if he was his biological father and said, "I just tried."

Smiling, Yvonne faced her son. "I'm going to marry Charles."

His smile broadened. "I'm down with that."

She embraced him and kissed the top of his short high-faded haircut. "I'm so proud of you."

* * *

Eleven months after the birth of Derrick, Charles and Yvonne were married. She moved into his semi-detached three-bedroom house and transferred the three framed Scriptures to their bedroom walls. Ten months later, she gave birth to twins. The boy was named Charles Jr., and the girl, Charlene. Both were born with reddish-brown skin.

"I wish my parents were alive to see them."

Yvonne was cradling the twins and said, "They can see them from heaven."

Charles faced her with his knees on the fluffy bedroom carpet. "I love you."

"I love you too. What's wrong? Your mind has been drifting for the past few weeks."

He avoided eye contact. "Nothing, I'm all right."

"C'mon Charles. What's wrong? I can see it in your face and hear it in your voice."

"Everything will be okay."

"What do you mean, everything will be okay?"

"Everything will be okay."

Yvonne frowned and tucked the twins in their cribs. "What is it?" she asked, with eyes narrowed and brows raised.

"I don't know how to say it."

"Just say it."

His eyes lowered with tears that followed, and muttered, "I-I have cancer."

"What? Cancer! Oh my God!"

Her voice woke the twins, who whiningly fussed.

She ignored the reverberation. "When did you find out?"

"Last month."

"What! Why didn't you tell me?"

"I didn't want to spoil your happiness."

42

"My happiness? I can't be happy if you're not happy. Charles, you can't keep things like that from me. Why did you do that?"

Teary-eyed, Yvonne used both hands to rock the blue and pink wooden cradles until the twins quieted.

Yvonne was on the phone telling Ruth that she would pick up Derrick in the morning. Charles was on the edge of the bed, his head down, when Mister entered the bedroom.

He peeked at the twins, and when his mother ended the call, he asked, "What's going on?"

"Charles has cancer."

Mister screeched, "Cancer? I thought only white people got cancer."

"That's because we only hear about the white people who die from cancer, but the disease attacks all races."

"Is Charles going to die?" he whimpered.

"We are going to do everything we can to keep that from happening, starting with prayer."

Mister shifted his eyes to Charles who was sitting without hope. "You can beat this. Have faith."

* * *

Diagnosed with prostate cancer and told that he had six months to live, the health insurance company compounded their problems with a letter that denied coverage.

Yvonne immediately responded. "Hi, this is Mrs. Dunbar. I'm calling for my husband, Charles Dunbar. We received a letter informing us that his insurance won't cover the treatments for cancer. I need clarification, please."

After she had given the policy number, the accommodating representative viewed the file.

"I'm sorry, Mrs. Dunbar, but Mr. Dunbar's illness is listed as a pre-existing condition as stated in the letter."

Furious, she shouted, "How was that determined?"

"I'm not sure. The information came from our investigative department. I can request another letter with more details. That's all I can do, Mrs. Dunbar. I'm sorry."

"Can I speak to a manager?"

43

"Sure, I will transfer you to my supervisor."

Elevator music sounded for ten minutes.

"Hello, this is Mr. Thomas. How can I help you?"

"Mr. Thomas, I'm calling for my husband, Charles Dunbar. Your company sent us a letter that states he's not covered for cancer treatments because he has a pre-existing condition. How was that determined?"

"Mrs. Dunbar, that was the findings of our investigative department. You will have to speak to them for additional details."

"Can you connect me, please?"

"I'm sorry, I'm unable. You will have to call directly. I can give you the number."

"I've called that number a million times, and all I get is a recording that doesn't return my call when I leave a message. This is some BS. You collect my husband's payment every month, and now that he needs you, your back has turned."

"I'm sorry Mrs. Dunbar. There is nothing more I can do."

"There is more you can do. You're just not willing to do it."

The conversation ended without her satisfaction.

The refusal of the health insurance company to honor its obligations forced them to pay full price for the treatments and prescribed medications. The cost, mercilessly expensive, gobbled their savings and added mounting debts. Despite their dilemma, the love rooted in friendship and steadfast faith sustained them. But as the days continued, one couldn't ignore that Charles Sr. was quickly deteriorating. It was as if Yvonne was caring for three infants.

When her husband could no longer get out of bed, Yvonne would put the twins in his arms. And when he became too weak to hold them, she held the twins for him to touch and kiss.

Mister watched with dismay and often cried as his stepfather's body withered.

Eight months after he had made his diagnosis known, Charles Sr. died, and the life insurance company refused to pay the $100,000 claim.

Incensed, Yvonne met with one of the executives. "Why did your company send this letter denying my claim? My husband didn't commit suicide."

"Mrs. Dunbar, it was the findings of our investigators that your husband's cancer was self-induced."

Enraged, she yelled, "Self-induced! How can prostate cancer be self-induced?"

The man ignored her valid point and repeated the company's decision.

"Well, I'm going to sue."

The man didn't respond, and Yvonne left the corporate office.

The saving grace was the $10,000 life insurance policy from Charles' employment at the sanitation department. Yvonne used that money to bury her husband with decency.

Left with insurmountable medical bills, a delinquent mortgage, and four children, Yvonne fell deeper into poverty. Unable to afford a lawyer or find pro-bono, she filed the lawsuit. But the piling on of legal fees thwarted the Herculean effort to represent her husband in court.

Loan sharks of many forms approached with Mister's future NBA contract as the collateral. But Yvonne refused every offer, even the ones that said there were no strings attached. She sold her car and added a part-time job to supplement her full-time salary, and worked every day except Sundays. She used the aged minivan as her transportation. Despite the tribulation, Yvonne kept her head above water.

Every night and morning, she read the three framed Scriptures on her bedroom walls:

He healeth the broken in heart, and bindeth up their wounds. (Psalms 147:3)

For we are saved by hope. But hope that is seen is not hope; for what a man seeth, why doth he yet hope for? But if we hope for that we see not, then do we with patience wait for it... And we know that all things work together for good to them that love God... (Romans 8:24-28)

For none of us liveth to himself, and no man dieth to himself. For whether we live, we live unto the Lord; and whether we die, we die unto the Lord; whether we live therefore, or die, we are the Lord's. (Romans 14:7-8)

45

CHAPTER 6

Monday through Friday, Beverly took care of the twins until Yvonne arrived after work. Ruth cared for Derrick until Mister picked him up after school. When Mister arrived home with his three-year-old brother, he cooked dinner, washed the dishes, put Derrick to bed, and completed his homework before his mother arrived home with the twins around nine p.m.

On Saturdays, Yvonne's sisters, Diane, Phyllis, and Stephanie, rotated babysitting duties while Mister minded Derrick and washed the clothes.

One weeknight, after a sixteen-hour workday, Yvonne was sitting at the dining room table with her eyes glued to the television. Mister moseyed upstairs from his basement bedroom and sat across from her. "Ma, I have to tell you something."

Worry replaced fatigue. "What happened?"

"Nothing bad happened. I just want you to know that I'm not playing basketball this year."

"Why? What's going on?" she asked.

"Derrick is about to start kindergarten. Who's going to watch him after school? Great-Grandma can barely walk to the bus stop; she can't pick him up. Grandma is babysitting the twins and doesn't have a car. If I'm playing basketball, I won't get home until six or seven. Derrick can't be home alone that long. It's only for one year. Next year, he'll be in school until three o'clock, and I can play my senior year."

Yvonne sighed and rubbed her face with the palm of her hands as if she was on the verge of a mental breakdown. "Oh, God. I've been thinking about this since the president cut the funding for child care. I'll find a way to afford his aftercare. I don't want you to stop playing basketball. Let me figure it out." She was already on a payment plan for her delinquent mortgage payments but fell behind when she decided to use the money to cover Derrick's aftercare.

Thirty days later, she received a letter from the mortgage company that threatened to foreclose if she missed another payment.

Unable to continue aftercare, Yvonne would leave work to pick up Derrick and take him to her grandmother and return to work. The problem appeared solved until her supervisor called her into the regional office.

"Yvonne, I received a complaint from one of your co-workers."

"Is it about picking up my son during my lunch break?"

"Yes."

"You know it's an emergency, Mr. Caldwell."

"I understand, Yvonne. You're my best manager, but I can't show favoritism."

"But you approved my request to change my lunch hour."

"Yes, but I'm told that you are away from work for almost ninety minutes."

"It takes that long to go to my son's school, take him to my grandmother, and then come back to work. I make up the time by working longer without overtime."

"I understand, but if I let you take a ninety-minute lunch break, I have to let everyone else do the same. I hope you understand."

"I-I understand," she said with the weight of another burden on her shoulders.

Uncomfortable, but without an alternative, she had to leave Derrick home alone from 12:30 to 6:30 most days. Mister taught him how to walk home after school and unlock the door.

Yvonne told Derrick, "Go straight home and don't talk to anybody. Don't talk to strangers or friends. Don't let anyone inside the house—and don't answer the phone. Just wait for your brother to come home."

A retired neighbor agreed to phone Yvonne every day when Derrick entered the house.

Mornings before school, Mister readied two peanut butter and jelly sandwiches for Derrick to eat when he arrived home and reiterated, "Don't let anyone in the house."

One morning after a Cream of Wheat breakfast, Mister was fixing the usual sandwiches when Derrick whined, "Can I have a butter apple sandwich? I'm tired of peanut butter and jelly."

"It's called apple butter. Not butter apple."

"Can I have apple butter sandwich?"

"It's all gone."

Derrick started crying.

"Shut up," Mister told him.

He halted his tears and pouted.

"I made some Kool-Aid for you."

"Your Kool-Aid don't taste like Great-Grandma's."

"Okay, I won't give you any."

"I sorry. I want some."

"Don't say, I sorry. Say, I'm sorry."

"I'm sorry."

"I'll be late today. I have a game. Don't let anyone inside the house. And study before you play."

"Okay, okay."

* * *

The following week, Mister arrived home early because of a canceled game. He had previously caught Derrick playing with his toys during study time, so he furtively entered the house through the basement door. The home was quiet. *He's either studying or asleep. I bet he's asleep.*

He stepped heel-to-toe up two flights of stairs to Derrick's bedroom, pausing along the way, when the floor squeaked.

When he approached the room, he heard what sounded like a bed squeaking and leaned his ear against the closed door.

Expecting to catch Derrick playing, he yanked open the door and saw Shirley, the ten-year-old daughter of the family that rented the house next door, straddled across his brother. She was holding Derrick's penis inside her vagina.

"What are you doing, girl?" he shouted, disgust etched on his face.

Shirley's black shoes and white ankle socks led her green plaid skirt and yellow blouse from the bed into a corner where she quivered.

48

Her inside-out Minnie-Mouse panties lay beside Derrick's head.

He was crying as if he wanted the world to hear.

When Mister stepped towards him, Shirley sped past and down the stairs.

Mister pursued and confronted Shirley on her porch. "Keep your stinky ass pussy away from my brother! I better not see you in my house again!"

She shrieked, "We were playing doctor!"

Their loud voices drew attention from the neighborhood. Children and adults were watching when Shirley's seventeen-year-old brother, J. T., recently home from juvenile detention, came from out of the house to defend his sister.

Shorter, but thirty pounds heavier, he stepped up into the face of Mister who had grown to six feet and seven inches.

"Motherfucker, who you think you are? You better stay away from my sister!"

"You better tell your sister to keep her hands off my brother."

"Fuck you, nigga! You don't run nuthin' around here."

"I run my house, and your sister isn't allowed in my house."

"Fuck you and your house! Get the fuck away from here, you bitch-ass nigga!"

"I'm not your bitch, and I'm not your nigga. Keep your sister away from my house."

When Mister turned to walk away, J. T. sucker-punched him, and the two fought.

The neighborhood youth gathered around and cheered. The adults watched from their yards, porches, and windows. It was the unspoken code of the community that no one stops a fight, so no one called the police. The wreck ended when the neighborhood patrolman intervened.

The onlookers closest to the action yelled, "Man... Mister kicked J. T. ass like he was a bitch!"

J. T. was humiliated because he had a rep in the neighborhood, and shouted as the officer pulled him away, "It ain't over, motherfucker!"

Mister didn't say a word. He went into the house and phoned his mother. Frantic, she hurried home, crying all the way.

When she picked up the twins, Beverly noticed her distress and asked, "What's wrong?"

"Nothing Ma. I'll tell you later. I'm in a hurry."

When she arrived home, Mister took charge of the twins, and Yvonne scolded Derrick before she took him next door.

Shirley's mom, also a single parent, was shocked when she heard what had occurred. "Shirley! Bring your ass down here!"

Upstairs in her room, Shirley was quiet.

"Bring your ass down here right now before I come up there!"

She sauntered down the stairs in tight jeans and a cut-off belly shirt.

"What did you do to her son?"

With her eyes down and thumbs squeezed into the pockets, she muttered, "We were playing doctor."

"You don't play like that! Look at them and apologize!"

She raised her eyes halfway. "I'm sorry. I won't play doctor with him again."

Further discussion revealed that Shirley had instigated previous sexual encounters with Derrick. Enraged by the confession, her mother slapped and kicked her until Shirley escaped the flurry of blows and ran upstairs.

Yvonne covered her son's eyes and said, "Your daughter doesn't need a beating. She needs professional help."

The riled woman turned from chasing her daughter, and with eyes bulging, yelled, "My daughter isn't crazy! What the hell do you know about her?"

"I'm not saying that she is crazy. I think she might've been sexually abused."

"Are you accusing my boyfriend?"

"No, I'm not. I was just sharing a possibility. I'm sorry if I offended you. Goodbye."

Yvonne returned home and sat at the dining room table. Derrick faced her. He was crying because of an expected spanking.

"Listen to me. What Shirley did to you was wrong and not your fault. I'm not mad at you because of what Shirley did. I'm mad because I told you not to let anyone inside the house. Mister reminded you every morning not to let anyone inside the house."

He whined, "I'm sorry, Mommy. I won't do it again, Mommy."

"Pull down your pants."

"I'm sorry, Mommy. I'm sorry. Please, Mommy."

"Pull down your pants."

With bubbled snot over his lips, he looked at Mister in the hope that he would save him from a spanking as he had done on previous occasions.

But Mister turned his face away and played with the twins.

"C'mon, hurry up and pull down your pants before I do it. It's gonna hurt worse if I have to do it."

Tears flowing, he slowly pulled down his pants. "I'm sorry Mommy. I won't do it again," he mumbled.

"This is gonna hurt me more than you," she said and slapped his bare behind four times with the palm of her hand.

Derrick jumped as if his feet were on hot coals. Tears mingled with snot ran over his lips.

"I'm sorry Mommy. I-I won't do it again, Mommy. I promise, Mommy."

She handed him a tissue. "Wipe your face."

To avoid the usual overflow at the emergency room on a Friday night, Yvonne phoned the family doctor, who accommodated her with an appointment for Derrick in the morning.

* * *

Mister had lost track of time playing soccer with the twins. "Ma, I got to go and meet Crystal."

"Okay, Tell her that I said hi."

"I will."

He grabbed his hoodie and sped through the darkness of long alleys.

Crystal, an aspiring actress with the face of an exotic West Indian, was waiting at the bus stop with a red book bag strapped on her thin shoulders.

"I'm sorry I'm late. Derrick got into trouble. Why didn't you call me?"

"My battery is dead. Is Derrick all right?"

"Yeah, he's fine. I was thinking you might have gotten tired of waiting and went home."

"I knew you were coming."

He smiled. "How did the audition go?"

"It went okay."

"Okay? C'mon. I know you did better than that."

She giggled. "I think I got the part. They will let me know on Monday."

"Yeah! I knew it!"

"How 'bout you? What happened to your lip?"

"I got into a fight with J. T."

"Why?"

"Nothing. I'll tell you about it later."

Their conversation continued as they strolled down the empty sidewalks.

Floodlights set up to deter drug sales and cars that moved in both directions lit the path. When they arrived at her three-floor apartment building, he said, "My mother's not working tomorrow. We can spend the day together without Derrick. You down?"

"Of course, I'm down. What time?"

"After I wash clothes. I'll call you at twelve. We can go to the mall and watch a movie later."

"Okay! You better call at twelve."

"I will."

"And call me when you get home."

"Of course."

He kissed her goodnight.

With a radiant face, Crystal backed-stepped to the building entrance.

Mister stood on the landing and returned her glow.

She blew a kiss and entered the building.

Mister danced his way back towards his house.

When he entered the long alley that led to the basement door, J. T. stepped out from a vacant garage. "Yeahhhh, what up now motherfucker!" he sneered before he pulled up his shirt and whipped out a gun.

Mister didn't flinch and said, "I'm not afraid."

J. T. puckered his lips and scrunched his nose and forehead. He fired four shots that struck Mister in the chest and walked away as if he had done nothing wrong.

Mister slumped in shock. He struggled to his feet in a desperate attempt to make it home and tried to yell, "Ma," with a voice that could only whisper.

He collapsed.

* * *

Yvonne felt a sharp pain in her heart and Derrick started crying for no apparent reason. She dialed Mister's cell. The phone rang until it went to voicemail. Concern turned to worry. *His phone is on. Why didn't he answer?* She hurried into her bedroom to get Crystal's number off her cell.

An anxious fist pounded on the front door.

Oh my God, what happened? Yvonne dropped the phone and ran to open the door.

Derrick was still crying. The twins looked at him with blank faces.

Yvonne yanked open the door, and the neighbor screamed, "Mister got shot in the alley!"

"Oh my God! Nooo!"

"I'll watch the kids for you," the elderly neighbor said with tear-filled eyes.

Frantic , thoughts racing, Yvonne ran down the steps of the back door. A large crowd had gathered around the body and blocked the view of other eager onlookers that pressed. But when they heard Yvonne's harrowed screams, a path opened.

She fell to her knees on the cratered concrete and embraced her son's lifeless body. Blood spewed on her clothing as she wailed in shock.

"Whyyy?" she screeched, eyes looking up at the moonless sky.

Moments later, red and blue lights circled her.

"Miss, you have to move away from the body," one of the officers politely said.

She ignored him.

"Miss, you're contaminating the crime scene."

She continued to disregard and pressed Mister's head against her breast.

The officer lost patience and tried to remove her forcibly.

"Get off me! He's my son! My son!"

A female officer with the face of a teen assisted, and they pulled Yvonne away from the body.

The female officer whispered, "I knew your son at the boys and girls club. He was an angel. He's gone back to heaven now. He's okay."

"Noooo!" Yvonne shrieked before she surrendered her body to the officer's will. Tears and painful screams poured out as she watched his body enter the white van.

"Let me take you home," the female officer said.

"I'm okay. I want to be alone."

She calmly pushed away from the officer's arms and slowly stepped towards the house. Her bloodshot eyes and puffy lids faced the sky.

"Why? Why didn't you save him?" she said.

Yvonne hazily entered the house. The neighbor was standing and gasping convulsively. The twins were asleep at the far end of the sofa. Derrick was sitting upright at the other end of the couch like a little man.

"Ma, where Mister?"

She tried to hide her expression and hugged him. "He's in heaven, baby."

"Heaven? Why Mister go to heaven without me?"

She sniffled, "Because God needed him."

"God need Mister to play on his basketball team?"

A smile crept across her face. "Yes. God needed Mister to play on his basketball team."

CHAPTER 7

Yvonne hugged Derrick as if she would never let him go.

She lifted her eyes to the neighbor. "Thank you for watching my kids."

With tears running down her cheeks, the neighbor's trembling hand gave Yvonne a list of the people who had called.

"Thank you," Yvonne said.

"I'm so sorry this happened. He was so good and respectful. If you need anything, please let me know."

Yvonne nodded with her eyes on her children.

The neighbor sobbed as she left the house.

Yvonne gathered her children into her bed. Charlene and Junior lay asleep in the middle.

With eyes on his mother, Derrick slid next to Junior and said, "Are we going to pray now? Mister made me pray before I sleep."

"Yes, we are going to pray."

After the prayer, Derrick smiled and said, "Mommy, how long will Mister stay in heaven?"

She held back tears and said, "He will stay there until God calls us to be with him."

"So I will see him again?"

"Yes, you will."

His smile broadened. "Goodnight, Mommy."

"Goodnight," she said and leaned across the twins to kiss his forehead.

There is a positive side to every negative thing, she silently repeated.

After a minute of reflection, she grabbed the cordless phone that sat on the night table and returned the calls of her mother and grandmother. The brief conversations ended with the request to be alone until the morning. Beverly fought against it, but reluctantly accepted.

Yvonne's woeful state of mind wouldn't allow her to sleep. She phoned Cynthia, and they cried together. Afterward, she phoned Crystal who answered in a teary voice.

"Mrs. Dunbar, I'm sorry."

"Why are you sorry, Crystal?"

A weeping voice answered, "Because if I hadn't asked him to meet me, he would still be alive."

"Crystal, baby, it wasn't your fault."

She hollered, "I loved him so much."

"I know you did... and he loved you. He told me."

She sniffled, "Why did he have to die, Mrs. Dunbar?"

Yvonne paused in search of an answer before she asked, "What did my son say tonight?"

Crystal wiped her tears with the back of her hand. "He told me that he loves you, Derrick, and the twins more than himself."

Yvonne's eyes swelled, and her lips protruded.

"He told me about what happened to Derrick. He said he was going to quit the team and ask his last two-period teachers if they could give him lessons to work at home so Derrick wouldn't be alone after school."

"What! Did he mean that?"

"I believe he did. He said protecting Derrick was more important than playing basketball."

For several seconds, the only sound heard over the phone was their tears.

"Thank you, Crystal. I love you. Goodnight."

"Goodnight, Mrs. Dunbar. I love you too."

A host of unanswered questions led Yvonne into daybreak.

She didn't consider who killed her son, only why did God allow him to die?

* * *

Yvonne was dressing the twins in the morning light that shone through her bedroom windows.

Derrick was in the bathroom brushing his teeth. Then, toothbrush in hand, he ran into his mother's room. "Ma, Ma, I saw Mister!"

"Calm down. Where did you see him?"

"In the mirror."

"That was your imagination, baby."

56

"My imagination?"

"Yes. It's natural to imagine seeing someone who just died that was very close to you. It's only your imagination."

"What's imagination?"

She hesitated, in search of a way to explain, and said, "Ahm, when you see something that's not there, or you want it to be there."

"Like, I want to see Mister?"

"Yes, baby."

He lowered his head, and his eyes leaned over a tummy that hung over his white briefs.

"It's okay, baby. Mister loves you and misses you too. Now hurry up and get dressed, we have to go to the doctor."

He lifted his head and ran back into the bathroom. When he didn't see Mister in the mirror, he cried.

The twins cried too, as if they knew the reason for Derrick's tears.

Yvonne called Derrick into the room, and she embraced her children.

When they left the house, Shirley's mother was sitting on the top step of her porch. Exhausted eyes were staring at oblivion, a cigarette in one hand, and a mug of coffee in the other.

Her deep thoughts broken when the front door closed, her head swung to Yvonne. "They arrested my son last night, but he didn't kill your son."

Yvonne didn't say a word. She led her children down the steps to the minivan parked at the front of her house, opened the back door, and strapped the twins in their car seats.

"He told me that he didn't kill your son!"

Yvonne opened the passenger's door for Derrick, and fastened his seatbelt.

"You know he didn't kill your son! Tell them that he didn't do it!"

Without looking at her, Yvonne entered the car and drove the mile to her mother's building.

She was glad to see the path void of residents because she wasn't in the mood to hear condolences of some who weren't sincere.

Her sisters embraced her with tears when she entered the apartment.

Beverly was bawling on the sofa, face down in her hands. Yvonne hurried over and cried with her. Her children and sisters joined the embrace.

Beverly raised her head and looked into her daughter's eyes. "Mister isn't dead."

Yvonne tightened her embrace. "I know. He is alive in Christ." She kissed her mother on the cheek. "I gotta go. Derrick has a nine o'clock appointment."

She hugged her sisters and said, "Thanks for watching the twins. I should be back by noon."

Diane said, "Take your time. We don't have anywhere to go."

Yvonne smiled. "I love y'all. Nothing can replace family."

* * *

When Yvonne returned to the complex, she parked at her grandmother's building. Without stopping, she acknowledged the many who expressed their condolences. She entered the apartment with a firm grip on Derrick's hand.

Ruth was sitting in her favorite chair. She quickly lowered the recliner and gripped the arms for support.

"No, Grandma, don't get up."

Derrick ran to her, "Hi, Great-Grandma."

She smiled and hugged and kissed him.

He climbed onto her lap.

She looked up at Yvonne. "What did the doctor say?"

"He's okay."

"Praise God."

She kissed him, and Derrick climbed down and ran into the bedroom to watch cartoons.

Yvonne sat on the sofa. "Grandma, what did I do to deserve this? Why is my son dead? Why is Cedric dead? Why is Charles dead? Life is not fair."

"Don't say that, Yvonne. When you say life isn't fair, you are saying God isn't fair. God is life, and God is fair. The Bible tells us that all things work together for good to those who love the Lord. What we don't understand right now, we will later. God doesn't forsake those who love him."

"Grandma, I believe those words, but I'm not seeing it right now. Mister is dead! Mister! Why is Mister dead? Tell me? Why is my son dead if life is fair?"

"Was life fair when God sacrificed His only begotten Son for us? Jesus was innocent, but His death gave us life. Out of death comes life. Mister lives in you. Cedric lives in Derrick. Charles lives in the twins."

Yvonne felt her heart pierced by the voice of truth. She lifted her head with renewed faith and used the sleeve of her pink fleece to wipe the droplets.

"You're right. I gotta believe. But it's hard, Grandma."

"There is great reward at the end of our trials and tribulations when we endure. I saw mine when you were born. I knew you would be special. I knew God had touched you. I was so proud of you. You were so smart. I knew you would be the first person in our family to get a college degree. I didn't tell you, but I cried all night when you told me that you were pregnant."

"You cried?"

"I cried for you. I prayed for you. I was afraid you would make the same mistakes as your mother and me."

"I might've if you hadn't made me promise to finish school."

"Talking means nothing if the person isn't listening. Thank God, you listened. Thank God, you kept your promise."

* * *

The news of Mister's death carried dismay nationwide, and donations in his name exceeded $90,000. Added was $50,000 from the life insurance.

With the money, Yvonne paid for her children's aftercare, removed the balance on her mortgage, purchased a new car, quit her part-time job, and hired a lawyer to sue the insurance companies that had denied Charles' benefits.

The medical insurance prepared for a trial. The life insurance settled.

She used the settlement to expunge her remaining debts, purchased a new car and sofa for her mother, funded her sisters' college tuition, provided a monthly canteen allowance for her incarcerated brothers, and paid for her grandmother's knee operation.

Six weeks after the settlement, investors were canvassing her neighborhood to buy homes for cash, and offered twice the amount Charles had paid for the home.

But he had told Yvonne about the regentrification that was coming, and that the property value would increase at least four times the original amount.

She shared that knowledge with the neighbors, but nearly all accepted the offer at hand.

The only other holdouts besides Yvonne were the neighbor that phoned her when Derrick entered the house after school and the neighbor who watched her kids the night that Mister died.

While Yvonne waited for her property value to increase, she noticed a change in Derrick's behavior.

"I don't have to tell you to do your homework and study anymore. Why?"

"Because I want Mister to be proud of me in heaven."

She smiled.

"Mommy, the imagination won't go away. I can hear Mister. He keeps saying, do your homework, study, read, and pray."

Her eyes narrowed at the seriousness on his face. *Is he really hearing Mister?*

"What's wrong, Mommy?"

"Nothing, baby. Keep listening to Mister."

"I will, Mommy."

Two years later, Yvonne sold her house for five times the purchased amount and moved into a mortgage-free, four-thousand-square foot, five-bedroom home inside a middle-class community. The only furniture transferred was Mister's bedroom.

Although she was still unable to erase the pain, confusion, and anger she felt over her son's death, she accepted her loss as the will of God.

CHAPTER 8

The days turned quickly into years. Derrick was nine-years-old and the twins neared seven.

Diane, Phyllis, and Stephanie had graduated from college, found jobs, and were childless. Steve and Ruben had another ten years before they were eligible for parole, but the money and gifts made prison comfortable.

Ruth was walking a mile every day. Beverly was visiting her sons twice a month.

The trial date for Yvonne's $20 million lawsuit against the health insurance company was still pending. But she believed a win was inevitable and promised her mother and grandmother a house of their own.

* * *

Another year had passed.

Yvonne was in her family room on a plush, oversized chair, reading a contemporary novel. Her white Ragdoll curled on the laminate floor.

Her sisters and their boyfriends were grilling on the patio where R&B music serenaded them. Charles Jr. was kicking a soccer ball in the fenced-in backyard. Charlene was standing in-between Diane's legs, eating a hot dog.

Derrick entered the family room with his eyes half-open and the side of his mouth slightly puckered. "Ma, tell me about my father?"

She smiled and closed the book. "I've been waiting for you to ask me about him. Why now?"

"I don't know. I guess because I'm bored."

She smiled broadly as she thought about a love that remained undiminished, and set the book on the arm of the sofa next to her.

"I never loved a man like I loved your father. I named you after him to maintain his lineage. That is why your last name is Williams."

"What was his first name?"

"Your middle name."

"Cedric?"

"Yes, Cedric."

"Where was he from?"

"Mississippi."

"Where in Mississippi?"

"Itta Bena. Your father has a daughter about seven years older than you. Her name is Erin."

"I have another sister?"

"Yes."

"Umm. What was my father like?"

"A dream. He was so charming and debonair."

"What is debonair?"

"He was a gentleman, and very stylish."

"Stylish?"

"Yes, he was always dressed sharp, even in uniform."

"Where is he at now?"

"He died defending this country."

"He's in heaven with Mister?"

Tears threatened. "Yes. He's in heaven with Mister. Your father was a good man with strong faith in God. He often quoted the Bible. He should've been a preacher. He told me the first law of human nature is self-preservation, and that self extends beyond you to family and friends. I agreed the family is an extension of self, but when I disagreed with friends, he quoted where Jesus said, 'There is no greater love than a man that lay down his life for his friends.'

"Your father is the one who told me to keep wisdom over love. That is why when I spank you, I say it hurts me more than it hurts you. Your father said the soul is thicker than blood. When I asked him to explain, he quoted Jesus again. I don't remember the exact quote, but it says something like: 'Whoever do the will of God is my mother, father, sister, and brother.' Your father was a biblical scholar. He loved to read and was always working towards the future."

"What did my father look like?"

"Like you without the chubby body."

"I'm fat?"

"You know you're fat. I'll show you a picture of him."

Yvonne sprung from the chair and scampered upstairs. She came back with a brown leather satchel. "This belonged to your father." She opened the satchel and took out pictures of Cedric.

"That's him?"

"Yeah. See how much you look like him?"

"Ma, why is he not fat like me?"

"Because he liked to exercise. Your father had the body of a world-class gymnast."

"I want that body too."

"You can have it if you exercise. Here... this is the Bible your father gave me. It's the Authorized King James Version."

He opened the hardcover and said, "Some of the words are highlighted. I like this Bible."

She took out a book that was titled *Black Wall Street*.

"Your father said, 'Every black man should know about *Black Wall Street.*'"

He took the book but didn't open it. He rubbed his palm across the cover as if he was feeling his father's hand on it.

She added cassette tapes of recorded music to his gifts, and singled out the one labeled, *Black Poets*. "Gil Scott-Heron was your father's favorite poet."

Derrick thought for a moment. "Ma, what is *Black Wall Street*?"

"You have to read to learn... and don't be lazy when you read."

"What you mean, don't be lazy when I read?"

"When you read a word that you don't understand or know the meaning of, don't try to guess and continue reading. Stop and educate yourself. Open the dictionary and look up the meaning. Learn how to pronounce and spell the word. That is one of the ways you gain knowledge."

* * *

Derrick held an immobile expression and took the books and tapes to his room. He listened to the lyrics of Gil Scott-Heron, The Last Poets, Mutabaruka, and Burning Spear, which raised his consciousness and motivated him to read about *Black Wall Street*.

When he opened the book, a piece of paper fluttered to the floor. He picked up the faded half-sheet and read what he believed was his father's handwriting. He rubbed a finger across his chin before he scuttled into his mother's room with the paper. "Ma, who is Peter New-rim-bird?"

She read the paper and said, "Peter Nuremberg was an occasional guest on a daily television program called, *Wall Street Today*. Your father told me that he took advice from him without doing research. His advice seemed like an easy and fast way to make money. If you bought stock from a particular company that he suggested, the value increased. But after a few months, that same stock devalued and investors lost their money."

"I don't understand."

Derrick scrunched his face.

"You have a dollar, but the value of your dollar has dropped to ten cents, and you sell your dollar to me for ten cents because you're afraid it might be only worth five cents tomorrow. Then, next month or next year, the dollar I bought from you for ten cents returned to its original value. That means I just earned ninety cents because I bought your dollar for ten cents."

"Ma, I would just keep my money until it's worth a dollar again."

She smiled. "That's the risk of investing in the stock market. Sometimes the price comes back and sometimes it doesn't."

At ten years old, Derrick added the stock market to his list of interests. He kept current with it, read, and studied about all stock exchange matters, including the history of *Black Wall Street*. The amazing thing was that he was able to comprehend at such a young age.

* * *

While Derrick was engrossed with the stock market, Charlene, at eight years old, was a loner like him. When she wasn't with her mother, she was often studying and reading with Derrick.

Charles Jr., nicknamed Junior, was the opposite. He was athletic and outgoing. At nine years old, he excelled in soccer with the extraordinary skill to guide the ball with both feet like Curley Neal dribbled a basketball.

Yvonne took advantage of the scholarship offers that Junior received from elite private schools and sent him to the top-rated school in the city, which was also among the top five in the country. The condition, which the school accepted, included a scholarship for Derrick and Charlene. The other perks included free transportation to and from school, free meals, and free aftercare.

The students accepted Junior with open arms because of his renowned soccer skills. But Derrick and Charlene were ridiculed by white and black classmates, who said, "You're dumb. The only reason you're in this school is because of your brother."

Charlene followed Derrick's lead and ignored them. They quickly detached themselves from Junior's coat tails and topped the Dean's list at the end of the first quarter.

Derrick had the aspiration to get a degree in economics from Princeton.

Charlene's goal was to attend Johns Hopkins and become a surgeon.

Junior, on the other hand, didn't study to make the honor roll. His focus was limited to meeting the minimum academic requirements to retain eligibility. His dream was to play soccer professionally after high school.

* * *

One morning, Yvonne was driving her children through their old neighborhood, and eleven-year-old Derrick noticed the difference in gas prices.

"Ma, why is gas cheaper in the rich neighborhood?"

"It's one of the many ways the rich get richer and the poor become poorer. It's called capitalism."

"Ma, is money the root of all evil?"

"No, the love of money is the root of all evil."

"Ma, why are white people so mean to black people?"

"All white people are not the same, like all black people are not the same. There are some good white people and some evil white people. There are some good black people and some evil black people. Our greatest enemy is within ourselves."

"What's that mean?"

"It means we have good thoughts and bad thoughts. The bad thoughts are the enemy."

"So, if I do what the bad thoughts tell me, I make the enemy my boss?"

She chuckled. "That's right."

"So that's why bad white people don't want good black people to be successful in business?"

"What do you mean?"

"In 1921, Black Wall Street was a successful business community in Tulsa. It was more successful than the white business communities. That's why the bad white people destroyed the community. Ma, didn't you read the book?"

"No," she answered with guilt.

"A plane dropped a bomb on that community."

"What? A bomb?"

"Yeah, Ma. Will the bad white people drop a bomb if I build a black community?"

She said what she didn't believe. "No. This country has changed a lot since 1921."

CHAPTER 9

After the nearly seven-year process that incurred substantial legal and court fees that depleted Yvonne's savings, the court ruled against her.

Stunned by the decision that didn't seem real, her biggest disappointment was the inability to remove her mother and grandmother from the projects.

Two months passed, and Derrick's twelfth birthday was near.

"Ma, for my birthday, can you open a stock market account in my name?"

"Oh, so you've decided to invest in stocks? Starting early."

"I'm thinking about the future, Ma. I'm living for tomorrow."

"Not only do you look like your father, you sound like him too."

He reached into the pocket of his pleated navy blue slacks and handed his mother a roll of cash wrapped with a red rubber band.

Curious, she tilted the roll. "How much is this?"

"It's $617."

"Where did you get it?"

"I saved it from shoveling snow and cutting grass for the past two years."

"That's good, Derrick. I'm proud of you. I'll add some money so you can invest an even $700. It will be your birthday gift from me."

"No, Ma. I can only use the money I earned."

"Why?"

"It's a feeling."

"Oh, okay. So, how do you want me to invest the money?"

He handed her a white index card with the name, address, and phone number of a company, and said, "Buy $317 of this penny stock."

"What kind of company is this?"

"It's a technology company. The owner is an idealist. His cousin is a classmate. He operates the company from out of his parents' garage."

"Garage? You sure you want to invest in that company?"

"Yes."

"Why?"

"Because Mister told me."

She narrowed her eyes. "Mister? You still see Mister?"

"No. I can feel him now. He's my instincts. My guardian angel."

Yvonne looked at her son with concern. *Do I need to have him checked?*

Derrick read her expression, and said, "You can still feel my father, right?"

"Umm, yes," she answered, trapped in thought.

"It's the same thing, Ma. I'm not crazy."

"Hmm. Okay, so what is penny stock?"

"Penny stocks are not listed on the NASDAQ because the company doesn't have enough capital. The stock is cheap because most operate out of a garage or bedroom. Some are scams."

"Okay," she said, skeptical. "What about the other three hundred dollars?"

He handed her another index card.

"I'm going to use my father's tip about Peter Nuremberg. I watched a company that he advocated rise from $17 a share to $109. The stock has now dropped under $2 a share because of an adverse rumor. I want you to buy 150 shares of that stock."

"What makes you so confident the value will come back?"

"My instincts. I also researched Peter Nuremberg. He and his business partners convince new investors to buy stock in a company, then they secretly spread a rumor, and when the stock falls, they take advantage of the fire sale and buy shares of low-priced stock that grows back to its original price and sometimes higher."

"So, that's what happened to your father?"

"Yeah."

She felt her son was making a huge mistake, but followed his directions.

Derrick monitored the stocks daily. Undaunted by the decreases, he continued to pour the bulk of his earnings from various jobs into purchasing additional shares of both companies. Instead of buying the latest brand-name sneakers and clothing, he bought his attire from thrift stores, and every penny saved was invested in stocks.

* * *

At fifteen years old, Junior stood six feet tall. The girls at the prep school raved about his dreadlocks and russet eyes. His fame and hip-hop lifestyle made soccer popular in the black communities.

With a pot of gold waiting after high school graduation, Junior lived the life of a teen idol. He traveled the world playing in soccer tournaments and won notable trophies, regaling his friends with stories of every sexual encounter.

National print and television proclaimed his greatness. Commercial offers were lucrative and abundant. But Yvonne denied the offers. She held onto the hope that he would change his mind and enter college.

Concerned about his cockiness, she had a private conversation with him.

"Don't let your confidence control you. Control your confidence."

"What are you saying, Ma?"

"In the game today, you had a teammate open for a shot equivalent to a layup in basketball. Instead of passing him the ball, you took a shot from thirty feet."

"Yeah, but I made it."

"Why did you take that shot?"

"Because I was confident I would make it."

"That's my point. You're letting your confidence control you. If you had missed that shot, the onus would've been on you. But if you had passed the ball, you would've been a hero regardless of the outcome. I was sitting directly behind the scouts, and even though they marveled at how you were able to make that shot, I heard them whispering afterward, 'He should have passed. That was a selfish play.' Junior, you have to understand that you are what you do. In the end, the scouts didn't see a great shot, they saw a selfish player. No one wants a selfish player on their team."

"What's the big deal? I made the shot. We would've scored the same point if I had passed the ball."

"That's right. So there was no benefit for you to take that shot other than to feed your ego."

"Ma, why are you talking to me like this? You should be proud of me. I'm going to be a millionaire when I graduate from high school."

"How many times have I told you that wisdom overshadows love? I'm not helping you if I don't tell you the truth."

"Grandma said I did the right thing."

"My mother was wrong. You didn't do the right thing. The right thing was to pass the ball for an easier shot. You only get one point in soccer regardless of how far the shot."

"I made the shot. That's the important thing. If I had missed, you could chastise me, but I made it. That shot earned me another five million dollars."

"Junior, what have I told you? Jesus said, 'What profit a man if he gain the whole world and lose his soul?' You are losing your soul."

"Ma, I don't want to hear that Bible stuff. I'm not losing my soul. God gave me this talent to showcase it. You should be proud of me."

"I am, Junior. I'm very proud of you. But you need to change your ways. You are a very selfish player."

"I'm not selfish. I pass the ball. I just felt like I could make the shot, so I shot it. That's not selfishness. It's confidence."

"That's right, and it's controlling you. That's why you should go to college before you turn professional."

"College? Aww, I'll think about it."

* * *

Charlene at fifteen was five feet and seven inches of cuteness in dress size twelve. She and Derrick were more like twins because of all the time they spent together.

70

When Derrick left home to attend college, Charlene was lonely and pursued her attraction to a classmate named James and staged a meeting with the football star.

James thought he had initiated the encounter, but she had already queried his acquaintances. So, when he introduced himself, she interspersed their conversation with specific questions related to his character. She already knew the answers. She was testing his honesty, and he passed.

That evening, he phoned Charlene.

"I might as well tell you," she said.

"Tell me what?"

"I'm a virgin."

"Really? You're a virgin?"

"Yes."

"Wow. You are way different than your brother."

"Are you still interested?"

"In what?"

"Me, stupid."

"Yeah, I'm cool with that."

"Don't get too excited 'cause I'm not having sex until I get married."

"Married?"

"That's right. After I become a surgeon."

"You gonna wait that long?"

"Yes. You can't wait?"

"Ahh, I don't know."

"So sex is all you want?"

"No. I'm not saying that. I think you're special. I can wait."

"You sure? I don't want a boyfriend cheating on me because I won't have sex. It's okay if you can't wait. We can still be friends."

"I can wait. I want to be your boyfriend."

The following sunny morning, Charlene and her mother sat on wooden chairs on the open deck. A cool breeze blew around them. Charlene shared her feelings about James.

"Why do you like him?" her mother asked.

"Because he's cute, smart, funny, and nice."

"He's cute? So that's the first thing you look for in a man?"

"No, Ma, but it's a close second." She chuckled.

Yvonne grinned. "Is he for real?"

"I tested him like you taught me. He hasn't contradicted himself."

"It's still early. Most teenage boys are only out for one thing. How does he feel about your virginity?"

"Oh, Mama, he told me that he doesn't want to do anything until I'm ready."

"Mm-hmm, I heard that before. How old is he?"

"Sixteen, like me."

"I know I'm repeating myself, but it's important that you hear this often. One, learn to be happy alone. If you're happy alone, you won't feel pressured to have sex before you're ready. Two, always love and value yourself. Do not seek validation from anyone. If a man doesn't value himself, he cannot value you. Three, don't ever let a man hit you or threaten to hit you. If he does, get as far away from him as possible. Do not believe him if he says, 'I'm sorry,' or 'I didn't mean it.' A threat will become action, and a hit will become another. Four, your body is precious. Whoever you decide to give your body to, make sure he's worthy of your trust, your heart, your mind, and every part of your body."

Charlene didn't want the feeling of her first love to end, so she allowed James to touch a little more each time they were alone, but kept restrictions.

One Friday night after the game, they were alone at his house. His jet-setting parents were in Ibiza. Cuddled on a plush sofa, they were watching television. The usual kisses and feels didn't satisfy James, and he became sexually aggressive.

"No! Stop!" Charlene repeatedly said.

But he didn't until she started crying.

Her panties halfway down, he said, "I'm sorry. I thought you wanted me to."

Tears rolled off her chin as she pulled up her panties and pants.

"I'm sorry, Charlene. I got carried away. I apologize. Please forgive me. I love you. Don't tell your mother, please."

"Take me home," she muttered.

"Okay. I'll take you home. I'm sorry. I love you. Please don't tell."

She hurried out of the house without a word. He nervously followed, and remotely opened the doors of his father's Bentley. Charlene wiped the tears with the palm of her hand, plopped on the passenger's seat, and slammed the door.

Shamefaced, James entered and said, "I'm sorry."

Her mouth didn't open, and she didn't look at him. He watched her out of the corner of his eye as he slowly backed out of the stone, semicircular driveway. Charlene faced the passenger's window as he drove down the street. The harrowing experience replayed in her mind as houses and parked cars flashed across her eyes.

James finally spoke, "I'm sorry, Charlene. I won't do it again. I promise. I love you, Charlene."

When they arrived at her house, he parked at the curb. She got out without a word and slammed the door.

He lowered the passenger's window. "Charlene, please don't tell. Please."

She didn't say a word, and didn't look back.

He quickly drove away.

Charlene peeked at her mother's car in the two-vehicle driveway before she paused under the bright porch light. She opened her purse and took out a hand mirror, wiped away the evidence of tears, and entered the house.

Her mother was reading a book in the family room, unable to see who entered. Charlene raced up the stairs.

* * *

Hearing Charlene go upstairs, Yvonne wondered, *What's wrong with her?*

She closed the book, scuttled upstairs, and opened the door to Charlene's bedroom.

Charlene was under the covers with her back to the door. "Are you okay?"

Charlene kept her face to the wall. "I'm okay, Ma. I'm just tired."

Yvonne knew something had happened and was tempted to press the matter but decided to allow her daughter the space she wanted.

73

* * *

Except for an occasional trip to the bathroom, Charlene stayed in her room the remainder of the weekend. She didn't eat and ignored the persistent phone calls from James.

When she went to school on Monday, James was very attentive, and she forgave him.

But when the weekend came, he made excuses for not seeing or calling her.

She sensed that he had lost interest but ignored her instincts because she loved him. Charlene convinced herself to believe his lies.

When James didn't meet her at the cafeteria during lunch break, she was suspicious and walked around the campus in search of him. Drawn to a group of football players and girls who were sitting on the bleachers, Charlene saw James kissing one of the cheerleaders under the bleachers.

Her heart felt like it had stopped. But she walked away as if the moment didn't affect her.

The whisperers and instigators tried to make her cry during the remainder of the school day, but she held back the tears and hid the pain of a broken heart until she arrived home.

CHAPTER 10

Derrick graduated valedictorian at the preparatory school and earned a four-year academic scholarship to Princeton. He didn't mention the status of his stock because no one in the family asked. Most assumed he wasn't profiting because he didn't talk about it.

But when he entered college, his penny stock was listed on NASDAQ and had grown from ten cents a share to $76 a share, and he owned ten thousand shares. The other investment in an Internet retailer had increased to $229 a share, and he held 421 shares.

As was his daily procedure, he phoned Charlene.

"Is everything okay with you?"

"Yes."

"How's Mom?"

"She misses you."

"How's Junior?"

"He's the same. Hardheaded and cocky. He's not training."

"I'm not surprised. He has to learn the hard way. How's Grandma?"

"Still spoiling Junior."

"Hmm. How's Great-Grandma?"

"She's fine. She told me to tell you to bring her a Princeton sweatshirt."

He chuckled. "She's got it. What's wrong? You don't sound happy."

"Nothing. I'm okay."

"No, you're not. Sound gives sight—I can see your face. You're sad. What's wrong?"

"I just miss you. I'm also tired of the girls at school pretending to be my friend so that they can get close to Junior."

"You sure that's all it is? 'Cause I'm feeling something more."

"That's all it is."

"Okay. I love you."

"Love you too."

"Tell everybody I love them, and I will see them on Thanksgiving."

"Okay."

* * *

On the first day of the last semester in his sophomore year, Derrick noticed a light-skinned woman with emerald eyes in the gorgeous face of a petite body. He assumed she had a boyfriend, so he didn't approach.

But she had apparently noticed *him* because on the fourth day of class, she introduced herself. "Hi, I'm Suzanne."

"Hi, nice to meet you. I'm Derrick," he said. His eyes focused on her skin-tight blue jeans accentuated by tan suede high-heel ankle boots. When she didn't respond, he said, "Why is it that white people look at you so curiously?"

"So you noticed. I guess they're trying to figure out my ethnicity. My mother is light-skinned, and my father is white, but I'm just another shade of black."

He smiled. "Another shade of black. I like that."

She tilted her side-swept short bangs and scanned him. "I guess I'm not your type."

"Why you say that?"

"Because you didn't speak when I gave you the opportunity. Am I too light for you?"

"No, you're not. I just know that guys approach you often. Didn't want you to count me as one of the many."

"Ahh. Mm-hmm. I like the way you think, Derrick."

"I get the feeling we think alike."

"What makes you say that?"

"Because of the woman I see in you."

"What woman do you see? We just met."

"This is the first time we talked, but we communicated from the first day of class. I felt the vibes you were sending me, and I'm sure you felt mine."

"So you're a mind reader."

"I wouldn't say that. I'm just a man who sees the realism in imagination."

After the two had exchanged phone numbers, they departed to their remaining classes.

Anxious to speak with Suzanne again, Derrick immediately phoned her at the end of his classes.

She surprised him by ignoring the unwritten rule to allow at least two rings before answering the first call from a suitor and answered before the first ring ended.

They talked for nearly two hours about their likes and dislikes.

Afterward, he mentioned the death of his brother.

"Was the guy caught?"

"Yes. He was our next-door neighbor. He's on death row. His family had to move because of the threats."

"From your people?"

"Nah. I have two uncles that would've killed him, but they're locked up. The threats came from the people in the 'hood. My brother was very popular."

Derrick felt tears coming and changed the subject. "What's your dream?"

"Clinical research."

"Is your focus patients or medicine?"

"Medicine."

"So, why are you in a social problems class?"

"Maybe to meet you?"

"Ahh, you see, we do think alike."

"Mm-hm."

"So why no boyfriend?"

"Who said I don't have a boyfriend?"

"You did when you approached me."

She paused then said, "Okay, so why no girlfriend?"

He peered as if he could see her. "Because I hadn't met a reflection of self until now."

"Now? You move quick. So I'm your girlfriend already?"

"Are you?"

"Um, if you want me."

"I want you."

Silence fell over the phone before she said, "What do you think about faith and hope?"

"Faith and hope?"

"Yes, faith and hope."

"Faith and hope are not assigned to a particular religion. I believe true faith is living a righteous life. Hope is the source of our faith to strive and fulfill dreams. I consider myself spiritual and not religious because I do not follow a denomination."

"Are you a Christian?"

"If the word means a follower of Jesus Christ, then I'm a Christian."

"Why did you answer that way?"

"Because many call themselves Christians but are not true followers of Jesus. I'm turned off by hypocritical people who claim to be Christians but aren't. One day, after church, my mother was trying to pull out of the church parking space, but some of the parishioners wouldn't allow her to get in front of them. They sped up when she tried to pull out. That's not the mind of a Christian. Then there are those who speculate about others' lives, spreading negativity which is manifesting wickedness. Gossip is no less of a sin than murder. That's just a couple of the reasons why I haven't been to church since I was eleven."

"Your mother didn't make you go to church?"

"She did until I showed the Scripture that said 'the church is the body.'" He sensed she wanted to hear more, and said, "There are many faiths in this world, and of every faith, there is some truth found. So there are many truths in life, but only one reality to life."

"Okay-y, so what's the one reality in your opinion?"

"For me, God is the one reality. Because God was, is, and shall be."

She asked, "How do you feel about white people?"

"I've learned that all white people are not the same. One day, it was snowing heavy and my mother's car got stuck trying to go up a hill. A white man and his two teenage sons pushed her car over the hill and followed us until they exited. Another situation was when my mother called the insurance company for a tow. A white man showed up with the tow truck, and instead of towing the car, he asked questions and tried to jump-start it. It didn't work, but he kept trying until it did. He didn't have to do that. But he did out of the goodness of his heart. The only difference between people is their race and culture. We all feel and think the same. Every race has good and evil, so you cannot judge a person by their race."

He paused, and when she didn't say anything, he asked, "You still there?"

"Yeah, just thinking."

"It's good to think."

CHAPTER 11

A few days later, Derrick was gazing out Suzanne's tenth-floor bedroom window as he lay under the sheets.

"Tell me what you're thinking?" she whispered as her fingers glided across the silky hair on his chest.

"The essence of life."

She turned and leaned on her arms. "What's the essence of life?"

He turned his head toward her. "Happiness, all the time, is the essence of life."

"All the time? You can't be happy all the time."

"Why not?"

"How can you be happy when someone you love dies?"

"Of course you'll feel sad because our flesh came before the spirit, so nothing can precede what the flesh feels, but the essence of life is the spirit of Christ—the gift of eternal life—that's our end. We need to use that knowledge to overcome the sadness and fear of death. We need to put our trust in things we can't see but believe will come. The saints glory in tribulation."

"Have you always been this way?"

"What way?"

"Every woman's dream."

"I'm sure I'm not every woman's dream. That's generalizing."

"Some things constitute generalization. Every woman dreams of a respectful, ambitious, and godly man. Most want someone cool, calm, and collected like you."

Suzanne curled her naked body under the sheets. Her eyes spoke feelings of love.

Derrick rubbed the tip of his index finger across her thin lips. "Being your dream is enough," he said before a passionate kiss turned into their first coital morning.

After they had showered together and eaten brunch on the patio of her off-campus apartment, Derrick's impulsiveness led them on a Saturday afternoon train ride to New York City.

En route he asked, "What was it like growing up biracial?"

"Ahm, my girlfriends were white because the black girls didn't like me."

"Why?"

"They called me a white girl. They said I was too light to hang with them. So I hung with my white friends and dated white guys mostly, but I'm attracted to black men. The darker, the better." She chuckled.

He smiled. "Why the darker, the better?"

"I don't know. I'm just attracted to dark men."

"There's a reason for that. What do you think it is?"

"I honestly don't know. Why are you always analyzing?"

"You don't like it?"

"I like it, but not all the time. Can't some things just be? Does it matter which came first, the chicken or the egg?"

"It matters. Which one do you think came first?"

"Are we going to do this now?"

"Yeah, why not? Which one came first?"

She bubbled her mouth with thought-provoking eyes. Her head turned slightly upward.

He faced her with his arms folded and back pressed against the window.

After a few seconds, she turned to him. "The chicken came first."

"Why?"

"I knew you were going to ask that. I'm ready for you. The chicken came first because the chicken makes the egg."

He grinned, and said, "I agree."

"Good. No more philosophical questions."

He smiled with his eyes and kissed her.

They paused, oblivious to the scenes that flashed from outside the windows of the fast-moving train.

He leaned back on the seat and closed his eyes.

She laid the side of her head on his shoulder and closed her eyes.

They stayed in that position until the conductor announced, "Grand Central Station."

Cuddled arm in arm, the couple stepped onto historic floors, surrounded by a crowd that represented people from all over the world.

Suzanne was wearing tight white jeans and a tucked, black, cotton-fitted blouse with black high-heel open-toe sandals, and bright red nail polish on her toes and fingers that matched her lipstick.

Derrick wore gray loose-fitting gabardine pants and black leather walking shoes. His untucked white cotton shirt had the first three buttons unfastened.

Heads turned to both.

"Where are we going first?" she asked with her hands clutched around his arm.

"Shopping in the Garment District."

"Then?"

"Times Square."

"Then?"

"A Broadway musical."

"Which one?" she asked.

"You choose."

"Okay. Then, what's next?"

"Harlem for soul food."

"Mmm, yummy. Then?"

He smiled. "I'm going to give you what you want, and I need."

"What's that?" she asked with eyes wide open.

"Me, and you."

* * *

On the next to last day of the social problems class, the professor stood at the front of his desk as the students entered. He held a stack of papers similar to the day of the midterm, which led the class to speculate he was about to hand out a final exam.

When the seventy-three students had settled in the seats of the amphitheater, the professor opened a small aging cabinet next to his desk and shoved the papers inside. With his eyeglasses flopped over his sloped nose, he said, "I've decided to allow the class to decide on whether you should have a final exam. The question is, do you want one? I'll be back in thirty minutes for your answer."

One of the students yelled, "*A quoi bon?*"

The professor turned with a pretentious smile towards the student that suggested he knew French and left the room.

"What's up like that?" one of the black students shouted.

"I think he's burned out," an Asian student replied.

"So what do we do now?" one of the white female students asked.

Various thoughts circled the room until an attention-grabbing student dressed as a stereotypical Ivy League schooler stood and said, "We vote. I'll moderate."

A vigorous debate ensued. Some didn't want a final exam, but others needed the exam to improve their grade.

Derrick and Suzanne were sitting next to each other and kept silent during the heated discussion.

With most suspecting an underlying reason for the question, the self-appointed class spokesman tried to convince them otherwise.

"Stop trying to overanalyze the situation. The professor gave us a simple yes or no question. He warned us about overanalyzing the simple. He's testing us to see if we will overanalyze a simple question.

"Can't you see that he doesn't want to give a final exam? That's why he threw the tests in his cabinet and left the room without answering any questions. He's looking forward to summer vacation as we are. If we ask for a final exam, we will piss him off, and he will fail us. But if we vote against a final exam, which is what he wants, he will give everyone an A."

Suzanne followed Derrick's lead and abstained from the vote.

When the class decided not to have a final exam, Derrick stood and said, "We should add a reason for our decision."

"The professor didn't ask for a reason," the spokesman said in defense of his position.

"But we should be prepared if he asks."

"Dude, the question is a yes or no answer. If the professor wanted a reason for our decision, he would have told us."

"One should always have an explanation for every decision, even if not asked."

Annoyed, the spokesman said, "You haven't spoken two words the whole semester until today. You abstained from the vote. *A Quoi Bon?*"

"I only speak when it's necessary. I abstained because it doesn't matter to me if we have a final exam or not."

Derrick said in fluent French, "To answer, *a quoi bon?* The point is that we need to have a reason for our decision."

The self-appointed spokesman was surprised that Derrick spoke French, and his expression showed a man backed into a corner. His head swung left to right. But every eye was on him, so he stood and challenged Derrick with the demeanor of an alpha male.

"If we give the professor a reason for our decision, he will fail us because we overanalyzed the simple. He told us that society often overanalyzes the simple, which causes social problems to increase. Dude, the professor gave us a trick question. Think about it. If he wanted us to have a final exam, why would he give an option? He gave us a way out because he doesn't want to grade the tests. We would be foolish if we didn't take it and run."

Derrick didn't stand down. "You can only overanalyze the definite. When the professor comes back into this room and asks us, and he will, for the reason behind our decision, we should have an answer."

As if he was reading from a teleprompter, the spokesman said, "If we should add a reason when the professor didn't ask for one, he will fail us for overanalyzing a simple yes-or-no question."

One of the white females stood and said, "What's the harm in adding a reason for our decision, just in case?"

The spokesman sighed and opened the floor to a vote.

But only Suzanne and eighteen others agreed with Derrick.

Livid, Derrick shouted at the opposing students, "Why are you so ignorant? Do you not realize the professor is testing us? If our decision is NO to a final exam, he expects a reason for that decision! If the decision is YES to a final exam, he expects a reason for that decision! The final exam is not the question, but the REASON for our decision!"

Suzanne left the room while he was yelling.

84

After the nearly two-minute-long tirade, he sat down and turned to look at Suzanne, but she wasn't there.

Where did she go? He feverishly looked around the room. *She must have gone to the bathroom.*

The professor entered.

The class whispered as he strolled to the front, twirling his eyeglasses as if prepared for a "gotcha" moment. He set his eyeglasses over squinting eyes and looked as if he had noticed someone missing. He scratched his ungroomed beard and asked, "What is your decision?"

All eyes turned towards the class spokesman.

He stood confident and said, "Under the democratic process, we voted against a final exam."

The professor said, "Hmm. So, what's the reason for the decision?"

The class gasped.

Derrick shook his head and left the room. "Where'd she go?" he muttered in the hallway.

He called her cell, but the phone was off. He went to her next class, but she wasn't there. He skipped his last two classes and searched the campus without success.

She must be home.

Confused and apologetic thoughts filled his mind as he continued to try to contact her while he rode in a cab to her apartment.

He stood at the building entrance and buzzed her apartment, but she didn't answer. He waited for someone to open the door, but lost patience and decided to check the loading dock.

The doors were open, and he rode the freight elevator to her floor. Multiple knocks on her door went unanswered.

Where is she?

Feebleminded, he squatted on the carpeted hallway with his back against the wall.

His eyes were glued to the elevators in the middle of the hall, hoping she would exit each time the doors opened.

Residents stared, and others smiled, at Derrick as they entered and exited their apartments.

After several hours and an abundance of unanswered calls and texts, Derrick returned to his dorm, unable to understand why Suzanne was avoiding him.

Restless, he continued his attempts to contact her until he fell asleep in the early morning light.

Hopeful to see her on the last day of class, he waited for the hour, but she wasn't there. His carefree world had turned upside down. An unchangeable moment brought sadness that melted his willpower, and made him believe it wasn't so.

CHAPTER 12

"Where is Derrick?" Beverly asked as she entered the passenger' seat of Yvonne's sedan.

"I talked to him this morning. He got held up at school. He will meet us there," Yvonne replied, concerned.

"Held up? He got robbed?"

"No, Ma. I think he had some work to do."

"School ended for the summer two days ago. He said he would be home for the twins' graduation. He need to start putting the family first."

"Ma, I told you that he's going to meet us."

"Yeah, but Junior and Charlene was expecting him to ride with them."

Ruth was sitting in the back seat and changed the subject.

Minutes later, Yvonne pulled into one of the school's four parking lots.

"I don't see Junior's limousine," Beverly said.

"It's probably in the back," Yvonne replied.

"Where are the chartered buses?" Beverly asked, looking around.

"We're early," Ruth said.

They stepped out of the car and joined the line of parents entering the front doors of the sloping open-air venue.

Shortly after they sat in reserved seats, the family members and friends who rode on the two chartered buses sat alongside and behind them.

The immediate buzz, "Where's Derrick?"

The classical music stopped, and the master of ceremonies approached the lectern.

Beverly, who sat next to Ruth, leaned over to Yvonne and whispered, "Where is Derrick? He gonna miss the graduation. I bet you he's out there sowing his wild oats."

She ignored her, but wondered, *where is he?* Her eyes discreetly circled the venue.

The music played and the graduates robed in green-and-gold caps and gowns marched in alphabetical order under the late afternoon sky.

When Charlene and Junior entered the amphitheater, Beverly stood and shouted, "You look good, Junior!" She ran down the aisle and blocked the view of parents as she took pictures without respect for others who were trying to take pictures of their children.

As if he was at the end of the procession, Derrick sat in the aisle seat next to his mother.

"I'm sorry I'm late, Ma."

Yvonne saw the pain in his face and knew his heart was broken. She placed her arms around his shoulders, kissed him on the forehead, and whispered, "It will pass."

His head lowered and tears erupted.

Beverly leaned over and said, "What's wrong with Derrick?"

Yvonne whispered, "He's okay. He's thinking about Mister."

* * *

After the ceremony, family and friends proceeded to the graduation dinner underwritten by Junior's off-the-books agent. The affluent restaurant showcased golden chandeliers, antique paintings, and seven-foot, white marble statues of various gods and goddesses. The dining table, designed for a monarch, accommodated all sixty-nine attendees.

Smiles and laughter infused the VIP room as most gobbled food they hadn't previously tasted.

Ruth clutched Yvonne's palm. "God has answered your prayers. You got a son at Princeton and a daughter going to Johns Hopkins, both on full academic scholarships. And Junior got the option to go to any college he wants or play soccer professionally. I told you God would not forsake you."

Yvonne smiled and kissed her grandmother on the cheek. "God is good."

"Yes, he is."

Frozen in a state of thoughts, Yvonne was reminiscing about her life's journey.

Derrick and Junior were pleasantly conversing at the front of the Jupiter sculpture.

Yvonne saw them and smiled. *I hope they are becoming closer.*

Her eyes turned in search of Charlene and found her dancing with a cousin.

Then suddenly, "Fuck you!" projected over the music and interrupted the festive mood.

"What's going on?" Yvonne shouted.

The music stopped.

Uh-oh, here goes Junior again.

Ruth grabbed Yvonne's arm and kept her from standing. "Don't interfere. They're both men now."

Derrick turned to the voice of his mother. "I was sharing some constructive criticism."

Junior scowled. "There's a difference between constructive criticism and disrespect!"

Derrick kept his eyes on his mother. "I didn't mean to offend him. I was just telling Junior that he should attend at least one year of college before he turned pro. I'm not going to tell him what he wants to hear. I'm going to tell him what I believe is the truth."

"You wanna hear the truth? The media project me as the number one overall pick. An overnight multimillionaire. Why should I pass that up for college? Ma, I know you want me to go to college, but school ain't my thang, and I might get hurt. Why should I make millions for some school when I can make millions to help my family? I'm gonna get—"

Derrick cut him off. "If I felt you were ready, I would be the first to encourage you to join the pros. But you're not ready, and I'm telling you this because I love you. I don't want you to get caught up in the hype and ruin your career by turning pro before you're mentally and physically ready. You're the athlete, but I'm the one with the six-pack."

"Fuck you."

Yvonne yelled, "Boy, if you curse again, I'm gonna knock you upside your head. Show some respect for the children and me."

"I'm sorry, Ma."

Beverly stood and interjected, "Derrick, why you believe Junior isn't ready to turn pro?"

"You honestly want to know?"

"Yeah, I do, 'cause I think he's ready."

"He's not ready because of his priorities, which are girls and parties. A professional player is a serious responsibility. You have to be disciplined and focused. He's okay right now because he's playing against boys. But when he turns pro, he'll be playing against men, and he's not yet strong enough, physically or mentally."

"I believe I'm ready, and it's my decision. I don't tell you how to invest in stocks, so don't tell me when I should turn pro. I can buy Grandma and Great-Grandma a house if I go pro."

Yvonne removed the grip of her grandmother and stood. "This should've been a private discussion but, since it's not, I agree with Derrick. Junior, you should go to college first, and I'll give you an example. At the twenty-one-and-under World Cup, those men manhandled you. I know you were only sixteen, but eighteen doesn't make you stronger. I believe you should play at least one year of college. But you're right, the decision to turn pro is yours. But don't use buying a house for your grandmother and great-grandmother as an excuse to justify your decision. If you turn pro, let it be because you want it. My mother and grandmother can wait another year or two."

"Okay, I'm turning pro because I want it. I'm turning pro because I'm tired of seeing Grandma and Great-Grandma in the projects. I'm turning pro so I can buy them a house and give everybody in the family some money. God blessed me with this talent to make things better for my family, and that's what I'm going to do. I'm turning pro."

Beverly broke the tension by leading a family toast to Junior's future as a professional soccer player.

Congratulatory hugs and well wishes followed, and the music started again.

Yvonne sauntered to Junior and hugged him. "I love you. I wish your father were here to see you."

"I love you too, Ma. I know you're disappointed I'm not going to college."

"Junior, you are a man now. It's not what I want; it's what you want. I will support you even if I disagree. I'm your mother."

She hugged him again, and Derrick and Charlene joined the embrace.

Ruth scooted to the DJ and requested a line dance.

The song had everyone on the dance floor. Even the infants were sliding in their parents' hands.

Afterward, Yvonne took Derrick aside. "It's not what you say, but how you say it. If I were Junior, I would've gotten upset too."

"I'm sorry, Ma. I took out my frustration on him."

"You have to think before you react. Be careful. It's not what you do, but why you do it. There's nothing wrong with speaking the truth, but you have to show respect for others. You have to be smarter than the love you feel for a person."

"I see why my father fell in love with you so quick. You're intelligent, faithful, and beautiful."

"The biggest part of being intelligent is the discipline to be silent, humble, and patient."

"I'm disciplined."

"Sometimes."

"Sometimes?"

"Yeah, sometimes."

* * *

When the festivity ended, Junior and Charlene climbed into a chauffeured white limousine and headed to the student graduation party.

At the unchaperoned gathering, Charlene sat in a metal chair at a matching round four-person table adjacent to the large Riviera pool filled with graduates and alumni. She was at oneness with the star that outshined the others in the moonless sky when James approached.

He sat and said, "Hi," as if all was forgotten.

"Hi," she replied without a visual change.

"I'm sorry for hurting you. I apologize."

She kept her eyes on the bright star. "I accept your apology. But I didn't thank you."

"Thank me for what?"

"For teaching me not to trust a creep like you again. Now go away, little boy."

Tongue-tied, he walked away to a chorus of laughter from the teens who were listening.

Charlene cracked a secret smile and went looking for Junior. She found him in the pool house.

He had two girls on their knees and a magnum of champagne to his mouth. After each swig, he took a puff of marijuana, and yelled, "I am the king."

Charlene turned her back to the tongues and fingers that were pleasuring him, and said, "I'm going home."

Naked, with white powder on his nostrils, he replied, "Why? It's not even eleven."

Without turning around, she said, "I'm outta here," and walked disgustedly to the limousine as techno music blasted the neighborhood.

Glassy-eyed, Junior twisted his nose, and took a long puff.

* * *

Neil Young crooned as Derrick lay on Mister's bed. The emotions of a lost love had saturated his thoughts when the footsteps of his mother on the basement stairs announced a needed moment. He leaned up and lowered the music.

His mother sat beside him on the twin bed. "Why haven't you told me about her?"

"We only dated a few weeks. It was too early."

"Obviously not. You're in love with her. What happened?"

"I think I embarrassed her in class."

"How?"

After he had replayed the scene, she said, "Just because you know something is right, doesn't mean you have to say it.

True wisdom knows what to say, when, and when not. What else happened after she left the class?"

"I went looking for her and waited a few hours outside her apartment, but she didn't answer the door or my calls."

She slapped her palms on her knees. "What! Tell me you didn't do that, did you, Derrick?"

"I only wanted to apologize in person."

"You scared the poor girl to death. She thinks you're a stalker."

"A stalker? She knows I'm not a stalker."

"Oh? Only after a few weeks, she knows you're not a stalker? I know your charm. Your ways are just like your father's. You were a real Prince Charming in her eyes. Then all of the sudden you turned into an Ogre. That's scary, Derrick. She had to take a step back so she could take a second look. She went into protective mode. I would've done the same thing.

"If you had been patient, she would've gotten over the initial shock and called you. But you kept chasing after her, so she kept running. The more you chased, the more she was frightened. You pushed her farther away. There are a lot of dangerous men out there. Women have to be careful. She might've had a bad experience before she met you."

"But I'm not dangerous."

"And how is she supposed to know that after only a few weeks? What's her name?"

"Suzanne. You think she will come back?"

"She might if you stop trying to contact her. When was the last time?"

"A few minutes ago."

His mother sighed. "Listen to me. I know you miss her. But if you want to see her again, don't bother her. Wait for her to contact you. Are you listening?"

"Yeah, Ma, I hear you."

"Hearing is one thing and doing is another."

"I won't try to contact her again. Do you think she found someone else?"

"No, but I'm sure she is trying to forget about you. And she will if you keep trying to contact her."

He grimaced. His head dropped.

She wrapped her arm around him and kissed the top of his head. "All relationships are not meant to be long term. Some come to heal, some to teach, some to motivate, and some to prepare for a better experience. Relationships start from moments that often come and go unrecognized. That's why it's important to seize every opportunity because there is no such thing as a coincidence. Your father called coincidence a secular word. What I am saying to you is this: Don't let a good woman pass by because you're waiting for Suzanne. I know you don't want to hear this right now, but she might not be your soulmate."

The thought of an unwanted possibility froze his mouth. His head sank into the palms of his hands.

She rubbed his back. "I know it hurts. I've been there before."

He lifted his head with the strength to restrain the tears he felt. "Thank you, Ma. The truth hurts, but it's the truth."

As she readied to go back upstairs, he said, "Ma, why haven't you asked me about my stock?"

With one hand on the banister she said, "Why haven't you told me?"

"Because you didn't ask."

She folded her arms and tilted her head to the side. "I shouldn't have to ask. You should've told me. But I knew you were earning money because you stopped buying your clothes from the thrift store. So how much have you earned?"

"Almost a million dollars."

"What? A million dollars! Wow!" She wobbled to her son and gave him a bear hug. "Your father would be so proud of you. Why are you so secretive?"

"I don't know."

"Yes, you do. Aren't you the one that said you need to have an explanation for every decision? So what's the reason for your decision not to tell me?"

He felt exposed. "I like to keep personal things to myself."

"You're just like your father. So what are you going to do with the money?"

"I'm going to be a venture capitalist."

"What's that?"

"I'm going to build economic empowerment for black communities."

She sat on the bed with an expression of the expected. "So you're serious about building black communities?"

"I'm very serious."

She put her right hand on his knee. "Wait." She hurried upstairs and returned with a book. "This belonged to your father. I read it."

He took the aged paperback from her hand. "*The Spook Who Sat By The Door*. What is this about?"

"You need to read it, know it, and understand it. Remember when I told you the world has changed since 1921?"

He nodded, looking down at the open book.

"Well, it hasn't. Even with a black president, racism remains prevalent."

Fascinated, he lifted his eyes to his mother.

"I felt the spirit of your father in you while you were still in the womb. I saw the spirit of your father in you the moment you were born. I wish he were alive to see you. But I know he and Mister are watching from heaven."

"I love you, Ma."

"And you know I will always love you."

* * *

Charlene entered a dark house. "I hope Derrick is still up," she whispered before she turned on the hallway light.

The music of Public Enemy led her to the steps of a dark basement.

Derrick turned on the table lamp beside the bed. He lowered the music and said, "I'm still awake."

Charlene skipped down the stairs.

Derrick sat up. "Back from the party already?"

"I'd rather be with you. You're leaving tomorrow. Why do you have to go so soon?"

"I was supposed to start last week. I can't delay any longer."

"Are you planning to work on Wall Street after college?"

"No, I'm just interning for the summer. I'm planning to build my own corporation."

"Oh, what kind?"

"Don't know yet. Enough about me. How are you?"

"I'm afraid you're going to move far away and the only time I'll see you is Thanksgiving or Christmas."

"I might move far away, but I'm always available for you. We can FaceTime every day."

Teary-eyed, she murmured, "I know," and sat beside him.

In the spirit of a surrogate father, he embraced her, and said, "I love you."

Her head fell onto his shoulder, "I love you too."

"I'm very proud of you, Charlene."

As if she needed to say something without him hearing it, she whispered, "James tried to rape me."

Derrick snapped backward. "What? He tried to rape you? Tonight?"

"No, not tonight. It was last year."

"Last year!" His hands flew up, and he stood gazed intently at her. "Why are you just telling me now?"

She lowered her head as if she stood before the altar, and said, "Because you told me not to date him, and I didn't listen. I felt ashamed."

"Ahh, Charlene, you can't keep things like that a secret from me. Does Mama know?"

"She knows. It's okay. He stopped when I cried."

"It's not okay. He sexually assaulted you. Did Mama file charges?"

"I begged her not to because he would've gotten kicked off the team and out of school. I didn't want that to happen. He apologized."

"Umm. You still a virgin?"

"I told you I'm not having sex until I get married."

"You said you wouldn't date James."

"All right, you got me there. But I'm lonely, Derrick. Most guys I like are uncomfortable with me because they say I'm too smart."

"That means they're insecure. You don't want a diffident man. Don't play dumb to keep a guy's interest."

"White guys are the ones asking me out. I like them, but I want to marry my own. I want a guy like you. You're the standard I use to measure my suitors. A man like you is hard to find."

"God didn't break the mold when he made me. Your soulmate is out there. Be patient."

She pouted like her mother, and said, "I'm lonely."

"I'm lonely too."

"You? Why?"

"I don't want to talk about it right now. Just remember, tomorrow will come and with it the fulfillment of dreams. Your dreams are coming true, my dreams are coming true, Junior's dreams are coming true, so our mother's dreams are coming true. Think about how much suffering she has handled. Without her endurance, where would we be? God is watching over our family, so cheer up."

"You always know how to make me feel better."

"Making you feel better has made me feel better. Let's dance."

They swayed to the beat of reggae, played Monopoly, and chatted until the break of dawn.

The love between a brother and sister replaced the loneliness they felt.

CHAPTER 13

Derrick had rented a furnished studio apartment. Dressed in a black suit, white shirt, red tie, and black closed-lace leather shoes, he walked the nine blocks to Wall Street and entered an art deco stone building. Metal pillars that sparkled like flawless diamonds stood in each of the expansive lobby's four corners.

He marveled unobtrusively at his surroundings as the sound of women's heels echoed off the spotless, buttercup marble tile.

"Can I help you, sir?" one of the three overweight security guards at the quartz lobby desk asked.

"Yes, I have a meeting with Mr. Jerry Romonowski," Derrick answered.

"ID, please."

He showed his identification, signed in, and was told to take the elevator to the twenty-third floor.

When he stepped out of the gold-plated elevator, a modest woman greeted and escorted him to the office of Mr. Romonowski, a short and hairless fifty-three-old with a bulbous beak.

Jerry, the right hand of the hedge fund manager who interviewed Derrick, sprung out of his high-back leather chair and extended his hand.

"Congratulations, Mr. Williams."

"Thank you, Mr. Romonowski. Please, call me Derrick."

"Okay, Derrick. Call me Jerry." He slapped his hand on top of Derrick's arm. "Have a seat."

Derrick sat in one of the two classic brown leather side chairs that faced the solid hardwood desk. The view from the floor-to-ceiling open windows of the corner office brightened Derrick's eyes.

Jerry sat in his chair and leaned back. His eyes seemed to search for deception.

After a few seconds, he said, "Mr. Williams, you should be proud to be selected out of 231 qualified candidates."

"I'm grateful. I believe it's a blessing. Please, call me Derrick."

"Oh, yes, I'm sorry, Derrick."

"I read your interview score sheets. You received high marks for your luculent answers."

"I try to be precise with my words. I believe it's important not to have any misunderstandings. Especially with those who entrust you with their money."

Jerry smiled like a person who couldn't, and said, "That's right! Are you excited to start?"

"Very."

"Good. Excitement is necessary for this business because it breeds motivation, and motivation leads to success. In this line of work, success is the only option."

"I agree."

"I read your cover letter, and I have a question. Why didn't you invest in the market since you were so interested at a young age? Your mother could've opened an account for you. With your understanding of how the market works, you might've been on your own ladder instead of trying to find one to climb."

Derrick's eyes smiled. "You're right. I didn't think about it. That's why I applied to be under your tutelage."

Jerry grinned.

Derrick widened his smile. *I got my own ladder, and it's higher than yours.*

After the thirty-minute orientation, Jerry escorted Derrick downstairs to the boiler room and introduced him to the workers.

Derrick had researched Jerry and knew he was an egomaniac, so he praised him in front of the guys, and called him "a real Lothario."

Impressed by the servile behavior that Derrick openly displayed, the next day Jerry removed him from the boiler room and volunteered to be his mentor.

Focused on learning the details of venture capitalism—the goods and asset markets, offshore tax shelters, and other financial loopholes—Derrick absorbed it all during the daily lunch breaks with Jerry. He also learned the secrets of insider trading and how the money on Wall Street controls the world.

On the third weekend of his internship, Derrick accepted an invitation to attend a private party.

Copper Jennings, a golden-haired, savvy, and brash twenty-three-year-old trader with the goal to earn a million dollars a day, hosted the gathering of upper-class twenty-somethings on the rooftop of his apartment building located in the affluent section of the Bronx.

Candlelight displays and sky lanterns sat on the rooftop's moonstone pavement. A full moon glowed in an orange and white sky that hovered over the heated pool with side Jacuzzis. A white canopy covered the portable bar and six high-back black leather bar stools. Round tables decorated with white linen and votive candles added to the chic atmosphere.

Derrick was standing in black linen shorts, a cream patterned short-sleeve silk shirt, and black woven sandals without socks, mingling with a crowd that held bottles of beer and translucent cups of liquor. In his cup was the champagne of cognac on the rocks.

He nodded to the beat of Bobby Nourmand and strolled along the poolside, where women were exposing their breasts for dead presidents. He watched for a minute before he continued to explore the spacious rooftop and noticed a well-dressed black man alone at one of the tables. His hairless face had a close haircut with a hook design at the front.

Drawn to the aura of his presence, Derrick approached. "Hi, I'm Derrick."

"What's up? Call me Blue."

"Nice to meet you, Blue. Do you work on Wall Street?"

"Nah, I'm not promoting that corruption. I was driving down Riverdale and saw the crowd, so I decided to step in to see what's up. What about you?"

"I was invited. I'm interning on Wall Street for the summer."

Blue waved a dismissive hand. "That's even worse."

Derrick didn't bite on the confrontation he sought but stood tall, and said, "Nice Rolex."

"Thanks, but to be honest, it's not real. I just wear it for the motivation to afford a real one without losing my heritage."

"Is it motivation or pretentiousness?"

Blue paused and stared. "So which part are you? The cookie or the filling? I see another nigga with his nose up the white man's ass."

Derrick narrowed his eyes. "You see what I want you to see. Have you heard of the spook who sat by the door?"

Dumbfounded, he answered, "No."

"Google it. You might learn something. Don't judge me until I allow you to know me."

Blue pulled out his cell to Google. "Oh snap! My bad. I'm down. So you're a summer intern. What school do you attend?"

"I'm entering my junior year at Princeton. My major is economics with a minor in investment banking."

"Ahh. I graduated two years ago from NYU. I majored in film."

"Another Spike Lee in the making?"

"Greater if possible."

"It's possible if you maintain your black identity as he did."

Blue looked at Derrick with an expression that requested acceptance into his world. "So what are you learning among the bulls and bears?"

"The things I thought to be so are confirmed. Congress is motivated and controlled by money, and US presidents often are indebted to Park Avenue."

"Continue, my brother."

"The country's wealth is controlled by one percent of the population through heavy influence of economic laws. Such as ensuring the tax codes are tilted to benefit their businesses, implementation of regulations designed to maximize their profits, and the existence of a carried interest tax code provision that allows billionaires and millionaires to avoid taxes or to be taxed at a much lower rate than a person that is a paycheck away from poverty."

"You truly are a spook who sat by the door."

"I have a dream to fulfill."

"What is it? You trying to start a revolution?"

"I might share it one day, but not now. I've shared enough."

Blue questioned him with his eyes.

Derrick answered the same way.

They exchanged contact information. And while they were discussing politics and worldviews, three loosely clothed young ladies approached and joined the conversation.

The five of them spent the next two hours talking, drinking, and gyrating.

Frisky from a buzz that teetered on intoxication, the women opened the door for sex, but Derrick called a cab and went home alone.

Blue stayed.

The next morning, he phoned Derrick and boasted about his sexual conquest with all three.

That afternoon, he picked up Derrick in his '99 Beemer and they rode through the Polo Grounds of Harlem.

A song played on the vehicle's CD player, and to Blue's surprise, Derrick knew the lyrics.

"How does a Princeton brother know about Mobb Deep?"

"I like old skool. My older brother had a collection that I inherited. Mobb Deep and Slick Rick were his favorites."

"Were?"

"Yeah, he was killed when I was five."

"Sorry to hear that."

"Don't let it kill the mood. My brother is alive inside me, and I know he's enjoying this song."

"Word. You heard Go-Go?"

"What's that?"

Blue chortled before he said, "The music of D.C., my hometown. I know you heard of Chuck Brown?"

"Yeah, I like him."

"Listen to this."

"Who's that?"

"Rare Essence."

"Man, I like Rare Essence! This beat will make a person in a wheelchair jump to their feet."

Blue laughed, and after the song played a speech by Minister Kabir.

Derrick said, "I heard him speak on television. The brother is deep."

"Yeah. He's speaking in D.C. next weekend for Black Awareness Day. You wanna go? You can stay with me at my parents'."

"Sure. I'm free."

"Cool."

"Can we visit my sister in Baltimore before we come back? She starts school next week."

"Sure. Is she at Morgan?"

"Johns Hopkins. She's studying to be a surgeon."

"A surgeon? Impressive."

"She's very impressive."

"I look forward to meeting her."

* * *

"Welcome to Washington, D.C.," the sign read.

Derrick said, "Welcome to Chocolate City!"

"Don't get too excited. Chocolate City is melting."

"What?"

"I'll show you what I mean."

Blue drove Derrick around the city.

"You're right. Chocolate City is melting."

"Yeah. It's like the Parliament Funkadelic song made the man mad, so he took his city back."

"Mmm-hmm, I think you're right."

The sun was setting when they arrived at the home of Blue's parents, who welcomed Derrick with the soul of hospitality.

Blue's sister, Xandra, a nineteen-year-old student at Howard University, eyed Derrick.

Drawn to her dark beauty, he returned the eye of attraction.

Xandra kept her eye on Derrick's six-foot-three-inch frame as Blue walked him up the carpeted stairs to the guest bedroom.

"Stop drooling," her mother whispered. "You're too obvious."

Xandra didn't turn her eyes away until Derrick entered the room.

"My sister digs you." Blue grinned.

"She's fine. She doesn't have a boyfriend?"

"Nah. She's pickier than me. You must be her type."

"But I'm already taken."

"Man, you gotta stop ailing over that girl. Somebody else is hitting that now."

"Maybe, but I know I still have her heart."

"But you don't have her mind."

"A woman's heart is her mind."

"Then you don't have her heart. If you did, she would've called you by now."

Derrick paused in that thought before he changed the topic.

* * *

The next morning, they rode an overcrowded subway downtown and walked to the National Mall.

Blue and Derrick were in front with his parents and sister closely behind.

The music of Backyard had the crowd of toddlers to seniors revved up in a tranquil atmosphere that radiated unified peace and love. The whiff of barbecue and fried fish made full stomachs hungry.

Derrick gazed over the multitude. He saw many shades of black. He lifted his head and stared as if he was looking beyond the blue sky. *I love you, Mister. I love you, daddy. Please keep watching over me.*

Xandra broke his concentration. "There isn't a cloud in the sky. What are you looking at?"

He smiled before he turned from her peering eyes, and said to Blue, "I'll be right back."

In the hope that he might find Suzanne among the many, he ventured into the crowd.

With the narrow room there was to maneuver, his feet swerved in every direction; his eyes roved for a light-skinned woman. Hope grew with every step. Anticipation mistook a few. And when the search seemed futile, a moment came.

Suzanne! Is that her? Locked onto a distant vision, he hurried his steps and slithered through the herd that faced him. Probability widened his eyes. Anxiousness compounded with the heat of the day added to his sweat. But when he got closer— *that's not her.* His enthusiasm vanished like a drop of water on hot pavement. His head slumped.

The festive bodies that circled him lifted his spirit, and his head spun with the realization that he didn't know his way back to Blue. He scanned his surroundings that exceeded five hundred thousand people. *Which way should I go?* His eyes roved for landmarks, but intuition led him back to Blue, who was dirty dancing with a hottie in red booty shorts.

Xandra abandoned the guy that she was dancing with and walked up to Derrick.

Spellbound by the thoughts in her eyes, he didn't resist when she twerked on his crotch. He embraced the move that was the norm around him.

When the song ended, she spun around, eyes wide. "I know you are feeling me. Why you running?"

"I'm not running. I just don't want to start something I can't finish. It's not fair to you."

"Let me decide what's fair. So you trying to be faithful to a girlfriend?"

"I don't have a girlfriend, but I'm in love with someone."

"Where is she?"

"We broke up before summer vacation. But I'm hoping to rekindle the relationship when school starts."

"Well, she's not here now, and I am. I can see you are attracted to me, and I'm attracted to you. I'm cool with a summer fling."

"I'm not. I want to wait for her."

Xandra swayed with a half-smile. "Really?"

"Straight-up. But I would be lying if I said I'm not attracted to you. I hope you can understand. I'm not ready to start another relationship."

"Okay, we can be friends and go from there."

"I can't be around you and pretend I'm not sexually attracted."

Her brows raised. "Then don't pretend."

A voice from the loudspeaker interrupted the moment. "Welcome to the stage, Minister Kabir!"

CHAPTER 14

Applause resounded over the grounds.

The sixty-three-year-old Minister stood in his traditional black suit, white shirt, and black bow tie. His face was as smooth as an infant's. His close-cut wavy hair didn't have a strand of gray.

Derrick clung to every word of the speech that ended on fourteen points of knowledge.

(1) Even as there is a natural inclination to be wise, there is a natural inclination to be foolish.

(2) A man cannot alter the world's future, but he can alter his own.

(3) Growth is not the number of experiences, but the learning from experience.

(4) Listening is also experiencing—because listening provides a frame of reference for and if a situation occurs.

(5) To believe is the seed of education, but to know is the growth of education.

(6) Growth is not the removal of childhood desires, but the realization of adulthood.

(7) There is no opinion to a fact.

(8) There are many ways to do the right thing.

(9) Where there are strengths and greatness in one, there is also weakness and faults. And where there are weakness and faults in one, there are also strengths and greatness. Therefore, no man is greater than the next in the kingdom of God.

(10) A wise person will not allow bad experiences to dictate their life.

(11) A wise person is objective with self and self-opinions.

(12) A wise person is not guided by what he sees, but by what he feels.

(13) A wise person prepares for the possibility.

(14) When one possesses a solid answer to every relevant question about a matter, only then can one be wise in their belief.

As the crowd dispersed, Derrick stayed in place. With renewed hope, his eyes scoured the grounds for Suzanne.

Xandra moved into his eyesight. "She's not here, but I am."

He lowered his eyes and smiled. Blue walked up to him. "This is Tamara. We're going to hang out with her."

"Can I go?" Xandra asked.

"No," Blue said emphatically.

"Why?"

"Because I said so."

Blue turned to his parents, who were chatting among a group of seniors. "We're rolling with Tamara. See you later."

His parents pardoned the interruption with a nod.

Blue and Derrick walked away with Tamara in-between.

Derrick felt Xandra's stare and looked back.

* * *

At the hour when most people are in their deepest sleep, Tamara parked in front of Blue's parents' house.

"Are you going to be able to make it inside?" she said with a hand on Blue's shoulder.

His head was pressed against the passenger's window. "I'll be all right," he slurred, and opened the door. When he stepped out, his body tilted to the side.

Derrick quickly climbed out of the back seat. "I got him."

Tamara lowered the passenger's window and watched as Derrick held Blue upright, and guided him up three concrete steps to a landing before five steps to the lighted front porch.

With Blue's body pressed against him, Derrick opened the unlocked screen door.

"Give me the key."

Blue's eyes squinted, and his body was swaying. He reached into his cargo shorts and fumbled for the keys. Derrick removed his arm from around Blue's shoulder to pick up the keys.

Blue tried to look down and lost his balance. He fell backward and landed on the front porch furniture.

Derrick quickly lifted him. "You all right?"

"Yeah, let me sleep here. I'll be good to go in a few minutes," he mumbled.

"You can't sleep out here. Which key is it?"

Blue struggled to open his eyes and became heavier to hold. So Derrick used the process of elimination to open the door. He raised a thumb to Tamara and she pulled off.

Blue whispered, "Don't turn on the lights."

Derrick obliged and guided him up the stairs to his bed. "Sleep it off," he whispered, and closed the door.

Tired but not sleepy, Derrick entered his room, turned on the ceiling light, and closed the door. He sat on the bed with his back against the wall. His mind was on Suzanne. *Who is she with? What is she doing right now?* A minute later, he heard a light tap.

Is that Blue? "Come in," he said.

Xandra entered wearing a sheer ivory chemise with lace cups and matching string bikini. "I waited for you," she said with a coy expression.

"Xandra, this ain't cool."

"Why? You don't like what you see?"

"I like what I see, but this ain't the place or time."

"I know that. I just wanted to give you something to think about."

"I see you don't lack confidence."

"I know what men want."

"But do you know what a man needs?"

She innocently stepped closer. "A man needs a woman who got his back. A woman at his side in sickness as she is in health. Every man needs a faithful woman. I don't play games. If I like someone, I let them know. If we start dating, I'm not dating

109

anyone else. I know you want me. I see the bulge. I'm feeling the same."

He peered beyond the body.

She read his expression. "I'm real on the inside too."

"I can feel that, but I'm in love with someone. Can you understand?"

"I understand you better than you realize. I appreciate your respect for my feelings. Most men would hop on the first woman that comes along after a breakup. I've never met a guy like you before. Didn't know someone like you existed. Your loyalty has made me want you more." She took two subtle steps closer. " Lock in my number." She gave him a seductive smile and left the room without closing the door.

The rear view urged him to follow, but he resisted the temptation. He rose from the bed, locked the door, and turned off the light.

Unable to fall asleep, he took out his iPod and earplugs and listened to tunes by Big L and Lawless Element until sleep took hold.

* * *

The smell of sausage links and bacon hung over Derrick's nose.

He stretched his body under the covers of the full-size bed and turned onto his back. His eyes opened at the ceiling. Thoughts of Suzanne held his feelings.

Blue's voice floated into his ears. It didn't sound like Blue had a hangover.

He turned on his side and listened to the joyous voices that lifted from the kitchen. Thoughts about his father surfaced behind the wholesome mouth of Blue's dad. After a minute, he rose, dressed, and ambled downstairs where the family sat around a curved-edge wooden table with the boughs of a willow tree dangling outside the kitchen's bay window the backdrop.

"Good morning," they said in unison.

Derrick grinned. "Good morning." He sat in the open seat across from Xandra.

Blue's mother smiled and asked, "Pancakes or waffles?"

"I'll have both," Derrick replied.

"How many?"

"Two of each."

"You want eggs?"

"No eggs."

She went to the granite countertop and poured mix into the skillet and double-waffle iron.

Derrick looked at Blue. "Why didn't you wake me?"

"I knew the smell would wake you." He chuckled.

Derrick's mouth curved up. "How are you feeling?"

"Man, I feel a lot better."

Blue's father interjected, "I fixed him a drink to cure his hangover."

"That's a good drink because he was out of it last night."

They laughed.

Derrick shifted his eyes to Xandra. She was leaning back in the chair, her brown eyes highlighted by naturally curled lashes and her lips slightly parted.

Blue and his parents saw the magnetism between Derrick and Xandra but acted as if they didn't notice.

* * *

Blue took the Baltimore-Washington Parkway en route to Charlene's school. Derrick was quiet, looking at the green foliage.

With his eyes on the road, Blue asked, "What are you thinking about?"

"My mind is always thinking. Remember when I said I have a dream to fulfill?"

"I remember. You ready to break the news?"

"No, but that's what I'm thinking about."

"You don't trust me?"

"It's not about trust. It's about timing."

"Timing?"

"Yeah, timing. The time hasn't come."

"So how do you know when the time will come? Is there some bell that rings in your brain?"

"Not a bell, but a feeling."

111

"Ahh, a feeling. So how can you distinguish the right feeling when every feeling brings a thought, and every thought brings a feeling?"

Derrick widened his eyes, and slid one of his fingers from the top of his lip to the bottom. "Um, the feeling comes from knowing. Like when you hear something that you hadn't heard before or even thought about but know it's the truth without the need to research. I call that the feeling without a doubt. That's the instinct I follow."

"That's a chancy instinct."

"Tell me what isn't taking a chance? We take a chance the moment we leave our house."

"Good point."

* * *

At the end of the fifty-one-mile drive, Charlene was standing at the security gate. Her hair was braided like an African queen.

"Wow! That's your sister?"

"That's my heart."

Blue lowered the window.

She leaned forward and pointed to the visitor's parking lot behind the gate.

"Show your ID and park over there," she said with a smile that lifted her high cheekbones.

Blue parked, and when Derrick stepped out of the car, she ran into his embrace.

"I missed you," she said.

"I missed you too. Has school gotten better?"

"No, still only first-year students here."

"What's wrong with first-year students?"

"I can't learn the ropes from them. But the upper class arrive today."

"I see. Okay, this is my friend Blue."

"Hi. Is Blue your real name or nickname?"

"It's a nickname that stuck since I was a kid. I've learned to like it."

"I like it too."

He smiled, showing his bright white teeth. "Thanks. By the way, my real name is Kevin."

"Which name would you prefer I call you?"

"Blue."

"Okay, Blue, nice to meet you."

"Very pleased to meet you, Charlene."

Derrick interrupted the conversation. "Where's your dorm?"

She positioned herself in the middle and locked arms. "Follow me."

They entered the co-ed building and rode the elevator to the fourth floor. Students lay on their beds with open doors and glanced as they walked by.

Charlene opened the door to her room at the end of the hall. On one of the two full-sized beds sat her roommate, a full-figured Caucasian who had her back against an aqua-colored wall covered with pictures of Taylor Swift and Justin Timberlake. A checkered orange and white laptop lay on her thighs.

Derrick said, "Hello," and walked towards her, hand extended.

"Hi," she jovially replied and set her laptop to the side. She stood and shook his hand.

"I'm Derrick. Your name?"

She blushed and removed her wide-lens eyeglasses from over a snub nose and said, "Judy."

"Nice to meet you, Judy. You mind if I sit on your bed?"

"I don't."

He sat. "Sit down, Judy. Relax. Did I interrupt you from studying?"

She chuckled softly. "No, I was on social media."

They entered into a conversation about social media.

Blue seized the opportunity. "Charlene, your brother told me that you're studying to become a surgeon."

"I am."

"Why have you chosen that career path? I haven't heard of a female surgeon."

"That's one of the reasons. But the main reason is to save lives."

One of Blue's eyes opened wider than the other. "You are an imposing woman."

"Thank you. So are you in school?"

"I graduated two years ago from NYU. My dream is to become a notable filmmaker. Right now, I'm directing low-budget commercials and documentaries."

"A struggling artist."

"More like a starving artist."

"You will become successful one day."

"What makes you say that?"

"Because I can see the determination in your eyes."

"What else can you see in my eyes?"

"Are you hitting on me?" she asked, grinning.

"I would be a fool if I didn't try."

She smiled and stared into his dark brown eyes. "I see talent, ambition, and—"

Derrick interrupted, "Charlene, I like your roommate. She's cool."

"I knew you would. Let's go and take a tour of the campus."

"Sound good. You coming, Judy?"

She had an unexpected smile, and said, "Okay."

After the hour-long exploration, they went to a popular off-campus bar that stood along a row of clubs and eateries on both sides of the street.

The four sat at a table three steps from the bar that stretched twenty yards like a coiled snake. They ordered hot wings and fries, and posted selfies and group photos. Country and western music played in the background.

Charlene nudged Judy to ask Blue to dance, and he accepted.

While they were shuffling cowboy and cowgirl style, Charlene said, "Junior decided to stay home and watch the draft with the family. Are you coming home to watch the draft with us?"

"Should I?"

"You know you should."

"Of course, I'll be there."

"Good. Now on another subject, I like your friend. Can I date him if he asks?"

"He's not for you."

"Why? He's with you; he must be a good guy."

"He's good but not for you. Just because someone is a friend of mine doesn't make him the right person for you."

"Why?" she pouted. "You know I'm lonely and want a brotha."

"I'm lonely too."

"You haven't told me why. I asked Mama, but she didn't tell me. So tell me, pleassse?"

His eyes turned away. A few seconds later, he faced her, and said, "I'm in love with someone I met at school. But I scared her away."

"What? How did you do that?"

"I embarrassed her in class. I've been trying to see her face-to-face to apologize, but she thinks I'm a stalker."

Charlene leaned over and hugged him. "She'll be back."

"I hope so. But back to your interest in Blue. You trust my judgment, right?"

"You know I do."

"So don't date Blue. He's not the man for you."

"Okay, okay, I won't."

"Good. Let's dance."

They joined Blue and Judy, who were following the moves of the people around them.

"Wahoo!" Blue shouted as he swayed and tapped his feet.

"Yahoo!" Derrick yelled with a lean to the side.

* * *

Late afternoon had turned into early evening when they left the country and western saloon.

Students honked horns as they slowly rode up and down the single-lane two-way street.

"Did your school win the lacrosse championship or something?" Derrick blurted.

Judy laughed and said, "No. Not this year. They're celebrating the last night of summer vacation."

"Oh. I still got another week before classes start."

Charlene grinned. "Future doctors start early."

115

Blue added, "Yeah, and party harder."

They chuckled and continued to walk down the busy, narrow cobblestone street that led to Blue's vehicle. Derrick and Judy were at the front. Charlene and Blue were twenty yards behind.

"Can I call you?" Blue asked.

"Umm, I like you, but I'm not interested in dating right now. I have to focus on school. If you're looking for sex, I'm not the one. I'm still a virgin and will stay that way until I'm married. And I'm not getting married until I finish medical school. So at least eight years from now."

"I can respect that."

"I heard that before."

"I'm sure you have, but I say it with sincerity."

She stopped and faced him with squinted eyes and tensed brows. Three seconds later, she said, "I can see your sincerity."

His eyes flickered. "I can wait for a soulmate. Maybe we can have dinner after you graduate from medical school."

The thought of possibility held her expression. She smiled. "Maybe."

CHAPTER 15

Blue was bobbing to the beat of reggae as he and Derrick rode Interstate 95 to New York. Derrick was leaning on the headrest with his eyes closed and his mind on Suzanne.

Blue said, "I know you thinking about that girl who broke your heart."

His eyelids half-opened, Derrick twisted his tongue from side to side before he said, "She didn't break my heart. I broke hers."

"She won't accept your apology?"

"She's avoiding me."

"That's because she still loves you."

His eyes widened and his body leaned forward as if he saw Suzanne in front of him. With his lips parted, he slowly turned his head towards Blue. A smile lifted his cheeks, and he said, "She still loves me."

"That doesn't mean she still wants you. She's trying to forget about you. You need to move on."

He turned away, head down. *I'm not feeling that.*

"Man, you got girls flocking to you like you're a celebrity, but you won't date them. What's up with that?"

Derrick kept his eyes forward. "I'm not like you. I'm looking for a soulmate."

Blue didn't reply, and stayed silent with his eyes on long lines of red lights. When he passed the congestion, his eyes rotated between Derrick and the road. "I'm looking for a soulmate too, but until I find her, I'm going to have fun the way a man should."

"Uh-huh, but I'm not a player."

"I'm not a player, Derrick. I'm a ladies' man."

Derrick chuckled wryly. "What's the difference?"

"I'll tell you the difference. A player lies to keep his women believing they are the only one he's dating. A ladies' man is straight up from the beginning. His women know they're not the only one."

"I'm not a player or a ladies' man. I want to get married and start a family after I graduate."

"You need to sow your oats first."

"Sowing oats is nothing but sex. That's unfulfilling to me because it satisfies the body but not the mind."

"Sex isn't supposed to satisfy the mind."

"That's why I don't like casual sex. There is a difference between having sex and making love. Sex satisfies the body. Making love satisfies the body and mind."

Blue kept his eyes locked on the road. "So when I fuck, I'm not making love?"

"Not if you and the woman aren't friends. Making love is the stimulating conversation after the sexual encounter—that's the orgasm of the mind."

"Orgasm of the mind? Never heard that before."

"After sex, have you ever felt that you're ready to leave, or want the woman to go?"

"A few times."

"That's because you don't like her. I never want to experience that feeling again. If I don't meet a woman that I want as a lover and friend, I'm not interested in a sexual relationship regardless of how fine she is."

"My brother, you are probably the only man on earth who feels that way. So, you gonna keep chasing after her?"

"I love her. I've decided to go back to school on Tuesday."

"Tuesday? Your internship doesn't end until Friday. What about the $5,000 bonus you will get if you stay until Friday? Are you going to forfeit that? Can't you wait a few more days to see her?"

"I don't care about that bonus. I don't need it."

"You tripping. You gonna throw away $5,000 for a bitch who doesn't want to see you? Man, fuck that bitch and move on."

"You need to stop calling women bitches. They're not female dogs unless you're a dog."

"All right, didn't mean to get you all riled up. But the chick hasn't called you all summer. She dumped you. You need to move on."

"Nah. It's not time yet. She still loves me. I can feel it."

Derrick knew the reporting day and time for the clinical research majors and returned to campus the night before. A restless night yielded to three hours of sleep.

Dressed in a black linen long-sleeved button-down shirt, cuffed tan linen pleated pants, and black dress shoes, Derrick boarded the 9:05 a.m. campus shuttle with a brown, saddleback leather briefcase hanging on his shoulder.

He walked to the back of the nearly empty bus, sat, closed his eyes, and turned on his iPod to block the conversations around him.

"Next stop, the student library and school of medicine," the high-pitched robotic voice announced.

He opened his eyes and turned his head as if he'd just woken from a deep sleep. He stood and eased his way through the students who were using the handholds and departed the shuttle.

At the library, he sat by the window facing the front door of the medical building across the street. When the minutes he waited became an hour, he left the library and jetted across an empty street where, next week at the same time, a flood of students would be, and he entered the school of medicine.

He anxiously searched every floor, and questioned everyone he thought might know her whereabouts but learned nothing. A dejected spirit carried him out of the building, and he sat alone on an iron bench at the shuttle stop.

His body had slumped like day's end with the stare of what-ifs when he heard, "Derrick!"

He turned to the voice that clearly identified a white female, and the sight of a familiar face lifted his spirit. "Amber, hi. How are you?"

"I'm good. Where you on your way to, looking all sharp?"

"I was at the library. I'm on my way back to my dorm. Have you seen Suzanne?"

"No. I heard she transferred."

"Transferred? Where?"

"Don't know."

"You have her number?"

"I don't have her new number. I sent her an email, but I didn't get a reply. I heard you guys broke up."

He looked at the ground. He knew that she knew he had scared Suzanne away. But after a few seconds, he lifted his eyes to hers. "Yeah, we broke up just before summer vacation."

"Sorry to hear that. You guys looked cute together."

"It's life, and you move on."

Amber tilted her head and slowly twirled a strand of streaked blonde hair while she moved her right leg slowly back and forth. "Sooo, what are you doing later?"

He couldn't ignore the pink neon yoga pants that parted her private lips, and a white, hot-girl belly shirt that gripped a perfectly chiseled body. Three seconds of staring felt like a minute before he said, "I'm sorry, I already got plans."

"What about now?"

"Uh..., I wish, but I'm meeting a friend."

"Oh, so that's why you're dressed up. I thought you were here looking for Suzanne. Okay, let me see your phone."

"My phone?"

"Yeah, silly, your phone."

He stood and handed her the phone.

She raised a brow higher than the other, and rubbed her index finger across his palm as she took the phone. "It's locked." She returned the phone and slowly slid her tongue across her upper lip.

Pushed by a desire that opposed his moral compass, he unlocked the phone.

She programmed her number. "Now you can call me anytime you're free. Late at night, early in the morning, or during the day. See you later, Derrick."

Her doll-face, puckered collagen lips blew an air kiss. She walked away wiggling her sultry rear.

He watched until she disappeared from view before he sat.

Suzanne transferred because of me! Damn! He turned his eyes and head away from each approaching shuttle. After several minutes, he aimlessly ambled around campus. His mind was an adhesive for the thoughts of heartache and loneliness.

Derrick entered a place called Prospect Garden, sat on an old stone bench in front of a flower bed of geraniums, and breathed the plants' carbon dioxide. That energy of life replaced his deadness.

Invigorated, he returned to his single-room dorm with hope alive, convinced he would see Suzanne again. He turned on his docking station and surround speakers and selected a playlist titled Nubian.

As he lay on his bed in the contemporary furnished room, the light of an early evening sun slithered through partially opened blinds with the music of Pharaoh Sanders the backdrop. When nightfall replaced the sunset, loneliness had soaked Derrick's mind. *I should call Xandra. But if I call her, I can't block Blue from dating my sister. Charlene is more important than my moment of need.*

He opened his contacts, and the first name was Amber.
Damn she's hot, but I don't like her.

He continued to scroll the list eagerly.

Unable to find one that met the moment of need, he called his sister and chatted with her until sleep took hold.

* * *

The weekdays passed slowly. The whereabouts of Suzanne heavy on Derrick's mind. But he found solace with Blue on the weekends.

Friday nights, they were in jazz clubs.

Saturday mornings, they worked out in the gym.

Saturday afternoons, they rode the Boroughs.

Saturday nights, they went club-hopping.

"What is this place?" Derrick asked as he and Blue entered an underground club on Staten Island.

"Looks like fifties night."

"Where are the black people at?"

Blue laughed. "Yeah, I don't see one so far. Wanna bounce?"

"Nah, I like this song by the Spaniels. We can stay a little while."

They sat in the back at a black, wooden square table.

A waitress that wore a fitted, white sleeveless blouse, black pencil skirt with red polka dots, and white Bettie shoes took their order.

The music of Jerry Lee Lewis packed the dance floor as Derrick downed a glass of cognac and Blue a beer.

"Let's bounce," Blue said.

"All right."

They were headed towards the front exit when they noticed two attractive, long-haired brunettes in poodle skirts and saddle shoes, dancing the twist.

They twisted over to them.

"I'm Derrick, and you?"

"Sherry."

"I'm Blue."

"Hi, Blue. I'm Pamela."

When Derrick and Blue left the dance floor with the women holding their arms, four men built like bodyguards approached.

"Niggers aren't welcome here," one said with the others leveled behind him.

Derrick's brows squeezed. "The definition of a nigger is an ignorant person. I'm not one, but I'm looking at one."

The man swung. Derrick ducked and countered with a right cross to the jaw. Screams and shouts mixed with overturned tables and broken glass replaced the music.

Out-manned, Derrick and Blue were under assault when a stranger jumped in and helped before the hesitant club security broke up the melee.

Derrick had a busted lip, swollen jaw, and knots on his forehead. Blue had a black eye you couldn't see and a missing front tooth.

The patrons who didn't flee jeered the four men as security escorted them out of the venue.

Derrick lifted a napkin from the floor and wiped his lip before he turned to the stranger. "Thanks for helping us."

"Yeah, thanks," Blue said, grimacing from the pain of a missing tooth.

"That shit was crazy. I just did the right thing."

"What's your name?" Derrick asked.

"Michael."

"Michael, you look like the reincarnation of James Dean."

"I hear that often. Mostly from grandmothers."

"Wow. Look, Blue, the resemblance is amazing."

"I know. He even got the same hairstyle."

Michael cracked a smile that he tried to hide. "Yeah, I Googled him, and since we favor, I decided to change my hairstyle."

Derrick said, "You more than favor him. Maybe you are the reincarnation?"

"Not all the way. I'm not bisexual. Women only."

"Cool. I'm Blue, and he's Derrick. You're good people for a white boy."

Derrick extended his hand. "Nah, he's good people period."

Sherry and Pamela rushed from the bar with small bags of ice. Derrick placed a bag on his jaw. Sherry held a bag to his forehead. Blue placed a bag over his eye, and he and Pamela searched the floor for the missing tooth.

"I found it," she yelled and wrapped it in a clean napkin.

The five sat, and the club returned to normal.

Holding a bag of ice over his jaw, Derrick said, "So, Michael, what do you do when you're not saving black guys from getting beat to death?"

He cracked a grin. "When I'm not with the ladies, I design and administer websites."

"You like that work?"

"I love it."

Blue curbed his smile. "Let's get out of here."

"Where to?" Derrick asked.

"Someplace other than here. I need a painkiller."

"We can stop at the pharmacy and go to my pad," Michael said.

"Cool. Ladies, you coming?" Blue asked.

Pamela eyed Sherry before she turned to Blue and said, "We're footloose and fancy-free."

Michael said, "Wait, the babe I was with left. I need a date." He scanned the club from his seat. Unable to get a full view, he stood with a five-foot-nine frame that weighed no more than

160 pounds. He lasered on two women who were sitting without male company.

Attired in black biker boots, inside-out cuffed blue jeans, white T-shirt, and a black windbreaker, he swaggered over to their table as the music of Fats Domino played.

Fixated on his approach, the two women held their glass of Long Island iced tea at their lips.

He placed his hands on the table and leaned forward.

They lowered their drinks. With a calm voice, he said, "I'm leaving, but I want to get to know you both. You wanna come?"

The blonde with brown close-set eyes, threaded brows, and blushed high cheeks said, "You didn't ask for our names?"

The other woman had dark eyes, short black hair, and puffed lips. She said, "And you didn't tell us your name?"

With his bad-boy persona, he replied, "I thought I'd save that conversation for the ride. You wanna come?"

The blonde lifted her brows. "Why do I get the feeling you mean something else when you say, come?"

"Maybe that's what you want."

The women turned to each other with coy expressions, and smiled. The blonde spoke for both and said, "Yeah."

He smiled, turned, and winged his arms. The women stood and interlocked. Michael escorted them to the parking lot. They lifted their circle skirts and squatted on his motorcycle.

Blue and Derrick followed with their dates.

CHAPTER 16

The morning sun beamed through the picture windows of Michael's loft. Derrick lay with thoughts of Suzanne on the sofa. Sherry was beside him. Blue and Pamela had made a bed on the hardwood floor. The back of his head lay on one of the sofa pillows. The side of her face lay on his chest and her arm was stretched across his stomach.

Blue yelled at the closed door. "Hey, Michael, let's go eat!"

Michael yawned with a naked woman on each side. "Okay. There's a spot on the corner. I'll be out in a minute."

Derrick and Sherry put on their shoes. Blue and Pamela stood up. Michael and the two women had smiles when they came out of the disheveled bedroom.

"Y'all ready?" he said, zipping his jeans.

Blue said, "Yeah."

They jovially walked to the corner cafe and entered a diner filled with Sunday worshippers. They waited on a plaid divan. Sherry was sitting on Derrick's lap and Pamela on Blue's. Michael and the two women had squeezed on the other side.

An elderly couple was about to exit when the double-chinned woman squinted. She paused, leaned her head back, and whispered to her husband, "Henry, that young man looks like James Dean."

"He does, Emma. Now let's go."

"Wait, I want to ask him something." She stepped up to Michael. "Has anyone told you that you look like James Dean? I guess you probably never heard of him. He was my teen idol."

"I heard of him. Seniors tell me that all the time."

"Uh. Lordy. If I was twenty years younger..."

Her husband interjected, "Twenty years younger? I think Alzheimer's has kicked in. You forgot your age. It's more like if you were fifty years younger."

Smiles and laughter lit the faces of everyone who heard.

"C'mon, Emma, let's go," her husband said as he tugged his wife's arm against her resistance.

"All right, Henry, but I need you to wear your James Dean outfit when we get home."

More laughter erupted.

The blonde had her head on Michael's shoulder and Googled James Dean. "Penny, look at this! He looks just like him."

Penny leaned over from the other side of Michael and put her hand on his thigh. "Oh my God!" She snatched the phone and stared at the picture openmouthed. She looked up at Michael and swirled her eyes back to the picture and whispered, "Jackie, we slept with James Dean."

* * *

After breakfast, the group of seven piled into Blue's car and rode to the nightclub where the women had left their vehicles. Sherry sat on Derrick's lap and whispered in his ear, "I'm not going to see you again, am I?"

His absent expression turned blank. Sherry turned away as if she wasn't disappointed. He felt the vibe and turned her face towards him. "I'm in love with someone, but we can be friends."

She forced a smile, and they exchanged contact information.

* * *

Blue pulled into the open parking lot where several cars remained, and all four doors opened.

Michael stood in-between Jackie and Penny with his arms around their waists and rotated kisses as they walked to the car. Blue and Pamela were hugging as they went in the opposite direction. Derrick was holding Sherry's hand in their steps behind.

After a long goodbye kiss, Pamela sat on the passenger's seat. Derrick tapped Sherry's lips and opened the door. They waved and drove away.

Michael opened the passenger's door for Penny and French kissed her. He hurried to the driver's side and did the same with Jackie. They waved to Blue and Derrick as they drove away.

126

"Michael, you the man!" Blue screeched with a high-five.

Without sharing his excitement, Michael said, "That was fun, but I'm looking for love."

"You sound like Derrick."

Derrick gave a slight grin. "Now you know I'm not the only young man in search of a wife."

Blue's eyes narrowed at Michael. "You just boned two red-hot chicks, and you want to get married?"

"I'd rather have a wife."

Derrick said, "I feel you, Michael."

"Hey, don't get it twisted. I'm looking for a wife too, but until I find her, I gotta share the bone."

"You see, Blue, that's what I'm talking about. You got the mentality of a dog. Share the bone?"

"We all got some dog in us, but you are too pussy-whipped to let the dog out. Michael, can you believe he passed up $5,000 so he could return to school three days early to see the woman who dumped him? Then he learned the bitch transferred."

Michael took a peek at Derrick before he turned his cool and calm demeanor to Blue. "I want to feel that way about a woman."

"Whaattt? You and Derrick been drinking from the same cup?"

With his natural inscrutable expression, Michael leaned back on Blue's car and folded his arms. "How old are you, Blue?"

"Twenty-four."

"I'm twenty-six. I've been screwing different chicks since I was thirteen. I'm ready for one woman the rest of my life."

Derrick rolled his eyes at Blue. "I wish you hadn't put my business out there, but I have no regrets about the five thousand. I'm not in love with money; I'm in love with her."

"I want to feel the same way about a woman," Michael said.

Blue ran his eyes across them both before he lowered his head. After a couple of seconds, he lifted watered eyes at Derrick. "I'm sorry for dissing you."

Derrick swung his arm around Blue's shoulders. "We're brothers. Apology accepted and we move forward together."

They cuffed their right hands and leaned into each other's upper body.

Derrick turned to Michael and said, "You're our brother too," and shared the same dap.

Blue did the same.

* * *

Eleven days later, Derrick flew home to be with his family on draft day. The bruises on his face were a thing of the past.

"Derrick!" Charlene yelled as she ran into a hug. "You haven't returned my calls or emails. Have you been with Suzanne?"

Expressionless, he answered, "Nah, she transferred."

Her head sunk deeper into his chest and she whispered, "It's okay. She'll be back."

"Derrick, where's your hug for your great-grandma?"

"Hi, Grandma Ruth." He dropped his overnight bag and embraced her with a kiss on the cheek.

"Where's my mother?" he asked as he looked around.

"She's upstairs with Junior."

His looked towards the stairs. *She's probably preparing him for the what if.*

After Derrick had shared hugs with family and friends, he sat and ate. Minutes later, his mother and brother walked downstairs to cheers. Derrick jumped from his seat and embraced his mother. After he and Junior dapped, he said, "You don't look excited."

Junior replied, "All of this is a formality. I already know I'm the number one pick."

Derrick smiled to hide his true feelings. *You won't be the number one pick.* He affectionately squeezed the top of Junior's arm and said, "No matter what happens, remember the Bible says, 'a brother is born for adversity.' I will always be there for you when you need me."

With exhilaration all around, they sought privacy in the basement seldom visited by Junior. Derrick turned on the music of Wale and sat on the edge of the bed. Junior walked over to a picture on top of a worn black wooden dresser with tarnished brass handles that stood next to the bed. The photo was of him, Charlene, Derrick, and Mister playing together in the snow on a Christmas morning.

"This is my favorite family picture. Look how chubby you were."

Derrick giggled. "We all have changed a lot since then."

Junior stared at the picture and held the frame as if hypnotized. "I was too young to remember that exact moment, but I can feel Mister's presence in my heart when I look at this picture."

"Mister was as good at basketball as you are in soccer. He sacrificed playing the game he loved to take care of me. His athletic skills live in you."

"Yeah, I feel it, Dee."

Derrick kept silent as the vibes of brotherly love circulated between them.

"I've always admired you, Dee. And I always wanted to be like you."

Derrick look up at him. "You admired me?"

"Remember when I was six and you told me to go home, but I didn't? Instead, I tried to follow you across the street and got hit by a car. I could've died, but I never regretted my decision because I wanted to be with you. You remember that day?"

Derrick looked deeper into his brother's eyes and saw a closeness he hadn't felt before. "Of course I remember that day."

Junior's eyes welled up. "You taught me more than you know. I never told you, but I love you."

Derrick embraced his brother. "We should've had this talk a long time ago. I apologize for neglecting you. I was too focused on my own thang."

"There's no need for apologies. When you tried to be there for me, I wasn't listening. I guess you got fed up with my hardheadedness. Can't blame you."

Minutes later, their mother yelled into the basement, "The draft is about to start!"

They hurried upstairs.

The sports network, granted permission to film Junior on draft day, had their camera on him. He was a beacon of smiles as he sat in front of the sixty-four-inch plasma television with eighty-three family members and friends cramped without complaint. The anticipation grew as the television announcers debated on who would be the first player chosen. Three of the four predicted Junior and the house roared their agreement.

The liveliness of numerous discussions inside the home turned silent when the league commissioner walked to the podium.

"With the first overall pick, Denver selects, Stan Jensen."

Silence held the house as if the commissioner hadn't spoken.

Grandma Beverly broke the quiet when she shouted, "That's all right! Denver gonna regret that!"

Junior said, "Stan Jensen? They took that white boy before me? That's okay. I don't want to play for that racist team."

Shouts of, "Yeah, that's right! They're racist!" followed.

"Stop it!" Yvonne yelled. "They aren't racist. Denver just believes he is better than Junior, but he's not. Don't forget television cameras are here, so keep your mouths shut until they call Junior's name."

Most were willing to bet their lives that Junior's name would be the next one called when the commissioner announced:

"With the second overall pick, New York selects, Rafael Horatio.

"With the third overall pick, Kansas City selects, Emilio Sanchez.

"With the fourth overall pick, Seattle selects, Jesus Rojas.

"With the fifth overall pick, New Jersey selects, Delvin Sanders.

"With the sixth overall pick, St. Louis selects, Charles Dunbar, Jr."

The house roared with the same enthusiasm as if Junior had been the first overall pick. But the congratulatory hugs and well wishes didn't lift the disappointment written on his face. The sixth overall pick to him felt like the final pick in the draft.

The reporter hurried to interview him, but Derrick intervened and led his brother into the basement. When Junior was out of the sight of others, he cried on his brother's shoulder.

After his tears had subsided, Derrick said, "Use this opportunity to prove to the teams who passed you over that they made a huge mistake. Make them remember what happened when Michael Jordan wasn't the first player drafted."

Junior lifted his sagging shoulders, and his face held an expression to hear more.

"The five players selected ahead of you were taken because the scouts doubt your work ethic and question your maturity. There is a Scripture that says, 'When I was a child, I spake as a child, I understood as a child, I thought as a child; but when I became a man, I put away childish things.'" (I Corinthians 13:11)

"Mama recited that same Scripture to me earlier."

"Take heed to what the spirit is telling you. You need to start training to strengthen your body and hone your skills. No matter how gifted you are, there is always room for improvement. I'm going to stay until the weekend to work out with you."

"What about your classes?"

"I can sacrifice a couple of days for my brother."

He dropped his gaze and lowered his head. "I should've been training like you told me. I should've gone to college like you said."

Derrick lifted Junior's chin with his fingers. "It's too late for what you should've done. Focus on what you need to do. You got three months before training camp starts. You need to get in shape."

Junior straightened. "All right."

"When they interview you, don't say anything negative about not being selected first overall. Admit your disappointment and apologize for the comment you made. Thank St. Louis for selecting you, and let the fans know that you intend to work hard and live up to their expectations."

"Okay."

The brothers hugged and walked upstairs with Derrick in front. When the door opened, the network camera was at the ready. With Derrick beside him, Junior said all the right words.

The next morning, Junior and his agent flew to St. Louis and signed a guaranteed five-year $20 million deal that added to his pre-draft worldwide endorsements worth $30 million a year.

He returned home the same day, celebrated with family and friends, and spent the next four days working out with Derrick from 6:00 a.m. to 9:00 a.m.

CHAPTER 17

Suzanne was still at the back of his mind when Derrick returned to school. He was in the school library, making up the days he had missed, when his cell vibrated.

"What's up, Blue?" he whispered.

"I got good news, brah."

"What happened?"

"I got a letter from a Hollywood producer. He's interested in my movie."

"Wait a minute." Derrick hurried down the flight of stairs and exited the building. He lifted his voice, "What movie? I didn't know you were pitching a movie."

"I've been sending my idea around for two years. You're not the only secretive person."

"Okay, you got me there. Congratulations! What's the movie about?"

"The story of Bass Reeves. You heard of him?"

"No," he answered, disappointed.

"Bass Reeves was a former slave that became a US deputy marshal. He's the one that inspired the *Lone Ranger* radio and television series. A friend of mine helped me write the script.

"The Lone Ranger was a black man? Tonto rode beside a black man?"

"Sho nuff. You need to read some books about blacks in Western times."

"You're right, and I will."

"You wanna go to the meeting with me?"

"When is it?"

"Thursday."

"Thursday? Thursday coming?"

"Yeah, they sent me two first-class tickets and arranged an overnight stay at the Beverly Hills Hotel."

"Sorry, I can't go. I have to make up three days of school. But good luck! I'm proud of you, Blue! You did it!"

"Not yet, but almost, my brother."

* * *

A chauffeured limousine picked up Blue at the hotel and took him to the Hollywood office of Warren Harlow. Blue wore a navy pin-striped suit, white collar shirt, sky-blue tie, and black spit-shined shoes. He sat stiffly in the modishly furnished reception area. Sweat dotted his forehead as the minutes passed.

"Mr. Wilson, Mr. Harlow is ready to see you now. Please follow me," the administrative assistant politely said. The woman of excessive makeup wore a thin dark-gray fitted dress and black heels. She led him into a commodious office.

Behind a framed black desk, a disembodied voice spoke from a high-back, black leather swivel chair that faced the picture window. "Please take a seat."

The woman gestured to a glass conference table and a particular chair.

Blue sat uncomfortably. *Stay calm. Don't stutter. Look him in the eye. He needs me more than I need him.*

The voice in the chair turned and faced him. The brown-haired and long-faced man had deep-set eyes, a fleshy nose, and a pale face, wearing a gray-and-white checkered suit, white collar shirt, and no tie.

He stood and walked over to Blue, and extended his hand. "Don't get up. Pleased to meet you, Kevin. I'm Warren Harlow." He shook Blue's hand, tapped him on the back, and sat at the other end of the twelve-foot table. "Let's get right to the point. I love the idea of your movie, but the way it's written doesn't have mass appeal."

"Sir, what do you mean?"

"No one wants to see a movie that tarnishes the legacy of the Lone Ranger. The television series goes back to the black-and-white days, and the radio version even further. Making a film about a black Lone Ranger is the same as a black man portraying the role of Superman. The idea doesn't translate into box-office success because it's not realistic. It's like... who wants to pay money to see a black Moses or Jesus? Not even black people, unless the movie is a comedy. Are you interested in changing the film into a comedy?"

"Absolutely not!"

134

"O-okay, calm down. I like the idea of a Lone Ranger movie, and the action and drama in your screenplay are excellent. But let's drop the Bass Reeves character and replace him with a white man, and I will finance the movie. You can co-direct. A white Lone Ranger will make the film a big hit."

"I'm sorry, Mr. Harlow, but I'm not for sale. I didn't fly three thousand miles to turn my movie into the continuation of a fairy tale. Thank you for your time, sir."

"Hold on there, boy. Be reasonable. I'm trying to help you."

"My name is Kevin Wilson, not boy. If you're not willing to finance my movie as I presented it to you, then you are not helping me. Again, thank you for your time."

Blue stood, shook Mr. Harlow's hand, and departed the room with his head held high. He stayed professional and left the building with a pretentious grin. When he entered the limousine, second thoughts surfaced. *It's the white man's world—I need to learn how to live in it. I might not get this opportunity again. I should go back, apologize, and accept the offer.*

But he didn't turn the thoughts into action. He phoned Derrick, who answered on the first ring.

"How did it go?"

"He offered to finance the movie if I changed the lead character to a white man, but I refused. He said a black Lone Ranger is like a black Superman: both would flop at the box office unless it's a comedy. Can you believe that racist asshole?"

"I've been thinking, Blue. How much would it cost to make a movie about Adam and Eve?"

"Adam and Eve? Who wants to see a movie about Adam and Eve?"

"I believe a lot of people if Adam is black and Eve is white."

"Okayyy. Sounds interesting now."

"Let's make a movie about Adam and Eve based on the Authorized King James Version of the Holy Bible. According to that version, God formed Adam from the dust of the ground. So if God created Adam from dirt, or anything you want to interpret the dust of the ground to be, his flesh was a shade of black. The same version says God formed Eve from Adam's rib, so her flesh would've been the color of a human bone. Based on the Scriptures translated by white men, you can reasonably conclude that Adam was black and Eve was white."

Silence took hold of the phone before Blue said, "Makes sense."

Excited, Derrick said, "How much would it cost to make such a film?"

"How far into the story do you want to go?"

"Not sure, but I'm thinking up to Noah if we can keep it low budget."

"Hmm. I know a lot of unemployed actors and actresses and some film production staff in search of work. Most of the animals and extras can be computer generated. But we need to buy some high-tech equipment. I think you can make a quality low-budget movie of that type for $700,000.

"It has to be quality. The actors and actresses, the cinematography, and the screenplay have to be top notch. The film has to have the feel of a big-budget movie. I'm not dissing the Bass Reeves story. I just believe the Adam and Eve tale will generate more revenue. Don't worry about finding a distributor. We can form our own company and distribute the movie independently."

"I don't want to rain on your parade, but you're getting too excited. Where in the world will we get the finances? We need some big investors."

"I'm the only investor we need."

"What? Are you getting the money from your brother?"

"Nah. The time has come for me to tell you a secret. I have over a $1 million in stocks. I started investing when I was twelve and got lucky. I've been waiting for the right time to liquidate."

"Are you sure you want to take the risk? A black Adam and white Eve is very controversial."

"That's what we want. Controversy gets people talking, and people talking generates interest, and interest makes people wanna see the movie. But if the movie sucks, social media will kill the interest, and the movie will bomb. But if the movie is good, social media will heighten the interest into worldwide sales."

Blue expressed doubt, "I don't know. It's a big move. I don't mind taking a chance with someone else's money, but not yours."

"If I'm not concerned, why are you? I've seen your commercials. The actors you choose are good! I've seen your documentaries. Your skill as a filmmaker is impressive. Your last documentary should've been nominated for an award. Moreover, if you weren't good at writing a screenplay, Hollywood wouldn't've called. You got unlimited potential. You only need an opportunity, and I'm giving you one."

Blue nervously shifted. "I don't want you to lose your money, and I don't want you to blame me if the movie flops."

"Like I said, I've seen your work. I know the reasons why our paths crossed. The invite to the Black Awareness Rally was one, but the main reason is the opportunity at hand. You ready to do this?"

Blue lifted his voice. "Let's do this."

CHAPTER 18

Eight days later, Derrick sat on a splintered wooden and cast-iron bench across from an old, dusky brown canopy outside a small colonial brick building on the Princeton campus. Bodies shivered as the frigid air searched skull caps, ear muffs, and scarfs for openings. A shoving wind claimed the smoke that floated out of open mouths. The group of eager students lined at the boarding point cheered when a headlight announced the arrival of the Dinky shuttle.

Derrick was the last to board and sat isolated on one of the aged brown leather seats. Five minutes later, he transferred and boarded the train to Penn Station. An hour and twenty minutes later, he departed the train and entered a cab. He gazed out the rear window at the trolley of people bustling up and down 42nd Street, and wondered why?

Moments later, his cell rang. "What's up, Junior?"

"Charlene told me that you're selling your stock to invest in a movie about a black Adam and white Eve. Why didn't you tell me?"

"I'm still in preliminary discussions."

"But you're planning to sell your stock, right?"

"I am."

"I heard you're starting your own film company."

"True."

"I want in. I want to invest."

"Junior, I'm taking a big risk. It might be better if you invest in something safer. I'll help you research a good investment."

"I like your movie idea. Charlene told me that you could use another $500,000. You know I got the money. Why didn't you ask me?"

"This is something I need to do myself. By the way, I like the houses you bought for Grandma and Great-Grandma."

"Thanks. I tried to buy Mama a new house, but she don't want. I also bought Phyllis, Stephanie, and Diane their own condo."

"I heard. That's good. But don't think you got money to burn. Have you made a monthly budget?"

"Yeah, I hired a financial planner."

"Good."

"But don't change the subject. I still want to invest in the movie."

Derrick placed his thumb at the bottom of a closed corner lip and slid the tongue side to side. He eyed the white lights in the rearview mirror and recalled forgotten memories.

"Derrick, you still there?"

"Junior, I've closed investments for the movie, but do you want to invest the 500k in the company?"

"Yeah."

"Welcome aboard, partner."

"Thank you. I called for another reason too."

"What?"

"Do you think Mama will move to St. Louis with me?"

Derrick slowly swung his head and pouted his lips. "I don't know. She loves North Carolina. But she might go with you. Ask her."

"Can you ask her for me? I asked her on draft day, and she said no."

"What makes you think that I can change her mind?"

"She listens to you."

"She listens to you too. Ask her again."

"Okay, I will."

* * *

When Derrick arrived at Blue's apartment door, he said a silent prayer before he knocked. Blue opened the door, holding a tuna fish sandwich

"You still down?" Derrick asked with a serious expression.

Blue took a bite of his sandwich and chewed. "Come on in."

They sat next to each other on a sunken couch. "I'm down. But you know you gonna get taxed big-time when you cash your stock."

"I'll be okay. I learned a few things on Wall Street. Let's put aside friendship for the moment and talk business. I have a budget of 900k to make the film, but I don't want to spend more than 700k unless it's necessary. My brother has solved our problem by investing 500k in the company."

"Five hundred thousand dollars?"

"Yes. Now we have extra for marketing, hiring staff, and any unforeseen expenses. Your job is to allocate the expenditures. You have control over all creative and artistic decisions. Since I'm shouldering all of the expenses for the movie, on top of my investment return, my share is 80% of the film's net revenue. Agreed?"

Blue turned and placed his sandwich on the white saucer that sat on the low indigo coffee table. He shifted to face Derrick and said, "Agreed."

"Now that my brother has invested in the company, all future business expenses and revenue will split three ways: 34% for me, and 33% for you and Junior. You will retain creative and artistic control over all projects. I will manage the company's finance and personnel departments. Agreed?"

"Agreed, but why is my percentage the same as Junior's? I'm not contributing a dime. Don't get it twisted, I'm not complaining, just wondering."

"You are the brain behind the company's success. I have one idea that I believe will get us on the fast track, but you have the know-how and skill to enhance it. Not Junior or me. With that said, my lawyer is drawing up the legal documents as we speak. We will formally sign on Monday."

"Cool. So what's the company's name?"

"You decide."

"Third Eye Films."

"I like the name!"

"Thanks. Are you renting office space for the company?"

"It's no longer me or you—it's us. For now, your apartment is our head office. We can use the expenses we incur as a tax write-off, including the rent."

"Cool. So, what do you think about hiring Michael as a consultant to design our website?"

"I think we're in sync. He's perfect. But we're not going to hire him as a consultant. We need him as a full-time employee. Do you know how much he's earning?"

"Nah."

"I'll call him."

Derrick dialed on his cell.

"Michael, I have you on speaker. I'm at Blue's. We're starting a business and want to bring you onboard as our website designer and manager."

"Hmm," Michael said, sounding unsure.

"We are giving you the freedom to implement your vision for the website and hire staff."

"That's a lot of liberty, Derrick."

"It is... and at the end, I see groundbreaking things."

"What's the business?"

"We're starting a film company. *The Untold Story of Adam and Eve* is our first movie. Adam is black and Eve is white. You have a problem with that?"

"No. Why should I have a problem? Is the movie rated R or PG?"

"We're making two versions. The R-rated version for theaters and an X-rated version for the DVD."

"I'm sure you know it's hard to get independent films into major theaters. So what's your plan for distribution?"

"We're working on it, and want you to be a part of that process. If you don't mind, how much do you earn?"

"Currently, around $60,000 if you add my side jobs."

"We're offering $75,000 plus bonuses and a yearly raise."

"Wow! I'm in."

"Great. Welcome to Third Eye Films, my brother."

* * *

Junior walked into the kitchen.

His mother was chopping onions and listening to the music of Nina Simone.

"Ma, please move to St. Louis with me."

"Junior, I've already told you that I'm happy here. I love this house. I'm in this house because of Mister. I'm not leaving. You decided to turn pro, and being on your own is one of the consequences of your decision. You'll be okay alone. Just stay focused and pray every day."

Junior's head fell. "I'm scared to be alone, Ma."

She stopped chopping. Her eyes watered beyond the onions. She lifted her son's head to her breast, kissed the locks of his hair, and rubbed his shoulders with one hand. "What are you afraid of?"

"I'm afraid to be alone. I'm only eighteen. I might go back to my old habits."

"Junior, it's too late to get discipline from me. That's something you have to do for yourself. You decided to turn pro. You are a man now. You have to be responsible, focused, and committed. If you want, we can FaceTime every day, and I will visit, but I'm not moving to St. Louis. What you really want is for me to cook and clean for you. If you hadn't bought a house for my mother, I'm sure she would've moved to St. Louis, but I doubt it now. You will be okay if you don't take any of your friends with you."

"What's wrong with my friends?"

"They're not your friends. I can see it. They are looking for a free ride but will walk away without helping when the tank is empty. If you take one of them with you, I won't come to visit."

"Okay, I won't. But can you do one thing for me?"

"What?"

"Stop working at the Eatery. I'm a millionaire, and my mother is still working at the Eatery."

"I like my job. Gives me something to do."

"Why don't you go and finish school?"

She paused, and smiled. "I will."

The next day, Junior tried again to persuade his mother, but he flew to St. Louis alone.

Two days later, with childish excitement, he video-chatted. "Ma, look at my house. I got six bedrooms, seven baths, a pool, a workout room, a home theater, two kitchens, three living rooms with fireplaces, and a six-car garage. Look at my dining room, Ma, I got a view of the river."

"The view is nice. The house is lovely, Junior. But why do you need two kitchens and all those rooms?"

"For when the family visits."

"How much did that mansion cost?"

"I'm renting. It's twelve thousand a month."

"Twelve thousand dollars a month! Junior, you could've bought a nice house for much less."

"Yeah, but I don't want to buy. At the end of my contract, I'm coming back to play for the home team. I'm not going to stay in St. Louis my whole career."

"But that's years away. Why don't you just get a cheaper place?"

"Ma, I'm a millionaire. I need to live like a millionaire. When I see this house, it reminds me of my accomplishment."

"But you still have to manage your money. A lot of rich athletes have gone bankrupt."

"I won't. I invested in Derrick's company, and I have a professional money manager. My monthly budget is twenty thousand. I got a savings account and a ten-million-dollar life insurance policy. You and Charlene are the beneficiaries."

"I'm glad to hear you invested with Derrick, but you're wasting money renting that home. Buy a smaller house and sell it when your contract ends."

"Ma, if I buy a house, I gotta get furniture and all that. Easier this way."

"The easy way is not always the best or right way. You can rent a smaller house or a furnished apartment and save a whole lot of money."

"Okay, if you move here, I will buy a house."

"Don't try to put a guilt trip on me. I told you when you decided to go pro you had to be ready for life on your own. You made a man decision, so be a man and take on the responsibility. I'm not moving to St. Louis."

When their call ended, Junior phoned his sister, and gave her a virtual tour. He followed up with a call to Derrick.

"Nice home, Junior. I feel a vibe, what's up?"

"I was waiting for you to ask how much it costs."

"That's none of my business. It's money you earned, so you can spend it as you see fit."

"Thanks, Dee. I needed to hear that. So how's the movie going?"

"We're working on the script right now. When it's finished, we'll start the casting calls. The film won't be ready for release until after my graduation."

"Another year and a half?"

"Somewhere around there. How's your training going? You got a gym in your house, so no excuses."

"Yeah, none so far."

"So far? That's not a good sign, Junior."

"Why? I'm training."

"You said, so far. That shows your mind is vulnerable to distractions. I'm concerned."

"I'm all right, Dee. I'm focused."

"I hear you, but you're not. I told you to stay with Mama until training camp opened so you wouldn't have any distractions. But I see you went out there early."

"I needed to find a place to live and get to know the community."

"You could've done all that during training camp."

"I'll be all right. Like Mama said, it's time for me to be a man."

"Do you know what a man is?"

"Of course I know."

"Tell me."

"A man is responsible, focused, and committed."

"True, but to accomplish those things requires discipline over the power of flesh."

"The power of flesh? What's that?"

"Nothing can precede what the flesh feels. That means the first thought that comes to our mind is the feeling and power of the flesh. The flesh has many good sides to it, but also bad sides like laziness, greed, selfishness, and lust, because every good thing has a negative side.

"The negative side of love is hate. The negative side of good is evil. The negative side of heaven is hell. The negative side of God is the devil. Human flesh by nature follows worldly things. That is why Jesus said we have to overcome the world, because the things of the world lead to evil if you don't have the spirit of control."

"The spirit of control?"

"The spirit is willing but the flesh is weak. So it takes a strong spirit to know and enforce your limitations—and prioritize. That spirit chooses need over desire and keeps you from misusing and abusing. You're not a man or a woman until you can control the negative thoughts of flesh. And you cannot control those thoughts that lead to evil actions without the discipline of faith. And that type of control doesn't come from prayer alone. It requires your volition."

Confused, Junior asked, "What's the meaning of volition?"

"Your self-will. The devil doesn't make you do anything. He only influences and tempts. You make the decision."

A realization held Junior's silence. *That's right. The choice is mine.* "Thanks, Dee. I'm not going out tonight. I'm going to bed early. Got training in the morning."

"Good decision. Stay focused."

When the call ended, Junior stared at the mirror he had installed on the ceiling above his Chelsea bed. Contrary thoughts brought feelings as he lay.

The minutes passed. Boredom took control and led him to a prestigious nightclub.

His face opened doors closed to his age, and he was escorted to the VIP lounge. Groupies quickly surrounded him.

* * *

An orange and black sky was the backdrop when the alarm on Junior's cell played Kendrick Lamar. *Shit, 5:30 already.* He blindly fumbled his hand across the nightstand. *Where the fuck is it?*

In the darkness lighted by the dawn, he snagged the phone and turned off the alarm as he lay there. His spirit interrupted the desire to go back to sleep, and he sat up with his back against the headboard.

He noticed the woman next to him. *Who is she?*

Awakened by the alarm, she turned on her side. One hand clutched the white satin sheet covering her nakedness. She looked up at him with the beauty of an Ethiopian.

Neither said a word.

Too intoxicated to remember her name, and too lonely to tell her to leave, he thought, *I'll train later*, and cuddled.

CHAPTER 19

Two days later, Derrick read a news report via social media:

Credible sources have informed me that Charles Dunbar Jr. will not be in the starting lineup for the season opener. We have not received an official reason, but speculation is his poor performance throughout training camp.

What? Derrick immediately phoned his brother, but the call went to voicemail. So he called his mother.

"Oh my God, I gotta move to St. Louis," she said.

"No, Ma. Moving out there is not going to help."

"He needs his family right now."

"I know. I'll fly out there on Friday after class."

"Okay, but I'm going to call him."

* * *

Junior was at home watching the sports channel when he heard the report. "What the fuck!"

He turned on his cell and was dialing the coach when he saw the incoming call from his mother. *Damn, she must have heard.*

He didn't answer, but listened to the voicemails from her and Derrick.

After he had stewed for a minute, he phoned the coach. The call went to voicemail. The same occurred when he called the general manager and the owner. Upset, he spewed vulgar messages on their phones throughout the night.

In the morning, he drove recklessly to the practice field and arrived an hour early. He stormed into the office of the coach, who sat behind his desk with an armed security guard on each side.

"What the fuck is going on?" Junior shouted.

"I don't know where that report came from. We just decided this morning to replace you in the starting lineup. I'm glad you're here early. I wanted to meet with you before the start of practice."

"Bullshit! You lying motherfucker!"

"I'm not lying. We just decided an hour ago. We feel you need more time to increase your strength and stamina, so we're going with Roberto to start the season."

"That's fucked up! You didn't respect me enough to tell me in person? I knew you were a racist motherfucker! I'm the best player on this team, but because I'm the only black, you feel like you can dog me because I don't have any brothers to back me. Fuck you and fuck Roberto!"

He eyed the security guards. "Fuck you too! You don't scare me!" Junior slammed his foot against the front of the desk and stormed out of the office.

I should go back home. Nah, they will think I'm a punk.

He went into the locker room with all eyes on him, but he didn't say a word. He changed and went to the field as if the news didn't bother him.

After practice, the reporters swarmed him. One of the male reporters asked sarcastically, "How do you feel about being benched?"

He answered without looking, "The same way you would feel if I punched you in your motherfucking mouth."

That comment led other reporters to yell questions, but he ignored them and left the field.

The herd hurried over to Roberto, a short, round-faced Hispanic from Central America.

Junior heard the interview and Roberto's comments on the car radio.

"Roberto, are you excited about your start in the season opener?"

"Sí."

"Do you think you're better than Charles Jr., or do you believe the coaches are using you to motivate him?"

"I-I better than he. Stronger. You see Junior World Cup? I play him good."

"Yeah, but he was sixteen, and you were twenty-one."

"No matter. Still better."

"Motherfucker ain't better than me," Junior said to himself.

One of the commentators said, "Charles Jr. was overhyped. He's lazy. That's why he fell to sixth in the draft. He should've dropped to the second round."

Junior shouted at the radio, "Fuck you, motherfuckers! I'm not a bust! I'll show you."

Later, Junior listened to Derrick's nineteen calls on his voicemail and ignored them. Embarrassed, he avoided his family and sought relief from depression with alcohol, women, and drugs.

* * *

The following day at practice, Junior fouled Roberto during the team scrimmage.

After a few seconds of rolling on the grass, Roberto jumped to his feet and yanked his arms into fists. He stepped towards Junior, his eyes swelled and chin raised, and pushed his short neck forward. "You foul purpose muthafucka!"

Junior smirked. "My bad."

"What bust feel like, homie?"

"Feels better than when your wife sucked my dick!"

"Fuck you, muthafucka... over-hyped bum!"

"Your wife didn't call me overhyped after I fucked her flat ass. Has the bitch learned how to suck dick yet? All I felt was teeth."

Roberto paused. "I'm gonna kill you, nigga... muthafucka you're dead!" he shouted in Spanish.

"Speak English, you fucking Indian!"

Roberto cocked his arm to throw a punch, but teammates intervened. "Let me go," he shouted in Spanish.

"Get off me," Junior yelled at the teammates who held his waist and shoulders.

"Your mother a *puta*," Roberto shouted.

"Fuck you! You probably suck dick better than your wife."

The fans at practice captured the scene on their phones, and the altercation went viral.

* * *

Derrick saw the video and phoned his brother for the thirty-fourth time. Concerned and angry, he flew to St. Louis. When the plane landed and slowly steered towards the arrival gate, he phoned Junior for the forty-seventh time without an answer.

He phoned again when he exited the plane, and the terminal, and when he entered the cab. The unanswered calls increased his anger, and he glared out the window the entire forty-minute ride.

An armed guard stopped the vehicle at the gated entrance and shined his flashlight at Derrick. "Can I help you?"

The driver lowered his window and Derrick leaned forward from the back.

"I'm here to visit my brother, Charles Dunbar."

"Your name?"

"Derrick Williams."

The guard narrowed his eyes. "I'll be right back." He stepped into the booth the size of a tiny house.

A black notebook in hand, he stepped out of the booth and leaned down at Derrick, who had lowered the back window. "I'm sorry, sir. He doesn't answer, and your name is not on the list of today's visitors. I cannot allow you to enter."

"I'm a day early. Do you have his visitor list for tomorrow?"

He opened the notebook and turned the pages. "ID please?"

Derrick showed his ID, and the guard raised the barrier.

He phoned his brother again as the driver drove past a row of mansions on both sides of the street. After a half mile, the cab turned left and entered Junior's stamped concrete driveway.

The house didn't have any visible lights.

"How much do I owe?" Derrick asked.

The driver pressed the surcharge button and the meter showed the total.

He paid with cash and added a ten-dollar tip.

"Thank you, sir. Do you want me to wait?" the driver said with an African accent.

"Nah, thanks."

Derrick stepped out of the cab, with his cell dialing. Voicemail again. He walked to the front door. He rang the doorbell and knocked several times.

Another call went unanswered. He sat on the stone front steps to wait. Twenty minutes later, gangsta rap assaulted his ears. He felt relieved and hustled towards the sound that led to a black-iron wraparound terrace that overlooked the pool area.

He looked up, and Junior was standing on the terrace with two alluring women. Both wore shades and bodycon dresses. The music was blasting out of the opened door that lit the terrace. Empty beer and liquor bottles lined the two-inch railing like trophies on a mantel. A white substance shaped like a miniature pyramid was on the small, round, glass table they circled.

Derrick yelled, "Junior," several times without being heard. He waited for the song to near its end and yelled again.

Junior scuttled to the voice. "Derrick! You came early. I'm coming down."

He opened the sliding patio door dressed in a striped red-and-black satin robe and black leather slippers. He greeted his brother with a body dap. "I got your messages, but you said you were coming tomorrow."

Derrick glared at him. "Why didn't you return my calls?"

Junior lowered his head and muttered, "I'm sorry. I felt ashamed. I didn't want to talk or think about it."

"Look at me. Why did you get benched?"

He lifted his head with a doleful expression. "The coach don't like me. He's racist."

"Why is he racist? What has he done to make you say that?"

"He benched me and didn't respect me enough to tell me in person. I found out on television."

"That doesn't make him racist. What did you do to get yourself benched?"

Junior raised his eyebrows. "What you mean? What did I do? I didn't do anything. I was at practice every day."

"So was the player that replaced you. Tell the truth. Did you train every day before training camp started?"

He didn't answer and averted his eyes.

"Junior, you were benched because you lack strength and stamina. You haven't been training every day. If you had, we wouldn't be having this conversation. You have to stop blaming others for your actions. Always point the finger inward before outward. When something bad happens or goes wrong, ask yourself, 'What did I do?' If you can honestly say, 'nothing,' then you can't be blamed. But in this matter, you're the reason for your situation."

Junior lowered his head.

"Look at me. It's after ten. You got practice in the morning. But what are you doing? You think women and drugs will solve your problem?"

"No, I just want to have some fun. I'm depressed. I've been playing organized soccer since I was seven, and I was never on the bench."

"The bench has now become a part of your reality. You can't escape reality with women, liquor, and drugs. You have to face your problem head on and solve it. That can't be done with vices. When the drugs, liquor, and women are gone, you still will be depressed. So what will you do? Because you're trying not to think about how you can solve your problem, you'll seek more drugs, liquor, and women to escape reality. That's one of the ways a person becomes an addict."

Shamefaced, he asked, "Is it too late?"

"It's never too late to change. The question is, are you willing to change? Can you trust yourself to change? Mama was ready to move out here when she heard you got benched, but I told her not to come because she can't help you change. Only you can make the change, Junior."

"What do I need to do?"

"What did the guys on the bench do when you were in the starting lineup? That's what you need to do now. Keep your head up. Be a class act. Support your teammates, especially the player that replaced you. Work hard before, during, and after practice. An opportunity will come. And when it does, be ready to take advantage."

Junior's eyes glistened as if something dormant had surfaced. "Wait. I'll be right back." He hurried upstairs and flushed the drugs down the toilet, trashed the empty beer and liquor bottles, and sent the women away in a cab.

He and Derrick sat on the terrace.

"It's hard to sit on the bench," Junior said. His eyes welled up with tears.

"Change is hard, especially when it makes you uncomfortable. But patience breeds maturity. Don't run from tribulation. Endure and receive the glory at the end of it. The Bible says, '...we glory in tribulations also, knowing that tribulation worketh patience; And patience, experience; and experience, hope.'" (Romans 5:3-4)

"You know I've never been into the Bible but I believe in God, and I can feel those words are true. I can feel God talking to me."

"If someone is telling you the truth, then God is talking to you. The question is, are you listening?"

Derrick sat among the crowd of over fifty thousand at the season opener. He focused fifty seconds of every game minute on his brother's body language.

* * *

Junior was the model teammate. He cheered and encouraged the players on the field. And when Roberto scored a goal, he was the first person from the bench that tried to congratulate him.

But he avoided Junior as if he didn't see him.

In the locker room after the game, Junior tried to apologize, but Roberto continued to evade him. Three players surrounded his locker to prevent Junior from getting close to him.

Junior yelled, "Roberto, I'm sorry for what I said. Please accept my apology."

Roberto didn't look. He continued to dress as if he had heard nothing and continued to evade Junior throughout the season.

* * *

On the strength of Roberto's outstanding performances, St. Louis entered the championship game. Even though Junior wasn't a starter or one of the regular substitutes, his mother, sister, and brother attended. Scoreless after two overtime periods, the outcome turned to penalty kicks.

Junior had proven during practice to be the best penalty striker on the team, so the coach selected him as one of the five, and positioned him to take the last kick if necessary.

The score was 2-2 and Junior had the opportunity to win the game. He calmly took the ball from the referee and placed it at the designated spot.

The goalie ran up to him and whispered, "Hey, bust boy, you nervous?"

The rants from the crowd, "O-ver-hyped!" grew louder.

The goalie smiled as if he was looking at a clown.

Junior knew what he was thinking, that he was going to use his right foot because he was too nervous to use his left.

The jeers drowned the cheers as Junior approached the ball with his right foot.

At the last moment, he rocketed the ball off his left foot into the upper corner of the net. His teammates went ballistic. Cheers replaced the jeers. Teammates and coaches who had despised Junior were jubilant and covered him with hugs.

While the players and their families celebrated on the field, Junior searched for Roberto and found him standing away from the celebration with his wife next to him.

"I'm sorry for what I said about your wife. I knew her before you were married. Please accept my apology."

Roberto scoffed and turned his back, with his wife in tow.

Junior watched them leave the field as confetti continued to float around him. He turned to search for his family and saw them standing in the midst of the celebration. He ran into his mother's outstretched arms.

"You did it, Junior! Praise God!" she shouted as they jumped and embraced.

Charlene was crying, with her nose and mouth between clamped hands as she leaned on Derrick's shoulder.

Junior looked up at the sky and yelled, "I finally did something right!"

With tears rolling down her face, Yvonne said, "I can tell you three things you did right before that kick. First, you didn't bring leeches with you to St. Louis. Second, you humbled yourself, and the Bible says 'before honor is humility' (Proverbs 15:33). Third, you believed in yourself."

CHAPTER 20

After the team parade, Junior traveled three weeks for increased commercial and advertising revenue. He broke his lease and went to stay with his mother for the remainder of the off-season.

Yvonne was sitting in her living room on a white leather, sectional sofa. Her Ragdoll was pacing around as if he was bored. Junior came downstairs from his room and sat beside her.

She turned to face him. "What are your plans for this evening?"

"I'm staying in, tonight."

"Whaaaatt? On the biggest party night of the year? I'll be okay alone. You can go out."

He twisted his nose with a thumb and finger. "Ma, I'm exactly where I want to be." He slumped deeper into the couch. "I see life different now. When I was on the bench, my friends stopped calling me. But now, they're blowing up my phone."

"The Bible says, 'every man is a friend to him that giveth gifts.' (Proverbs 19:6). You gave a lot of gifts."

"So, I was stupid?"

"No. They were stupid for not being a real friend to a true friend. Maturity has made you see the things you didn't want to see before."

"Yeah, I see a lot of stuff I didn't see before. You and Derrick were right. I wasn't ready to turn pro."

"The important thing is that you're ready now."

"Yeah, I'm ready now. Thank you, Ma."

"Always remember, everything has a purpose and meaning. Learn the purpose, and you will have the meaning."

"Ma, you're starting to sound like Derrick."

"Maybe, Derrick sounds like me."

He paused before he asked with inquiring eyes, "Who is your favorite?"

"My favorite what?"

"Child?"

"I don't have a favorite child. All of my children are special to me."

"C'mon Ma. I know it's Derrick."

"Why do you think it's Derrick?"

"Because when I was little, I heard Grandma Beverly talking about how much you loved his father. That's why you spoiled him."

"Uh-huh. Let me answer you this way. You and Charlene are twins, but one came before the other. Let's say a race between four people ends with a tie. They share the victory as equals. But if you examine the thousandth of a second, one of them won the race. That is how I see my children, as equals."

"But using that example, there's a first among equals."

"That's right. Mister was the first."

He smiled. "I love you."

"And I love you."

"Ma, I was going to ask Derrick, but since he's busy with the movie, I want you to have financial control of my money."

"Ah, Junior, I think you should manage your own money. I feel you are responsible enough now."

"C'mon, Ma. It'll be one less thing for me to worry about. I want to focus my attention on honing my skills. Is it okay if I give you power of attorney?"

She studied him. "Okay, Junior. I've been bored since I resigned from the Eatery, so that will give me something to do after school."

"After school?"

"Yes, I'm going to finish my college."

"Why? I'm rich, so you're rich. You don't need to work another day in your life."

She leaned back. "Wasn't it you that said I should finish school? I'm getting my degree to fulfill a dream. I never dreamed of being rich or my children being rich. My dream was for my children and me to graduate from college. I knew education would lead us from poverty, and keep us from returning."

Junior's eyes sparkled. "I'm going to get my degree too."

"Why?"

"Because I want to fulfill your dream."

156

With a smile that brightened her eyes, she said, "I don't have to ask if you're serious. I can see you are."

They hugged.

"Now that I'm going to be handling your finances, I need to change my major to business management."

"Are you going to open a bakery for Grandma Ruth?"

"Derrick told me to wait until he finished his secret project. But if you want, I will."

"I want, but let's wait for Derrick."

"Okay. Are you sure you want me to control your money? I'm going to cut your monthly allowance in half."

He shifted his body to face her. "You're stricter than Derrick."

"That's right. So you sure you want me to control your money?"

He laughed. "I'm sure."

"You better be, 'cause it's too late to take it back now."

Five minutes before midnight, Yvonne went into the kitchen and grabbed a chilled bottle and two champagne glasses.

When the ball dropped, their eyes turned to each other, and they simultaneously said, "Happy New Year!" and clinked glasses filled with apple cider.

"I love you, Ma."

"Not more than I love you."

* * *

Junior stuck to a vigorous training schedule during the off-season.

One day after his daily workout at the community center, he returned to the house and was bored of watching television.

He surfed the Internet for entertainment and was intrigued by an adult site that featured free chats with cam-girl models and entered the chat room of a model with the screen name FantasyGirl4U.

A curvaceous woman lay on white sheets and pillows in a room that appeared to be her bedroom. She was peering through black full-rimmed, rectangular-shaped eyeglasses, at an opened book. V-shaped peach colored panties on a plump rear with a matching lace bra that lifted the succulence of her breasts adorned her golden-honey skin.

Focused on what she was reading, the model waited a few seconds before she turned to the beep that signaled an online visitor, and saw his screen name Phenom.

She typed, "Hello."

Junior, unsure of the procedure, typed, "Hello."

She replied, "hru?"

"Um... ok"

"im joy. wat ur name?"

"Junior. Is Joy ur real name or work name?"

"real name"

"R the glasses 4 need or style?"

"both"

"So wat u doing?"

"study 4 class"

"Oh... ic... wat school u attend?"

"sdsu"

"Wat's that?"

"San Diego State University."

"Wat's ur major?"

"sociology"

"So y u work here? This place 4 whores ryt?"

"If u lookin 4 whore... go 2 another room. (BLAH emoji attached) BYE!"

"W8. im sorry. i didnt mean 2 offend u. never been on site like this b4... i thought all girls here r prostitutes. glad u not. Please 4give me."

"hmm... so wat u want? wat u looking 4?"

"I don't know. i like 2 talk 2 u"

"can't talk long n free chat. u wanna take me prvt?"

"u expensive... 3.99 a minute. I can get a lap dance 4 $5."

"then go get a lap dance or find cheaper girl"

"I want 2 chat with u"

"ok... (laughing emoji attached)... take me prvt"

"ok... brb."

He left the chat room, purchased $200 of minutes, and returned.

"WB (smiley face emoji attached)"

He clicked the private icon.

She turned on the audio so they wouldn't have to type.

"Can I see you?" she asked sitting frog style.

He hesitated and muttered, "Umm."

"So you shy, Mr. Phenom?"

"No."

"So let me see the face behind the name."

"I'm ugly."

"Don't say that. You can only be ugly on the inside."

He grinned and clicked the cam-2-cam icon.

"You look good, hon. Why are you here?"

"What you mean?"

"Most men I meet here are old and lonely. You're not old, and you're too cute to be lonely. So why are you here?"

"I'm bored."

"Why? A good-looking guy like you don't have a girlfriend?"

"Nah, I don't. I've been ballin since I was twelve, but never had a girlfriend."

"How old are you, Junior?"

"Nineteen. How old are you?"

"Twenty."

"You seem like a nice girl. You shouldn't be working here."

"I have to do what I have to do. I work here part-time to pay for school and my apartment."

"Why not work part-time as a waitress, or in a store?"

"Because I can earn in one day more than I would make in two weeks if I worked as a waitress or in a store. I'm not ashamed to be seen naked. Nobody can touch me. I only touch myself. I'm not a slut. I don't lie to the customers like some girls here, and I don't ask favors."

"Hmm... you like this job?"

"No, but it pays for my apartment and school. I guess you can say I've gotten used to it."

"So men pay $3.99 a minute to watch you play with yourself?"

"We play together sometimes. It's like phone sex. Have you had phone sex?"

159

"Nooo, that's for perverts," he said with his face scrunched. "I only do real sex."

"So you calling me a pervert?"

"No, the men are perverts."

"So what am I?"

He shrugged. "I guess a poor girl the perverts exploit."

"All the men that come here aren't perverts. What's the difference between them and you? You pay for lap dances."

"But that's different. That's live entertainment."

"Am I live right now?"

"Yeah, but you can't give me a lap dance."

"I can give you something more than a lap dance."

He narrowed his eyes. *Is she trying to get me to jerk off?*

She sensed he was uncomfortable and said, "So what do you do, Junior? Are you in school?"

"I play professional soccer. I turned pro after high school."

"Is your name Charles?" she asked with her head turned to the side and slightly downward.

"Yeah. You heard of me?"

"Yeah," she excitedly said. "My girlfriends talked about you. They're soccer fans, but I like real football."

"Ah-mm. So what your girlfriends say about me?"

"That you're hot."

"That's it?"

She laughed before she smiled and said, "They also said you're a great player. They won't believe me when I tell them that I met you here. Oh, but if you want to keep it secret, I won't tell them."

"You would do that?"

"Of course. What happens here can stay here if you want."

"Even if I leave your room right now and don't come back again?"

"Yes. I'm respectful of others, and I want them to be respectful of me. What you do unto others will be done unto you."

"Word. I like you, Joy."

"Thanks, Junior. I like you too. You seem like a nice guy."

A friendly conversation continued until the minutes expired.

160

Anxious to continue, Junior purchased sixty minutes of her private time.

Their video-chat was a daily occurrence, even when Joy wasn't working.

* * *

Junior was sweating as he ran the final yards of his daily early-morning five-mile run. He entered the kitchen and plopped on one of the table chairs with his eyelids half-opened.

His mother was cooking omelets. The light of a rising sun shone through the windows that faced her as she stood in front of the sink.

"Your stamina is increasing. You're not panting," she said. She flipped the omelet, and grinned.

"Ma, I'm going to San Diego this weekend to visit a friend."

"A girlfriend?" she asked, handing him a plate with two omelets and a glass of orange juice.

His face turned blank. "I'm not sure. Never had a girlfriend before."

"Where did you meet her?"

His mouth closed and his eyes swung downward. *I can't tell her where we met. She will look down on her.* He considered a lie before he lifted his eyes with a straight face and said, "She's a cam girl."

"Ahh, my best friend was a stripper. She worked at a gentleman's club to pay for school. After she got her degree, she found her dream job and moved to Atlanta."

He bellowed, "Ma, that's like my friend! She's working to pay for school. I was getting ready to lie because I thought you wouldn't respect her. Snap, Cynthia was a stripper?"

"Yes, Cynthia was a stripper. I'm glad you didn't lie to me."

"I was afraid you was going to look down on her."

"What's her name?"

"Joy."

"So she's the reason you cut your hair and stopped wearing your jeans under your butt?"

He smiled with his eyes. "I decided it was time for me to look and dress more sophisticated. She's only a year older than me, but she made me feel like a youngin."

"That's because girls mature quicker than boys."

"Why?"

"Because while boys are running around, girls are thinking, and thinking leads to maturity. You are her fixer-upper."

"Fixer-upper? What's that?"

"A man that a woman sees with potential but needs a little push or guidance. Maybe a little cleanup sometimes might be necessary."

"Cleanup? I wasn't dirty."

"Cleanup doesn't necessarily mean poor hygiene. Cleanup can be different things. In your case, you needed to stop wearing your pants below your butt. I told you that was stupid. I'm grateful Joy has turned you towards maturity. You have a picture of her?"

He opened his phone and showed pictures that Joy had sent.

"She's gorgeous. I like her because I can see the positive influence she has on you."

"Thanks, Ma. I really like her. Should I take her a gift?"

"No. Send her a gift the day before you arrive. That will enhance her excitement to see you."

"What gift should I send?"

"Flowers."

"Roses?"

"You can never go wrong sending roses. But any arrangement of colorful flowers will do."

"Thanks, Ma."

"Now eat your food before it get cold."

* * *

The next day, after Junior completed his daily afternoon workout with the machines and free weights, he was walking across the community center field towards his car. His mind was preoccupied with thoughts of Joy.

"What's up, Junior?" an acquaintance said as he headed towards the center's entrance.

"It's all good," he replied before the sound of squealing brakes drew his attention to a vehicle with tinted windows that blocked his path.

Who's that?

The passenger's window lowered, and a Hispanic man aimed a silver gun at his face. One shot that sounded like a cannon blast threw him backward onto the frozen grass.

Screeching tires replaced the boom.

Screams and cries followed as life became death an instant later.

CHAPTER 21

Like a string of hair burning, the news of Junior's death traveled worldwide. Charlene was walking to her dorm when she received a text from Grandma Beverly: "Junior got shot!" With tears and trembling hands, she texted back, "OMG! Is he okay?"

"Hurry home!" was the reply.

Charlene phoned her mother five continuous times without an answer before she checked social media and saw the report. She didn't believe it and phoned Derrick.

"Hello," he answered with drowsiness.

Hysterical, she said, "Tell me it's not true, Derrick, please!"

He mumbled under the sheets, "What are you talking about?"

"Junior was shot!"

Derrick jumped to his feet with a hand that brushed the top of his head. "What?"

"They say he's dead."

"Who said that?"

A cracked voice answered, "I saw it online, but I don't believe it."

"Have you talked to Mama?"

"I can't reach her. Grandma Beverly texted me. I'm on my way home."

"I'll meet you there."

* * *

Judy drove Charlene home and both cried the entire six-hour ride. Added to Charlene's dismay was her inability to speak to her mother. When they arrived at the house, cars had covered the lawn.

Charlene didn't wait for Judy to double park. She jumped out of the car and sprinted into the house.

"Ma!" she yelled, over and over, as family members tried to console her.

"Where's my mother?" she screamed and stomped both feet with full-blown tears.

"Upstairs in Junior's room," Grandma Ruth said.

Charlene ran upstairs faster than her feet could carry and stumbled. She ignored the throbbing pain in her knee and hobbled into Junior's room.

Like a child in fear, she cried, "Mama! Mama!"

Yvonne was sitting at the foot of the bed, staring into space. Her body rocked back and forth. Her fingers clasped together. "It's my fault," she kept repeating.

Charlene wiped her tears and kneeled at her mother's side. "What's your fault, Ma?"

As if she could only hear and not see, Yvonne faintly said, "Junior's death."

Charlene shrieked, "Junior's dead? Oh my God! Nooo, Ma... his death isn't your fault."

Yvonne's eyes rolled as if trying to escape from the sockets. "Yes, it is, yes it is."

Charlene positioned herself directly in front of her mother with a hand on each arm. "Nooo, Ma, it's not!"

With tears rolling down her cheeks, Yvonne lifted her eyes towards the ceiling as if she could see beyond.

"I should've gone with him to St. Louis. He would still be alive. I didn't sacrifice my comfort for my son. I did the same with Mister. I left them alone by themselves and Mister died. I failed as a mother. I failed Mister and Junior. I failed Charlene and Derrick. I'm the blame. God has cursed me. I should've told Mister that Justin was his father. I should've taken him to the funeral. God took Mister from me because of my selfish love. I'm the reason he died in the alley like his father. Oh Lord, Dear God, please forgive me."

"Ma! Look at me! Look... at... me, Ma!" Charlene shouted as she rubbed her mother's arms. "Ma, I love you; we love you." She unfastened her mother's hands and kissed her forehead. "I love you. Your children love you."

As if a closed door in her mind had opened, Yvonne looked straight at her daughter and smiled. She cuffed her daughter's hands firmly. Silence held the room a few seconds as they stared into each other's eyes.

Charlene sensed Derrick's presence and looked over her shoulder at him standing outside the open door. He gestured for her to continue.

"Ma, Derrick is here. You haven't failed as a mother. Listen to me, Ma. Because of your guidance, I'm studying to become a surgeon, and Derrick is fulfilling the dream of his father. You dedicated your life to see your children break the family chain of generational welfare, and we did it for you because we love you. How can that be a failure as a mother?"

Yvonne placed the palm of her hands on the side of her daughter's face and slowly slid her fingers to the shoulders, smiling.

"Listen to me, Ma... You couldn't prevent Mister's death. If you had quit your job and moved us into a shelter, maybe something worse might have happened. If you had told Mister about his father, maybe his father would've influenced him the wrong way. A wayward Mister would have led Derrick into waywardness, and Junior and I would've followed.

"Junior didn't die because you weren't there for him. He died because the evil of envy and jealousy murdered him. You told me the Bible says all things work together for good to those who love God. No one loves God more than you, Mom.

"God sacrificed His own Son to save us. Maybe Mister's death was a sacrifice for Derrick to fulfill God's purpose. Maybe Junior's death is a sacrifice for me to accomplish God's purpose. All I know is that God loves you Ma, and you're not the reason for their deaths. The blame is on the evil in this world."

"Where's Derrick?" Yvonne whispered.

"He's here."

Charlene looked over her shoulder and nodded to him. He entered expressionless, and kneeled beside his sister.

Their mother slid the palm of her hands along the sides of their faces. She smiled like a lantern in darkness and said to Derrick, "In your face, I see your father and Mister alive." She looked at Charlene. "In your face, I see your father and Junior alive." She smiled at both. "I see death as the start of a new life. I can feel my sadness turning into happiness. I see a new beginning at every end."

Charlene felt the spirit of the moment. She stood and yelled, "Everyone come up here, now."

As if her voice was a magnet to steel, the family and friends crowded into the room and held hands. Grandma Ruth sung a spiritual song and led the prayer.

The room went silent for a few seconds before Yvonne said, "At the funeral, I want everyone in the family dressed in white. We're celebrating Junior's life and not his death, so let your tears be those of joy because he's with Mister and his father in the kingdom of heaven. We have a lot to be thankful for because of Junior. Even though he isn't physically with us anymore, we can see him every day in us. Because of him, I don't have to work another day in my life. Because of him, everyone in the family has been taken out of the projects. Junior loved his family, and he showed it by sharing his wealth without anyone having to ask."

She looked at her brothers, Steve and Ruben, who had recently returned home after twenty-three years of imprisonment. "Put the word out that I don't want any mess at the funeral. I know y'all want revenge, but it's time to turn the corner."

She turned to her son. "You too, Derrick. I see your eyes and feel your heart. Leave justice in the hand of the Lord. Please do that for me."

* * *

Roberto was the prime suspect but had an iron-clad alibi. He was in Central America with his wife at the time of the shooting. The vehicle described by multiple witnesses was found torched in a black community, and the police turned their suspicions to gang-related.

Junior's funeral drew a massive police presence because the governor, state senators, mayor, and other high-ranking city officials were present among the thousands.

The governor, a burly man without a chin and low-lidded eyes, was the first person in the condolence line that veered from the closed casket to Yvonne, who sat in the first row with

Derrick beside her, followed by Charlene, a nurse, Grandma Beverly, Grandma Ruth, and Cynthia.

Behind them were rows of family members and close friends dressed in white. Wide eyes, open mouths, and intense gazes were on the faces of every family member except Yvonne and Derrick when Roberto and his wife appeared in the line.

Charlene quickly linked arms with Derrick and whispered, "Don't you do it. Think about Mama." She turned to the row behind and whispered to her uncles Ruben and Steve, "Don't forget what my mother said," before she whispered the same to Grandma Beverly.

Roberto's body language at the casket was that of a person disappointed he couldn't see the body.

His wife stood to the right of him with a wistful expression, and discreetly rubbed her hand across the casket.

When Roberto turned to walk by, Yvonne smiled as if she was happy to see him and leaned forward.

Dumb bitch doesn't know I had her son killed. With a pretentious smile, he lowered his head and leaned towards her.

She whispered in his ear, "You're not the only one who knows killers, but vengeance is mine saith the Lord. My son is in heaven, where will you be?"

He backed away as if frightened. His smile melted; his eyes reflected paranoia.

His wife inconspicuously tugged him away.

That was a moment seen by every member of the family.

Moments later, Yvonne recognized Joy lingering at the casket, weeping. She sprung from her seat and hugged her like a family member and whispered, "I'm so glad you came. I'm Junior's mother. I want you to sit with us. I need to talk to you."

Joy cried on her shoulder, lifted her head, and nodded solemnly. Yvonne led her by the arm and sat her between Charlene and the nurse. The family was left to speculate, and made the consensus that she was Junior's girlfriend.

* * *

Joy rode to the interment in the limousine with Yvonne, Derrick, Charlene, and Cynthia. Thoughts were abundant, but

168

not a word was said. After the burial service, the same group rode to the repast held at Yvonne's home. Punctuated by a few sobs from Charlene and Joy, silence continued.

When the first of nine limousines arrived, Yvonne stepped out with Joy's hand in tow. She entered the house and hastily went upstairs to her bedroom without a word.

Derrick was curious and stood at the bottom of the stairs. He leaned against the banister with one foot on the bottom step and his head pointed to the top.

Steve and Ruben approached.

"We got friends in St. Louis. You want us to end his days?" Ruben asked.

"Nah. I want vengeance, but I don't want his blood on my hands, or your hands. My mother is right, let the Lord handle it."

Steve said, "But that motherfucker had the nerve to come to the funeral. He spit in our face."

Derrick stepped away from the stairs. "Yeah, I know he did, but my mother spit right back into his face. He's gonna get what's coming to him. Karma is real. The days of an eye for an eye and a tooth for a tooth are over. Thug life is not the way. I need you and Ruben to put those days behind and don't look back. I got a job for both of you at my film company. But straight-up, if you're still trying to keep that thug in you, you can't roll with me. I'm not bringing that lifestyle. I'm trying to end that mentality in our communities. You can bring the music, but don't live the words. Can you get with that?"

Steve and Ruben looked at each other with blank expressions. They turned back to Derrick and nodded.

"Yeah, we're down with that," Ruben said.

Derrick led them to the basement for a private conversation.

* * *

Upstairs, Yvonne said to Joy, "I want to thank you for being such a positive influence on my son. He told me you were the first woman that he felt like he could love. He wanted to pay

169

your tuition and apartment, so you wouldn't have to work anymore on that site, so, on his behalf, I will honor his wish."

Joy's eyes were bloodshot, her eyelids puffed, and she sniffled.

"I-I, don't know what to say. I'm happy and sad at the same time, Mrs. Dunbar."

Joy leaned into Yvonne's embrace. Trying to talk while crying, she said, "I know I hadn't known your son long, but I loved him."

"I know you did. You wouldn't've come all the way from California if you didn't. Did you speak to him on the day he died?"

"No, ma'am. I was in class. We were planning to video-chat later."

"Okay, thank you for loving my son."

After they had discussed the details of Junior's wish, they locked arms, and Yvonne introduced Joy to the family as Junior's girlfriend.

She ate with the family and mingled a few hours before she was chauffeured back to her hotel.

* * *

In the fourth hour of the repast, Derrick sat beside Charlene in the family room. He was consoling her and, at the same time, trying to assuage his own guilt because he partly blamed himself for Junior's death. But when the voice of reason chimed, he stood and called everyone into the family room.

Those who couldn't find a seat, sat on the floor or stood in the adjacent room. "Junior's death didn't alter his future. The killer's future is the one that changed."

Grandma Beverly threw up her hands. "Derrick, you speaking over our head again. What do you mean by that?"

"In the story of Cain and Abel, Cain murdered his brother, but the killing didn't remove Abel from his lineage as a son of God. The murderer was cursed and cast out, and the birth of another son renewed the seed of Abel. That son was called Seth."

Grandma Ruth shouted, "Amen. That's right!"

Yvonne was sitting on the other side of Charlene, and said, "Where will the seed come from to replace Junior? I'm too old to have another child."

Derrick shifted his eyes to Charlene, and said, "Charlene will have a son."

Charlene's eyebrows raised, but she didn't say a word.

Straight-faced, Yvonne said, "Derrick, you're starting to sound like a prophet. Do you think you're a prophet?"

"I'm not a prophet. I'm expressing my thoughts. Just like Mister lives through me, Junior lives through Charlene. That's why I want a wife, so I can bring a seed for Mister, like Charlene will bring a seed for Junior."

CHAPTER 22

At the end of the nine-hour repast, Charlene and Cynthia were asleep upstairs. Yvonne and Derrick, the only others in the house, were sitting in the living room.

"Joy's a nice girl," Yvonne said while petting her cat.

"She seems nice."

"Pretty too."

Derrick grinned. "Matchmaking again?"

"I'm just saying. She's nice, pretty, and smart. I saw how you looked at her in the limo."

"I was just curious. I didn't know who she was."

"The curious look was at the funeral. The look you gave her in the limo was all about attraction."

Surprised his mother had noticed, he narrowed his eyes. "Okay, she's very attractive, but I'm waiting for Suzanne. Besides, she loved Junior."

"What better replacement than his brother who he was trying to emulate? You're the one who said you need a wife to have a seed for Mister. Well, aren't you the one always repeating that there is no such thing as a coincidence?"

"You need to stop, Ma. When I see her, I see Junior. She's not the woman for me."

"I think she is if you give her a chance. I told you, don't let a soulmate pass because you're waiting for someone who has moved on."

"Ma, I believe I will see Suzanne again."

"Maybe you will, but that doesn't mean you should stop your life for her."

"I haven't stopped my life. I'm in school, operating a business, and I date."

"But you're not giving any of the women you meet a chance, are you?"

"If I meet a woman who makes me forget about Suzanne, I'll give her a chance. Until then, I'm focused on school and fulfilling my dreams."

"Maybe you're not allowing yourself to forget about her. I hope I'm still alive when you find a wife for the seed of Mister." She stood and went to her bedroom.

Maybe I should move on.

* * *

A few weeks later, Derrick, Blue, and Michael met to discuss the movie.

"Have you read the screenplay?" Blue asked.

Derrick and Michael shared the enthusiasm and said, "Yes."

"Do you have any corrections or suggestions?"

Michael, with his laid-back demeanor, replied, "I don't."

Derrick skimmed through the pages then said, "The voice of God is the star of the movie. Who's playing the voice of God?"

"Michael found him for us."

"He's a tennis chair umpire. I was watching a tennis match and heard his voice. Sounded like the voice of God to me, so I told Blue, and he contacted him."

Derrick leaned back in the chair, stretched his legs, and locked his hands behind his head. "Can I hear the voice?"

"Sure." Blue grabbed one of the compact discs off the coffee table in front of him and played it on his laptop.

Derrick leaned forward. "He sounds like the voice of God! He's perfect!"

Energized by Derrick's approval, Blue quickly showed the screen tests of the actors and actresses selected for the roles.

Derrick's eyes widened. "Outstanding selections. Eve and Cain are perfect."

Blue played another video.

"Great scenery. Where's that?" Derrick asked.

"In Arizona. It's called the Wave, a sandstone rock with thousands of linear carvings. I've identified places in this country that most people haven't seen to use in the movie. With technology, we don't actually have to be at the location when filming. We can put the actors inside the picture." Blue showed an example.

"Wow, I like that. It looks like the actors are actually there."

Blue smiled. "The cinematography is critical to the success of this film. The audience must feel like they are experiencing the beginning of days. The opening scene of creation has to dazzle. Here are some of the sites I identified for the opening." He turned on a video that showed more locations. "The Fire Rainbow in Idaho, the northern lights in Alaska, the Appalachian Highlands along the Blue Ridge Parkway in North Carolina, Niagara Falls, Mount Washington in New Hampshire, Glacier National Park in Montana, the Onondaga Cave in Missouri, and the Assateague Island in Maryland."

Derrick asked, "Where's the Garden of Eden?"

"Hawaii would've been perfect, but it's too expensive to take the entire crew for a month or two of filming."

"Can't you just impose the actors into the scenery?" Derrick asked.

"No because the Garden of Eden requires actual touching of the surroundings. To be realistic, we had to find another place, and Michael discovered a location in South Florida. He knows someone who owns five thousand acres of land outside Miami. I've seen it. It's perfect for the Garden of Eden and the bulk of the film. But there are still some places the actors and crew have to travel."

"Where?" Derrick asked.

"The Arches and Zion National Parks in Utah. I've received written permission to film on location and use all the footage we've discussed."

Derrick leaned back. "Nice presentation. So how much more will it cost?"

"We need to expand the budget to at least a mill," Blue said.

Derrick leaned forward. "That's three hundred thousand over budget."

"If we are going to do this, we need to go all the way."

Derrick looked over at Michael, who calmly said, "I agree."

Derrick turned back to Blue. "Approved." To Michael he said, "Update me on the website."

"We're ready to launch twenty hours a day, seven days a week. Since we are dedicating the film in memory of Junior, we kept his social media tags active with footage from when he scored nine goals at age ten up to the moment he scored his last goal."

With his hands on his knees, Derrick leaned forward. "Show me what you got."

Michael played the video. "Junior was killed because of envy and jealousy. We have an interactive section on the website where people can discuss their experiences with envy and jealousy. The page also advertises the movie as the beginning of envy and jealousy."

"I like it," Derrick said, and followed up with a fist-pump.

Michael continued, "I have ten colleges lined up for a free on-campus screening the day before we release the movie."

"Where?"

"Morehouse University, Jackson State University, Grambling University, Howard University, Miami University, the University of San Francisco, UCLA, TCU, the University of Paris, and the University of Tokyo."

"Paris, France, and Tokyo, Japan?" Derrick said, surprised.

Michael stood with pen and paper in hand. "Yes, we're going international. Without backing from a major studio, the doors to the major theater chains are closed to us. Our best option is to create a buzz on social media and let the millennials spread the word. We're good with the independent theaters, but as you know, they are very limited. So DVD sales are the key."

Blue interjected, "That's right. We're releasing the R-rated version to the independent theaters, and online we're selling the R-rated and NC-17 versions. On the night of the campus screenings, we'll have a hundred thousand DVD copies available at $15.99 each, with free shipping. We estimate a minimum profit of $9.00 per DVD."

"Excellent work. I estimated the same. Where are we holding the red-carpet opening?"

"On the campus of Howard University," Blue said.

"And the after-party?"

Michael said, "TBA."

* * *

Eighteen months later, Blue submitted the film in two versions to the Motion Picture Board. As expected, the two movie versions received R and NC-17 ratings.

Derrick had graduated from Princeton among the top of his class and was living in his mother's basement, overseeing the film's release from a makeshift office. One Saturday morning, he lay on Mister's bed, meditating, when his mother entered the basement carrying a bamboo hamper.

"You okay?" she asked as she took the clothes to the laundry room.

Looking at the ceiling, he answered, "I'm okay, just a lot on my mind. I don't show it, but I feel the pressure."

While separating the whites from the colors, she replied, "Your father told me pressure makes or breaks you. I'm sure you won't allow it to break you."

He turned his head to the side at her. "No, I won't allow the pressure to break me."

"Good," she said and loaded the whites. She had poured bleach and detergent into the washer. "Why did you waste money by mailing me an invitation to the screening?"

He leaned up on his elbows. "I wanted everyone to receive a formal invitation."

"The invitation is nice. Very classy and unique. Where did you find a passport-style invite?"

"I had it specially made."

"It's sharp. Makes you want to go even if you don't feel like it. Why only a single invite? Most invitations allow you to bring a guest."

"Yeah I know, but I wanted each to have their own souvenir."

"So, did you send Cynthia an invitation?"

"Yes."

"I would like to bring someone."

His eyes widened. "Of course, who is it?"

"A friend."

"A friend?" *Must be a man she met at church.* "Okay, I look forward to meeting him."

176

"Who said it was a *he*?"

"Whoever. I look forward to meeting your friend. Give me the name and address, and I will send an invitation."

"I'd rather give it personally."

Hmm. Must be someone special. "Okay. I'll give you one."

"Thank you. Can you put the clothes in the dryer? I don't want to disturb you."

"Ma, you're not disturbing me."

"Yeah, but still, so I won't have to come back down."

"Okay, sure."

* * *

The night of the screening, Derrick had finished an interview with the university radio station and was standing alone at the entrance of the auditorium when his mother arrived on the red carpet with Joy beside her.

The sight of Joy captivated him. *Damn, she looks good.*

She held her almond-shaped eyes on him, and he couldn't turn away.

When the two approached, Yvonne smiled, hugged her son, and said, "Congratulations. Oh, there's Charlene. I'll be right back." She lifted the side of her gold full-length silk dress and walked over to Charlene and Judy.

He turned to Joy. "I wasn't expecting to see you when my mother told me that she was bringing a friend."

She tilted her head to the side with a half-smile. "Are you disappointed?"

"Of course not. Just surprised. Did you graduate?"

"Yes. I'm officially a social worker."

"A social worker? You don't look like a social worker."

She rubbed her tongue over her lips. "Sooo, what does a social worker look like?"

Never seen a social worker as fine as you. "Let's just say you look like a young, high-powered attorney."

She chuckled softly. "Ah, okay."

Xandra walked over wearing a black halter gown that covered her heels and stood in-between them. "Ahm, Derrick, a reporter for the student newspaper has a few questions for you."

He looked over her shoulder and smiled at Joy. "I'll be back. Duty calls."

She returned the smile and nodded.

He walked over to the reporter, who was standing at a two-person high-rise table with a recorder in hand.

* * *

After Derrick sat at the table, Xandra turned around and said to Joy, "Who are you?"

Joy brightened her smile. "A friend of the family."

"A friend of the family or a friend of Derrick?"

In a womanly posture that telegraphed her sophistication, Joy placed her purse strap over the shoulder of her sleeveless, white and gold-trimmed fitted dress. "Actually, this is the first time I've spoken with Derrick. Are you his girlfriend?"

"Let's just say I'm a girl and a friend."

"I see. Well, I'm a woman who hopes to be his friend. You got a problem with that?"

Xandra rolled her eyes and smirked. *Bitch.* She turned and walked towards Derrick. *I know she's watching.* She glided her fingers across his shoulders, and leaned against him with her eyes on Joy.

Yvonne walked over to Joy and whispered, "She's not a threat."

A few minutes later, the lights flickered and the guests went to their designated seats inside an auditorium that seated three thousand people.

Yvonne switched her seat to allow Joy to sit next to Derrick.

* * *

The auditorium darkened.

Written on the screen under the Third Eye emblem, which was an all-seeing eye: "Derrick Williams Presents, The Untold Story of Adam and Eve, a film directed by Kevin (Blue) Wilson, and dedicated to Charles (Junior) Dunbar."

178

The audience clapped, and the movie opened with a pitch-black screen.

After three seconds, the voice of God said, "Let there be Light." The screen immediately brightened with footage of the northern lights that turned into a Fire Rainbow. The voice of God said, "I name this, Day."

The rhythmic bass drums behind angelic soprano voices lowered as the light subsided into darkness and the voice of God said, "I name this, night."

The first three minutes of the movie followed that pattern for the six days of creation. On the seventh day, the voice of God said, "This is my Sabbath and your day of rest. Keep it holy."

The movie ended with the voice of God commanding Noah to build an ark as a refuge from the flood. The screen faded to black, the surround sound mimicked the feeling of a great deluge, and words slowly scrolled up the screen:

For forty days and nights, rain from heaven fell upon the earth and destroyed every living thing save that which Noah had entered into the Ark.

His three sons replenished the whole earth with the seed of an African, Arab, Asian, European, Hispanic, and Indian.

But envy mingled with jealousy hardened the heart of mankind and restored hate in a world made for love.

The movie credits followed and the auditorium lights ignited a rousing standing ovation with shouts of, "Oscar for Best Picture and Director."

* * *

Michael approached Derrick as the applause entered the second minute and whispered, "The movie is blowing up on social media. Online sales for the NC-17 version are spanking."

When the applause subsided, Derrick introduced Michael as the third member of the team. Blue introduced the cast and crew. When he announced the actor who portrayed the voice of God, the shy man received a stirring standing ovation with shouts, "Oscar for Best Actor."

Joy timidly hugged Derrick. "Congratulations. Your film is exceptional."

"Thank you. What part did you like most?"

Standing tall with one hand over the other, she slowly twisted side to side. "Mmm, so hard to pick just one part. But if I have to, I would say I liked how Adam and Eve's relationship was before she ate the forbidden fruit."

Yvonne and Charlene waited until Derrick ended his conversation with Joy before they congratulated him with a hug and kiss and quickly departed.

With Joy at his side, Derrick walked through an excited crowd who stopped him often for selfies. As he neared the auditorium exit, he turned towards Joy with his signature smile, and said, "Are you going to the after-party?"

In an open-ended look, she said, "Will I be wasting my time?"

He paused, pondering, then he lowered his head as he continued to walk.

After a few moments, he lifted his head and looked at her. "I like you, but I'm in love."

CHAPTER 23

All showings of the movie were sold out weeks in advance as twenty- and thirty-somethings flocked to the independent theaters.

Those unwilling to wait went online and purchased the theatrical version. The majority of those who watched at the theater went online afterward and bought the NC-17. Online sales worldwide exceeded ten million copies in less than five days.

The film depicted three main controversies: (1) The introduction of a black Adam and white Eve, (2) a white Cain and black Abel, and (3) the sisters of Cain and Abel. Those hullabaloos added to the film's popularity. And because of the swelled demand, the major theater chains paid Third Eye Films for the rights to show the movie.

But religious leaders heavily criticized the film, claiming it to be an inaccurate portrayal and a "shameful pornographic version of a divine story."

"This movie is filth! Blasphemous and Satanic," one prominent white religious leader claimed during a nationally televised interview. "Derrick Williams has twisted the Scriptures with a serpent's tongue. We all know the Bible doesn't say anything about Adam and Eve with daughters. We all know Ham was a black man and not a white man as the movie depicts."

Derrick, Blue, and Michael watched the broadcast together inside the man cave at Blue's $5 million home on Long Island.

"I think we need to beef up security," Blue said as he twisted open a beer.

Derrick paused at the thought with one brow raised. "Nah, they'll get over it in a few weeks. Michael, what did you do with your bonus?"

"I'm trying to spend it, but $3 million is a lot of money to spend in less than two weeks."

Derrick and Blue chuckled.

"Not for me it ain't," Blue said. "What's up with you, Derrick? I haven't seen you try to spend a dime. Why you still living at your mother's?"

Derrick swerved his head, smiled, and took a sip of cognac. "I don't spend until I see what I want. Both of you need to make sure you save some money. Don't spend it just because you have it. I was holding it as a surprise until our staff meeting next week, but I'll tell you now. I found a building that's perfect for our headquarters."

Blue's eyes widened. "Where?"

"In Brooklyn on Flatbush Avenue. The building needs renovation but has three floors and a huge basement. The architect is coming to our staff meeting. I have another surprise; you might not like this one."

Blue's and Michael's expressions turned blank.

Derrick leaned forward. He propped his elbows on his thighs with his fingers clamped. "I want you guys to know that I won't be around much. I have a dream to fulfill... the movie was the springboard for another direction."

"Another direction? W-what's up?" Blue asked attentively.

Michael's laid-back image changed. His naturally narrowed eyes widened, and his mouth opened slightly.

Derrick swung his eyes to both as if he could hear their thoughts. "I am not leaving Third Eye Films. I'm starting a new business."

Blue frowned. "What kind of business?"

"A venture capitalist. I'm going to finance small black businesses and build black communities across this country."

"That's a huge project, and a dangerous one," Michael said wild-eyed.

Blue lowered his head. "So what about our plans?"

"I'll continue to handle the finances and oversee personnel. It's not like we won't communicate. I just won't see you in-person as much. You have the vision to take Third Eye where it should be. We will continue our weekly staff and monthly one-on-one meetings. It just might be by Skype."

Michael lifted his body off the purple velvet sofa and extended his hand. "I want to thank you for what you gave me.

In two years, my salary has doubled. I never dreamed that I would supervise a staff of ten. Thanks for believing in me."

With his tongue twisted to the side, mouth closed, and lips pursed, eyes locked on Michael's, Derrick stood. "I didn't give you anything. You earned it. We're brothers. I hope nothing comes between that."

They leaned forward, clasped hands, and each put an arm around the other's shoulders. Blue stood and shared the same dap.

"Now begins the hard part," Derrick said as he sat.

"What's that?" Blue asked. "Your cut has to be over three hundred mill after taxes. You can do a whole lot with that."

"Money isn't my concern. I need to find some prime land to buy."

Michael slowly ran a hand through his auburn-brown hair. "Noah mentioned he was interested in selling his land."

"Who's Noah?" Derrick asked with his arms prepared to spring him from the sofa.

"Noah Wynn, the man who owns the land where we filmed the movie in South Florida."

"Really? That land is perfect. It's only two miles outside of Miami. You sure?"

"He told me during the filming. You should talk to him."

"Thanks, I will."

* * *

Derrick registered his development company as a private business under the name The Unity Corporation and leased office space in upper Manhattan. He purchased a $29 million Central Park penthouse, renovated the property, and hired an interior decorator to meet his specifications before he flew to the home of Mr. Wynn, a lanky, seventy-nine-year-old Native American.

"I liked your movie, Mr. Williams. You didn't forget about the Indian."

"Thanks. I hope that helps with the negotiation."

Mr. Wynn chuckled with resistance. "I have a firm price, sir. Twenty thousand dollars an acre for all five thousand acres. That's a good price. I can easily get twenty-five an acre."

Derrick leaned forward in the vintage wood-carved chair at the polished log-cabin dining table. "How long have you owned this land?"

"Oh, it goes back to before the Civil War. The only reason the land wasn't stolen is because a white man was among our greats." He chuckled. "I'm the last of the lineage. I'd like to sell so I can move to Hawaii and enjoy my last days with my nineteen-year-old wife."

"Well, here's my offer, Mr. Wynn. Ten thousand dollars an acre in cash."

"Ten thousand dollars an acre? Aww, you gotta do better than that, Mr. Williams. Tell you what, since I like you, fifteen thousand. That's a bargain. The market value is thirty thousand an acre."

"I know the market value, Mr. Wynn. But that is only for a third of your land. The other two-thirds aren't appealing to developers because of zoning. The majority of that area can only be used for nature preservation and farming. The most you can earn if you sell to another developer is $48 million, but you'll be stuck with two-thirds of the land that you still have to maintain. I'm offering you $50 million in cash with a way to claim less than the amount received to reduce federal taxes. Or, if you're conscience-ridden, my company has a nonprofit arm. You can donate the other two-thirds and earn a tax write-off. But my offer comes off the table in thirty seconds."

Mr. Wynn held a frozen stare with his lips slightly open. His eyes narrowed.

When Derrick had silently counted thirty seconds, his hands gripped the arms of the chair and pushed it away from the table.

"Wait!" Mr. Wynn said with his arm stretched out. "We got a deal, Mr. Williams."

CHAPTER 24

Derrick had hired a private investigator to locate the mother and daughter of his father, and flew from Florida to Mississippi. He rented a car at Medgar Wiley Evers Airport and drove to Itta Bena.

What should I say to Mrs. Williams? Will she believe me? Maybe I should've called first to introduce myself? Those were some of the questions that circled his mind during the two-hour drive. He turned off the interstate onto a road that lined boarded-up homes and dead trees on both sides. *She can't live here.*

"Your destination is five hundred yards away on the right," the navigation system said.

He slowed and scanned for the address.

"You have arrived at your destination," the system said.

He pulled over to the curbside. The house to the right had broken windows and a tin roof. The house on the left had a tattered sofa on the weather-beaten wooden porch. His head leaned back with closed eyes, thinking about his father.

A barking dog interrupted his thoughts, and his eyes opened. A group of teens that stood on the corner were scrutinizing him as he exited the car and walked on the cracked pavement to the front door of the shabby, one-level, white wooden home. The pit bull inside the makeshift fence at the house next door was threatening to escape.

He anxiously knocked, with his eyes on the dog.

"Who is it?" a strong and pleasant voice asked.

"My name is Derrick Williams. Is the mother of Cedric Williams home?"

She opened the door and her eyes widened.

He saw the resemblance and said, "Hi, I'm your grandson. My mother was engaged to your son when she got pregnant. My name is Derrick Cedric Williams." He smiled at the joy written on her face.

"Come on in," she said with teary eyes. "What is your mother's name?"

"Yvonne Baker."

"He told me about her, but he didn't say she was pregnant."

"He didn't know. She found out after his deployment but was unable to contact him."

"Y-you look just like him."

She led him by the hand to a plastic-fitted floral sofa in the living room. The outside appearance of the house didn't match the inside. The home was neat and well kept.

"You look just like my son," she said with a tear rolling from each eye.

He hugged her and saw a picture of his father in uniform hung over the hallway mirror.

After they had chatted for several minutes, he asked about Erin.

"How do you know about her?"

"My father told my mother that he had a daughter named Erin."

Ms. Williams phoned Erin and left a message.

"Are you hungry?"

"Not really," he answered.

"That means you're hungry."

She went into the kitchen and seasoned pork chops that she placed in the oven, then returned to the living room to continue the conversation as they looked through photo albums.

An hour later, Erin, a beautiful, tall and slender, light-brown-skinned woman, ran into the house and immediately hugged him. She held his hand with a huge smile and said, "You look just like my father. Wow! Big Mama said you're the one that made the Adam and Eve movie."

"I'm the one that produced the movie."

She turned to Ms. Williams. "Big Mama, it's amazing. He looks just like my daddy. God has brought back the spirit of my son and your father," she said teary-eyed.

Erin turned her eyes back to Derrick. "My husband and I saw your movie. It was really good! How come I don't see you on television? I see the movie director."

"I like to stay in the background."

"Why?"

186

"You sound like me. That's exactly what I would've asked."

Erin smiled and tilted her head. "So why?"

"I just don't like the spotlight."

"So, you're shy?"

He chuckled lightly. "Nah, I'm not shy. It's just the way of my spirit. My life is like the Scripture that reads: 'As a servant earnestly desireth the shadow, and as an hireling looketh for the reward of his work, So am I made to possess months of vanity, and wearisome nights are appointed to me.'" (Job 7:2-3)

"You sound like my father. I remember him reciting Scriptures to me."

"I remember that Scripture. My son marked it in his Bible."

"That's where I found it, Ms. Williams. My mother gave his Bible to me."

She cried, and Erin embraced her.

Derrick watched the solemn moment.

"Let's eat," Ms. Williams said, wiping the tears with her fingers.

They sat at the covered dining room table and ate pork chops and black-eyed peas.

Erin broke the moment of silence. "My father's life insurance paid for my college degree. I'm married, with two children, and teach fourth grade."

"Where is your husband?"

"He's home with the kids. He owns a convenience store in Greenwood."

Derrick leaned back in the cushioned wooden chair with his eyes on both. "I didn't just come to meet you. I also came to fulfill dreams of my father."

"What dreams?" Ms. Williams said with brows tensed and eyes narrowed.

He gazed at her. "His dreams were for his family to be freed from poverty and his daughter to graduate from college and have a happy life. His death fulfilled the dream for his daughter. I've come to fulfill the dream for his mother and the dream of my sister."

His eyes shifted to Erin and then back to Ms. Williams. "My father told my mother that when he became rich, he was going to buy you a dream house in Itta Bena. I'm fulfilling that dream. I brought you two acres of land to build the house of your dreams. My lawyer's name is Mustafa Holmes. He will contact you to schedule a meeting with the architect and has set up an account in your name to furnish the home. That same account provides a monthly allowance of $10,000 until the day you die. If you currently have any outstanding bills, let him know, and he will pay the balance."

Ms. Williams wept with her head lowered. Erin caressed her shoulders. She lifted her head and cried, "Thank you, Lord. Thank you, Derrick." Her wet face fell onto Erin's shoulder.

"Thank you for your kindness," Erin said with grateful eyes.

"I have a gift for you too."

Her eyes widened. "Me?"

"Yes. I'm giving you two million dollars in cash to do as you will. My lawyer will contact you to make arrangements. Forward all of your outstanding bills to him, and that includes the bills of your husband."

Her head snapped back with raised brows before he had finished those words. Her open mouth turned into an opened smile. Her fingers covered her nose and mouth. She stood. Tears rolled down her fingers.

Ms. Williams stood. "Thank you, Jesus."

They embraced him as he sat. He caught the reflection of the three of them in the mirror on the wall behind them.

* * *

Derrick flew from Mississippi to Detroit and then to Washington, D.C., where he purchased property before he attended a prestigious black economic empowerment con-ference in Chicago.

"The economic growth of black America has stalled because we're not united. We were a united people in our fight for civil rights, but after we won the war, we celebrated. And when the party was over, systemic racism had set stumbling blocks. Drugs infested our communities, and crime became a temptation," said one of the workshop presenters, a tall, stout man of reddish-brown skin with wide-set eyes.

Derrick, seated among the three hundred plus in the room, raised his hand.

In a tailored gray pinstriped suit, the presenter stepped towards him and said, "Yes sir, you have a question? Please stand." His eyes stared as if he recognized Derrick but couldn't recall.

Derrick stood among whispers of, "That's the Adam and Eve producer."

The presenter said, "Yeah, it's Derrick Williams. Welcome. What's your question, sir?"

"What's the solution?" he asked.

Silence hung over the room as the presenter turned his back and walked to the middle of the posh-carpeted floor before he pivoted with a deep thoughtful expression. "Good question," he said and locked his eyes on Derrick. "The solution is a change of mentality, and for that to occur, we need a culture shock. Mr. Williams, would you like to come forward and share a few words?"

"Thank you for the invitation, but I respectfully decline. I didn't come here to speak. I came to learn from you and others at this conference."

Rapid applause erupted into a standing ovation.

Derrick nodded and sat.

Pats on his shoulder and pointed smiles greeted him.

At the end of the workshop, he shook hands and posed for pictures, before he approached the presenter. "Mr. Milton, your presentation was excellent."

"Thank you, Mr. Williams. You can call me Paul."

"You can call me Derrick."

"I'm glad to see you here, Derrick. Are you staying for all three days?"

"No. I came for your workshop and to network. I'm flying home tomorrow night."

"Wow. I feel special. What is it about me?"

"I'm building a school for grades pre-K to twelve that will offer preparatory college classes and vocational training. I need someone to oversee a project that will expand into other cities. I'd like to offer you the job."

"Without an interview?"

"The question I asked during the presentation was the interview."

Paul smiled. "I earn $300,000 a year on workshops and speeches."

"I'm offering $400,000 a year plus travel expenses."

"I need to talk it over with my wife. How soon do you need an answer?"

"Before I leave tomorrow."

"When is the start date?"

"Immediately."

He walked over to a corner and phoned his wife, and after a brief conversation, he and Derrick shook hands and exchanged contact information.

When Derrick stepped out of the room, an enthusiastic crowd had gathered. Among the horde, he noticed a couple who stood away from those taking selfies and requesting autographs, and he graciously made his way towards them.

"Mr. and Mrs. Greene?" he said, uncertain.

The woman, dressed in Afro-centric garb, nodded with a smile. "Yes, we are."

Mr. Greene, who stood six feet and six inches and what looked like a solid 260 pounds, wore a baggy canary suit. With a baritone voice he said, "Have we met before, Mr. Williams?"

"We haven't. I saw you and your wife on television. I was hoping I would see you here. I share your vision. Please call me Derrick."

"Ahh, I see. Well, it's good to see you here, Derrick. You can call me Xavier, and this is my wife, Gladys."

Derrick extended his hand. "Nice to meet you, Gladys." He turned to Xavier and extended his hand. "Nice to meet you."

Xavier smiled with his coffee-colored face and gray goatee. "Do you have plans this evening?"

Derrick grinned. "Nothing important."

With his shoulders held high and a palm that covered a fist, Xavier said, "Would you like to join my wife and me later in our room?"

"Sure, what time?"

"How does eight o'clock sound?"

He glanced at his watch and said, "I'll be there. What's your room number?"

"Room 3104."

"See you at eight."

* * *

At 7:59 Derrick knocked. Gladys opened the door, attired in a different Afro-centric garment. The music of Donald Byrd serenaded the presidential suite.

Xavier wore brown satin pajamas and terry-cloth slippers and was sitting on a cream leather, semicircular couch with his legs stretched across a matching ottoman, a glass of Scotch on the rocks in his hand.

"Heyyy, glad you came," he said without moving from his comfort.

Derrick smiled and nodded.

Gladys escorted him to a seat on the couch, directly across from her husband. "Would you like a drink?" she asked.

"Cognac."

Gladys turned off the music and opened a glass cabinet. She returned with an unopened fifth, a small glass of ice, and a chaser. She set the items on an oval, glass table and sat beside her husband.

Derrick leaned forward, fixed his drink, and took a sip before he leaned back. "I don't believe in coincidences. Everything happens for a reason."

Xavier twisted pursed lips. "Everything happens for a reason, you say? What about the good people unjustly killed every day? What is the reason for their deaths?"

Derrick looked at him with a neutral face before he turned to Gladys with the same. He quickly shifted his attention back to Xavier and leaned forward. "It's written, 'The righteous perisheth, and no man layeth it to heart; and merciful men are taken away, none considering that the righteous is taken away from the evil to come.'" (Isaiah 57:1)

Silence hung over the room a few seconds before Xavier said, "Amen."

His wife asked, "Are you a biblical scholar?"

He turned his head towards her. "I am, but I'm still studying."

Xavier leaned forward and set his glass on a marble coaster. He leaned back. "So if we use your philosophy on coincidence, why did we meet?"

"That is yet to be determined, but I'm sure my instincts didn't lead me here in vain."

With her legs womanly crossed, Gladys interjected, "How did you raise the money to finance the Adam and Eve film?"

After he had shared his life story, he told them about his dream to develop the land in South Florida and to build black communities across America.

"You are a very ambitious man, Mr. Williams. You haven't completed your first project and you're planning to start new ones. Maybe you are a little too eager," Xavier said with his naturally stern face.

"There is foresight to ambition and eagerness. I'm not starting new projects. I'm buying available land for development later. What's available today might not be available tomorrow."

Xavier leaned forward with his head down. He opened a solid gold case that sat on the table and took out a Unico cigar. He lit it, blew a circle, and leaned back. "Folks think I'm paranoid... but I'm always on the alert for the existence of possibilities. That awareness keeps me a step ahead of my enemies."

Derrick leaned forward with a frown of concentration. His eyes asked Xavier to continue.

"You can't prevent something from happening unless you are aware of the possibility and take proper precautions. Many have failed to rebuild Black Wall Street because they weren't paranoid enough. A wise man is paranoid because he assumes that he's under surveillance even if he's not. That way he'll always be steps ahead. A wise man controls his paranoia and doesn't allow it to control him. In this country, a black man must know how to pretend. He must know how to make everything in the eyes of the powers that be appear to be less than it truly is."

192

Derrick leaned back. His eyes tried to peer into Xavier's mind. *He's the partner I need.*

Xavier returned a look that seemed to ask whether Derrick realized the danger that lay ahead.

CHAPTER 25

Xavier puffed, lifted his chin, blew two circles, and his eyes followed the smoke with an inscrutable expression. Seconds of silence passed as if the room was empty.

Derrick leaned forward, took a sip, and leaned back, unfazed by the disposition.

Xavier slid a thumb under his chin and rubbed the top of his goatee with the side of his index finger. "I'm fifty-six years old. I was too young to prance with Dr. King, but I'm ready to get up into the mix of action to empower black communities. My concern is you. I'm not sure you realize what's ahead."

"I know what's ahead. It's life or death."

"That's right! And in-between are people, places, and things. You can't trust a man because he's black. You can't trust your brother because he's your brother. On this road, your ilk isn't flesh, or blood, but soul. And it's not easy to decipher a person's soul on this path because unfamiliar faces are professionally trained to make you believe their lies are true, and some of the familiar faces are turncoats."

Derrick's ears were attuned to every word. "I know why we met."

Looking straight at Derrick, Xavier leaned forward and thrust his cigar into the unfinished glass of Scotch. He clasped his hands. "Why?"

"I've read books and attended seminars, but none of that knowledge can compare to you. I need a partner. I believe it's you. I'm the spook who infiltrated the CIA. You're the one when he left."

Xavier's and his wife's eyes both widened. They looked at each other, then Gladys turned to Derrick and cracked a smile. "You saw the movie?"

He shook his head slowly. "No, I read the book."

Xavier leaned back and folded his arms. "I'm impressed."

Derrick took another sip. "I've been planning since I was ten. I'm not turning back."

With his fingers in a V, Xavier scratched his goatee. "So you really want to do this? What if your mother turns against you?"

"She's the one that gave me the book."

He and his wife smiled before she excused herself.

"I'm curious. How did you pull off the deal that allowed you to sell DVDs while the movie was in the theaters?"

"Our agreement with the independent theaters was to sell the movie online because their theaters were few. They were happy with being sold-out for all showings for a month."

"Smart business move. And the deal with the major chains?"

"We were paid millions to stop all online sales in the US for forty-five days."

"Brilliant. You're a strong negotiator. A necessary skill for the road ahead. Let me tell you a personal story. In the twelfth grade, I was working part-time in an after-school program funded by the government. I cleaned offices and toilets. One day a friend I had met on the job who worked in the copy room was shooting the breeze with me outside the building. We both were wearing smocks, mine of course because I was a janitor, his to protect his clothes when he changed the toner.

"We saw this sophisticated sista walking from the subway. He hollered at her, but she kept on walking. Then he said, 'Can I give you my office number?' She stopped dead in her tracks and turned around. A few seconds earlier, she wouldn't give him the time of day, but when he mentioned he had an office number, she immediately changed. I said to myself, 'That's fucked up.' But that was the emerging mentality among some educated black women. A trash man wasn't worth a look.

"I didn't attend college. I graduated from a vocational school and went to work busting my ass for the white man. I was a good worker. I was never absent or late. One day I was shoveling rocks and saw this fine sista walking up the sidewalk. Of course, I spoke. I was polite and gentleman-like, but she didn't even say hi to me. She turned up her nose and kept walking. I said to myself, 'I need my own business.' So I quit my job and became a contractor. I wasn't making much, but I was earning a living. Still, the women looked down on me because I didn't have a degree. So I thought about going to school to get my degree, but said, 'Nah. I need a woman who will accept me for who I am and not for who she wants me to be.'

"Then I met Gladys, and when she told me that she had a doctorate from Stanford, I expected her to dump me when I told her that I was only a high-school graduate. But she didn't. And on our second date, I said, 'You are twenty-six with a doctorate from Stanford, why do you like me?' You know what she told me?"

Eager to hear more, Derrick asked, "What did she say?"

"She said, 'Because you represent the essence of a black man.' I was twenty-nine years old. We got married when I was thirty. We celebrated our Silver Anniversary last March. You heard the saying, 'Behind every successful man there is a woman?' It's true."

Derrick put his clutched hands behind his head and sat there, contemplating.

Xavier allowed him a few seconds to his thoughts before he said, "Several years ago when my father died, I inherited eleven thousand acres of farmland. The problem is that I can't develop the land into a business community because the location is too rural. I've been waiting for an opportunity to use it as a farm, and I might have found one."

"Not might, you have. I came to this conference with the hope that I would meet you. Your construction firm garners the bulk of city contracts in Philadelphia. I'm looking to build, and you have the expertise. As I develop land and communities across the country, I want to use the service of one construction company, and I can provide the capital to make you that company."

Xavier exhaled. "I knew one day that someone like you would come along, but I didn't expect to be alive, like I didn't expect to see a black president. But here you are, right before my eyes, and I think you're serious. Call me, Obe."

"Obe?"

"Yeah, that's what my close friends call me. It's short for Obadiah, my middle name."

"I'm honored, Obe, to be considered a close friend so soon."

"I also do not believe in coincidences. I think you are the future. I'm just not sure the future is now. I'm not sure if we should be partners yet. You're still wet behind the ears."

Derrick smiled and sipped his drink. "David was wet behind the ears when he slew Goliath."

Xavier slid forward and clamped his hands and locked eyes with Derrick. "Development often nurtures bribery and backroom deals. When a white man does it, he's a great businessman. When a black man does the same, he's a crook. Are you ready to get your clean hands dirty?"

"If I can wash my hands clean afterward."

Xavier tilted his head slightly. "On the road we're headed if a person is not with you, he or she is against you. So those on the fence are against you."

Derrick extended his hand.

"What's the shake for?"

"You said, on the road we're headed. So your spirit has accepted our partnership."

Xavier's eyes glistened. "Okay, Derrick."

They shook hands.

Xavier said, "Let's design a nation," and called Gladys.

As if she knew the reason, Gladys exited the bedroom with a laptop, writing pads, and pens. They stayed up all night and fleshed out the partnership details, and verbally agreed.

Derrick would serve as the Chief Executive Officer and oversee the financial department and human resources. Xavier would serve as Chief Operating Officer and oversee planning and development, which included securing all necessary licenses, building code requirements, and regulations. Gladys would be the Executive Director and manage public relations and marketing, which included vetting all potential investors, and serving as the liaison for all approved investors.

Derrick said to her, "I need you to identify three thousand African-American business people, celebrities, and athletes that are financially able to invest a minimum of $1 million."

She replied, "Phase One is only projected to cost $100 million. Why do we need three thousand names?"

197

"If we start at three thousand, the vetting will probably reduce the number to half. And out of fifteen hundred, I'm confident we can get a hundred to commit $1 million each."

"How in-depth do you want the vetting?"

"Like your husband said, 'If they are on the fence, they are against us.'"

Xavier added to the notes: "We will take advantage of available government funds and avoid taxes with the same loopholes utilized by major corporations. But instead of pocketing the savings, we will use it to develop additional jobs for the communities."

That was the inception of The Unity Corporation.

* * *

While the lawyers were finalizing the partnership, Xavier and Gladys returned to their estate in Philadelphia. Derrick went to Long Island to visit Blue.

"Wow, Blue, this is a nice recording studio. I was wondering what you were going to do with your basement."

"Thanks. I decided to start my own record label. I know some talented artists in need of an opportunity, so I signed them. Figured I introduce them on the *Bass Reeves* sound-track."

"Good idea. How's the movie coming?"

"Like I said the last time we spoke, which was almost a month ago by the way, I'm busy with the cable sitcom. We should start filming in a few months. No rush. We're still making money from *Adam and Eve*."

"Yeah, but we signed a three-movie deal with the major theaters. I know we got a four-year deadline for two new movies, but we need to get a movie out. We have an audience waiting, and I want to end that contract early. I apologize for not keeping our weekly staff meetings. Handling the finances for two companies is more challenging than I expected, but that's not an excuse. I'm sorry. I'll do better."

"Cool. On a business note, Entertainment Television is trying to schedule an interview. They want to know how we feel about being snubbed by the Oscars."

"You've been doing all the television interviews. They don't need me."

"They are asking about you specifically. They're trying to get an exclusive. Everyone wants an interview with the man behind the movie."

"Well, I don't have the time. You handle it. Just stay positive on the questions. Don't let the public know how you truly feel. Let our fans do the ranting for us. How's Michael doing?"

"Ohhh, you won't believe it. He's hooked up with Judy."

"Judy who?"

"Judy, your sister's friend."

"Really? When did that happen?"

"It started at the party after the screening. Ain't that some crazy shit? He has his choice of international models, and he chose a heavyweight."

"That just proves my point. Real beauty lies within. What you see inside a person is what you see on the outside. Who cares what other people see? The only thing that matters is what you see."

* * *

After they had chatted a few hours, Blue drove Derrick home in his custom-built 740.

"Thanks, Blue," he said as the doorman opened the passenger's door.

"Good evening, Mr. Williams." The doorman tilted his hat and opened the door to the Central Park West building.

"Good evening, Mr. Brisett."

He rode a private elevator to the twenty-ninth floor, the first of his two floors, and entered a huge high-ceilinged white-marble foyer that led to walnut ombre flooring stretched across a sunken, capacious living area. Floor-to-ceiling, vertical, fixed-paned windows spaced the expanse on both sides with panoramic views of Central Park and the Manhattan skyline. A double-sided fireplace divided the broad area with contemporary furniture.

Five fully furnished bedrooms with sprawling walk-in closets and multicolored marble bathroom suites each with a hanging chandelier were side by side. A roomy marble-panel guest bathroom with a chandelier was at the north, and another at the south. The area also featured an island kitchen stove with six burners, double oven, white marble countertops, and chrome appliances and fixtures.

The thirtieth floor was accessible by elevator and a platinum, two-person, spiral staircase, and featured an inlaid marble, sixty-foot baronial entrance. The master bedroom had his and her walk-in closets and bathroom suites with soaking tubs and dual steam showers, each with in-wall televisions. The top level also featured four terraces, one adjacent to the master bedroom, one enclosed as a solarium, one that overlooked Central Park, and one designed for a party in the sky.

At twenty-four years old, Derrick had an enviable lifestyle. But Suzanne continued to weigh heavily on his mind, so he buried himself with work to erase the thoughts.

His loneliness persisted, and female companionship became a necessity, so he dated women who wouldn't get emotionally attached.

CHAPTER 26

Two years had passed when the list of three thousand names became 973 potential investors. Gladys was the lead for the individual presentations and Xavier for the groups. Thirteen million was committed out of the first twenty-four approached.

But despite the good news, Derrick was depressed.

On his bedroom terrace, he peered into the sunset with Suzanne at the forefront of his mind. *Why has God given me everything but her?* Restless, he rode a cab to Times Square.

Darkness covered the sky, and millions of lights illuminated his path as he sauntered through the densely crowded streets looking into the unknown faces of many, wondering if any were as lonely as him. The strangers he sought to find comfort among became obstacles in his steps to nowhere, so he squeezed himself through the congestion but was drawn back by a voice quoting from the Holy Bible.

The bearded man, dressed in white, ancient Hebrew garb, had a gathering of fifteen people. The sound of overfilled sidewalks and jammed vehicles faded from Derrick's consciousness as he focused on the seemingly biblical scholar's emotional speech.

Three men with similar clothing stood like bodyguards, one behind, and one on each side. Except for an occasional exclamation, "Amen," or "Preach on, brother," the men were silent.

Are they affiliated with Xavier's church? Derrick stepped closer but stayed at the back.

When the gathering thinned, he noticed a middle-aged white man who stood in front of the preacher, still and silent like a servant.

After a few more Scripture recitations, the preacher shouted, "White people are the devil, and are cast out from the kingdom of heaven. God has cursed all white people!"

But the white man didn't move. He said, "I believe you. How can I be saved?"

The preacher yelled over the man's head, "Jesus is a black man! God will only save the black Jews!"

The white man's expression became one of consternation. "I believe! I believe Jesus is a black man! Can I be saved?"

The preacher continued to look around as if he didn't see the man in front of him and kept his rhetoric aimed at recruiting the blacks at the gathering and those who walked by. "The kingdom of God is for black people only!"

"I believe you. Please tell me how I can be saved!"

His question went unanswered, but he continued to listen as if the preacher was his last hope of salvation. Seconds later, he turned to the gathered faces with the hope that one might answer the question. His clothing was covered with mud and dirt. A tear from each eye slowly rolled down the cheeks of his ruddy face.

But no one said a word, so he turned his short dumpy body towards the preacher and begged, "Please tell me how I can be saved? Please? I believe. Please tell me?"

Annoyed, the preacher leaned his neck towards the man. "You cannot be saved! No Gentile can be saved! Only the Black Hebrews will enter the kingdom of God!"

The man's face turned from pink to red. His head drooped as if he believed he couldn't enter the kingdom of God.

Derrick lifted up his voice to the preacher and asked, "Are you affiliated with prophet William?"

The minister didn't open his mouth but looked at Derrick with an expression that said, No!

"Read Romans 1:16," Derrick calmly said.

The preacher's face turned blank. His beady eyes stared at Derrick while his fingers turned the pages.

Derrick held the eye contact.

The preacher lowered his eyes to the book, flicked a few pages, and recited the Scripture. He lifted his eyes to Derrick and shouted, "Do you know who the Greeks are?"

With an unchanged expression, Derrick said, "Yes. The seed of Alexander the Great, a white man."

The preacher took up the challenge. "Let me educate you, my brother, with the words of Jesus Christ himself." He turned to the Bible and read: "These twelve Jesus sent forth and commanded them, saying, Go not into the way of the Gentiles," (the preacher emphasized *Gentiles*), "and into any city of the Samaritans enter ye not; But go, rather, to the lost sheep of the house of Israel." (St. Matthew 10:5-6)

The preacher lifted his head as if he had proven his point and won the debate.

Derrick heard murmurs from a crowd enlarged by the curiosity for a biblical dispute. And in his peripheral vision saw the white man waiting anxiously for his reply. He took a couple of steps forward.

The white man moved to the side as if a physical altercation was about to occur. The bodyguards took a step closer, and the crowd grew.

Derrick said, "If you don't tell the whole story, you lied. Read what Jesus said to his disciples after he rose from the dead. Read the last chapter of St. Matthew, verses sixteen to twenty."

The crowd was quietly waiting to hear the Scriptures when another Black Hebrew who sat undetected in the back of the van parked behind the preacher emerged. The towering, mysterious man stepped forward with the aura of the group's leader and whispered to the front man. Without a word, the men climbed into the van and departed.

A tall, slim black woman who stood behind Derrick tapped him on the shoulder. "What's written in those Scriptures?"

The white man's ear was attentive, and Derrick answered, "Jesus told his disciples, 'All power is given unto me in heaven and in earth. Go ye therefore and teach all nations, baptizing them in the name of the Father, and Son, and Holy Ghost. Teach them to observe all things whatsoever I have commanded you.'"

"Thank you!" the woman said and walked away from among the crowd that had swelled.

Rejuvenated, the white man shouted, "Amen, Amen! Thank you, brother... thank you so much! I'm saved!"

As he started to walk away, Derrick asked, "What's your name?"

He turned, as if it had been a long time since someone asked for his name, and proudly said, "My name is Ryan Mendendorf."

"Nice to meet you, Ryan. My name is Derrick Williams. Would you like to eat with me?"

Ryan's round face sprung a hesitant smile, and he nervously said, "Yes. Thank you for the invitation."

"Thank you for accepting."

They walked side by side in silence up the crowded street.

Derrick headed towards the door of a posh restaurant. Ryan scurried behind him as if he was a part of Derrick's body, with his head down.

The aged hostess apparently thought he was trying to sneak inside and yelled, "You can't come in! Our bathrooms are for customers only."

Derrick turned to her. "He's with me," and wrapped his arm around Ryan's shoulders.

The hostess forced a grin. "I'm sorry, I thought..."

"I know what you thought. Table for two, please."

Ryan looked up at him with wet eyes. "Thank you, sir."

"Ryan, call me, Derrick."

"Okay, Derrick."

She led them towards an isolated table.

"Excuse me. We're not sitting there," Derrick said and pointed to a table that had a view of the street. "We want to sit there."

She tried to hide the smirk and seated them as requested.

"Your server will be with you shortly," she said with a curled lip.

"Excuse me. I don't appreciate the attitude," Derrick said.

"Sir, I don't have an attitude."

"I wouldn't've said it if it wasn't obvious."

"I apologize if I gave you the wrong impression."

"Apology accepted. Thank you."

She turned away with a masked smile.

"I could've eaten fast food, Derrick. I'm not welcome here. People are looking at us. I feel uncomfortable."

"First, I don't have a taste for fast food. Second, they are the ones that feel uncomfortable. Don't allow them to make you feel what they feel."

A few seconds later, a broad-smiled waitress came to the table with two menus and asked, "Can I get you something to drink while you look over the menu?"

"Bottled water. What do you want, Ryan?"

His face was buried in the menu. He looked up with eyes that told a story of dereliction.

"I'll have soda," he timidly said.

"What kind?" the waitress asked, pointing to the list.

"Any kind."

When she left, Derrick leaned forward with his hands clamped and arms on the white linen. "Don't be shy, Ryan. Get whatever you want, and as much as you want. I can afford it."

He lowered his head to the menu. Derrick smiled and put his phone on vibrate.

The waitress returned quickly with the drinks, and politely asked, "Are you ready to order?"

Derrick ordered the well-done T-bone dinner.

Ryan ordered the medium-rare filet mignon dinner.

Derrick said to the waitress, "Double his order."

"Okay." She turned to Ryan and smiled. "Would you like a refill?"

"Yes, thank you."

She returned with the pitcher and filled his twenty-four-ounce glass. "Your food will be ready soon."

"Thank you," Ryan said and turned his weary face to Derrick. "Mr. Derrick, why did you invite me to eat with you?"

"Ryan, please, just call me Derrick."

"Okay, Derrick, I'm sorry."

"Ryan, there is a story in the Gospel of St. Matthew (15:21-28) about a woman of Canaan who begged Jesus to save her daughter, but he said, 'I am not sent but unto the lost sheep of the house of Israel.' So the woman worshiped Jesus, and said, 'Lord, help me.' But he answered, 'It is not meet to take the children's bread, and to cast it to dogs.' The woman said, 'Truth, Lord; yet the dogs eat of the crumbs which fall from their masters' table.' Then Jesus said, 'O woman, great is thy faith; be it unto thee even as thou wilt.' And the woman's daughter who the devil vexed was made whole in that very hour. You are the same as that woman."

Appreciation lit Ryan's face. "Are you Jesus?"

"No, I'm not Jesus. But his spirit lives in me, and in you, and in all who accept him as Lord and Savior."

"Amen," Ryan said with his brown eyes brightened. "I'm blessed to have met you."

"I feel blessed to have met you."

"Why? I'm nobody."

"Everybody is somebody. Every living thing has a soul."

"Every living thing? Do plants and trees have a soul?"

"Plants and trees are living things like fish and birds. The Bible says, 'In God's hand is the soul of every living thing.'" (Job 12:10)

Their conversation about God continued until the waitress placed their food on the table.

"Is there anything else I can get for you two gentlemen?"

"Ryan, you want anything else?"

"No," he answered with a mouth full of food.

Derrick turned to the waitress. "We're good. Thank you."

"If you need anything, just signal."

"We will," Derrick said as he watched Ryan gobble. He smiled, dumped sauce on his steak, and sliced. "Tell me about yourself?"

Ryan looked up as he chewed his filet. He swallowed and said, "I was the CFO for a hedge-fund manager on Wall Street when I lost my job because of a company scandal. I was wrongly convicted of embezzlement and spent six years in federal prison. Not one time during my incarceration did my wife visit, or accept my calls. When I got released four years ago, I found my home was foreclosed and resold, and I couldn't locate my wife and two daughters."

"What about the other members of your family?"

"My parents died more than twenty years ago. I'm the only child. The people I thought were my family and friends disowned me. It was akin to being abandoned in the middle of the desert without food or water. Everyone I knew as family and friends turned their backs on me."

206

"That's because they were never truly your family or friends. So how long have you been homeless?"

His face drooped. "Since I got out of prison."

"Where did you meet your wife?"

"I met her at a party hosted by my former boss. He introduced her, and we fell in love. She's from Ukraine and was in America on a school visa. She was twenty years old when we married, and I loved her so much. I just can't believe she left me." His face turned red with a burst of tears.

Derrick stretched his hand on Ryan's shoulder. "God hasn't abandoned you." He removed his hand and said, "I remember hearing about that scandal, but I didn't follow it closely. Were you the only one convicted?"

"Yep."

"Why not your boss?"

"I don't know. At first, I thought he had set me up to be the scapegoat. But he testified as a character witness on my behalf. Someone in that office framed me, but I don't believe he was involved."

"Mm-hmm, so what happened to your boss?"

"I heard he's managing a new hedge fund company."

Derrick narrowed his eyes. "Convenient." He calmly chewed a piece of meat. After he had sipped his water, he looked at Ryan. "With your knowledge and experience, why haven't you found a job?"

With the last piece of meat on a fork headed towards his mouth, Ryan looked at him. "I'm a branded criminal. I can't get a job in finance. I don't know how to do anything else. I tried every day for nearly three years to find a job... any job. I couldn't even get hired to wash pots and pans, so I decided to give up on life. I gave up hope on finding my wife and children. I just wander around every day, waiting for someone to kill me because I'm too much of a coward to take my own life."

"Ryan, do you really want to die?"

"What do I have to live for? My wife and children are gone. I have no family or friends. It's like someone pushed me out of the world and locked the door. God has cursed me for my sins."

"Why do you believe God has cursed you? What have you done to offend God?"

"I've broken his sacred commandments. I cheated on my wife with whores. I was cocky and insolent as New York's top accountant. I saw people, some of whom were my neighbors, being fleeced, but I didn't say anything. I just looked the other way. Although cooking the books is standard practice on Wall Street, it's still wrong. But I didn't care if it was wrong. I did it because my boss asked me.

"And as a result of my dishonesty, a lot of families lost their savings and homes, for which I am truly sorry. I can't blame anyone else for my sexual misconduct. I can't blame my boss for my participation in wrongdoing. I should've allowed my moral compass to guide me, but I didn't. So, God took my family away and scarred my reputation for life. Although I didn't embezzle, I'm just as guilty."

Derrick allowed Ryan's confession to settle before he said, "Every person who loves God deserves a second chance, and God will provide that chance."

"I can't have a second chance. I can never work in accounting again."

"Yes, you can."

Ryan's eyes sparkled. "How? What type of work do you do?"

"I'm part owner of an independent film company. Have you heard of Third Eye Films?"

"No."

"What about the Adam and Eve movie?"

"I heard about that. I saw the advertisement in Times Square. You made that movie?"

"I produced it. Want to work for me? I need a good finance man."

Discombobulated, Ryan spilled soda over his asparagus. "You're serious?"

"I'm always serious about business."

He jumped from his seat. "Praise God! Thank you, Lord! Thank you, Jesus! Thank you, sir!"

Frowns, blank faces, and smiles came from the patrons and employees.

Ryan sat. "I'm sorry if I embarrassed you."

"You didn't embarrass me."

With tears in his eyes, Ryan said, "This can't be real. Am I on a reality TV show?"

"This is reality, but not a television show."

"Why me? I'm a sinner. I've done bad things. I helped destroy people's lives."

"Ryan, all are under sin, but the grace of Jesus Christ is the forgiveness of sins. The Bible tells us that to whom much is given, much is required. A man is not made rich for himself, but to help the poor and downtrodden. I ask you, which one is the greatest between hope, faith, and charity?"

"Faith," Ryan said confidently.

"It's charity: I Corinthians 13:13."

"Are you a minister?"

"All are born to be ministers in the love of God. I'm just a man trying to live a righteous life. People who have heard of me think I have all that I need, but I'm lonelier than you."

Ryan scrunched his forehead. "How is that possible?"

"You have memories of a wife and children. I envy your memories because as an existence of human flesh, a wife and child are the most important in my life. I want to have those memories. I want to feel those moments. I want to experience that love."

Ryan stared as if he was looking at an angel.

Derrick signaled the waitress for the check.

She quickly came and handed him a leather holder trimmed with solid gold.

He opened his wallet, took out a black card, and placed it inside the pouch without viewing the bill. When she returned with the receipt, he asked, "What's your name?"

"Adelita."

"Hablas Español?"

"Sí."

Derrick asked in Spanish, "Are you in school?"

"Sí. Segundo año en St. John's University."

He nodded twice, opened the book-style holder, and signed a $2,000 tip.

Her head jerked back. "Wow. Thank you. But I'm not sure if the restaurant will approve that amount."

"That's a black card. The restaurant will accept it. If not, I'll bring you cash. What is your major?"

She answered with jubilance, "Business management."

He handed her his Third Eye business card.

"You're the 'Adam and Eve' Derrick Williams?" she asked wide-eyed.

"That's me. I want you to work for me when you graduate."

"Really?"

"Yes. I appreciate the respect you showed for my friend. That told me all I need to know about you."

"Thank you, sir."

"Call me Derrick."

"Thank you, Derrick."

She blissfully walked away.

"God is with you," Ryan said.

"God is with us all. I didn't give her a $2,000 tip. God gave it. He used me as his hand. He rewarded her natural kindness. He rewarded me by bringing her into my life, as he brought you into my life. The Lord knows I need to be surrounded by people with good hearts. But let's talk about your situation. My company owns a three-bedroom condo on Ocean Avenue. We use it as a temporary stay for out-of-state hires. You can stay there until you get your place."

Ryan's eyes closed and an onslaught of tears followed. "I-I'm, j-just, s-so, happy." He wiped his eyes with the back of his hand. "Thank you."

"Don't thank me. Thank God. Now let's go and buy you some clothes and toiletries."

CHAPTER 27

The next day, when human resources input Ryan's social security number into the system, Arthur Kornish, Ryan's former boss and council member for the powers that be, was alerted because Ryan was on their tracking list.

"What is this?" *Ryan's working for Third Eye Films? How did he get there?*

Arthur ordered an investigation, and within thirty minutes, received folders about Third Eye Films, Derrick, and Blue.

He opened the Third Eye folder and learned the company had sold over fifty-nine million DVDs of the Adam and Eve movie worldwide, and netted over $320 million in box-office revenue. *What are these niggers doing with all that money?*

He opened Derrick's folder and saw that he had graduated from Princeton among the top of his class with an economics degree, purchased a $29 million penthouse, and owned a development company.

Arthur raised his bushy brows. *What is this nigger planning to do with a development company?* Suspicion swirled when he read that Derrick had purchased land in South Florida. But when he saw the restrictions on the majority of the property, his concern subsided slightly. Still alarmed by Derrick's wealth, he read his college thesis.

He's a smart, toady nigger—a bootlicker. No threat. He didn't dig any further.

In a search for what brought Ryan to Third Eye Films, Arthur opened Blue's folder and discovered a link. A friend of Blue, incarcerated at the same prison as Ryan, was recently released and employed at Blue's record label. *Ryan must have been that nigger's bitch. They're probably using him to help launder drug money.* He ended his investigation on that thought and sent an encrypted report to Erich Hornsby, the chairman of the One Percent Leadership Council.

The report, if interpreted, read: "Lots of money here but small potatoes like most niggers. Family members and associates are two-bit thugs. In their search for a little piece of the American pie, the coons got lucky. There is no threat here, but got 24/7 on RM, waiting to get inside."

Two days after Ryan's hire, Third Eye posted an immediate opening for his administrative assistant. Arthur submitted a doctored resume of a full-time high-end call girl who, during lulls in service to affluent clientele, worked as a webcam model.

When the young operative received confirmation, Arthur thought Ryan was in charge of the interviews and directed her to wear a short, body-hugging dress that accentuated the breasts.

But Derrick, assisted by staff from an outsourced human resources company, oversaw the process and rejected the candidate.

Arthur texted Erich Hornsby, "Wrong key. Still waiting for help from the 24/7 locksmith."

"Keep calling," Hornsby replied.

* * *

Leather flooring and a path of mosaic tile led to an elaborate sixty-four-seat theater inside the home of seventy-six-year-old Fred Davis, a wealthy music producer and outspoken advocate for black economic empowerment.

Xavier stood in front of the 120-foot movie screen as an A-list of forty-nine potential investors that included businessmen and women, past and present celebrities and athletes, entered the brightly lit room and sat on brown leather cup-holder recliners. He wore a custom three-piece suit. His lubricated bald head glowed like a crown of distinction.

After he had introduced himself, his wife, and Derrick, he said, "The Unity Corporation, in four phases, is building a black community two miles outside of Miami. We are in need of investors for all four phases, starting with Phase One. The investors of Phase One are given priority for all future investment opportunities. At the end of a brief presentation, I will open the floor to questions."

The room sat silent and turned their attention to the screen that detailed the architectural layout for all four phases. Xavier remotely flicked to the list of streets that read: Hope Boulevard,

Faith Lane, Charity Road, Endurance Avenue, Comfort Street, Prosperity Circle, and Salvation Parkway.

He felt the group at attention and clicked to the next slide. "A black-owned credit union will lead the four phases. The executive directors of the credit union are the investors of Phase One.

"Phase One includes the construction of five hundred single-family brick homes bound by the policies of a homeowners association to prevent property and grounds' neglect. Construction has begun on an additional two hundred homes for low-income families, under the same homeowners association.

"We are offering home buyers who choose to finance through our credit union either a lower interest rate or a discount on the purchase. To be determined on a case-by-case basis."

He sensed a growing interest and said, "A government grant will absorb the cost of installing a solar grid for the community. The solar company contracted to provide the service is a subsidiary of the Unity Corporation, which will add revenue on the front and back ends for investors.

"The final parts of Phase One is a 150,000-square-foot public community center with a spa and Olympic-sized pool, adjacent athletic fields, green space, a dog park, and a three-thousand-seat amphitheater. The homeowners association monthly fee of $350 and $150 for the low-income residents will cover the cost of a private maintenance crew and twenty-four-hour security. Now let's take a peek at Phase Two."

He clicked the next slide. "This building is a state-of-the-art charter school for pre-K through twelfth grade. The school will offer vocational training and introductory college classes."

"Ahh" and "Uhh," sounded the room.

He clicked the next slide with an inward smile. "Phase Three is a health center, a 24/7 one-stop superstore, three twenty-four-pump gas stations, an open-air mall that includes four restaurants, a food court, and a sixteen-screen movie theater—all owned by the Unity Corporation."

A potential male investor interrupted, "In today's integrated times, what is the likelihood that residents will conduct the bulk of their activities within this community no matter how beautiful?"

From the expression on the man's face, Xavier sensed wolfish intent. He smiled to keep his true thoughts hidden. "Please hold all questions until after the presentation. But since you asked the question, I will address it. The amenities are a convenience for the residents. But the goal is to attract people outside the community to spend their money inside. Our gas prices, for example, will be a dollar per gallon less than our competitors. We will become the gas provider of choice for all residents within fifty miles of Miami. The lure of cheap gas will introduce consumers to a community that meets their shopping, food, and entertainment needs. We will discuss more when investments for Phase Three begin."

Xavier could feel the heightened interest to know more about the low gas prices but quickly clicked to the Phase Four slide.

"This is a twenty-three-floor luxury building that features condominiums, a private fitness center, a family-oriented luxury public spa with poultice rooms, and residential and commercial leasing space. Phase Four includes an eighteen-hole public golf course. The cost of which to be absorbed by the state under a federal grant, because the golf course is open to the public on property that provides affordable housing. The Unity Corporation's construction company is contracted to build the four phases."

Feeling the room's urge to ask questions, he skipped to the slide that read, "Investors' Reward." He faced the group of men and women, took a sip of water, and cleared his throat.

"The single-family homes will sell from $450,000 to $550,000. If we sell all five hundred homes at the low end, we will generate a sales amount of $225 million. The two hundred affordable houses subsidized by the state at $200,000 each adds another $40 million in sales, for a low-end total of $265 million. After we deduct construction costs, marketing, insurance, and corporate taxes, the investment group can expect a minimum of 20% on their return within the first two years after the completion of Phase One, and a minimum of 40% within three years. Each phase will generate significant investment returns, but we are currently seeking investors for Phase One only, at a minimum investment of $1 million. The cost to complete Phase One is $100 million."

Xavier sensed a downward turn in the room. He read skepticism in the faces of most. "It's shameful that we as a people have yet to empower ourselves economically. The dollar circulates only once in the black community, but many times in the white and Asian communities. The reason is that they create and invest in their own. The time is overdue for us to do the same.

"As a race, we have been programmed to embrace others' cultures, others' histories, and others' futures. I once heard a wise person say, 'It's harder to unlearn than to learn.' That is sadly true for our people and three hundred years of indoctrination under slavery contributed.

"The Unity Corporation is born to move our people forward. We own property in Philadelphia, New York, Los Angeles, Chicago, Detroit, Atlanta, and Washington, D.C. We have plans to develop communities in each of those cities. If you decide to invest, the revenue after expenses is divided among the corporation of investors based on the amount of their investment. All investments made for Phase One will apply solely to the costs and revenue from Phase One. But Phase One investors receive a bonus package because they will benefit from all of the credit union's business endeavors, which are continuous and worldwide."

With the sense of impatient queries mounting, Xavier asked, "Any questions?"

A potential woman investor stood. "I have two questions. Are the homes more expensive than the value of the property, and is it public transportation accessible?"

"The property value is currently lower but will increase significantly after the completion of all four phases. We are targeting homebuyers attracted to living in a black community that offers luxury housing, a charter school, a health clinic, one-stop shopping, gas stations without intermediary costs, a mall, a community center, green spaces, and an eighteen-hole golf course. To answer your second question, yes."

215

She followed up, "Is the public transportation on the property?"

"It's currently across the street from the property but will eventually become a stop on the property. The property management service will provide a daily shuttle that stops at every location on the property. The thirty-six-passenger shuttle is scheduled to operate seven days a week, and run every fifteen minutes between the hours of 6:00 a.m. to 10:00 p.m. Two shuttles will be operating."

Another potential woman investor asked, "What happens if I invest, but unforeseen circumstances obstruct the project?"

"We addressed all known areas of bureaucratic red tape before we started pursuing investors. The zoning and building permits for all of our properties are signed, sealed, and delivered by local, state, and federal governments. All we need now are the investors."

A potential male investor asked, "The Unity Corporation has its own construction company?"

"We do."

"You mentioned that your construction company would build everything. By law, all government-funded developments require a bid. How can you guarantee the Unity Corporation will win the bid?"

"That's a very good question, as were the previous. There are a lot of sharp minds in this room, and your questions are the evidence. That is why we want you to become a part of the Unity Corporation. To answer your question, we won the bid because we low-balled the competing bids by removing the profit margin. The Unity Corporation also has a nonprofit arm among its many subsidiaries."

Another potential male investor asked, "How much money is actually needed to complete Phase One, and how much have you raised? A hundred million dollars seems very high for what you've outlined for Phase One."

"The majority of the money will go towards opening the credit union. As for the other part of your question, we are still in the early stages of seeking investors."

Another male asked, "Low-income families bring thugs and drugs into the community. What steps are you taking to prevent undisciplined youth from taking over the neighborhood?"

"First, I disagree with your broad negative characterization of low-income families. With that said, the homeowners association has a written agreement with the Housing Authority to remove families who violate community rules. Next question?"

"Can white people live or own a business in the community?" another male asked.

"Residency is open to all races, but our marketing strategy targets black families and individuals. The homeowner must live on the property; he or she cannot lease or rent their home. All other properties in the community are under the ownership of the Unity Corporation, which is forever black-owned as written in the bylaws. White people can own a business on the property, but they have to lease the space. However, as is our strategy of marketing our homes, our priority and first choice for renting commercial space are for black business owners. We are providing an opportunity for small black businesses to start and expand."

That answer prompted a follow-up question. "Can white people invest in the Unity Corporation?"

Xavier smiled broadly. "The Unity Corporation is the investment group for the black community development projects. The investment group is for black investors only. We employ without prejudice of race, creed, and religion, but we reserve the right, as a private corporation, to select our investors. We specifically targeted 973 African-Americans with the hope that one hundred will commit $1 million each towards Phase One.

"I must admit, after approaching more than four hundred potential investors, we are very disappointed by the lack of overall support and enthusiasm, which we interpret as fear. Many are apprehensive of the unknown, so they avoid the risk. If you are afraid to take the risk to gain knowledge, then your ignorance will remain. And if your ignorance continues, then your actions can only result in piffle works."

The room hushed with the air of several offended.

Xavier narrowed his eyes and looked over the group. "If the truth offends you, the truth is not in you. Is a black president the end of our struggle for change? Or should he be the inspiration to continue the change? I believe he should be the motivation to step forward and accomplish that which no one thought could ever happen. We are asking you to help us initiate bold change that hopefully in the future will, among other things, lead to a major reduction in black-on-black crime, poverty and unemployment, juvenile delinquency, and youth pregnancies.

"Because we are black men first and businessmen second, we have deliberately avoided accepting investment commitments from high-powered Arab, Hispanic, and other nonwhites until we have completed our targeted list."

The room sat silent for a few seconds before Mr. Davis stood. "I've already committed $2 million. I'm committing an additional three."

The monarch of professional basketball stood. "I'll match that three."

Of the remaining group, only ten committed.

Some said, "I need to think about it," or, "My money is tied up right now."

Others kept quiet.

CHAPTER 28

Gladys had gathered the eleven new investors into a corner of the room. Xavier was standing beside Mr. Davis at the bifold scenescape door that led to a concave lawn. They both held a glass of Scotch on the rocks. The uncommitted were mingling around the buffet table at the back of the room. Derrick stood at the front. "Can I have your attention, please?"

All eyes turned towards him. Most were expressionless.

Composed, he said, "Why not have our own major television network when shows that star black people are the number one shows on television? Why not have our own basketball league when blacks are the ones the fans pay to see? Those are giant steps we should be willing to take. But we are not asking that today. We are asking you to take a small step that is no different than any other legal investment. It's not against the law to build a black community. We are not preventing whites from owning a home or operating a business in our community.

"But I sense the fear of being labeled a black nationalist is holding most of you back. Some of you I have admired from the time I was ten. The honor I felt in being black because of you is more than words can say. As a kid, I dreamed of meeting some of you, so in a way, you helped with my motivation to be where I am today. But I'm shocked by the reluctance I've witnessed.

"We made this presentation confident that thirty-one of the forty-nine attendees would commit. We based it on things you had said publicly. But I've learned that money is the controlling force in this world. If one of us gets too loud with the truth, to the point of influencing many, the white man will ask, 'Does he have a job?' If he doesn't, he'll give him a job and the man will shut his mouth. If the man already has a job, he'll give him an avenue to earn more money, and the man will shut his mouth. But if the man is pure in heart and righteous of mind, his soul can't be bought, so the oppressor will kill him. I can't change a man's thinking. I can only show him the light. The Unity Corporation has shown you the light."

Some of the faces turned downward in shame. Others simply stared tight-lipped.

Derrick confronted them. "The situation that has provided us with wealth and incredible opportunities came primarily from generations of black men and women who made the sacrifice of sweat, tears, and blood—many of whom we will never know, because their names were not written in history books. What is it that we owe the millions of unknown freedom fighters? What does it mean to you to be free? For me, it means using my God-given ability to honor those who helped me get to this point and to do what I can to make things better for my people.

"Freedom in America for blacks is economic empowerment. Why should I pay to live in a house that someone has built for me when I can build a better home that costs less? Is there fear that I might upset the builder and he becomes my enemy? Dr. Martin Luther King Jr. stood without fear! Rosa Parks sat without fear! Harriet Tubman walked without fear! And because of their willingness to act on their beliefs, look at what they accomplished, and their greatness thereof."

A voice from among the offended shouted, "You got lucky with one film, and now you believe everything you touch will turn to gold. What you're proposing to do has already been done and failed. Remember Rosewood and Tulsa—what happened? You think we are free? We're not free! All we have is a place the white man has given us. If we step out of that spot, he will take it from us because he can. There is no new Africa here. We are Americans, and your position to exclude whites from investing is racist.

"I prefer to invest my money and not waste it on an idea. I help the black community with donations to college funds and other nonprofits that help black youth. I know my place, and staying in it has made me very rich and able to help the less fortunate in my own way. To tell you the truth, I have no desire to live in an all-black community. Martin Luther King Jr. had a dream about black and white people holding hands together. In your dream, you only hold black hands. That's racist. Open the Unity Corporation to whites, and I will commit $5 million today."

Derrick glared at the man he had admired since the age of eleven. "I invested every penny I had to make a movie about God's love for every race of man on this earth. So don't misrepresent me. Keep your money. You have just shown an example of why it is harder to unlearn than to learn. The Unity Corporation is nonwhite for valid reasons that I see no need to repeat. Black residents are the priority, and we are offering our commercial leasing space to black businesses first.

"You were correct when you said Dr. King's dream included unity among black and white people. I too believe in that dream. There were white people, and others, who risked their lives to save us from slavery. White people, and others, joined with black people during the civil rights struggle. White people, and others, helped elect the first black president. White people are not my enemy. White racists and foolish people are. *And you're one of the foolish.*

"Why is it that some black people only feel secure if a white man heads the table, or has nodded approval? We are not excluding, we are empowering ourselves as a race without stealing or murdering. The Emancipation Proclamation granted us forty acres and a mule, which we haven't received unto this day. Now that we have purchased our acres and mules to accomplish that which we were freed from slavery to do, we are told that we are out of our place? We are not out of our place. We are stepping into our place, which has been unoccupied for over a century.

"The people of Rosewood and Tulsa had it right! Was it not the white racists' realization that they had to destroy the Rosewood and Tulsa business communities because they were so much better than the white businesses? So much so that whites had begun venturing into Rosewood and Tulsa to purchase from blacks because the items were better and cheaper.

"Surely you don't seek to destroy your competition unless you perceive it to be a serious threat, which in time, will overpower you, all things remaining equal. I'm not asking you to invest in an idea. I'm asking you to invest in your heritage."

The man gave Derrick a death stare. Derrick stood without fear.

Xavier stepped in front of Derrick, gripped his arms, and whispered, "Reginald West has strong ties to gangland."

Derrick maintained his confrontational posture, and spoke loud enough for Mr. West to hear, "I'm not scared of that Uncle Tom, or his associates."

"Muthafucka, who you calling an Uncle Tom?"

"You."

Reginald West pushed forward but was held back by the two men with him, and he held an ill-natured eye on Derrick as they led him out onto the lawn. Several of the attendees followed closely behind.

* * *

The Unity Corporation had flown under the radar. But after the presentation at the home of Mr. Davis, the news of Derrick's plan came to the ears of Erich Hornsby. Mr. Hornsby, a stone-faced, sixty-one-year-old neo-Nazi, was known for having a sense of entitlement and for being narcissistic, unremorseful, without conscience, misogynistic, manipulative, a pathological liar, exploitative, an egomaniac, unforgiving, addicted to power, and a murderer.

His residence was on Park Avenue, but the world was his playground, with castles and mistresses on five continents. Through ruthless underhandedness, he profited $20 million a day worldwide. As chairman of the One Percent Leadership Council, his power was unimaginable for most. He secretly sat above the US president, and with a hidden hand directed the highest authorities. His cohorts were the heads of every major bank, investment firm, and corporation in America.

Everything put into the system was made known to them because they controlled it. They are Big Brother, and live by the art of gaslighting with abstract reality and alternative facts. To them, not getting caught in a lie is the same as telling the truth.

The news of Derrick's plan to become a significant player in the American economy without their approval ignited immediate action. Mr. Hornsby ordered twenty-four-hour surveillance on the Unity Corporation that included family members and friends and summoned Arthur to his home on Park Avenue.

"You dumbass! You told me there was no threat here!"

Arthur lowered his head like a scolded child. "I'm sorry, sir. I underestimated that nigger."

"How could you underestimate a Princeton nigger?"

"Sir, did you read his thesis?"

"His thesis? The nigger has half a billion dollars and owns a development company. That should've alerted you. Schedule an executive council meeting for nine in the morning."

"Sir, some of the members are out of the country."

"I don't give a rat's ass! Schedule an emergency meeting!"

At 9:00 a.m. sharp, the meeting started with six of the nine members in-person, and three by an encrypted video call.

Erich Hornsby sat on a cushioned, solid-gold chair at a gold, oblong table in a windowless, soundproof room, and said, "Gentleman, we have the threat of niggers who think they can own a major conglomerate." He pounded his fist. "We cannot allow that to happen!"

The members were silent with anticipation.

Hornsby leaned forward. "If this Williams nigger succeeds with his plan, he will eventually remove us from the top of the business world by undercutting our prices. That is a serious conundrum."

Samuel Hindenburg, a seventy-one-year-old billionaire said, "Let's kill them as we have done before. The only good nigger is a dead nigger."

Hornsby replied, "We need to be cunning. This nigger seems smarter than most. We don't want to make another martyr. We just need to sway his investors. We cannot allow blacks to dream too big. I knew that nigra president would inspire them. But this jigaboo wants more than his own cable channel, or professional sports team. He wants meaningful power. This nigger wants to replace us."

Daniel Stevens, the owner of the largest bank, asked, "What do you suggest?"

"Destroy his character. Arthur informed me that Ryan Mendendorf, of all people, now works for Williams. If

Mendendorf helps us to gather inside information, we'll let him back into the world."

Stephen Silverton, a bold-natured member, said, "Send him a big ass white woman. No nigger can resist that."

"Duly noted," Hornsby said before he closed the meeting with a 1960 quote from Fred Koch. "The colored man looms large in the Communist plan to take over America."

* * *

The council initiated a smear campaign through payoff shills with established reputations in the black community, who strongly refuted the viability of the Unity Corporation.

"The homes cost more than the property is worth. It's an investment not based on common sense. I believe it's a Ponzi scheme," said one prominent black community leader during a nationally televised interview on a network with worldwide syndication.

"As Americans, we shouldn't be attempting to separate ourselves from America. We're not a part of a black America or a white America. We are one America!" touted another highly respected black leader.

"The dream of the Honorable Dr. Martin Luther King Jr. was one America. With the election of the first black president, we now have Dr. King's dream fulfilled. We don't need division. We shouldn't give birth to the same racism we fought against," said another trusted black clergyman over the airwaves.

In search of dirt, the council traced Derrick's background from birth to present but came up empty-handed. In checking his college phone records, they learned about his obsession with Suzanne.

"Find her and send an agent to befriend her. I'm sure she's still his weakness. We can use her to our benefit even if she isn't on board," Hornsby ordered. He covered another angle and gave a dossier on Derrick to one of the whores from a stable reserved for kings and presidents. "Become the woman he fancies, and take him down without delay."

CHAPTER 29

"Hi, Gladys. It's Benjamin."

"What can I do for you, Benjamin?"

"I'm sorry I didn't commit at the Miami presentation. You know I'm comfortable with you and Obe, but I wasn't sure about Mr. Williams. Now with all the negative publicity circulating, I feel it's time for me to show my support. But first, I would like to get to know Mr. Williams a little better before I commit. I'm having a small gathering at my home, and I have a couple of friends who are also interested. Can you invite him to attend?"

"Who are the friends?"

"Richard Walker and Jeffrey Parker."

"They didn't return my calls. What changed their minds?"

"Like me, the bad publicity has motivated them to support the cause."

She paused.

Benjamin said, "All three of us are thinking about investing at least three million each. I'm leaning towards five."

She stayed silent.

"Gladys, are you there? Gladys?"

"I'm here. What day is your gathering?"

"Thursday at seven. Of course, the invitation extends to you and Obe."

"Thanks, but we won't be able to attend. We have a presentation in Houston. I can't commit that your investment will be accepted. The corporation is not accustomed to accepting investors that initially said no."

"I didn't say no. I told you that I had to think about it. Richard and Jeffrey hadn't returned your calls because they wanted my opinion. Now that I'm on board, they are willing to join. We want to invest in all four phases."

She waited several moments before responding, "I'll ask Derrick and get back to you."

"Thank you. I can speak for Richard and Jeffrey—we are excited about the opportunity to join your team."

"I'll let you know."

She phoned Derrick.

"I just got a call from one of the people at the Miami presentation who said he and two of his friends, who didn't return my calls by the way, want to invest."

"What changed their minds?"

"He said the bad publicity."

"What do you think?"

"My husband and I have known Benjamin for more than twenty years. He didn't say no, but I believe we should stick to the rule and count everyone who was undecided as a no."

"How much are they willing to invest?"

"Collectively, a minimum of nine." When Derrick didn't respond immediately, she broke the silence. "I'm not in favor, but it's your call."

"You and Obe have known him for more than twenty years. He has been very outspoken about the need for economic empowerment."

"Yeah, but he was on the fence with this one. And the rule is that if you're on the fence, you're against us."

"I know, but there is an exception to every rule. Maybe he's the exception."

"And maybe he's not."

A few seconds of silence passed before Derrick said, "You still there?"

"Yes. It's your decision. Benjamin wants you to attend a social at his home on Thursday. I can tell him to change the date so Obe and I can go with you."

"Naw. Don't change it. I'll go. There's no harm in hearing him out."

* * *

Derrick flew to Los Angeles, rented a vehicle, and checked into his hotel before he drove to the Hollywood Hills home of Benjamin Summers.

Mr. Summers, a freckle-faced, copper-skinned redhead, was dressed in a Dashiki. "Welcome, Mr. Williams," he said before the exchange of a body dap. "Let me introduce you to the

226

guests." He wrapped his arm around Derrick's shoulders and led him into an opulent open space of modern furnishings that featured enlarged 24k gold-framed pictures of Tommie Smith and John Carlos on the 1968 Olympics medal stand, and Malcolm X at the microphone.

Among the guests were two of the Unity Corporation's investors, who tried to speak at length with Derrick.

"I'll bring him back to talk to you, but I have to introduce him to a few others first," Mr. Summers said cheerfully.

He took Derrick onto the patio, and along a crescent stone path to an igloo-style solarium decorated with tropical trees and plants. A woman sat alone at the end of a white sofa. She was listening to the speech of Minister Kabir that came from the surround speakers hidden by the top leaves of eight-foot fern trees.

"Ahh, Derrick, this is Olivia."

Derrick immediately noticed her stunning orange, fitted, slash-neck party dress and black four-inch ankle-wrapped stilettos.

"Hi, Derrick. I've heard so much about you. It's an honor to meet a man who walks the talk," she said without a hint of flirtation. "If I had a million dollars, I would invest."

Even if you did, you couldn't. Derrick grinned. Intrigued, he asked, "Have you met the Minister?"

"No, I haven't, but I would love to. My ex-boyfriend introduced me to his speeches, and I fell in love with his teachings. The Minister has such a dynamic flair. Have you met him?"

"No, but I saw him at a rally in D.C."

"Oh snap! I was there with my ex—the black empowerment rally on the National Mall, right?"

"Yeah," he answered with a full smile.

"Seems like you two have something in common, so I'll let you chat. I have to get back to the party," Summers said. "Relax, Derrick. We'll talk later. The two friends I told Gladys about haven't arrived yet."

As Summers turned to leave the room, Olivia nonchalantly said, "Would you like to sit down?"

"Thank you. I'd like to hear the remainder of the speech. Is this the latest?"

"I think so. I try to keep current."

She held a frown of concentration throughout the speech. When it was over, she clapped. "Thanks, Derrick, for keeping me company."

"Thank you for the invite."

She opened the CD player that sat on the blue table beside her and placed the CD in a case. "My gift to you. I have another copy."

Derrick gave her a huge smile. "Thank you. I appreciate it."

She lifted her black purse from the coffee table and stood.

He discreetly scanned her from head to toe. *Man, she is tight.*

She turned to him and smiled as if she had heard his thoughts. "Bye, Derrick. Nice to have met you. God is with you, so I do not doubt your success."

Man, she is nice. "Thanks again for the CD. It was nice meeting you too."

Instinctively, he turned as she walked towards the door. *Wow, her ass is banging. Where did a white girl get that ass from?* He watched her glide to the patio door, hoping she would look back, but she didn't. *It's time to move on from Suzanne.*

A minute later, the urge to see Olivia led him to the house. He looked around for her. *I hope she hasn't left.*

The two investors approached and initiated a conversation, but he only devoted a third of his attention to them. He periodically searched for Olivia.

When Mr. Summers entered the room that featured a life-size, handcrafted wooden elephant with an upturned trunk and pure ivory tusks, a hand-crafted life-size wooden lion, hand-crafted African artwork, and gold-plated framed portraits of what appeared to be Moorish kings, Derrick excused himself and walked over to Mr. Summers. "Is Olivia still here?"

"I haven't seen her since I left you with her," he said loud enough for the room to hear and quickly entered into a conversation with another guest.

Derrick assumed that she had left and sought solace in the vacant piano room. He slumped on a yellow-green and white accent chair in the dimly lit space. *God, give me the strength to stop hesitating and move on from Suzanne.*

At a party without music, he listened to the words of a song in his head that overshadowed the chatter and laughter of the guests who were outside the doorless room. He took out a picture of Mister and him that he had carried since he was nine. It brought tears to his eyes.

He looked up at the sound of footsteps. "I heard you're looking for Olivia?" He didn't recognize the middle-aged man.

His eyes widened, and he perked up. "Yes, have you seen her?"

"I saw her go towards the study."

"Where's the study?"

"At the back of the house." He pointed.

Derrick scooted through the Japanese garden that led to a secluded area of the home. The glass double doors of the study were open, and Olivia was sitting on a mahogany leather couch, searching the Internet on a large screen mounted over the unlit fireplace.

At the sound of his footsteps, she shifted her body. One of her dark almond-shaped eyes partially covered by strands of jet-black hair posed a tantalizing picture.

"I've been looking for you."

A long red nail removed the hair that dangled over her eye. "Hi, I've been thinking about you too."

He smiled. "What are you doing?"

"I'm searching for King Tutankhamun. Are you familiar with him?"

"King Tut? I know he was crowned king at eight years old and married his sister."

"Well, you know more than me. I just started reading *Coming Forth By Day*. Have you read it?"

"The Book of the Dead? A few pages. What drew you to Egyptology?"

"I like to read. Minister Kabir has opened my mind to seek the truth. I've found lots of truth in Egyptology, but I'll remain a Christian."

The sparkle from her eyes engaged him, and he asked, "What's your nationality?"

"I'm Greek," she answered with one eyebrow raised higher than the other. "Anything wrong with that?"

"No, I was just thinking."

"What are you thinking, Derrick? There's a reason for every thought."

He smiled at her display of knowledge and charisma. *She's a wise black woman in a white woman's body.*

He sat beside her and began what became an in-depth conversation centered around God and philosophy.

She listened intently to his every word, and what he saw led him into a sensual kiss.

Suddenly, he withdrew from their erotic embrace and said what his flesh didn't feel. "I can't do this."

"Why? I like it," she replied with eyes that spewed lust.

With a will greater than his own, he physically backed away from the sexually charged moment. "I'm sorry, I can't."

"But I want it, Derrick. You want it too. Your mouth is saying no, but your body is screaming yes," she cooed, and gently squeezed his erection. "I want some of thisss," she whispered, and leaned towards him with fingers that measured the length.

But as if a spirit had yanked him, he jumped off the couch. "Not now. Maybe another time and place. I'm sorry."

"It's okay. I understand. I respect your strength and discipline that few men possess. Can we just sit and continue our conversation about God? You know I found it very thought-provoking."

"Of course," he said with a freefall of feelings.

She smiled, stood, and said, "I'll be right back. I have to use the ladies' room."

He nodded blankly.

She went into the comfort room to the left of the fireplace. His instincts guided him away from the couch, and he sat on one of four high chairs to the right of the fireplace.

What's wrong with me? I like her. I want her. Why am I holding back? I gotta move on from Suzanne.

Thoughts circled and his phone vibrated with Gladys requesting FaceTime. The moment he tapped the screen to accept, a vision from the corner of his eye diverted him. Olivia had stepped out of the bathroom, naked. He forgot about the call, and focused on Olivia. He inadvertently pushing the mute button when he lowered the phone to his side.

She slowly moved towards him with olive skin and a shaved triangle. He stood and backed away from the pointed natural breasts and rivet curves that faced him. Her eyes locked on his.

He continued to back away. "This isn't going to happen. I'm leaving."

The only exit was at her back, so she continued to advance in silence. Backed against the wall-length bookshelf, he tried to step around her, but she cut off his path and stood with a trained fighting position.

She's crazy. "Get out of my way!"

Her brows tensed. She bared her teeth, ruffled her hair, and with a demonic gaze, punched her own jaw to swell and nose to bleed. "You tried to rape me, but I fought you off. Who do you think they will believe when I start screaming?"

His eyes, locked on hers, didn't reflect the anxiety he was feeling. He instinctively knew that he couldn't show fear and held an unworried expression. But inwardly, he cried, *God, please help me.*

A voice in his head whispered, "Gladys." He smiled and turned away.

She leaned her head to the side and gave him a dumbfounded look.

He lifted the phone with the hope that Gladys was still there and pointed it at her. Olivia's expression told him that she was, and he quickly returned it to his side.

She doesn't know the phone wasn't recording. "Go ahead and scream as loud as you can. They will believe me, because from the time you came out of the bathroom, my phone recorded everything you said and did. And Gladys was a witness."

Olivia paused with her eyes locked on him. He matched her unblinking expression for over a minute. Then her eyes lowered, and she went to retrieve her clothes.

Composed, he left the room and found a secluded area in the garden where he exhaled a huge sigh of relief. *Thank you,*

God! He unmuted his phone and told Gladys what had occurred.

"You cannot leave yet," she said. "The person behind this isn't in that house. When she reports to whoever sent her, they might call your bluff. They can still claim that you attempted to rape her and were frightened away. You have to remove all doubt before you leave. Calm yourself and use the same technique that set you free. You got the edge. They're not expecting you to come back. That move will convince the person who sent her that you are not bluffing."

Derrick ended the call and went in search of Mr. Summers. He found him in the piano room, with guests, listening to a poor rendition of Stevie Wonder. He casually walked up from behind, discreetly gripped Summers' arm, and whispered, "Come with me, you bastard."

Mr. Summers followed Derrick without a word.

When they entered the study, Olivia was clothed, and talking on her cell.

Derrick shouted, "Put down the phone!"

She spun around wide-eyed and mouth agape.

"I said, put down the phone unless you're talking to the police."

She lay the phone next to a gold sconce on the desk behind her.

Unaware that Erich Hornsby was listening on the other end, Derrick yanked Mr. Summers over to her and yelled, "You see her bruises? They were self-inflicted, and I have the audio and video recording on this phone to prove it."

Mr. Summers turned to her as a picture of guilt.

"I hope you're not underestimating my intelligence and thinking of how you can prevent me from leaving this house with my phone, because I've already sent a copy to family and friends. If any accusations are made against me after I leave, my evidence will convict you both of conspiracy. I don't want to involve the police. I've got too many important matters to handle. I don't need the distraction. But I might change my mind."

Olivia stood silent and expressionless. Summers had become a picture of worry.

Derrick turned and slowly walked out of the room, back towards the guests, and waved goodbye before he left the house.

When he entered the car, his body trembled.

He leaned his head back and sighed. *Thank you, Jesus.*

Without turning on the engine, he phoned Gladys as directed.

* * *

Olivia and Summers watched from a darkened window as the vehicle sat in the U-shaped driveway of the circular home.

"He's calling the police," Mr. Summers said, panicked. "You better tell the police I didn't have anything to do with this. I'm not going to jail. I will tell everything if I have to." With frightened anxiety, he ran upstairs.

A moment later, Olivia was on the phone with Erich Hornsby, who heard every word.

"Has he driven away yet?" Hornsby asked.

"He hasn't turned on the engine," she answered, concerned.

"What is he doing?"

"I can't see behind the tinted windows."

"So he wasn't bluffing. He's either calling the police, or trying to decide if he should."

"What should I do?"

"Don't panic. Stay on the phone. I can handle the police. My concern is that nigger Benjamin."

"The car is leaving," Olivia said.

"Good. Continue to stay out of sight, and wait fifteen minutes before you leave."

"What about Mr. Summers?"

"I'll take care of him."

CHAPTER 30

Derrick spent the next four days alone at home, conscious of the dangers that lurked all around him, and prepared a new strategy. He agreed to a live interview on the major network controlled by the One Percent Leadership Council.

The long-faced host with bluish-gray eyes and balding brown hair said, "Mr. Williams, thank you for accepting our invitation. I must admit that I was surprised you accepted. It's my understanding that you have denied invitations from other shows that are more friendly because of their liberalism. So I have to ask you, why did you choose my show?"

"Why did you invite me?"

"You're answering my question with a question."

"Because the answer to my question is the answer to yours. Let me say it this way—if I can convince your audience that I'm not the man that you and others of your ilk have labeled, the war to discredit my name is over."

"Well, it does appear that you are practicing reverse discrimination. Can you set the record straight? Why is it, the Unity Corporation doesn't allow white investors?"

Derrick leaned forward with his fingers clamped and arms on the round glass table. "The Unity Corporation is a black-owned private enterprise, no different from the many well-known American corporations that, by the way, are underhandedly designed to be owned by whites only. As a private entity, we also reserve the right to select our investors. Discrimination is blocking whites from living or operating a business on our properties. That is not happening."

"But you are preventing whites from investing? Can we be clear on that?"

"There are other options for investment. Join our credit union. Live on the property. Operate a business on the property. Shop in our stores."

"Okay, Mr. Williams, let's move on. Your corporation has received federal dollars to help support the development of the community. Is that a fact or not?"

"A fact."

"So, isn't that a violation of the law when you refuse white investors?"

"The Unity Corporation has not and will not violate any laws. The federal grants provide support for the affordable housing located on the property, and to promote energy efficiency. Those grants are available for the development of any community project that complies with the grant requirements. Again, you are harping on something that is not relevant to violating existing laws."

"What do you have to say about the allegations that you are operating a Ponzi scheme? Two-thirds of the land you own in South Florida is restricted. Aren't you selling the investors a pie in the sky when you claim that you're going to build in four phases, but clearly do not have the available land to accomplish all the things proposed?"

"That isn't true. I'm surprised you haven't done your research. We are exempt from the restrictions because we provide public housing. Therefore we can expand land development for a school, community center, athletic fields, golf course, shopping, etc."

"Mr. Williams, are you a Marxist?"

"Before I answer, let me ask you a question. Is the owner of this network a Marxist?"

The host hid his grimace with a smile. "I'm proud to say this network is an institution of the American Dream. With that said, I am sure the owner is a Capitalist like me."

Derrick leaned back and grinned. "I'm a Venture Capitalist. The difference between me and others is that I believe in sharing my wealth to empower the needy. While others bank on the greed of excessive profit, the Unity Corporation uses its surplus to add more jobs and programs to strengthen the community, beginning with a strong educational system."

"That is very honorable of you, but many believe your philanthropy is a front for terrorist networks. Are you secretly planning to overthrow the government?"

Derrick cringed. "What? I'm not a terrorist. I don't have any affiliations with terrorists. I am not breaking any laws. I am a black American trying to help my fellow black Americans escape poverty. If anything, I'm helping American society by empowering black people to remove themselves from the welfare and unemployment lines. I am providing an opportunity for black youth to reach their God-given potential without roadblocks. By accomplishing those things, I will contribute to significantly decreasing the crime rate in America."

"Your words say one thing, but your actions speak another. I understand you purchased a penthouse in New York City from a Middle-Easterner for $29 million less than the value of the property. $29,000,000! Who would sell their property for $29 million less than the value without receiving something in return? Please explain how you were able to get such a great deal, Mr. Williams?"

Derrick's spiritual eye peered at a rancorous heart, and he said, "I was in the right place at the right time. Her husband died, and she was in a hurry to sell and return to her family in Saudi Arabia. It was an excellent investment opportunity. By the way, her husband served in the cabinet of a former US president."

The host couldn't hide his chagrined expression. He abruptly ended the interview.

Derrick's straightforward responses and clear vision generated a groundswell of support within the black communities. A prominent bishop in North Carolina led his advocacy group. Derrick followed up that interview with multiple day and night talk-show appearances.

* * *

Erich Hornsby was fuming. "Is everyone incompetent? He's a smart nigger, but still a nigger!" He phoned Arthur. "When are you making contact with Ryan?"

"Sir, Williams is going to Hawaii in a few days. When he leaves, I will meet with Ryan."

"What's that coon doing in Hawaii?"

"Sir, he's buying more land."

"Make that meeting quick. If Ryan doesn't come on board, release the story. Persistent aspersions will eventually bring that nigger down."

"Sir, should I release the insider trading allegation too?"

"That story doesn't have legs. Williams didn't make any trades while he interned, and after, he sold blue-chip stock that went up in value. We don't want to make it appear like we're throwing things at him to see what sticks. The Ryan story is solid if we cannot get inside."

* * *

"Wow, this place feels like the original Garden of Eden," Derrick whispered as he entered the Hawaiian night air. His imagination soared, and he felt the realization. He entered one of several cabs aligned outside the airport terminal and gazed at the serenity of paradise as he rode to the hotel in Waikiki.

But during the ride, he saw people living under trees, and the projects visible from the highway. *Even into paradise has poverty spread.*

When Derrick entered the hotel room, he was captivated by the sight that faced him. He left his wheeled luggage where he stood and went out onto the balcony, and marveled at a huge full moon that sat at the edge of the ocean as if you could sail into it. The tranquil moment was interrupted when his phone beeped the news alert: *Benjamin Summers, an energy magnate, and renowned black activist was found dead at his Hollywood Hills home from an apparent self-inflicted gunshot wound. Early reports indicate that Mr. Summers had been depressed after he and his girlfriend, socialite Arianna Kasparov, broke up recently.*

What? He quickly phoned Gladys.

"Hello," she slurred.

"You asleep already? It's only a little after nine."

"It's 3:00 a.m. here."

"Oh, sorry. I forgot about the time change. Have you heard about Mr. Summers?"

She yawned, "No, what happened?"

"He was found dead in his home. The report said it was suicide."

"Hmm."

"Should I come back?"

"Just a minute..."

Derrick waited.

When she came back, she said, "I woke Obe and told him. I have you on speaker. If you come back, they will know you're scared. You cannot show any sign of fear. We're dealing with animals in human form. If you run when they approach, they will chase you. But if you stand your ground and become as big as you can, they won't charge. Everything is okay. They are just getting rid of a loose end. Relax and have fun. There are a lot of beautiful women in Hawaii. Maybe you will find your soul-mate."

"Or another Olivia," he said, concerned.

"Don't worry about that. If they send another woman, she will be someone you know. Some good news for you: we have sixty-nine million in the bank and another sixty-four names on the list. Obe has a group presentation tomorrow, and I have individual presentations on Friday and Saturday."

"That's very good news."

"So stop working and have some fun... and don't forget to bring me some white chocolate macadamia nuts. Have a good night, Derrick."

"Thanks. Goodnight, Gladys."

CHAPTER 31

Derrick stood on the balcony of his room, hands on the silver iron railing, and gazed out at the sun rising above the ocean and waves lapping onto the beach below. Birds tweeting their praise for the dawn. On the left, mountains of thick dark clouds slowly moved across the purple sky; on the right were heavy white clouds. Both headed towards the rising of the sun, as if hell was on the left and heaven on the right.

In that mystic moment, Derrick's mind was on Mister and Junior, and his eyes followed the white clouds into the sunrise. "Thank you, Jesus, for the life that you have given me. I pray that I can join my brothers in the kingdom of heaven." He closed his eyes and bowed his head in a moment of silence before he left the room and went to breakfast.

A steady flow surrounded the buffet tables as he approached.

A woman dressed in a dazzling printed Kaftan recognized him. "Honey, that's Derrick Williams."

Her husband looked in the direction she pointed. "That is him, honey."

With his plate half-full, the short, bald, distinguished man approached him. "Derrick Williams," he said.

Derrick held an empty plate and nodded. "Your name?"

"Raymond, and this is my wife, Loraine," he said, eyes widened behind full-frame spectacles.

"Nice to meet you both. Where are you from?"

"Wyoming," Raymond answered.

"I didn't know blacks were living in Wyoming."

"Oh yeah, we're everywhere," he replied. "Can you join us for breakfast?"

"Sure."

The three sat outside on a spacious deck at a six-person circular table robed with white linen. In the background, the sound of waves pounding against the rocks added to the ambiance. Raymond was talkative, but Loraine with her cute dimples was reticent.

"Is this your first time in Hawaii?" Raymond asked.

"It is."

"When did you arrive?"

"Last night."

"How long will you be here?"

"Until Saturday morning."

"Oh, you have time to visit all the islands," Raymond said.

"I think I'll just rest mostly. I'll probably tour this island before I leave."

"My wife and I saw the Bass Reeves movie last week. Another excellent film."

Loraine broke her silence. "Who portrayed God's voice in the Adam and Eve movie?"

"We hired a black professional tennis chair umpire for that role."

She smiled. Her dark brown eyes seemed to sparkle. "I loved his voice. I felt God when he spoke."

Raymond interjected, "I'd like to know more about the Unity Corporation."

After Derrick outlined the four phases, Loraine nodded twice at her husband.

"I'd like to invest."

"What's your line of work?" Derrick asked.

"I own a trucking company that transports equipment and supplies to businesses across the mountain and West Coast areas. I net around $2 million a year."

Trucks. He's valuable. How was he overlooked? Derrick perceived him to be trustworthy and extended his hand. "Welcome to our family. Gladys Greene will contact you to finalize your investment."

He gave Derrick his contact information. "You know, I'm eighty years old, so now I can die knowing I have a stake in something that will become historic."

"Eighty years old? Raymond, you can't be eighty. You don't look like a day over sixty. I'm serious."

"Thank you, but I'm eighty."

Loraine proudly added, "I'm seventy-three."

"What! You look almost as young as my mother. And I'm not just saying that to flatter. I'm serious..."

Raymond interjected, "Well, you know what they say about us. We don't age like some other people."

"True," Derrick replied with a slight chuckle before another piece of pancake entered his mouth.

After more conversation and a second helping, Derrick returned to his room. He phoned Gladys via FaceTime and shared Raymond's information. "How did we overlook him?" he asked.

She checked her records. "He wasn't a millionaire when we started the vetting process, but he's a good find. I received a call from Benjamin's two friends who said they still want to invest three million each."

"So what did you say?"

"I told them, no. I know you're the boss, but if I'm in charge of screening investors, you got to trust my decisions. We have one strike. In this game of life and death, two strikes and you're out. I hope you're not offended."

Derrick paused for a second and said, "If the truth offends you, the truth is not in you."

"Good. Another thing, Raymond is a good find, but moving forward, don't bring anyone on board without my approval first."

"Okay," he said, humbled.

* * *

When the moon had replaced the sun, Derrick stepped out in search of a life-changing moment, garbed in cuffed, royal blue, pleated linen pants and a white, long-sleeve, mandarin linen shirt and black suede slip-on shoes. His instincts led him down a two-way street lit by tiki torches and into an oceanfront club where he listened to a live performance by Vaihi.

After two glasses of cognac, he continued his journey to no place in particular and entered a lively dance venue. He found a seat at the circular bar as if reserved for him.

One of three cheerful bartenders that wore tan Daisy Duke shorts approached. "What can I get you to drink?" she asked. Her cleavage held his attention for a moment.

He lifted his satin eyes and smiled. "This is my first visit to Hawaii. What drink do you recommend?"

A white hand towel over her shoulder, she smiled with the presence of a twenty-one-year-old. "Lava Flow."

Derrick ordered the drink and quickly had two.

The club was rocking to house music when he noticed a woman at a table across from the bar. She was sitting in-between two other females. He patiently waited for their eyes to meet. When the bodies of patrons blocked his sight, he maneuvered his head to keep an eye on her as he slowly sipped his third drink.

Seconds that seemed like minutes had passed before their eyes connected. Derrick stood and stepped towards her with purpose, avoiding bodies as obstacles in his path.

Her friends noticed his stare in her direction. He leaned over the table and without a spoken word, gently took her hand, and led her to the dance floor.

* * *

Captivated, she followed his lead. *Why am I allowing him to take me?*

She didn't have an answer and submitted her will. He led her into the world where eye contact, the touch of a hand, and facial expressions are the spoken words. Their bodies swayed to the beat of Thievery Corporation as he sensuously slid his hands along her arms, around her waist, and on her thighs.

Like a sexually suppressed woman set free, she encouraged his tasteful fondling and positioned the divide of her rear at his crotch, with both hands on the back of his head. In a biosphere of their own, he spun her to face him, and their tongues stroked passion.

When the amorous kiss ended, she wanted to speak but couldn't, her mouth kept shut by his sagacious eyes. Her mind filled with the comfort every woman wants in the presence of one they desire.

An up-tempo beat didn't interrupt the slow rhythm that led to another zealous kiss. Surrounded by energized bodies flailing, he suspended their movement, and soothed over the loud music, "What's your name?"

Her emboldened eyes lifted with a raised voice. "Vanessa. What's yours?"

"Derrick."

"I like your name," she said as she slowly swung his hand.

"I like you, Vanessa, but you already have a boyfriend."

"How do you know?" she asked.

"I felt it after the second kiss."

She stopped swinging his hand. "Are you a mind reader?"

"No. But I trust what I feel and not what I see."

"I'm not married, or engaged."

"But you love your boyfriend more than you realize, and I don't want to come between that."

"What do you mean?"

"We can leave right now and go to my room. But in the morning you'll wake up beside me and feel like you're in love, but I won't be able to return the same feelings."

She removed her hand from his grip and tilted her head to the side. "So, you only see me as a one-night stand?"

"If I only saw you as a one-night stand, I wouldn't have told you what would happen in the morning. I like you. I respect you. I don't want to interfere with your relationship. You love your boyfriend more than you know."

"How can you say that?"

"Because if you didn't love him, you wouldn't've felt guilty after our second kiss."

"How do you know I felt guilty?"

"I saw it in your eyes."

Her eyes tilted downward as if the truth had struck her heart. After a moment of silence, she lifted her head with a sympathetic half-smile. "Ah, okay." *He could've taken advantage of me.* "So what do we do now?"

Derrick extended his hand. "I'm leaving, and you're going back to your friends. Thank you for the dance." He gave her his business card. "Invite me to the wedding."

She shook his hand, turned, and squeezed past moving bodies. *He's right. I feel guilty. I really do love Evan.*

243

She sat with a bewildered face, and was immediately questioned by her two companions. But she ignored as if they were speaking to someone else. Her mind was elevated above the surroundings with her eyes in search of Derrick.

For a brief moment, their eyes met with undiminished attraction as he stood among bodies dancing to the beat of Klaves.

He smiled and left.

* * *

He continued his stroll along the streets of Waikiki and entered a picturesque hookah lounge that serenaded downtempo and deep house music. He sat next to a black woman at the V-shaped bar. Five shot glasses, two empty, sat in front of her—probably tequila.

"Hi, I'm Derrick."

"Hi, I'm Shareese. You have a beautiful smile, Derrick."

"Thank you. I wish you would smile. Why so sad?"

"Men. They think women are stupid. They tell lies even when they don't have to. Like, 'I didn't get your text because I lost my phone.' Nigga, please! Why are men always lying?"

"Shareese, you're generalizing. All men aren't liars. Some might lie when they're afraid to tell the truth, just like women."

She turned her plus-size body towards him. "What do you mean?"

"For example, if your boyfriend fails to give you an orgasm, and when he asks if you had one, you will lie, because you don't want to hurt his feelings, right?"

"No, I won't. If he gets his rocks off without satisfying me, he better get it back up or start going down," she said with a smirk.

He laughed.

She continued, "I believe in real talk. Fuck all the bullshit. If a guy wants to get with me, just tell me. I don't need all those rehashed pick-up lines he got from his father."

He laughed again, in love with the personality of this down-to-earth woman.

244

She continued, "My bad, forgive my French. I don't even know you and I'm cussing. You probably think I don't have class," and downed the third shot.

He poised himself. "Nah, I think you're real."

"I'm real all right. I'm real fat and ugly."

He turned serious. "You're not ugly."

"Yeah, yeah, Mr. Nice Man. I know I'm not attractive."

"Says who?"

"Real talk. I look into the mirror. I'm not delusional like some who think they look as good as Beyoncé. Guys want to have sex with me but don't want to be seen with me in public. But I ain't taking no BS just to keep a man."

"Real talk. True beauty is found where the heart and mind is. A real man looks for the beauty within, because what he sees of a woman internally is what he sees of the woman externally. I sat beside you because I like what I sensed from you as a person. I found that to be attractive."

"Oh, so you saying you will date someone like me?"

"What I am saying is that you are not unattractive to me. I'm not ashamed to be seen with you. Am I sexually attracted? No. But friendship is more important than sex. I can marry a woman that I'm not sexually attracted to if she is my best friend. I've met and seen women who are attractive on the outside but not the inside. They are conceited and phony. You can feel the vibes of a person's character without speaking to them. It's called using your spiritual perceptions."

Shareese smiled. "You a cool brotha. The world need more guys like you."

"You know what, Shareese? It's much easier to find a good woman than it is a good man, and that bothers me."

She downed her fifth shot, and the two left the seats at the bar and sat on a red velvet couch. A four-person hookah pipe was on the black table in front of them.

"You smoke," she asked.

"Nah."

"Why you in here?"

"I like lounge music," he said with his legs stretched and the back of his head pressed against the couch.

She ordered another shot and downed it. "I was dating this guy right," she said, "and I finally decided to give him some. Man, he had this little dick. I said, 'What you gonna do with that?' He covered his dick with his hands. I said, 'You only need your baby finger to cover that,' and started laughing. I called him broken pencil dick. 'Pencil dick, Pencil dick.' He got mad and left."

Derrick tried not to laugh, but he couldn't help himself.

Tipsy and comfortable, she said, "I dated this one brotha who had a big dick. I mean a foot long. I got excited. Mmm—I knew I was gonna get it good that night. But the brotha didn't know how to work it. I told him, 'You need to give that dick to me because you don't know how to use it.' He got mad and never called me again."

Derrick couldn't stop the laugh that led to tears.

She turned the conversation to the Adam and Eve movie. "I stood in line with friends for three hours to watch that movie. Have you seen it?"

"No," he said.

"What! You the first black person I know who hasn't seen the movie. That movie was the bomb! And Adam, that brotha was hot and hung like a donkey. I bought the NC-17 version too."

Derrick interjected, "I heard Eve was a blue-eyed blonde."

"Yeah, but that didn't bother me. I found it believable in the way the story was told. My favorite part was when Eve ate the forbidden fruit and the devil guided her to seduce Adam with an erotic dance before she pawed and sucked his dick. That was a very steamy scene not shown in the theater."

"Wow, I need to see that movie."

"You do. The movie is deep, very deep. I don't wanna say anymore 'cause I don't want to spoil it for you."

"Nah, you won't spoil it—tell me more."

"Okay. When God cast out Cain, Eve and her fair-skinned daughter went with him because God temporarily separated the races. The ominous music during the scene when Cain received the mark of the beast was awesome. I could feel Cain's spirit and got scared.

"Cain and his family were living in caves, and Adam and his family were living under tents, until the races came together again. They used scriptural references for the scenes throughout the movie. Genesis 6:1-2 was used to show the races coming together again. But what I think was the deepest part of the movie is when the voice of God said, 'Behold, the man has become one of us, to know good and evil.' The movie implied that man is a god, and that God Almighty looks like man 'cause man was created in God's image and likeness. I guess when you think about it, man is god with the small g."

Derrick whispered, "I got a secret to tell you."

"What?" she asked, prepared to light the hookah pipe.

"My name is Derrick Williams. I produced the Adam and Eve movie."

Her jaw dropped. "You lyin' ass nigga! I told you all men are liars. Why you frontin? You got me all-up-in-here looking like a fool, telling you about your own movie!"

Her expression and demeanor made him laugh, and he said, "I'm sorry. If I had told you the truth, I might not have gotten the honest feedback I wanted."

"Yeah, yeah, but you still a lyin' ass. Come on over here and give me a hug! Wait, you ain't lyin' again are you?"

He reached into his pocket and pulled out his wallet. "Here's my ID."

"Just because your name is Derrick Williams don't mean you're the Derrick Williams that made the movie. You might be using his name as a pick-up line."

"I'm the Derrick Williams who produced the movie."

He opened his cell and showed a video clip from a television interview.

"What you talking about!" she shouted with a fist-pump. "Got-damn! I'm sitting here with Derrick Williams. Oh, you owe me a kiss for lying to me. I ain't talking about no tongue action, but I ain't talking about no cheek either. I want a selfie with our lips touching."

Derrick laughingly complied, and Shareese posted several pictures of her and him on Instagram. The two chatted for the next couple of hours about their backgrounds, music, politics, and God.

"I'd like you to join the Unity Corporation."

"Me? You want me to work for you? I've heard the name, but what is it?"

"It's a private enterprise focused on economic empowerment for black communities."

"You serious? Why you want me to work for you? You falling in love with me or something? Just kidding."

"Yeah, I'd like you to work for me. You have the spirit needed for my company. You just need to clean your mouth a little."

"Uh-huh. Umm, what's the position?"

"I haven't come up with a name yet. Let me think about it. Are you interested?"

"Umm, how much is it?"

"How much do you earn now?"

"I ain't about telling people how much I make."

"Okay, so how can I offer more if I don't know how much you make?"

"Okay. Forty-four thousand."

"I'll pay you fifty-four thousand."

"Fifty-four thousand dollars! Snap! I like that. Can I be myself?"

"That's why I want you to join my team. I want you to be you, but keep the profanity out of the workplace."

"Okay, I'm down. Where is it?"

"New York City."

"New York City! Wow! They got some fine brothas in New York City—starting with Jay-Z. When do I start?"

"My HR department will contact you on Monday with the details."

The two exchanged contact information and continued to chitchat until closing time. Derrick escorted Shareese to the cab.

"You sure you don't want to take me to your hotel? I will rock your world."

He chuckled. "Remember, for every woman, there is a man exclusively made for her. The key to finding him is patience. You will know him when you see a reflection of yourself in his eyes. But be careful, because there are pretenders."

He kissed her on the cheek and they hugged. She entered the white cab and waved goodbye.

Derrick walked along the nearly empty streets to the hotel with warmhearted thoughts of the night's events.

Shortly after he entered his room, he received a text from Shareese.

"btw... i only make 34" (smiley face emoji attached).

He texted back. "I still would have offered 54 (smiley face emoji attached).

CHAPTER 32

Ryan was walking briskly down a narrow street towards a cigar bar in Soho for his usual Thursday evening visit. Arthur stood in plain sight at the front of a fruit vendor's cart.

"Arthur?" Ryan yelled.

Arthur turned. "Ryan, is that you? Oh my God! Where have you been?"

Ryan scampered towards him, and they embraced.

"My God, it's so good to see you again. Why didn't you call me when you got out? How's your wife and kids?"

"I don't know. I've spent the past four years looking for them. Do you know where they are?"

"I don't have a clue where they might be. Why didn't you call me when you got out?"

"I called you, but your number had changed. I went to your home, but you had moved. I heard you were managing another company, but no one told me the name. Besides, what could you do? I can't work on Wall Street again."

Arthur put his arm around Ryan's shoulder and gave him a sad look. "I could've given you money and helped you get back on your feet, but you look like you're doing very well for yourself. Where are you working?"

"I work for Third Eye Films. Have you heard of it?"

Arthur clutched Ryan's arm and led him away from the vendor. "Yes, I have. That's the company owned by a radical named Derrick Williams. How did you get connected with him?"

"I wouldn't call him a radical. He's a very good man, Arthur. I think you would like him."

"Hmm. Let's talk about you. I've missed you. I'm still trying to discover who set you up. My theory is Joel."

"Joel! Joel Stanberry? I can't believe it. Why do you think that?"

"After you were convicted, he committed suicide. I believe the guilt got to him."

"Oh, not Joel. He was my best friend."

"In a dog-eat-dog world, friends quickly turn to enemies."

"I know what you mean, Arthur. When I got out of prison, my family and friends abandoned me. They wouldn't answer my calls or knocks on their doors. I felt like a man with a deadly contagious disease. I was living on the streets the past four years when I met Derrick Williams."

"What! You were homeless?"

"Mm-hmm. I was one of the forgotten."

"My God, Ryan," Arthur said with pretentious tears. "I wish I had known. I wish you had tried harder to find me. I blame myself for not keeping up with you. I apologize for not writing. My lawyer told me that it might be construed the wrong way. But let's forget about the past and focus on the future. You're back now. I'm glad to see you. I'm sure your former colleagues would love to see you. Do you have plans for Saturday?"

Ryan smiled. "Nothing special."

"Good! I'm having a small gathering on my boat with some of your former colleagues. Maybe someone will have information about your family. I'll send a car to pick you up at the back of your apartment building."

Ryan raised his eyebrows. "How do you know I leave my apartment from the back? And how do you know I live in an apartment?"

"Everyone in New York lives in an apartment. I assumed, since you are a convicted felon and work for the controversial Derrick Williams, you leave your home from the rear like everyone else who is trying to avoid the tabloids. Just a lucky guess. What's your address?"

Ryan believed him. "I'll write it down for you."

He opened his briefcase and took out a pen and pad. They reminisced and joked for several minutes.

"Would you like to join me for a cigar?" Ryan asked.

"I'm sorry, Ryan, I stayed too long already. The wife is waiting for these peaches to make a cobbler. You know how she is when I'm late."

"Okay, see you Saturday. And tell your wife I said hi."

"I will... and I will ask around about your wife."

Ryan held a smile as Arthur entered the chauffeured vehicle illegally parked.

He carried that face into the bar. *I might find out on Saturday where my kids are.*

* * *

At 4:00 p.m. on Saturday, a chauffeured limousine drove Ryan to the marina. Loud music led him on the Chelsea Piers to Arthur's mega-yacht. Topless women in thongs and heels paraded on two decks.

Ryan stopped halfway to the vessel. *I don't want to be here.* He looked behind him and wondered if he should just leave. *But someone might know where my children are.* That thought persuaded him to board the boat of unfamiliar faces. He looked for Arthur.

A young woman in an apricot-colored thong and black spike heels approached. She had her auburn hair in a ponytail and facial makeup like that of a model.

"What's your name?" she asked with the voice of an eighteen-year-old and gently rubbed the back of his hand with her thumb.

Ryan yanked his hand away, gave her an unwelcome look, and turned to leave the boat.

"Ryan! Wait!" Arthur yelled from the upper deck. He ran down the six steps, stumbling at the end. "Don't leave. I'm sorry I wasn't down here to meet you."

Ryan didn't say a word and felt uneasy. Arthur placed his right hand on Ryan's shoulder. "Are you okay?"

"No, I'm not."

He led Ryan by the arm. "Let's go somewhere where we can talk." They went below deck to a private space the size of a five-star three-bedroom villa. "Let's talk in my office."

Ryan followed him into a transformed bedroom and sat on an oversized wool chair in front of a walnut desk.

Arthur sat on a brown high-back leather chair behind the desk and leaned forward with clasped hands. "What's wrong, Ryan?"

"I'm very uncomfortable, Arthur. I became a born-again Christian in prison. I thought this was a small gathering of old friends."

"It is, Ryan. As soon as your former colleagues arrive, we will sail without the girls. They're only here to entertain some clients who will be leaving soon. You know how our business works."

"Arthur, I think I'd better leave. Being here reminds me too much of my past."

"Wait a few minutes. I have someone coming with information about your family."

Ryan leaped from the chair. "What? You found my children?"

"What are friends for if they can't help when needed? When you told me you couldn't locate your family, I hired a private detective, and he's bringing some information today. I don't know if he has found exactly where your family is, but I think he has an excellent lead."

"Praise God! Thank you, Lord! Thank you, Arthur! How can I repay you?"

"Repay me? What? That's an insult. You're one of my best friends. I owe you for your loyalty."

"Thank you, Arthur. When will the detective arrive?"

Arthur leaned back in the chair. "Within an hour or so. In the meantime, relax and have a drink. You can stay down here if it makes you more comfortable. Heck, I'll stay with you, and we can talk."

"Uh, I-I don't want to keep you away from your party."

He raised a finger to his lips. "Shhh. The only good thing about this party is that you're here."

"Thanks, Arthur."

"Let's have a drink."

"Nooo, not me, you go ahead. I stopped drinking."

Arthur stood. "Ah, c'mon. You can take a small sip for the occasion. Let's toast to God for bringing us together again."

"O-okay."

Arthur opened the double-door cabinet that matched his desk and took out a chilled bottle of champagne that had tiny twenty-four-karat-gold flakes floating among the bubbles.

He popped the cork and filled two crystal flutes. "Here's to God for returning my friend to my life."

Their glasses clinked, and they sipped.

"Arthur, thank you for your friendship. May God continue to bless you and your family."

"Ryan, I will always be your friend. I love you like a brother. Out of my concern for you, I looked into Third Eye Films and learned the Feds are watching everything associated with Derrick Williams. I was told the Unity Corporation is a vehicle for laundering money to support terrorist groups."

"Nooo, that's not true!"

"I'm just telling you what I heard. How did you meet Derrick Williams?"

"I was on the street, and he invited me to eat with him. He took me to a restaurant. During dinner, I told him about my life. He offered me a job, took me shopping for the bare necessities, and provided temporary lodging."

"What an unbelievable story."

"I know. God is good."

"God is good, but aren't you suspicious about how you met? It's not normal for a man to just walk up to a homeless stranger and do all the things you said that he did. Ryan, I believe he recognized you. I believe he is using your mastery to hide his criminal activity."

"I don't believe that, Arthur. I know firsthand of his honesty."

"You also thought that about Joel, and look at what happened. Trust me, Ryan. I'm your old and proven friend. This man is trouble, and I don't want you to go back to prison. I believe he's a scammer and a terrorist."

Ryan paused.

"The Feds are coming after Mr. Williams, and you're going down with him if you don't get out before it's too late."

"Arthur, I can't do that. I can't abandon the company."

"Yes, you can. Think about your wife and children. Now that you're close to finding them, do you want to end up back in prison?"

"No, I don't."

"Okay then, let me help you."

"How?" he asked, torn between belief and disbelief.

"I have an idea. If you provide the Feds with classified information, I guarantee they won't implicate you, and you'll be able to work on Wall Street again."

"I can't betray Derrick."

"Why not? He lied to you. He knew who you were. Think about it. He pretended not to know you to gain your trust by masquerading as a godly man. He has convinced a lot of people into believing he is an angel sent from God. But he's no angel of God. He doesn't even go to church. What person is going to do all that you said he did for a stranger on the street? My God, Ryan. He put you in charge of his company finances, knowing that you were convicted of embezzlement. Not even Jesus Christ would do that. Trust me, Ryan, this man is using you. I heard he's planning a trip to the Middle East. Is that true?"

"Yes, but that's a deal to purchase oil for his gas stations."

"That's what he told you. But I have it from a reliable source that he's meeting with the representative of a terrorist organization. Mr. Williams is taking advantage of the many opportunities opened up by that nigger in the White House, who some believe is guiding him. Somebody's got to be helping that neophyte—that young nigger can't be that smart!"

Offended by Arthur's words, Ryan stood. "I'm leaving."

"Why? You can't leave yet. The information about your family hasn't arrived."

"I have to go, Arthur. You know where to reach me. I'd appreciate it if you call me with any information you might have, but I can't stay here any longer. I'm not going to betray Derrick. I believe him. I trust him. I'm willing to take my chances and stand with him. I remember when you told me, 'Everything and everyone has a price.' Well, I don't have a price to sell out the only man that cared when the world turned its back on me. You weren't living with me on the streets while thousands of people every day eyed me with disgust. You weren't there when Derrick defended me against a preacher who condemned me. You'll never know the sincerity in his eyes or feel his honesty when he first spoke to me. I'm ready to die for him, Arthur. The same as I would for Jesus Christ.

"Thank you for trying to help me find my family. But at this moment, if I have to decide between my wife and Derrick, I choose Derrick. I don't give a damn about my wife. It's obvious she never loved me. I'm at peace with that now. I want to see my children again. I hope you can still find it in your heart to help me find them."

Ryan stood with a nearly full glass of champagne, set it on the desk, and headed towards the steps.

"Ryan. If you leave, I won't be able to save you from what lies ahead."

He calmly turned and said, "Christ will save me. I'm human, so I'm scared. But I believe I will be with Christ at the end of it all."

He went up the steps and down the ramp, ignoring familiar voices that shouted his name as he walked to the waiting vehicle.

CHAPTER 33

The day before Ryan went to Arthur's boat, Derrick woke that morning undecided as to how he would spend his last non-business day on the island of Oahu. After room-service brunch, he showered, dressed, and video-chatted with Charlene for an hour on the balcony.

Attired in an untucked long-sleeve white cotton dress shirt that had the first three buttons unfastened, loose-fitting blue jeans, and tightly woven dark-brown leather sandals, he left the room and sat at the round, two-person, black wrought-iron table at the sidewalk cafe connected to the hotel.

His square-shaped sunglasses blocked the intense rays of an afternoon sun. His tapered and faded haircut highlighted a well-groomed man. He was reading the newspaper and periodically glancing at the multitude of passersby when he noticed in the distance a woman serenely walking towards him.

Taken by the uniqueness of her graceful gait, he focused on the stylishly attired lady who sauntered in a bright yellow sleeveless dress that complemented her yellow wide-brim summer hat, and strappy yellow sandals. A large lime-colored woven purse hung from her shoulder. A sheer white scarf of lime and yellow polka dots billowed with the summer breeze. Lime hoop earrings drew attention to an Asian face.

He kept his eye on her but wasn't able to see if she was looking his way because of the butterfly sunglasses that finalized her impressive attire.

She's dressed to be noticed. And when she came into range, he scanned her left hand. *She's not married.*

She stopped near his table, the second over from the sidewalk, and turned her back as if she was searching for something in her purse.

He removed his shades. *She's got back. Never seen an Asian that wasn't flat. She stopped right in front of me, so she's interested. But she might be another Olivia.* He hesitated.

After a few seconds, she continued to stroll without looking his way.

Derrick felt the window of opportunity about to close and decided to seize the moment. He sprung, cutting off people in their path, and scurried towards her. "Excuse me, miss."

She turned.

He peered into her dark sunglasses and said, "I wouldn't be a man if I let you pass without asking for your name."

She blushed and removed her sunglasses to reveal an alluring set of monolid eyes.

"My name is Juna," she said with an accent.

"Nice to meet you, Juna. I'm Derrick." He extended his hand.

She shook it briefly.

He sensed her nervousness and said, "I'm safe."

She cracked a slight smile that broadened her beauty.

He smiled. "Do you have a few minutes to talk?"

"Yes," she said with a touch of hesitation in her voice.

He escorted her to his table and pulled back the chair. She sat with the sophistication of her attire. He pushed her chair forward and sat facing her.

"Can I order you something?"

With a shy smile, she answered, "Water."

He signaled the waitress and ordered. "A liter of bottled water and two glasses."

"Do you live on the island?" he asked.

"I live in Philippines. Here visiting my sister and husband. Where you from?"

"I was born in North Carolina. I live in New York. This is my first trip to Hawaii. I came for a mini-vacation and business meeting."

"What your business, sir?"

"Please call me Derrick."

"Okay, Derrick. What business you do?"

"I'm a developer."

"You build buildings?"

"I'm working on building a community."

She incredulously asked, "A whole community?"

"Yes. Seriously. I'm not lying. I'm building a black community in Florida. I came here to buy some land to develop."

"You building a community here too?"

"I'm planning to build a resort. You speak good English."

"English is the second language in my country. But sometimes I am shy to speak."

"Why?"

"Just shy. Filipino shy."

"What is your work in the Philippines?"

"I am, how you call this, accountant at Manila airport."

"An accountant? You look too young to be an accountant."

"I am nineteen when I graduate college. How you say this... I am CPA two months later."

"Wow! You graduated college at nineteen and a CPA at the same age. You are an extraordinary woman. How old were you when you graduated from high school?"

"Fifteen," she answered proudly.

"Fifteen! I was a sophomore in high school. How old are you now?"

"Twenty-two."

"I'm twenty-seven. Tell me more about yourself? I'd like to know."

"I grew up in province Bulacan. I am oldest of six sisters and one brother. I am taller than them. I am tall for a Filipino."

"How tall are you?"

"Five foot five inches," she proudly said.

"Five foot five inches? That's tall in your country?"

"Filipino short."

"Okay, so tell me more about your life."

"My father was a lawyer. How you call this, we were middle class. But when he die of cancer, we become poor. We live without electricity and running water. Because I am the oldest, I had to fetch water every day from well to bring home to cook and clean dishes. I wash our clothes at well and take shower when it rained. I studied with candlelight because we do not have electricity. I pray a lot and go to Mass every Sunday. My mother the reason for my faith. She had cancer, but God cured her."

"Your mother had cancer?"

"Yes. She survives breast cancer."

"What's your mother's name?"

"Emy."

"Your mother is a blessed woman. How did you escape poverty?"

"The priests help me, God helps me, get scholarship for top school in Manila because I make honor roll every year since first grade."

"Is this your first time in America?"

"Yes. I visit Europe and Asia a lot, but first time in America. My sister marry a good man and they have new baby, so I visit. But Hawaii not feel like America."

"No? What is America supposed to feel like?"

"New York." She shyly giggled.

"To only be twenty-two, you have traveled the world. Your life story is amazing. God has blessed you."

"God bless me because I always pray. Tell me your life?"

"I was born in poverty. At twelve, I invested in the stock market with money I earned from odd jobs. Like you, I received an academic scholarship to attend a top university. During a summer internship, I met a friend who had the dream to become a movie director, so we decided to make a movie. I sold a million dollars' worth of stock and invested every dime into the movie."

"You had a million dollars of stock?"

"Yes. God blessed me too."

"You sold all of it?"

"Yes."

"You took big risk. You not scared?"

"I was scared, but not afraid. You cannot escape poverty without taking a risk."

With intense interest, she asked, "What happened to the movie?"

"Have you heard of a movie called *Adam and Eve?*"

"Oh, yes! You make that movie?"

"I invested the money to make it."

"That movie not shown in my country, but I heard about it. How you call this, it is controversial. You famous man. What a coincidence to meet you."

"I don't believe in coincidence. If God delivers all things, then the things we call a coincidence are purpose and fate."

"I believe that," she said with her thin arched brows raised.

Derrick shifted the topic. "What have you heard about black men?"

She chuckled softly and shyly said, "Nothing."

But he sensed otherwise. "Tell me what you've heard."

She lowered her head. "I am shy."

Not pressing any further, he asked, "Do you have a boyfriend?"

"I do not have, but I am not virgin."

"I'm not a virgin either. Do you have children?"

"No. That will never happen before I marry. You have kid?"

"No. I don't want kids until I'm married."

She grinned as if he had said what she wanted to hear. "You have girlfriend?"

"No."

She blushed and smiled.

"How can a woman as beautiful as you, not have a boyfriend?"

"Maybe same reason you do not have girlfriend."

"I like the way you think, Juna. What are your plans for the day?"

"I do not have plans. How you say this... I am sightseeing."

"Does your sister live nearby?"

"No, she drops me. I call her later when ready."

"Would you like to tour the island with me?"

"Okay," she said, enthused.

He smiled and paid the check. They ambled down the busy street to the tour bus stop and joined a line of vibrant tourists. He purchased the tickets and led her by hand to the top of the double-decker.

The radiant sunshine highlighted the grins and laughter that came out of their conversation, and the destinations became secondary. At the end of the three-hour tour, Derrick led Juna off the bus. They stood on the sidewalk lighted by tiki torches as darkness began to settle at early evening.

"Would you like to have dinner with me?" he asked.

"Yes, but I have to call my sister."

While she phoned, he went back to the empty bus and discreetly asked the tour guide, "Can you recommend a romantic restaurant?"

"There is a great place on the other side of the island. I'll write the name down for you," she said with a smile and a wink.

"Thank you." He added a hundred dollars to his original twenty-dollar tip. Spirited, he returned to Juna, who stood like a picture of elegance.

She pointed the phone to show him to her sister.

He smiled, waved, and said, "Hi, your sister is in good hands."

Her sister smiled. "She better be."

Derrick and Juna chuckled.

"What's your name?" he asked.

"Nenita."

"I hope I get to meet you in person."

"If you're a good boy, you will."

Juna laughed and covered her mouth with her hand.

Derrick chuckled, and said, "I am. I'm a very good man."

He faced Juna. *Today is the beginning of something that will last.*

She promptly ended the call.

Unspoken words held the moment as their eyes mirrored the start of a new relationship. Derrick smiled and signaled a cab.

They shared life stories during the twenty-five-minute ride to an oceanfront restaurant nestled among exotic flowers and sixty-five-foot palm trees. A lighted courtyard led to an elevated boardwalk.

Juna smiled. "How did you find this place?"

"I asked the tour guide."

She removed her sunglasses. "You are too good to be true."

"If you are true, then I am true, because you are also too good to be true."

He led her by the hand into the opulent restaurant.

The Japanese hostess escorted them to the garden patio surrounded by tropical plants, and seated them at a two-person table with beige rattan chairs. The square table was covered with fine ivory linen. White votive candles inside clear azure glasses circled the fresh bouquet of flowers at the center.

"Can you stay in Hawaii after your meeting tomorrow?"

"I'm sorry, I can't. I have to fly back to New York to prepare for a presentation on Monday, and I have guests arriving on Sunday afternoon."

* * *

While they were eating, Juna was wrestling with indecision. *If he asks me to go hotel, I not go. If he likes me, he wait. But I want to go with him.*

As if he had heard her thoughts, he said, "After the boardwalk, I'll send you back to your sister. I have an early morning meeting, and need to finish some work."

She tried to hide her stunned expression and lowered her head. "Okay, thank you."

"You sound disappointed."

She swallowed brown rice and lifted her head. "No, I am not. I understand."

"What do you understand?"

"I understand you busy man."

"Yeah, maybe I'm too busy. Maybe I need to find more time for me."

"You should. All work, no play, waste life."

"You're right, and I feel the change coming."

She batted her lashes and ate a piece of milkfish.

"I like you, Juna."

"I like you too," she replied with a look that didn't want to be hurt.

"I'm serious. I don't play games. I'm not looking for a one-night stand. I want a meaningful and lasting relationship."

Her eyes met his. *I believe him.*

Juna's head rested comfortably on Derrick's shoulder as they slowly walked arm in arm on the boardwalk.

God, I think I love him already.

A light breeze enhanced the tranquility, as they sauntered in the night lighted by tiki torches that lined both sides of the boardwalk.

Their silence ended when Juna lifted her head and said, "Why you like me?"

Derrick halted and faced her with a hand on each arm. "I like you because when I look into your eyes, I see a reflection of myself. I see a woman no man has discovered."

"Woman no man has discovered? Who she?"

"She's virtuous, faithful, clever, and focused on fulfilling her dreams. She is the heart of a devoted wife and disciplined mother. She is a woman who has never been satisfied sexually because her satisfaction doesn't come from her vagina. Her orgasm comes from the mind."

She sunk her head into his chest. "Tell me more," she whispered.

He led her to a silver-railed iron bench where leaves from a tropical tree hung over them like a nature-made bivouac. She laid her head against his shoulder and they watched the veil of the moonlight shine over the rapid waves of the ocean.

He continued, "A woman's heart isn't her vagina. It's her mind. So it takes the knowledge and understanding of life to capture a woman's heart. That comes from the wisdom to discern the spiritual world on earth—the things we call imagination, coincidence, and dreams. That is how we see the hand of God. When a man captures a woman's heart, she won't take it away unless he abuses or misuses. I'm sure you heard that opposites attract. Not so with all things, because a wise woman is only attracted to a wise man, and a wise man is only attracted to a wise woman."

She looked up at him. "I sorry I not virgin. But I only sex once."

He tilted his head down. "Where did that come from?"

"You man of God. I know you like virgin. But I only sex once."

"I don't care if you had sex once or a thousand times. I believe a virgin in the eyes of God is a virtuous woman. I believe every time a woman has her menstruation, she's cleansed and made a virgin again, even if she has kids, or is a whore."

"A whore! How can a whore be a virgin?"

"The Bible says, '...if any man be in Christ, he is a new creature; old things are passed away; behold all things are become new.' (II Corinthians 5:17) That Scripture says all things are made new."

Juna looked at him with smiling eyes. *I want to spend the night with him. I hope he change his mind and asks me.*

"I need to get back to my hotel. I will call you after the meeting."

He must have seen her sadness because he leaned into a long, passionate kiss. After, he said, "I will call you later tonight."

They exchanged contact information and walked arm in arm to the cab line outside the front of the restaurant. He kissed her again and opened the cab door. She reluctantly entered, hoping to the last second that he would take her with him.

Her eyes were locked with his as the cab drove away.

* * *

He questioned his decision from the moment she entered the cab and carried that regret back to his hotel room.

Unable to concentrate on business, he phoned Juna on his computer.

Their video-chat lasted until almost two in the morning, and during the conversation, Derrick said, "I want you to think about this and answer me honestly. If I become crippled, amputated, or disfigured, would you still love me?"

Her lips slightly parted before she said, "If I love you now, I would still love you."

"Why? I understand if I was that way before we met, but why would you still love me if that situation occurred later?"

"Because I love the man inside. Those things don't affect the person inside. I see lots of good-looking men that are ugly inside. I see men, how you call this, that people say are not attractive but are to me because they have good heart. You a good-looking man, but I like the man inside more."

He felt a heartbeat unlike any before. *She's the one.*

CHAPTER 34

At 6:00 a.m., Derrick toured the two thousand acres referred by his friend Nootau Wynn and agreed to buy the land.

He phoned Xavier. "I love this place, Obe. We can build a six-star resort."

"That's what I'm talking about! I've got some good news—we have eighty-one million. The last forty-three names will be in New York for the Black Entrepreneurs conference and have confirmed to attend the presentation at your home. We should be over the top on Monday night."

Derrick exhaled. "It's coming together, despite the opposition. Praise God."

"Yeah, but I'm sure they will make another media play on Monday."

"Why wait till Monday? If they've got a move to make, why don't they use it now before the conference?"

"Weekend stories get buried. They have something up their sleeve. I'm sure of it. But we're ready. On another note, my son is back from South Africa. Is it okay if he stays the week with us at your place?"

"You didn't have to ask. Of course he's welcome. You've kept him secret long enough. I look forward to meeting him and learning more about the church."

"I look forward to meeting your mother and sister. Have a safe flight back."

* * *

Derrick had a two-hour window before his chartered jet departed at 10:00 a.m., so he phoned Juna on FaceTime. She answered her tablet on the first ring, dressed in a white-laced bra and matching V-shaped panties.

"Whoa! I thought you were shy."

"I forgot what I wear. Wait, I put on clothes."

"Nooo, don't change. I like what I see."

She giggled.

"I want to see you before I go home. I want you to ride with me to the airport."

She paused. "If I go to airport, I am getting on plane too," she said with a joking tone.

"You can. I chartered a jet."

Her lips parted in surprise. "Okay! I get ready. When you get here? You remember address?"

"Yes, I have the address. I should be there in about thirty minutes."

With a wide smile she had never shown, she said, "Okay my love!"

The words struck his heart. "See you shortly," he said.

* * *

Juna put on her robe and ran into the room where Nenita and her husband were watching the Filipino Channel. She spoke in her native language, Tagalog. "I am going to New York!" She jumped up and down like a child with a dream gift on Christmas morning.

Her sister replied in Tagalog, "You are going with Derrick?"

"Yes!"

"But you just met him. Shouldn't you play a little hard to get?"

"He's got me already."

"Okay, go for it, big sis."

"I feel so happy. I gotta call Mama."

She ran back into the bedroom, dressed, and packed her luggage before she called the Philippines.

On FaceTime, her mother spoke in Tagalong as well. "He's white American?"

"No. He's black American. Very handsome and fears God."

"Oooh, fears God, that's good, Juna. How old is he?"

"Twenty-seven, Ma."

"What's his work?"

"He a developer, Ma. Very rich. Respectful. He not like that judge who likes me to be his property."

"Uh, good! I'm happy for you."

"Ma, I will call you back when he gets here."

"O-kay."

When the doorbell rang, Juna, dressed in a white, free-flowing summer dress, got nervous and ran upstairs into the bathroom. Nenita opened the door and introduced Derrick to her husband, a Filipino with a heart of gold who naturally sheds his kindness and generosity towards everyone.

After a brief conversation between the three, Derrick asked, "Where is Juna?"

"She is upstairs getting ready. I will get her."

Nenita went upstairs to calm her sister while Derrick and her husband discussed healthy living.

"Why am I shy? How do I look?" Juna asked in Tagalog.

"Filipinos are always shy. You look beautiful."

"Should I change my dress?"

"No, your dress is cute."

"What about my shoes?"

"Your shoes are cute. Stop wasting time and come on, he's waiting."

Juna walked closely behind her sister down the carpeted stairs.

"Juna, you look more beautiful today than yesterday," Derrick said. "I'm sure you will look more beautiful tomorrow than today."

With some of her insecurity removed, she sat beside him on the sofa. Nenita sat next to her husband. A few minutes later, Juna phoned her mother on FaceTime and introduced him.

In Tagalog, her mother said, "Tall and handsome."

Juna said, "Ma, speak English."

"O-kay."

"Hi," Derrick said with an amiable smile.

They quickly entered into a conversation about faith, and she was impressed by his knowledge of the Scriptures. She told him about her charitable work and spiritual writings, he said, "You are a saint."

"I am not a saint. How can I be a saint?"

"God ordains saints, not man. I believe everyone who accepts Jesus Christ as their Lord and Savior is a saint by their works."

Her other sisters, also cute, were speaking in Tagalog, as they peeked excitedly over their mother's shoulder to catch a glimpse of Derrick.

Juna abruptly ended the call because of their flirtatious behavior, and said, "We go now."

* * *

They boarded a flying five-star hotel suite that had silk carpet, stone flooring, and granite surfaces.

Juna gaped. "Why you get this big plane?"

"I like space, and I can deduct it on my taxes as a travel expense."

The stewardess led them to a beige leather love seat with personal touchscreens on each side. Two small square cream-streaked granite tables separated a fifty-five-inch 4K television mounted on lacquered panels.

Derrick paired his phone and turned on a playlist heard from the overhead speakers as the jet ascended. He opened his black leather satchel, took out the laptop, and set it on the table in front of him. Juna watched as he connected to the onboard Wi-Fi and video-chatted with Xavier and Gladys.

When the lengthy conversation ended, she said, "You sound, how you call this, stress."

"The presentation on Monday is critical. We are nineteen million dollars short of our goal, and they are the last group."

"How much money you got?"

"You mean personally?"

"Oo, I mean, yes."

"Uh-mm. Cash on hand?"

"Oo, yes."

"Somewhere around two hundred million."

"Two hundred million dollars! You serious?"

"Give or take a little."

"Why you not give the nineteen million, and your problem gone?"

"I can't do this alone. My money is the seed to purchase property, open businesses, and help strengthen small black businesses. I'm opening a chain of superstores, gas stations, movie theaters, among other things. The project in South Florida is the first of many. Two hundred million is not enough. I need five hundred billion to do everything I want."

"Oh, I understand now."

"I don't think you do. This country operates under capitalism, which harbors a soul of greed and selfishness that exploits the poor and working class. This type of exploitation is happening all around the world, and America is the leading culprit. The powers that be are only one percent of the country, and they control the government. I'm a threat, not because I'm advocating for black empowerment, but because I bring to light the possibility of a spiritual and social revolution. Those who control this country saw what most didn't in the Adam and Eve movie. They are afraid of my influence, so I'm being watched 24/7.

"Most believe the number-one priority of the FBI is to prevent terrorism, but it's not. It's the impeding rise of a Black Messiah, which they perceive I might represent. I'm telling you this because I want you to know who I am and where I'm going. Powerful men are seeking to ruin me, even kill me if necessary. You need to know this before you fall in love with me like I have fallen in love with you."

She looked straight at him and said nothing, the meaning of his words clear on her face.

"I know this might have burst your bubble, but I need to be straight-up with you. I'm not a Black Messiah. But that doesn't matter if the powers that be believe I am. So they are coming after me with everything they got, and being around me can put you in danger."

She sighed, lowered her head, and turned away. Then she looked back at him. "If you are with God, I am with you."

"Do you believe without a doubt that I am with God?"

"What you said is scary, but I not doubt you with God. I am just frightened."

"It's natural to be frightened. I'm scared. But I'm not afraid."

"What the difference?"

"When you're afraid, you won't walk through the valley of death. When you're scared, you'll take precautions along the way."

"You like the perfect man. But I am not perfect."

"What is perfect? In St. Matthew 5:48, Jesus commanded us to be perfect even as our Father in heaven. How is that possible? I define perfect as correcting your mistake and not repeating the same error.

"In our heart is the truth, but in our mind is the knowledge of good and evil. That is where the war to maintain the truth is fought. It's easy to say that our mind must accept the truth, but it's very hard to do because of human nature. Human nature brings the feelings of envy, jealousy, greed, selfishness, and other things that lead us from righteousness. Every feeling brings a thought that wants to become action. So when we feel envy and jealousy, what is the thought? When we feel greed, what is the thought? When we feel selfishness, what is the thought? Didn't the Bible show us at the beginning of days those feelings led Cain to act on the thoughts of hate and murder?

"The heart knows that we are made to be righteous. It's the mind that must accept the truth, or the heart will become wicked."

He felt her want and leaned into a long and passionate kiss.

After, they stared into each other's eyes until Derrick broke the moment of silence.

"Let's eat," he whispered.

They used their touchscreens and ordered fresh crab cakes and rice. Derrick ordered a glass of cognac, and Juna had pure coconut water.

After they had eaten, they cuddled, watched the Adam & Eve and Bass Reeves movies, and slept clothed on the queen bed at the back of the plane.

For dinner, they ordered salmon and rice, and continued to bond with love and like until they arrived in New York around 2:00 a.m.

* * *

Derrick hadn't told her that he lived in a penthouse.

When the doorman opened the taxi door and greeted him by name, she thought Derrick had made reservations at a frequented hotel. The thought of a playboy came back to mind, and she felt downhearted.

He must have noticed her expression because he said, "This is where I live."

She embraced him.

"I bought this place to sell it later. But if you like it, I'll keep it."

She stayed silent and tightened her embrace as they stepped on the marble floor that continued into the private elevator that sped to the twenty-ninth floor.

When the door opened, her mouth froze open at the sight of a huge living space with modern furnishings and artwork.

"Welcome to my home."

"Wow!" she screamed and ran up the spiral staircase.

Derrick followed. Childlike, she ran onto the terrace that had the view of Central Park and blissfully whirled in the darkness of early morning.

"What a beautiful place! I love it! All this yours?"

"It's ours."

"Ours?"

"Yes, ours. You're my girl now."

"I am? I am your girl now?"

"If you want."

"I want." She wrapped her arms around his waist and planted her head on his chest.

He lifted her chin, and with eyes that stared into hers, he said, "We were born for this moment."

Her eyes showed the feelings of love, and they leaned into a short, passionate kiss.

"Let me give you a tour."

He led her by hand around the penthouse.

"How do you keep this place clean?"

"I contracted a black-owned cleaning service. They come every Friday, and to my offices, Monday through Friday."

"This like the whole floor of a hotel."

"It is."

The master bedroom was the last stop of the tour.

"You got his and her bathrooms and walk-in closets."

"One for me and one for you." He pointed. "You can shower in that one. There are robes and slippers in the bathroom closet."

"Okay."

A solid hardwood floor led her to the bathroom's mosaic marble floor, and a crystal chandelier automatically lit when she entered.

She turned and said, "You have remote control everywhere."

He smiled.

She looked out the windows behind the bed. "Nice view, but people can see us."

"No, they can't. You can see out but not in. All of my open windows are that way."

She smiled. His eyes gleamed with reverence. She turned and closed the door.

Wow. She marveled at the size of the bathroom, the floor, the chandelier, the white ten-foot-wide double basin vanity, and the oversize bright-moon marble bathtub with matching glass-enclosed dual shower.

She placed her clothes inside a white hamper, grabbed one of the washcloths and towels that hung on the double glass shelf mounted above, and entered the shower that had a rainfall head, and a separate head for steam.

After the shower and steam bath, she wrapped her body in a white towel and covered her hair with a towel. She opened the double door closet and saw white terry-cloth robes and matching slippers. She checked the slippers sizes. *Hmm, sizes six to nine.*

She slipped on size eight and a half, and danced over to the vanity mirror. *Will he like me without makeup? What if I don't satisfy him? What if he too big for me?* Her insecurity mounted and she lingered. *Maybe I stay here till he sleep.*

She thought about turning on the in-wall television to kill time, but decided against it, and sang to herself while she searched to see if a woman had left something in the room, but found nothing.

His maid clean good. I know he had other girls here, and we always leave something behind.

She made silly faces in the mirror, removed her hair towel, and practiced sexy poses.

He hasn't called my name or knocked. He must be sleep. She leaned her ear against the door and heard nothing. *He sleep.*

She gently turned the knob and opened to a dimly lit spacious room.

He wasn't on the king-size platform bed. *Where is he?*

She walked towards the front of the bed and saw him on the terrace with the same robe and slippers, staring at the bright stars in the approaching dawn over a stellar view of the Manhattan skyline.

She went and stood beside him. "This feels like America. I'm happy, Derrick."

He faced her and placed his hands on the sides of her face. His eyes twinkled, and he kissed her.

"Do you believe in love at first sight?" he asked with the light of dawn his backdrop.

Her mouth didn't open, but her eyes radiated the feelings of love.

He led her by hand to a white leather chaise longue on the terrace. They lay and faced a full moon in the deep blue sky. One bright star was still visible.

"Is this going to end after a few days?" she asked.

"This will not end until you want it to end."

She tightened her embrace and sank her head into the chest of his robe.

"My feelings are real, Juna," he whispered as he stroked her long silky hair.

"You promise?" she said.

"I promise."

They kissed, cuddled, and fell asleep.

* * *

274

An hour later, the rays of an early morning sun settled on his face. He squinted his eyes open and turned to Juna, who was sound asleep. *Man, she is beautiful in the morning.*

He watched her for a minute before he quietly rose, then stood at the terrace railing and stared at the sun. Thoughts of Mister, Junior, and his father surfaced.

He turned around and looked at Juna, surprised the sunlight hadn't woken her. He smiled at the innocence written on her face before he went into his bathroom suite, removed his robe, and entered the spacious dual shower.

He turned on the steam-mist, and sprouts of water vapor dispersed around his six-three athletic frame. In less than a minute, steamed had clouded the glass door. Covered with sweat, he stretched his arms against the marble wall with his back to the door.

The vapors entered his breath, and he lowered his head with thoughts of happiness and sadness. Flashes of memories circled his mind.

He heard the shower door open, but he didn't move. Juna entered with soft, catlike footsteps and rubbed a hand across his firm, rounded ass. The other hand slid gently down the indents on his stomach and took hold of a semi-erection.

"Big," she whispered, and gently rubbed his arousal to fullness.

He leaned his head back as she cupped the tip of his penis. The louder he moaned, the quicker she jerked, until he ejaculated euphorically. She continued to yank as if to drain him of semen.

Enthralled by her sexual prowess, he turned and faced her chestnut skin.

His eyes lowered to the moisture on her round breasts that appeared as if no man had touched them, and he sucked on the softness.

Her eyes closed; her head tilted back, and he slowly slid the tip of his tongue up her chest, around her neck, over her jaw, across her lips, and into her mouth.

Like feathered pillows, his fingers sank into her rear cheeks, and she wrapped her legs around his waist with her nails pinned to the sweat on his back.

Their tongues were a lesson in the art of the French-kiss. With that embrace, he sat her succulent body on the stone sauna seating at the back of the shower.

Her moist legs slid off his waist and she spread with no hint of inhibition.

He kneeled with a lustful stare, gently bit and sucked her inner thighs and flicked the tip of his tongue around her trimmed pubic hair.

Her back leaned against the marbled wall, mouth open, moaning with pleasure.

His lips covered her clitoris while he continued to please her with his tongue, and her ecstatic moans grew. She wrapped her legs around his neck and squeezed as if she didn't want his head to move.

Like an infant to a bottle, he sucked the lips of her warm core. Her body writhed and shook as he tasted.

"I love you too much," she whispered.

He lifted his head. "I love you too, Juna."

Confused, she asked, "Was that love or lust?"

He held her hands and gazed into her eyes. "It was both. You can't be fully satisfied sexually without both."

They kissed in an impassioned embrace.

CHAPTER 35

Consumed by the possibility of seeing his children and unable to rid the doubt that Arthur had planted, Ryan had a restless night. Torn, he sought solace and decided to walk across the street to the 8:00 a.m. Sunday Mass instead of waiting for the 10:00 a.m. service at his church. He returned to his apartment the same as he had left, double-minded. He prayed again as he had for the past sixteen hours. "Lord, please guide me in the right way."

At 9:27 a.m., Ryan phoned Derrick.

"Hi, Ryan, what's up?"

"Hi. Are you still in Hawaii?"

"No, I arrived home early this morning."

"Did you enjoy the trip?"

"I did. What's wrong? I can feel you want to talk about something other than my trip."

"Umm, I went to an outing yesterday hosted by my former boss. He told me that your trip next month to the Middle East is a cover to meet with terrorist leaders."

"Do you believe him?"

"To be honest, I was starting to. I'm sorry."

"What else did he say?"

"He said the government is coming after you. He told me that I'm going down with you if I don't help the Feds. But I can't betray you."

"That's good to hear, Ryan. Thank you."

"I'm scared, Derrick."

"I'm scared too. Like I told you before, being scared won't stop a man of faith from walking through the valley of death, but being afraid will."

Confused, Ryan asked, "But why are we scared if we have faith?"

"Because nothing can precede what the flesh feels, and the flesh fears the unknown. It's natural to be scared like it's natural to feel jealousy. Even God feels jealousy. It says that in

Exodus 20:5. When God created man, the physical body came before the spiritual body.

"The Bible tells us that we have a natural body and a spiritual body because 'the first man, Adam, was made a living soul; the last Adam was made a quickening spirit.'—I Corinthians 15:44-45. The Bible also tells us, in I Corinthians 15:47 that 'The first man is of the earth, earthy; the second man is the Lord from heaven.' So you cannot overcome fear without feeling the threat of fear. You cannot overcome death without feeling the threat of death. But if we trust that our God is omnipotent, then we are not afraid of the unknown, because we know our God is greater than anything found in the unknown."

Juna was in the room when the call ended and showed her concern by wrapping her arms around him and laying the side of her head on his shoulder. They tapped lips, and he opened the stainless steel refrigerator and took out a carton of eggs and bottle of orange juice.

He set the juice on the round eight-person, marble table, and the eggs on the kitchen island countertop. Juna stood beside him and watched as he cracked eggs over seasoned ground beef in the frying pan, and stirred.

"Can we go to Mass after breakfast?" she asked.

"I'm not a church person, Juna."

"Why not? You man of God."

"I am, but I believe our body is the church."

"Me too, but I still like Mass."

He placed the eggs and beef on the serving plate with fried ham, sunny-side-up eggs, and toasted wheat bread.

"Maybe another time. You know we have guests coming."

"That not till later. C'mon, it's only an hour."

"Only an hour? I like that."

"So we going?"

His pressed his lips together. "Ahh, another time. I don't feel like putting on a suit and all that."

"You can go as you are."

"I can wear my shorts and LeBron James jersey?"

"Yes."

He smirked. "People will look at me like I'm disrespecting the church."

"No. Catholic church not like that."

He pointed. "So you can go like that?"

"That would be disrespectful. I only wearing your dress shirt. I need to put on bra and shorts."

"Okay, we can go after breakfast."

* * *

A little over two hours after they had returned from Mass, Derrick and Juna were in the twenty-ninth floor kitchen. He was frying fish and cooking fresh broccoli while watching the baseball game on a 55-inch television mounted on the wall that separated cabinets and marble backsplash.

Juna was sitting in a chair at the table, watching Filipino television on her tablet.

A chime sounded throughout the residence.

"What that?" she asked, looking around.

"A call for the elevator."

Derrick pressed a button on the television remote, and a split screen showed his mother holding her Ragdoll cat and Charlene with a rolling suitcase in each hand. He voice-activated the elevator, and when they entered, the screen switched to the inside camera.

Juna grabbed a broom and started sweeping.

"What are you doing? Give me that!" He yanked the broom from her hands. "You're not my maid."

He returned the broom to the closet, led her by hand into the foyer, and introduced her as his wife to be.

"Wife to be?" Yvonne said excitedly. She lowered her cat to the floor and hugged Juna.

Charlene followed.

Yvonne turned to her son. "This is a surprise." Her eyes shifted back to Juna. "How long have you known each other?"

Derrick said, "Today is the third day."

Yvonne narrowed her eyes at him. "Three days only? Have you closed that other door?"

"I have."

"Good. Lock it, and throw away the key."

Charlene interjected with a slight chuckle, "You're quicker than your father."

"I believe in love at first sight. Ma, you told me that you fell in love with my father at first sight."

"I did. But that's a rare occurrence."

"Maybe it's rare because few are aware of the moment. I know I see life differently than most, but to me, I see life as God meant for man to see it. Not as a natural man, but a spiritual man. The Bible tells us in I Corinthians 2:14, 'But the natural man receiveth not the things of the Spirit of God; for they are foolishness unto him: neither can he know them, because they are spiritually discerned.' That's why I use my imagination, follow my dreams, and don't believe in coincidences. And in II Peter 3:8, '...beloved, be not ignorant of this one thing, that one day is with the Lord as a thousand years, and a thousand years as one day.' I interpret that to mean we cannot know the number of days the earth has been in existence. And that if we walk with the Lord, then every second of every day has a purpose and meaning. If I can fall in love with Jesus at first sight then I can also fall in love at first sight with the woman that He has sent to be my soulmate. Some fairy tales are real, Ma."

Juna stood quietly.

Yvonne hugged her son. "I'm happy you found your soulmate. So when is the wedding?"

"Soon, Ma. But don't go planning for a big wedding. It will be private."

With exuded glee, Yvonne and Charlene took hold of Juna's arms and led her to the terrace that had an enclosed solarium with plants and trees like a botanical garden. The three sat around a circular table and chatted private girl talk.

Minutes later, Xavier, Gladys, and their son Amari arrived. After introductions, Derrick met privately with the Greene family while his mother and sister continued their conversation with Juna.

After dinner, the group of seven attended a Broadway musical that starred Crystal, Mister's teenage girlfriend. When they returned to the penthouse, Xavier and Gladys entered their guestroom. Yvonne, Charlene, and Amari entered their respective bedrooms.

Derrick led Juna by hand to their bedroom and she went directly into her bathroom suite.

A minute later, she came out joyfully in a pink lace bra and matching V-shaped panties and embraced Derrick under the covers, with her hand in search of an erection.

"I'm tired, Juna."

"I know. You sleep now."

They slept with three sides of an astral view of the city that never sleeps.

* * *

At 7:00 a.m., the One Percent Council released a story that bolstered scurrilous claims about the Unity Corporation.

XOF Breaking News: *"We have learned that Ryan Mendendorf, a former Wall Street accountant who spent six years in a federal prison for embezzlement, is the chief financial officer at Third Eye Films, a company owned by Derrick Williams, who also heads the Unity Corporation. Mr. Mendendorf is reported to be masterfully skilled in 'cooking the books.' Early reports indicate an elaborate Ponzi scheme operating under the name of the Unity Corporation. A source has informed us that Third Eye Films is also under federal investigation for money laundering and terrorist affiliations."*

Xavier was watching the morning news on the bedroom's wall-mounted television, and woke Gladys. He hurried upstairs to Derrick's room and knocked.

* * *

"Who is it?" Derrick asked, fatigued.

A troubled voice said, "It's me. Turn on XOF news."

Derrick scooted up against the headboard and voice-activated the 65-inch television on a black tempered-glass and chrome-framed stand that faced the platform bed.

Juna raised herself up with worry on her face.

"There is no doubt in my mind that he is funding terrorism and operating a Ponzi scheme that has defrauded

the government, and I blame the president because his administration has paved the way for him," said one contributor to XOF News.

Derrick jumped from the bed and ran into his closet. He stepped into a pair of jogging shorts and put on a Steph Curry jersey.

Juna remained on the bed.

"Get dressed and come downstairs," he said as he hastily left the room.

Derrick dashed down the spiral staircase—Yvonne, Charlene, Xavier, Gladys, and Amari were sitting on the sectional sofa and accent chairs in a space designated as the library. All eyes turned away from the television to him.

He stolidly walked over and sat on the end of the sofa facing Gladys. Juna scampered down the stairs and she sat next to him.

Gladys broke their moment of silence. "We can handle this. We have a cadre of public relations experts to combat these types of things. Will get a retraction on the Unity Corporation statements. Derrick, I took the liberty to speak with the public relations manager at Third Eye. I have a team working with her, but there is nothing we can do to squash the story right now."

He nodded and turned his attention back to the television, ignoring all phone calls except from Blue, Ryan, and Michael.

* * *

Before noon, the innuendos about the Unity Corporation were debunked and retractions announced. Gladys appeared on live television to shore up the current and targeted investors. But the untoward scrutiny had cast further doubt on the Unity Corporation's legitimacy, and some investors bolted, and all but four canceled their attendance at the presentation.

"The contract is binding. We don't have to give the money back," Gladys said with the hope that Derrick would agree.

"I know, but I don't want anyone among our investors who aren't with us all the way. Give them their money back."

Before 3:00 p.m., the Unity Corporation returned $21 million.

The group of seven sat at the steel dining table on the first of Derrick's two floors. Gladys said, "It's time for plan B."

"What is plan B?" Yvonne asked.

Gladys turned to Derrick with an expression that asked if she should answer.

He nodded.

"Plan B is to recruit investors from Jamaica and Africa."

Yvonne turned to her son and said, "I think it's time that you allow your family to invest. You need our help."

He leaned forward and into the shadow of sunlight on the floor. "Ma, I don't want you to use Junior's money for this. We can get the necessary investors."

"What about my money? You know I have $5 million from Junior's life insurance."

Charlene said, "Me too."

Derrick leaned back and looked over at Gladys and Xavier with his eyes narrowed and brows raised.

He leaned forward with an intense expression and faced his mother and sister. "I'm the target and I want it to stay that way. Investors are not the target, but if I allow my family to invest, you will become targets. Right now, my enemies believe my family doesn't think like me because they know you have the money and haven't invested. That also bolsters their claim that I'm operating a Ponzi scheme. That's the negative part, but the way I want it. I don't want them to come after my family in their pursuit to remove me. If anything happens to me, I don't want it to carry over into my family."

His mother tensed. "What do you mean if anything happens to you? Are they trying to kill you?"

"No. They're just trying to scare off my investors and discredit my name. Today is a setback. But you taught me there is a positive side to every negative thing. We have four potential investors still coming. That is a positive side. We have a plan B. That is a positive side. We have each other. That is a positive side. We have faith, and that is the strength to overcome all things."

Yvonne raised her voice, "Family is faith."

He leaned back and stared at his mother. Seconds passed without a word before he said, "It's my decision. I don't want my family involved."

Yvonne smacked her lips and went to her room. Charlene frowned and followed.

Juna sat as if she didn't understand what was going on.

Xavier, Gladys, and Amari sat prepared.

* * *

Four potential investors, who were rap music moguls, arrived as scheduled. They passed on the presentation and made online transfers of $5 million each.

Derrick shouted, "Let's eat!"

The group of eleven sat at the rosewood dining table and ate a catered meal.

After they had eaten, Yvonne, Charlene, and Juna went shopping. Derrick, Xavier, Gladys, and Amari sat in the library with the four investors, where Gladys spoke to them.

"I officially welcome you to the Unity Corporation. As you know, we are very excited about the future of this project and are pleased to have you as members of our family. I am your personal point of contact. I'm available twenty-four hours a day and seven days a week, so please do not hesitate to call me even if you need me at four a.m."

Derrick added, "I want to thank you for not becoming alarmed and discouraged, as did many others. We started with 973 names, needing only a hundred to invest one million dollars each, so our optimism was very high. I'm sure you can understand our disappointment. We profoundly appreciate your contributions to this great cause that will benefit you and the black community. We expected to be over the top at this time, but the news report set us back. Your generous investment has lowered the shortfall to where it began today. For that, I am very grateful.

"To update you, I'm in the process of buying additional land and properties. I want you to know what I am doing with my money so you won't be alarmed when they begin caustically criticizing me for not putting up my own money to meet the shortfall. The vision of the Unity Corporation is much greater than the project in Florida. We are focused on becoming a major player in the American economy. Ultimately, we will own a bank in-line with our credit union as we pursue business dealings worldwide. Thank you for joining the Unity Corporation. We are no longer tenants. We are landlords."

They toasted with chilled bottles of champagne on the terrace that overlooked Central Park.

Shortly after that, the new investors departed.

* * *

Excited about the $20 million, Xavier and Gladys each filled a large bowl with some leftover shrimp and crab legs from the catered food and went to their bedroom, while Derrick and Amari conversed in the library.

Amari stood five-ten at 230 pounds with dreadlocks and a triangular-shaped face.

"How is it stepping into the shoes of your father at such a young age to oversee churches in North America, South Africa, and the West Indies? That's a big task for a young man."

"My task is no more than yours. The Scriptures say the young shall lead them."

"Touché."

Amari took a sip of apple juice and asked, "When did you receive your calling?"

"At the age of ten, but I believe it came earlier. I just didn't hear it."

Amari chuckled.

"There is a Scripture in Jeremiah 17:9 that reads, 'The heart is deceitful above all things, and desperately wicked: who can know it?' What is your interpretation?"

"To me, it means the heart, which is a part of the flesh, cannot be trusted on its own. Because love which comes from the heart is blind without the wisdom of the mind that comes from the spirit. So the meaning is to know wisdom is greater than love. That is why the Scriptures say, God is love, but love not the world, neither the things in the world."

"Great answer," Derrick said, impressed.

"Now I have a question for you. Can you fry ice cream?"

Derrick paused before he said, "Fry ice cream? You mean freezer ice cream?"

"Yes."

"Good question, Amari. I like your philosophical thoughts. You can fry ice cream in a pan, but the purpose of ice cream is to be eaten frozen or thawed a little if preferred, so what is the logic in frying ice cream? Hence, anything without logic is nothing more than an existence."

"Good answer," Amari said, nodding.

"Now I have another question for you, Amari. Is there an opinion on everything?"

"No. There is no opinion to a fact. The Patriots won the Super Bowl, that's a fact. There is no opinion as to who won the Super Bowl. But there is an opinion as to how and why they won."

"Another excellent answer."

"I like philosophy. It keeps the mind sharp. A true man of God bathes in philosophy."

They continued their conversation until Yvonne and Charlene returned with Juna.

With a glow like the new Jerusalem, Juna stood with her hands full of shopping bags.

"Are all those bags yours?" Derrick asked.

"Um, oh," she said, shyly.

"Don't worry, she didn't spend your money," his mother interjected.

"I'm not concerned about the money. I'm just surprised she bought so much."

"Dee, you know when girls go shopping, it's on," Charlene said and snapped her fingers.

"That right, sis," Juna said before she pursed her lips.

Derrick grinned. "Sis? You calling her sis already? You just met."

"Uhh, how you say this... we like that."

He laughed at her newly acquired black dialect, and smiled over the bond she had established with his mother and sister so quickly.

Anxious to model her new outfits, she pressed him to go to their bedroom. Derrick turned to Amari with Juna tugging his arm. "We will continue our conversation tomorrow. I'd like to hear more about Prophet William and the lost tribe of Judah."

"Tomorrow it is," he replied.

* * *

"I think your mother is playing matchmaker," Amari said to Charlene after the others had left.

Charlene giggled and said, "Father knows best, and He hasn't given me an answer yet."

Surprised by the depth of her spirituality, he asked, "Does the Father speak to you often?"

"He's my intuition."

"Not only are you cute, but you're also smart and vigorous. I can feel it."

"What else can you feel?"

"Are you flirting?"

"Is that a question or an answer?" she asked

"An answer. I believe I'm time enough for you."

"You better be, 'cause I have no time to waste."

Taken by her directness, he said, "This is the first conversation I've had with a woman who stimulated my mind. You might be my soulmate."

"And you might be mine. Time will tell." She leaned back on her side of a white leather couch and tilted her head towards him. "If you could change anything in this world, what would it be?"

"The powers that be in this country."

"Ahh, so what would you replace it with?"

"A nation that is truly under God. A government that knows the church and state cannot be separate because it's written of Christ, the government shall be upon his shoulder as it says in Isaiah 9:6."

She smiled at him.

* * *

Derrick was sitting on the bottom of the mattress leaning back on his elbows. Shopping bags were to his left and right. Juna came out of a closet the size of a two-car garage and modeled a white, long-sleeve crop-top blouse, skin-tight blue jeans, and black sandal heels.

"You like it?" she said, bubbly.

"I like it. What did you talk about with my mother and sister?"

"Uh, we just girl talk."

"What's that?"

"You know, how you call this... stuff."

"What kind of stuff?"

She quickly grabbed a small red shopping bag. "Your mother choose this lingerie for me. I try it on."

"Whaatt? My mother picked it out for you? What does she know about lingerie? You probably got a pair of bloomers in there."

He chuckled and skimmed through some of the bags while she was changing.

Moments later she scurried out in a robe and grabbed a large, shiny white shopping bag that he hadn't nosed into yet. "Your mother pick this outfit too. I wear it."

He smiled at her excitement and let his eyes follow her into the closet.

I like her ass. "Thank you, God," he whispered, and fell backward with his arms stretched out.

"Don't go sleep," she yelled.

He sat up and removed the bags from the bed. Voice-activation dimmed the lights and played the music of Tory Lanez.

Juna's cat eyeliner peeked into the room. "You ready for me?"

"Yeah. Show me what you got."

She stepped out in a black, fitted thigh-length, V-neck silk dress with black sheer stockings, and posed. Black high-heel silk pumps elongated her frame.

"Wow, you look gorgeous! My mother picked that?"

"Yes, and everything under."

Aroused by the thought of the unseen, he leaned forward and whispered over the music, "Come here."

She twirled like a child until she stood between his spread legs.

"Turn around," he whispered.

She turned with her hands down at her side.

He slowly unzipped the dress and slid it off her shoulders. Lust guided him to suck beneath her black silk strapless bra.

Her eyes rolled upward, and her arms reached back as her dress fell at the feet of her curvy, petite body. He gazed at black silk panties tailored to grip the cheeks of a rounded rear.

Heightened desire took hold, and he yanked down her panties, and used his thumbs to lift her marshmallow cheeks into his mouth. She flinched, but spread her legs.

His head lowered and he moved his tongue across her female lips. Her soft sensual moans mingled with the music captured the sensual moment.

He lowered the cups on her bra and used his thumbs to harden her nipples. Her head swung back; her hair dangled across his face.

He stood and pressed his erection against her crevice. She bent over.

He unsnapped her bra, pressed his hands against her pointed breasts and stood her upright.

"I love you," she whispered.

He turned her body to face him and whispered, "What do you see in my eyes?"

"Love."

Their tongues twirled into a deep and long kiss.

"Jacob, lights off," he said, and the only illumination was the night sky outside the open floor-to-ceiling windows.

He pulled her down on top of him, and engulfed her breasts.

She unbuckled his belt, and opened his pants.

He turned her underneath and moistened her nipples with the tip of his tongue.

Her eyes rolled backward with a wet core, and her knees lifted.

He rose from the bed.

She grabbed his arm, and cooed, "Where you going?"

"To get a condom."

"Nooo. I want to feel all of you."

She knelt, unbuttoned and removed his shirt, and pulled down his pants and fitted boxers. She scooted her body to the middle of the bed, and spread-eagled there in lace-top thigh-high stockings and heels.

He stood with a nine-inch erection, removed his shoes, and stepped out of his pants and briefs. He removed her heels, and leaned over her, licking and sucking on her navel and across her flat stomach.

She grabbed his arousal and inserted it.

"Arrgh! Arrgh!" she said with painful pleasure. "It hurt," she whispered.

"You want me to stop?"

"No. Push it."

He pushed his phallus deeper, but slower, into her warm core.

"Arrgh. Feels good. Don't stop. Stretch it," she moaned as her soft folds expanded.

"Deeper. Harder," she cooed. "Feels too good."

In less than an hour, there were three orgasms and enough semen for the birth of ten babies.

* * *

Derrick lay on his side and watched Juna as her eyes opened. The morning sun glowed on her face. Her natural beauty ignited another coital moment.

"I'm ovulating," she said afterward.

He smiled and reached into the bottom drawer of the night table on his side of the bed and took out a small black case and opened it. "I bought this ring for my soulmate. I believe you are the one. Will you marry me?"

Her hands, pressed together as if in prayer, clutched her nose and mouth with teary eyes. "You make me so happy. I love you too much. Yesss, I marry you!"

Derrick placed the ring on her finger.

"It fit! How you know my size?" she said with happiness written across her face.

"I didn't. Most would call it a coincidence. I call it destiny."

"You sure you want me?" she asked.

"I have no doubt. Why, do you?"

"Because your mother told me 'bout Suzanne."

"What did she say?"

"She afraid you might still love her. Do you love her?"

His tongue twisted side to side; his eyes closed and opened. "I still love her, but I'm not in love with her."

Her face soured. "What is difference?" she asked with a tear.

He sat upright and gripped her arms with the sunlight on their naked bodies. His eyes locked on hers. "When you love, that means you have care and concern, which is something we should feel for everyone. When you are in love, that means you feel the need for that person because she or he is a necessity in your life. You are a necessity in my life. I'm in love with you, not her."

"But you thought she your soulmate. What happen if you see her again?"

"It took some time, but I finally realized that she wasn't my soulmate. If she were, God would've sent her back. But He didn't. He sent you. I've met lots of women since I last saw Suzanne, and none of them took my mind away from her. But you did. You made me forget about her. If I see her again, I don't know what I'll do. But I know what I won't do."

"What that?"

"Leave you."

She embraced him with tears of joy. "I love you too much. You love me?"

"Not only do I love you, I'm in love with you, Juna."

CHAPTER 36

Juna, Yvonne, and Charlene spent the week planning the wedding.

Gladys scheduled meetings with potential investors in Jamaica and South Africa.

Derrick, Xavier, and Amari spent the week working on plan C.

On Saturday morning, the group of seven attended a Jewish-Christian church in Brooklyn to hear Amari preach. The men of the church didn't wear yarmulkes. They wore white suits and shoes, a white shirt, brown bow tie, and multicolored rosettes on their lapels. The women wore long, white, pleated dresses and shoes, a slim sky-blue necktie and belt, a multicolored rosette, and a sky-blue bow on the left side of their hair.

Service started promptly at 9:00 a.m. when one of the ministers blew the trumpet. Everyone stood, swayed, and sang the church anthem. Derrick, Juna, Yvonne, and Charlene stood and listened. After the song, everyone remained standing, and a twelve-year-old boy led the recitation of St. Matthew 6:9-13, followed by the Seven Keys and Ten Commandments.

They continued to stand while the ministers stepped down from the pulpit and saluted the members of the choir with a kiss on the lips.

Derrick whispered to Xavier, who was standing next to him, "Why are they touching lips?"

"It's ancient Hebrew custom to greet with closed lips. Arabs salute with a kiss on the cheek. We salute on the lips. It's Proverbs 24:26. 'Be not sensitive to a man's touch, but wise to his intent.' Jesus taught us that lesson during the Last Supper when one of the apostles was leaning on his bosom in St. John 13:23. You're not a member, so it's okay to shake hands."

Derrick, Juna, Yvonne, and Charlene were all uncomfortable with the touching of lips and shook the hand of the person to their left and right. The thought of a cult crossed their minds, but they continued to observe and listen to the voices that embraced every race as saints of Christ.

The four had planned to leave after Amari had preached. But because of the a cappella voices, prancing, testimonials, and hospitality, they decided to stay until the Sabbath service ended at sundown, which was at 8:39 p.m. that summer day.

* * *

While Derrick was at church, Ryan received an encrypted call unbeknownst to him.

"Hello."

"Mr. Mendendorf?" a male voice asked.

"Yes, I'm Ryan Mendendorf."

"Mr. Mendendorf, I work for Arthur Kornish, and he instructed me to provide you with the address for your wife and children."

Ryan withheld his excitement and paused. *Is this real?*

"Hello, Mr. Mendendorf, are you there? Hello?"

"Yes, I'm here," Ryan said as he struggled to stay calm.

"Sir, are you ready for the information?"

"Wait a second." He nervously retrieved a pen and paper. "Okay, I'm ready." His hand quivered as he wrote the address.

When he repeated the information, the caller said, "Correct. I pray you have a good reunion with your wife and children."

Ryan was shocked, fidgety, and puzzled. He was excited and afraid at the same time. On the brink of an anxiety attack, he phoned Derrick for guidance, but the call went to voicemail. He didn't leave a message. *I'll call back later.*

Over the next hour, he wrestled on whether he should go to the address. His brain scrambled with indecision. He called Derrick again and received the same notice. *I'll just call back.*

Two more hours had passed, and he was still unable to reach Derrick, so he decided to take a cab to the address. When the taxi arrived, he was standing at the front of the building, but acted as if he wasn't the person who called the cab. The driver finally lowered the passenger's window. "Sir, are you the one who called for a cab?"

Ryan didn't say a word and had his head turned upward.

The driver honked twice. The beeps broke his daze, and he looked at the driver but still didn't move. The driver started to pull off.

"Wait! I'm coming!"

Ryan entered the vehicle with racing thoughts and emotions. *Why did my wife abandon me? What should I say when I see her? Will my daughters remember me? What should I say to them?*

He phoned Derrick again as he rode across the Verrazano Bridge, but voicemail continued to answer. The driver entered an area in New Jersey where the homes were spread out, and dropped off Ryan at the front of a gnarly house. A luxury SUV was in the driveway.

Hesitant to walk up the steps and knock on the door, he phoned Derrick and voicemail answered again.

"Hi, Derrick. I called earlier but didn't leave a message. Arthur sent me the address of my wife and children. I'm outside their home now, but I'm afraid to knock on the door. Just calling to get your advice. Talk to you later."

A strong wind that signaled an impending storm motivated Ryan to walk up the cracked brick steps. He stood at the weather-beaten front door, panted, and exhaled, before he rang the doorbell.

The voice of a young girl yelled, "The pizza man is here. I'll get it." She opened the door.

Ryan smiled at a face that he hadn't seen in ten years and kindly asked, "Is your mother home?"

"Mom, someone's here to see you," she yelled, without turning her eyes from him.

He broadened his smile, and she invited him inside without closing the door.

Her mother was in the living room, unable to see the foyer. When she turned the corner and saw Ryan, her mouth was frozen open and her eyes wide. After she had recovered from the initial shock, she said to her daughter, "It's okay, Jenny. You can go now."

Jenny skipped playfully towards the back room.

Ryan ignored the sight of his wife and watched every step of his daughter, amazed at how beautiful she was.

"What are you doing here? How did you find me?" his wife asked.

"Arthur told me where to find you."

"Arthur?" she said with disbelief. "Arthur would've never given you this address. How did you find me? Did you do something to Arthur, you bastard!"

Two frightened girls—his daughters— ran from the back room into the hallway and flung their arms around their mother's waist.

"Jenny, Samantha, I'm your daddy," Ryan said as if he expected a warm reception.

The two girls stepped back, and pulled their mother with them.

"Stop! Everything is okay. Go back into the room."

"How does he know our names, Mommy?" Jenny asked.

"He's an old friend. He knew you when you were babies. Go back into the room and watch television. I'll call you when the pizza comes."

With their eyes on Ryan, the girls turned and left.

Ryan was perplexed as to why his wife didn't confirm who he was to them, and with a raised voice said, "Why are you hiding my children from me?"

With the stare of disgust planted on her face, she didn't respond.

"Why do you hate me?" he viciously yelled.

The pizza man walked up the steps. She paid for the pizza, closed the door, and called her daughters.

"We're coming, Mommy," Samantha and Jenny responded in unison. "Pizza! Pizza!" they excitedly yelled and reached for the box.

"Take it upstairs. I need to speak privately with an old friend."

"Okay Mommy," the girls said and ran upstairs.

With a blank expression, his wife invited him into the cluttered living room where he sat on a blue suede couch.

His wife excused herself. He could hear her making a phone call but didn't know to who.

Ryan, bewildered, wanted answers. When his wife returned, she sat glumly on a chair across from the couch. He repeated his unanswered questions.

She turned away with contempt and stared at the wall. His constant pleas ignored, he went over to the chair and shook her arms. "Answer me?"

"What?" she shouted. "What do you want, Ryan? Why are you here? You're not supposed to be here."

"I'm not here to see you. I'm here to see my children."

"Your children? You don't have any children, Ryan. Samantha and Jenny aren't your children! They're Arthur's daughters."

He froze, then took a step back, "Why are you lying to me?"

"It's the truth, Ryan. I only married you because Arthur arranged it. I was paid to fuck you, and I hated each time because I love Arthur. Now you know the truth. Is that what you came to hear?"

"You whore of Babylon! You disgusting slut!" he shouted.

Drained of emotion, she asked, "How did you find me? You weren't supposed to find me."

"You're lying. Arthur hired a private detective to find you. If the children were his, he wouldn't have done that."

His wife sobbed. "I'm not lying, Ryan. Arthur is the father of my children."

Moments later, there was a triple ring of the doorbell, followed by rapid knocks. His wife sprinted to the door. Her daughters excitedly ran down the stairs, screaming, "Daddy, Daddy!"

Ryan sat dejected. His eyes and face downward, unable to comprehend the moment at hand.

With her daughters at her side, she opened the door.

Ryan heard a man say, "Arthur sent me to bring you and the kids to him. Is Ryan still here?"

"Yes, he's in the living room," she said. "Please come in."

"Thank you," the man said as he stepped inside and closed the door. "Please go upstairs and pack a suitcase. Arthur has a new home for you."

Ryan listened but didn't move. He heard three gunshots and jumped up from the couch and ran into the hallway. "What was that?" he hollered before he saw the gun pointed at him.

"Turn around and walk slowly towards me," the man ordered.

His body was trembling, and he followed the command.

Tears ran down his cheeks when he saw the bodies sprawled at the bottom of the stairs. "Why did you kill them? They're kids," he sobbed.

"Shut up, and keep walking."

When he had reached the exact spot where the intruder had stood to assassinate his wife and her children, the man said, "Stop."

With the barrel of the gun firmly against the back of his head, Ryan closed his eyes and prayed. In an instant, the man placed Ryan in a choke hold with his left arm and rendered him helpless. With his gloved right hand, he forced Ryan to grip the gun's trigger, and in one continuous motion, made him fire a shot into each of the bodies before a fatal shot went into the side of Ryan's head.

* * *

Across the bridge, the sky was clear into nightfall. When the group of seven returned from church, everyone except Charlene and Amari went to sleep.

When the sun had risen, Gladys, Yvonne, Charlene, and Juna were on the top floor preparing breakfast. Xavier and Amari were sitting at the kitchen table debating for the fun of it.

Derrick walked through the open living space that led to the island kitchen, and said, "Good morning."

"Good morning," everyone replied.

He went to Juna, who was cutting fresh pineapple, and pecked her lips before he sat at the table and turned on the sports channel.

Yvonne was flipping pancakes. "I thought you were a Raiders fan?"

"I am. I'm wearing this Colin Kaepernick jersey out of respect for the man."

"Ahh, okay."

Gladys said, "The omelets are ready."

Charlene took the last of the bacon from the frying pan and placed the platters of breakfast meats on the table.

While they were eating, the sports show ended, and Yvonne asked, "Can I watch the news?"

"Sure." Derrick flicked to the nine o'clock local news.

Breaking News: "*Sometime last night, in this home behind me, an estranged husband shot and killed his wife and two daughters, before turning the gun on himself. The names of the wife and children have not been officially released, but a source has informed me the husband is Ryan Mendendorf. Mr. Mendendorf is the chief accountant for Third Eye Films, which is currently under federal investigation for money laundering.*

"*Sources have also informed me that the wife and her two young daughters, ages thirteen and eleven, moved to New Jersey after Mr. Mendendorf was sent to prison for embezzlement. The source said that she was abused by her husband and feared for her safety.*

"*At this time, police don't know how, or when, Mr. Mendendorf discovered their whereabouts but according to sources, he had desperately been searching for his wife and kids since his release from prison. We will keep you updated as new developments occur.*"

Silence permeated the vast space except for the television. Worry reflected on every face.

With an intense stare at Xavier and Gladys, who sat next to his mother, Derrick said, "Their gloves are off."

Yvonne's eyes widened at her son. "What do you mean?"

He shifted his eyes to her. "Ma, Ryan didn't murder his wife and children. They staged it as a murder-suicide, and I'm the next target on their list."

She pushed away from the table and stood. "Oh, no! I'm not burying another son! You're not next on their list. You were first on the list, but you outsmarted them. Now they want to kill you? Let me tell you something. They have to kill me before they can kill you. All of this mess just to stop you from raising a hundred million dollars? Okay, they failed. You don't need plan B. I'm overriding your decision and joining the corporation."

Charlene interjected, "I'm investing too."

Every eye was on Derrick, waiting for his reply. With an unblinking expression, he paused at each face but didn't say a word.

Yvonne broke the silence. "It's time to fight back as a family. This isn't about vengeance. It's about self-preservation. If you die, I die, and I'm not ready to die. Amari recited Scriptures from the book of Psalms during his sermon yesterday. I asked him this morning where could I find those words. He showed me. That's why the Bible is on the table. I don't think you were listening close enough to the sermon."

"I was listening."

"Well then act like it. I don't want to hear a defeatist attitude. You sound like a person who has given up." She lifted the Bible off the table and read Psalms 57:1, "'Be merciful unto me, O God, be merciful unto me; for my soul trusteth in thee. Yea, in the shadow of thy wings will I make my refuge, until these calamities be overpast.' What happened to your faith, Derrick?"

"I haven't lost my faith. I admit I had a moment of weakness, but you strengthened me."

"That's what family and friends are for, son. Listen to this: 'They have prepared a net for my steps; my soul is bowed down. They have digged a pit before me, into the midst whereof they are fallen themselves.' That's Psalm 57:6. God spoke to you through Amari."

Her eyes glinted with the love of a mother and friend. She closed the Bible. "That pit they dug for you, they will fall into it. You are doing righteous work. You're not leaving this earth until you finish that work. They are stronger and mightier. We don't have the muscle to defeat them. But we don't need muscle. The only thing that can stop us is fear. If we do not fear, we will win like we won the war for civil rights. How did we win that war? Not with violence, but the peace of God."

She opened the Bible to Philippians 4:7, and like a realization had struck, she looked at Juna and said, "Maybe the Philippians are the people of the Philippines." Yvonne paused with everyone considering that thought before she read, "'And the peace of God, which passeth all understanding, shall keep your hearts and minds through Jesus Christ."

Derrick leaned back in the chair with his head resting on the palms of clasped hands. His eyes stared into his mother's, and he saw one greater than him.

Silence held the space for a few seconds.

He unclasped his hands and rested them on his thighs. He turned to Juna, who was sitting next to him with a tear rolling from each eye. He shifted his body to face her, and wiped the tears with his thumbs. "My mother is right. I cannot die until I finish God's work, and that includes seeing the birth of my son. You see how God works? I lost an accountant, but gained a wife and accountant in one."

Her closed mouth curved upward and her eyes seemed to want to smile and cry.

He kissed her, and held the eyes of love until she smiled and opened her mouth, and he kissed her again.

His eyes shifted to Obe, Gladys, and Amari. "It's on," he said.

Charlene was sobbing.

"Let those tears be tears of joy," Derrick said. "God has sent you the man that you prayed for."

He looked at his mother and nodded.

TO BE CONTINUED

CPSIA information can be obtained
at www.ICGtesting.com
Printed in the USA
FFHW022318080819
54162761-59874FF